W9-DGS-911

A SCIENCE FICTION READER

A SCIENCE FICTION READER

edited by

Harry Harrison

editor *Year's Best Science Fiction*

Carol Pugner

English Department
Chairman Journalism Department
Montgomery High School
San Diego, California

Charles Scribner's Sons New York

A–11.72(C)

Printed in the United States of America
Library of Congress Catalog Card Number 72–2210
SBN 684–13023–8

Acknowledgments

"Mirror of Ice," by Gary Wright, copyright © 1967 by Galaxy Publishing Corp.; reprinted by permission of the author.
"Sunjammer," by Arthur C. Clarke, copyright © 1964 by Boy Scouts of America; reprinted by permission of the author and his agents, Scott Meredith Literary Agency, Inc.
"Escape the Morning," by Poul Anderson, copyright © 1966 by Boy Scouts of America; reprinted by permission of the author and his agents, Scott Meredith Literary Agency, Inc.
"If," by Harry Harrison, copyright © 1969 as "Praiseworthy Saur" by Galaxy Publishing Corp.; reprinted by permission of the author and his agent, Robert P. Mills, Ltd.
"Prone," by Mack Reynolds, copyright © 1954 by Mercury Press, Inc.; reprinted by permission of the author and his agents, Scott Meredith Literary Agency, Inc.
"The Yellow Pill," by Rog Phillips, copyright © 1958 by Street & Smith Publications, Inc.; reprinted by permission of the author's Estate and their agent, Scott Meredith Literary Agency, Inc.

"Light of Other Days," by Bob Shaw, copyright © 1966 by Street & Smith Publications, Inc.; reprinted by permission of the author.
"Who Can Replace a Man?" by Brian W. Aldiss, copyright © 1959 by Brian W. Aldiss; reprinted by permission of the author.
"Heavyplanet," by Milton A. Rothman, copyright © 1939 by Street & Smith Publications, Inc.; reprinted by permission of the author.
"Grandpa," by James A. Schmitz, copyright © 1955 by Street & Smith Publications, Inc.; reprinted by permission of the author and his agents, Scott Meredith Literary Agency, Inc.
"Surface Tension," by James Blish, copyright © 1952 by Galaxy Publishing Corporation; reprinted by permission of the author and his agent, Robert P. Mills, Ltd.
"Traffic Problem," by William Earls, copyright © 1970 by Universal Publishing and Distributing Corp.; reprinted by permission of the author and the author's agents, Scott Meredith Literary Agency, Inc.
"Nightfall," by Isaac Asimov, copyright © 1941 by Street & Smith Publications, Inc.; reprinted by permission of the author.
"The Cold Equations," by Tom Godwin, copyright © 1954 by Street & Smith Publications, Inc.; reprinted by permission of the author.

Contents

This Strange Beast

That wonderful Englishman, H. G. Wells, was the father of science fiction, and he started writing it at the end of the last century. He was well ahead of the rest of the world when he did this so that the SF engine only idled for a number of years, until the 1930's in the United States when the science fiction pulp magazines burst upon an unsuspecting world. This was well before comic books, before television too, a time when *all* of the bang-zowie entertainment was in the pulps. Cheap magazines with garish covers and shredding pages. The most garish—and shreddiest—of all were the SF mags. They promised great wonders on the outside, and then delivered these wonders inside.

Science fiction is still delivering its wonders. And it still has a lot of bang-zowie left. It might be called a literature of ideas, presenting those ideas in an adventurous package. But "literature of ideas" sounds stuffy, and good SF is never stuffy. Look at some of the ideas presented in this book and you will easily see why. Get aboard the largest sailing ship ever made and sail it—to the moon! Or find out what it feels like to live on a planet where the gravity is so immense that the hardest steel becomes as soft as putty. A literature of ideas like these *cannot* be stuffy.

SF is also about the real world of the present, and about the tomorrow that is already coming into existence. Other kinds of fiction have not yet caught up with rocket ships—while science fiction authors stopped writing about rockets years ago. As the pace of science and technology—and pollution—increases daily we are slipping faster and faster into this science fictional future. SF, by examining possibilities and futures, gives us something to grab on to in our flight through time.

Science fiction is many things. Fantasy and adventure, monsters and rockets, distant stars and close-up robots. A literature of ideas, yes—but always a literature of entertainment as well.

Harry Harrison

A SCIENCE FICTION READER

Mirror of Ice

by Gary Wright

Gary Wright is an avid winter sportsman from Vermont—and a naval architect as well so that machines have a special life of their own for him. These traits combine perfectly to produce this wonderful invention of a totally new sport—rocket-driven sleds—and tells about the kind of men who drive these dangerous vehicles.

They called it the Stuka. It was a tortuous, twenty-kilometer path of bright ice, and in that distance—12.42 miles—it dropped 7,366 feet, carving a course down the alpine mountainside like the track of a great snake. It was thirty feet wide on the straights with corners curling as high as forty feet. It was made for sleds. . . .

He waited in the narrow cockpit and listened to the wind. It moaned along the frozen shoulder of the towering white peak and across the steep starting ramp, pushing along streamers of snow out against the hard blue sky, and he could hear it cry inside him with the same cold and lonely sound.

He was scared. And what was worse—he knew it.

Forward, under the sleek nose of his sled, the mountain fell away abruptly—straight down, it seemed—and the valley was far below. So very far.

. . . *too far this time, buddy-boy, too far forever* . . .

The countdown light on the dash flickered a sudden blood red, then deliberately winked twice. At the same time two red rockets arced out over the valley and exploded into twin crimson fireballs.

Two minutes.

On both sides of the starting ramp, cantilevered gracefully from the mountainside, brightly bannered platforms were crowded with people. He glanced at the hundreds of blankly staring sunglasses, always the same, always turned to the ramp as if trying to see inside the helmets of these men, as if trying to pry into the reasons of their being there waiting to die. He looked back to the deep valley; today he wondered too.

. . . *just one last time, wasn't that what you told yourself? One last race and that's the end of it and good-bye to the sleds and thank God! Wasn't that your personal promise?*

Then what in hell are you doing here? That "last race" was last month's race. Why are you in this one?

No answer.

All he could find inside were cold questions and a hollow echo of the wind. He gripped the steering wheel, hard, until cramps began in his hands; he would think about his sled. . . .

It was his eleventh sled, and like the others it was a brilliant red, not red for its particular flash, but because of a possible crash far from the course in deep snow. He wanted to be found and found fast. Some of the Kin had never been found in time.

. . . *they didn't find Bob Lander until that summer—*

He forced himself back.

Empty, the sled weighed 185 pounds and looked very much like the body-shell of a particularly sleek racer but with a full bubble canopy and with runners instead of wheels. It was a mean-looking missile, low and lean, hardly wider than his shoulders, clearing the ice by barely two inches. He sat nearly reclining, the half wheel in his lap, feet braced on the two edging pedals—and this was the feature that made these sleds the awesome things they were. They could tilt their runners—four hollow-ground, chrome-steel "skis"—edging them against the ice like wide skate blades. This was what had changed bobsledding into . . . *this*: this special thing with its special brotherhood, this clan apart, this peculiar breed of men set aside for the wonder of other men. The Kin, they called themselves.

. . . Someone once, laughing, had said, "Without peer, we are the world's fastest suicides."

He snapped himself back again and checked his brakes.

By pulling back on the wheel, two electrically operated flaps—actually halves of the sled's tail section—swung out on either side. Silly to see, perhaps. But quite effective when this twelve and a half square feet hit the airstream at eighty mph. A button under his right thumb operated another braking system: with each push it fired forward a solid rocket charge in the nose of the sled. There were seven charges, quite often not enough. But when everything failed, including the man, there was the lever by his left hip. The Final Folly, it was called; a firm pull and, depending on a hundred unknown "if 's" and "maybe's," he might be lucky enough to find himself hanging from a parachute some three hundred feet up. Or it might be the last voluntary act of his life.

He had used it twice. Once streaking into the tall wall of the Wingover, he had lost a runner . . . and was almost fired into the opposite grandstand, missing the top tiers of seats by less than four feet. Another time six sleds suddenly tangled directly in front of him, and he had blasted himself through the overhanging limbs of a large fir tree.

But others had not been so lucky.

Hans Kroger: they finally dug his body out of eighteen feet of snow; he'd gone all the way to the dirt. His sled had been airborne when he blew–and upside-down!

Jarl Yogensen: his sled tumbling and he ejected directly under the following sleds. No one was certain that all of him was ever found!

Max Conrad: a perfect blow-out! At least 350 feet up and slightly downhill . . . His chute never opened.

Wayne Barley:—

He jarred himself hard in the cockpit and felt the sudden seizure of his G-suit. He wanted to hit something. But he could feel the watching eyes and the TV cameras, and there wasn't room in the cockpit to get a decent swing anyway.

His countdown light flickered for attention and blinked once, and a single red rocket flashed into the sky.

One minute—God, had time stopped?

But that was part of it all: the waiting, the God-awful waiting, staring down at the valley over a mile below. And how many men had irrevocably slammed back their canopy in this lifetime of two minutes and stayed behind? A few, yes. And he could too. Simply open his canopy, that was the signal, and when the start came the other sleds would dive down and away and he would be sitting here alone. But, God, so alone! And he would be alone for the rest of his life. He might see some of the Kin again, sometime, somewhere. But they would not see him. It was a kind of death to stay behind.

. . . and a real death to go. Death, the silent rider with every man in every race . . .

He frowned at the other sleds, sixteen in staggered rows of eight. Sixteen bright and beautiful, trim fast projectiles hanging from their starting clamps. He knew them, every one; they were his brothers. They were the Kin—but not here. Not now.

Years ago when he was a novice he had asked old Franz Cashner, "Did you see the way I took Basher Bend right beside you?"

And Franz told him, "Up there I see nobody! Only sleds! Down here you are you, up there you are nothing but another sled. That's all! And don't forget that!"

. . . and it had to be that way. On the course sleds crashed and were no more. . . . Only later, in the valley, were there men missing.

Of these sixteen, chances were that nine would finish. With luck, maybe ten. And chances also said that only fourteen of these men would be alive tonight. Those were the odds, as hard and cold as the ice, the fascinating frosting for this sport. Violent death! Assured, spectacular, magnetic death in a sport such as the world had never known. Incredible men with incredible skills doing an incredible thing.

Back in the Sixties they claimed an empty sled with its steering locked would make a course all by itself. An empty sled here would not last two corners. The Stuka was a cold killer, not a thrill ride. And it was not particular. It killed veterans and novices alike. But there was $20,000 for the man who got to the end of it first, and a whole month before he had to do it again. Money and fame and all the girls in the world. Everything and anything for the men who rode the Stuka.

Was that why they did it?

. . . *yes, always that question: "Why do you do it?" And before he had died on the Plummet, Sir Robert Brooke had told them, "Well, why not?"*

And it was an answer as good as any.

But was it good enough this time?

No answer.

He only knew there was but one way off this mountain for him now and that was straight ahead, and for the first time since his novice runs, his legs were trembling. Twelve and a half miles, call it, and the record was 9 minutes, 1.14 seconds! An average speed of 82.67 mph, and that was *his* record. They would at least remember him by that!

His countdown light flashed, a green rocket rose and burst, and there was a frozen moment . . . the quiet click of the release hook, the lazy, slow-motion start, the sleds sliding forward in formation over the edge . . . then he was looking once again into the terrible top of the Stuka—that 45-degree, quarter-mile straight drop. In six seconds he was doing over sixty mph, and the mouth of the first corner was reaching up.

. . . *Carl's Corner, for Carl Rasch, who went over the top of it nine years ago; and they found him a half-mile down the glacier . . . what was left of him. . . .*

He glanced to his right. It was clear. He eased his flap brakes, dropped back slightly and pulled right. The leading sleds were jockeying in front now, lining for this long left. Brakes flapped like quick wings, and they started around, sleds riding up the vertical ice wall and holding there, ice chips spraying back like contrails from those on the lower part of the wall as they edged their runners against the turn. He came in far right and fast, riding high on the wall and diving off with good acceleration.

The ice was a brilliant blur underneath now, and he could feel the trembling rumble of his sled. They rattled into the Chute, a steep traverse, still gaining speed, still bunched and jostling for position. He was in the rear but this was good; he didn't like this early crowding for the corners.

The sheer wall of Basher Bend loomed, a 120-degree right that dropped hard coming out. He was following close in the slipstream of the sled in front of him, overtaking because of the lessened wind resistance. The corner came, and they were on the wall again. With his slightly greater speed he was able to go higher on the wall, nearly to the top and above the other sled. His G-suit tightened. They swarmed out of the corner and into the Strafing Run, a long, steep dive with a hard pull-out.

A roar rose from the mountain now as the sleds reached speed, a dull rumble like that of avalanche . . . and that is actually what they were now—an avalanche of sleds, and just as deadly.

He pulled ahead of the other sled in the dive and hit the savage pull-out right on the tail of another, and the next turn curved up before them: Hell's Left, a double corner, an abrupt left falling into a short straight with another sharp left at the bottom. He was still overtaking, and they went up the wall side by side, he on the inside, under the other. He eased his left pedal, using edges for the first time, holding himself away from the other by a safe six inches. The course dropped away, straight down the mountain to the second half of the corner, and he felt the sickening sudden smoothness of leaving the ice—he had tried it too fast, and the course was falling away under him. . . .

. . . old Rolf De Kepler, "The Flying Dutchman," laughing over his beer and saying, "Always I am spending more time off the ice than on, hah? So this is more easy to my stomach. Already I have four G-suits to give up on me." . . .

. . . and he made his last flight three years ago off the top at the bottom of Hell's Left . . . four hundred yards, they claimed.

He held firm and straight on the wheel and pulled carefully, barely opening his brakes. The sled touched at a slight angle, lurched, but he caught it by edging quickly. The other sled had pulled ahead. He tucked in behind it. The second left was rushing up at them, narrow and filled with sleds. They dove into it less than a foot apart. Ice chips streamed back from edging runners, rattling against his sled like a storm of bullets. There was an abrupt lurching, the quick left-right slam of air turbulence. A sled was braking hard somewhere ahead. Perhaps two or three. Where? He couldn't see. He reacted automatically . . . full air brakes, hard onto his left edges and steer for the inside; the safest area if a wreck was trying to happen. His sled shivered with the strain of coming off the wall, holding against the force of the corner now only with the knifelike edges of its runners. But the force was too great. He began to skid, edges chattering. He eased them off a little, letting the sled drift slightly sideways. Two others had sliced down to the inside too, edges spraying ice. For a moment he was blinded again, but the corner twisted out flat, and he was through and still on the course, and he knew he was too tight, too hard with his control; he was fighting his sled instead of working with it. . . .

. . . a tourist once asked Erik Sigismund how he controlled his sled, and he answered, "Barely." And even that had failed when he flipped it a year ago and four others ran over him.

An old, lurking thought pounced into him again . . . he couldn't stop this sled now if he wanted to. There was no such thing as stopping, outside of a crash. He had to ride until it ended, and he was suddenly certain that was not going to be at the bottom. Not this time. He had crashed before, too many times, but he had never had this feeling of fear before. Not *this* fear. It was different, and he couldn't say why, and he was letting it affect him. And that was the greatest wrong.

They were thundering into the Jackhammer now, three hundred yards of violent dips. Every sled had its brakes out, and there were fast flashes as some fired braking rockets. But where the walls of the course sloped upward the ice was comparatively smooth. He eased left, to the uphill side, and leaned on his left pedal, holding the sled on the slope with its edges. Then he folded his air brakes and started gaining again. It was necessary; one did not hold back from fear. If that was one's style of life, he would never be a sledder in the first place.

Suddenly from the middle of the leading blurs a sled became airborne from the crest of one of the bumps. It hit once and twisted into the air like something alive. Sleds behind it fired rockets and tried to edge away. One skidded broadside, then rolled. A shattered body panel spun away; the two sleds were demolishing themselves. Someone blew out, streaking into the sky, canopy sparkling high in the sun—and that meant another sled out of control. He pulled full air brakes and fired a rocket, the force slamming him hard against his chest straps. His left arm was ready to fire the charge under the seat. But if he waited too long. . . .

. . . *Kurt Schnabel was proud to be the only man who had never ejected . . . but the one time he had tried he had waited the barest fraction of a moment too long, and his chute came down with his shattered corpse.*

The three wild sleds whirled away, spinning out of sight over the low retaining walls. He folded his brakes. There was a trembling in his arms and legs like the slight but solid shuddering of a flywheel out of balance, involuntary and with a threat of getting worse. He cursed himself. He could have blown out too. No one would have blamed him with that tangle developing in front. But he hadn't . . . and it was too late now.

. . . *only one man had ever blown out without an apparent reason and gotten away with it: Shorty Case in his first race. And when he was asked about it afterward, asked in that overcasual, quiet tone, he had answered, "You bet your sweet, I blew! 'Cause if I hadn't, man, I was gonna pee my pants!"*

But he didn't blow out that day on the Fallaways, the day his sled somersaulted and sowed its wreckage down the course for a half mile . . . and him too. . . .

No, there were no quitters here; only the doers or the dead. And which was he going to be tonight?

. . . *Drive, don't think. . . .*

The Jackhammer smoothed out and plunged downward, and they were hurtling now into the Wingover at over ninety mph. Here were the second biggest grandstands on the course, the second greatest concentration of cameras.

Here two ambulance helicopters stood by, and a priest too. The Wingover. . . .

Imagine an airplane peeling off into a dive . . . imagine a sled doing the same on a towering wall of ice, a wall rising like a great, breaking wave, frozen at the moment of its overhanging curl. . . . The Wingover was a monstrous, curving scoop to the right, nearly fifty feet high, rolling the sleds up, over, and hurling them down into a sixty-five-degree pitch when twisted into a 6-G pull-out to the left.

. . . "Impossible!" When Wilfrid von Gerlach laid out the Stuka that is what they told him about the Wingover. "It cannot be done!"

But von Gerlach had been a Grand Prix racer and a stunt pilot, and when the Stuka was finished he took the first sled through. At the finish he sat quietly for a moment, staring back at the mountain. "At the Wingover I was how fast?" he asked thoughtfully. They replied that he'd been radared there at 110 mph. He nodded, then made the statement the sledders had carried with them ever since.

"It's possible."

He watched the leading sleds line up for that shining, sheer curve and felt the fear freeze through him again. A man was little more than a captive in his sled here. If he was on the right line going in, then it was beautiful; if not, well. . . .

. . . the brotherly beers and the late talk . . .

"Remember when Otto Domagk left Cripple's Corner in that snowstorm?"

"Ya, und ven him vas digged out–Vas? Two hours?–he vas so sleeping."

"And not a mark on him, remember?"

. . . Remember, remember. . . .

He followed in line barely four feet from the sled in front of him and felt the savage, sickening blow as the wall raised and rolled him. A flicker of a shadow, a glimpse of the valley nearly upside-down, then the fall and the increasing shriek of wind and runners, and he was pointing perfectly into the pull-out, still lined exactly with the sled ahead—but there was one sled badly out of line. . . .

And someone pulled their air brakes full open.

Sleds began weaving in the violent turbulence of those brakes. Rockets flashed. A sled went sideways, rolling lazily above the others, and exploded against the wall of the pull-out. He pulled the ejection lever . . . nothing happened!

He was dead, he knew that. He saw two sleds tumbling into the sky, another shattered to pieces and sliding along the course. All that was necessary was to hit one of those pieces . . . but the corner was suddenly gone behind. The course unwound into a long left traverse. He remembered to breathe. There were tooth chips in his mouth and the taste of blood. He swerved past a piece of wreckage, then another. . . .

. . . *How many were dead now? Himself and how many others? But it wasn't fear of death—what was it? What was it that he'd walled off inside—that something secret always skirted as carefully as a ship veers from a hidden reef, knowing it is there—what? And now the wall was down, and he was facing. . . .*

His sled shuddered. He was driving badly, too harsh with his edge control. He narrowly made it through the Boot and Cripple's Corner, spraying ice behind him, but it was not the sled that was out of control. It was him. And he was diving now straight for the gates of hell at over 110 mph.

It was called the Plummet. It began with an innocent, wide left, steeply banked, then the world fell away. It dove over a half mile headlong down a fifty-degree slope straight into a ravine and up the other side, then into a full 180-degree uphill hairpin to the right, a steep straight to the bottom of the ravine again, and finally into a sharp left and a long, rolling straight. It had killed more men than any other part of the course.

Here were the biggest grandstands and the most hungry eyes of the cameras. Here there were three clergy, and emergency operating rooms. Here . . .

. . . *Here he would complete the formality of dying.*

He came into the left too low, too fast for the edges to hold. The sled skidded. He reacted automatically, holding slight left edges and steering into the skid. The sled drifted up the wall, arcing toward the top where nothing showed but the cold blue of the sky. He waited, a part of him almost calm now, waiting to see if the corner would straighten before he went over the top. It did, but he was still skidding, close to the retaining wall, plunging into the half-mile drop nearly sideways. He increased his edges. The tail of the sled brushed the wall and it was suddenly swinging the opposite way. He reversed his wheel and edges, anticipating another skid, but he was not quick enough. The sled bucked, careening up on its left runners. It grazed the wall again, completely out of control now—but he kept trying. . . .

. . . *And that was it; you kept trying. Over and over. No matter how many times you faced yourself it had to be done again. And again. The Self was never satisfied with single victories–you had to keep trying.* . . .

And he was empty no more.

The hospital. How many times had he awakened here? And it was always wonderfully the same: gentle warmth and his body finally relaxed and he would test it piece by piece to see what was bent and broken this time; and always the newsmen and the writers and the other assorted ghouls, and always the question and answer period. Punch-lining, they called it. . . .

"How did it happen?"

"I dozed off."

"Why didn't you eject?"

"Parachuting is dangerous."

"When did you realize you were out of control?"

"At the starting line."

"What will you do now?"

"Heal."

"Will you race again?"

. . . "It's possible."

Outside, the wind was blowing.

■ ■ ■

For a Journal Entry . . .

A good story *demands* some kind of reaction from the reader. You have to talk or write about it just to share it or, maybe, to explore it further. After each story in *Science Fiction Reader*, there will be a journal entry suggestion for you to examine in relationship to the story, to your world, and to yourself. Set up a notebook to use as a journal, making entries as you read each story or as something of interest comes up. It may become a valuable record to look back on.

Why do you climb a mountain? Because it's there. Why do you run in a race? To move as fast as possible, to win, if that is possible. Challenges are important in making us what we are. What kinds of challenges have you faced? What kinds of challenges do you think you will face—and how well do you think you will face them?

For Your Consideration . . .

1. What is Gary Wright's purpose in having his character think about other races and other racers as he awaits the start of the Stuka?
2. There are two kinds of death in "Mirror of Ice." One is the death we all face; the other, something different. What is this other death, and why is it important to the story? Would it also be important in real life?
3. Ultimately, what is the real reason the sledder returns to race again after he has promised himself that he would not?
4. What kinds of physical detail does the author use to make the race more vivid?
5. The next to the last line of the story is "It's possible." It is a repetition of an earlier line. How are the lines connected? Do you think "It's possible" in this context really means, yes, he will race again? Would you race again? Why or why not?
6. Why is the story called "Mirror of Ice"?
7. Unlike other stories in this collection, "Mirror of Ice" is not obviously science fiction. It does not take place on some exotic planet, nor does it involve space or time travel or other familiar trappings of standard science fiction. Why then do you think it is included in *Science Fiction Reader*?

Notes

PAGE

3 *kilometer*—5/8 of a mile
3 *alpine*—high mountains, like the Alps
3 *cockpit*—compartment in a plane, or in this case, sled, where the pilot sits
4 *crimson*—deep red
4 *cantilevered*—supported (as with a beam or bracket)
4 *canopy*—a cover over the cockpit

4 *runners*—the metal skis the sled moves on
5 *peer*—equal
6 *irrevocably*—unchangeably
6 *projectile*—missile
6 *novice*—beginner
7 *jockeying*—maneuvering for position
8 *slipstream*—lower air pressure area formed behind a fast-moving object
8 *avalanche*—snow or mud slide
9 *air turbulence*—rough air currents, as in a storm
10 *demolishing*—destroying
12 *ravine*—large gully
13 *careening*—lurching or tilting sideways

Sunjammer

by Arthur C. Clarke

Arthur C. Clarke is from Somerset in England, although he now makes his home in Ceylon on the other side of the world. He is well known for his television appearances commenting on the moon flights, as well as for the motion picture *2001: A Space Odyssey.* Yet his reputation rests first upon his excellent science fiction novels like *A Fall of Moondust* and *Childhood's End,* as well as classic short stories such as "The Billion Names of God" and "The Star." He writes here about a different kind of spaceship powered by sails, and how these spaceships race to the moon.

The enormous disc of sail strained at its rigging, already filled with the wind that blew between the worlds. In three minutes the race would begin, yet now John Merton felt more relaxed, more at peace, than at any time for the past year. Whatever happened when the Commodore gave the starting signal, whether *Diana* carried him to victory or defeat, he had achieved his ambition. After a lifetime spent in designing ships for others, now he would sail his own.

"T minus two minutes," said the cabin radio. "Please confirm your readiness."

One by one, the other skippers answered. Merton recognized all the voices—some tense, some calm—for they were the voices of his friends and rivals. On the four inhabited worlds, there were scarcely twenty men who could sail a sun-yacht; and they were all here, on the starting-line or aboard the escort vessels, orbiting twenty-two thousand miles above the equator.

"Number One, *Gossamer*—ready to go."

"Number Two, *Santa Maria*—all O.K."

"Number Three, *Sunbeam*—O.K."

"Number Four, *Woomera*—all systems go."

Merton smiled at that last echo from the early, primitive days of astronautics. But it had become part of the tradition of space; and there were times when a man needed to evoke the shades of those who had gone before him to the stars.

"Number Five, *Lebedev*—we're ready."

"Number Six, *Arachne*—O.K."

Now it was his turn, at the end of the line; strange to think that the words he was speaking in this tiny cabin were being heard by at least five billion people.

"Number Seven, *Diana*—ready to start."

"One through Seven acknowledged." The voice from the judge's launch was impersonal. "Now T minus one minute."

Merton scarcely heard it; for the last time, he was checking the tension in the rigging. The needles of all the dynamometers were steady; the immense sail was taut, its mirror surface sparkling and glittering gloriously in the sun.

To Merton, floating weightless at the periscope, it seemed to fill the sky. As it well might—for out there were fifty million square feet of sail, linked to his capsule by almost a hundred miles of rigging. All the canvas of all the tea-clippers that had once raced like clouds across the China seas, sewn into one gigantic sheet, could not match the single sail that *Diana* had spread beneath the sun. Yet it was little more substantial than a soap-bubble; that two square miles of aluminized plastic was only a few millionths of an inch thick.

"T minus ten seconds. All recording cameras *on*."

Something so huge, yet so frail, was hard for the mind to grasp. And it was harder still to realize that this fragile mirror could tow them free of Earth, merely by the power of the sunlight it would trap.

". . . Five, four, three, two, one, *cut!*"

Seven knife-blades sliced through the seven thin lines tethering the yachts to the motherships that had assembled and serviced them.

Until this moment, all had been circling Earth together in a rigidly held formation, but now the yachts would begin to disperse, like dandelion seeds drifting before the breeze. And the winner would be the one that first drifted past the Moon.

Aboard *Diana*, nothing seemed to be happening. But Merton knew better; though his body would feel no thrust, the instrument board told him he was now accelerating at almost one thousandth of a gravity. For a rocket, that figure would have been ludicrous—but this was the first time any solar yacht had attained it. *Diana*'s design was sound; the vast sail was living up to his calculations. At this rate, two circuits of the Earth would build up his speed to escape velocity—then he could head out for the moon, with the full force of the sun behind him.

The full force of the sun. He smiled wryly, remembering all his attempts to explain solar sailing to those lecture audiences back on Earth. That had been the only way he could raise money, in those early days. He might be Chief Designer of Cosmodyne Corporation, with a whole string of successful spaceships to his credit, but his firm had not been exactly enthusiastic about his hobby.

"Hold your hands out to the sun," he'd said. "What do you feel? Heat, of course. But there's pressure as well—though you've never noticed it, because it's so tiny. Over the area of your hands, it only comes to about a millionth of an ounce.

"But out in space, even a pressure as small as that can be important—for it's acting all the time, hour after hour, day after day. Unlike rocket fuel, it's free and unlimited. If we want to, we can use it; we can build sails to catch the radiation blowing from the sun."

At that point, he would pull out a few square yards of sail material and toss it toward the audience. The silvery film would coil and twist like smoke, then drift slowly to the ceiling in the hot-air currents.

"You can see how light it is," he'd continue. "A square mile weighs only a ton, and can collect five pounds of radiation pressure. So it will start moving—and we can let it tow us along, if we attach rigging to it.

"Of course, its acceleration will be tiny—about a thousandth of a g. That doesn't seem much, but let's see what it means.

"It means that in the first second, we'll move about a fifth of an inch. I suppose a healthy snail could do better than that. But after a minute, we've covered sixty feet, and will be doing just over a mile an hour. That's not bad, for something driven by pure sunlight! After an hour, we're forty miles from our starting point, and will be moving at eighty miles an hour. Please remember that in space there's no friction, so once you start anything moving, it will keep going forever. You'll be surprised when I tell you what our thousandth-of-a-g sailing boat will be doing at the end of a day's run. *Almost two thousand miles an hour!* If it starts from orbit—as it has to, of course—it can reach escape velocity in a couple of days. And all without burning a single drop of fuel!"

Well, he'd convinced them, and in the end he'd even convinced Cosmodyne. Over the last twenty years, a new sport had come into being. It had been called the sport of billionaires, and that was true—but it was beginning to pay for itself in terms of publicity and television coverage. The prestige of four continents and two worlds was riding on this race, and it had the biggest audience in history.

Diana had made a good start; time to take a look at the opposition. Moving very gently. Though there were shock absorbers between the control capsule and the delicate rigging, he was determined to run no risks. Merton stationed himself at the periscope.

There they were, looking like strange silver flowers planted in the dark fields of space. The nearest, South America's *Santa Maria*, was only fifty miles away; it bore a resemblance to a boy's kite—but a kite more than a mile on its side. Farther away, the University of Astrograd's *Lebedev* looked like a Maltese cross; the sails that formed the four arms could apparently be tilted for steering purposes. In contrast, the Federation of Australasia's *Woomera* was a simple parachute, four miles in circumference. General Spacecraft's *Arachne*, as its name suggested, looked like a spider web—and had been built on the same principles, by robot shuttles spiraling out from a central point. Eurospace Corporation's *Gossamer* was an identical design, on a slightly smaller scale. And the Republic of Mars' *Sunbeam* was a flat ring, with a half-mile-wide hole in the center, spinning slowly so that centrifugal force gave it stiffness. That was an old idea, but no one had ever made it work. Merton was fairly sure that the colonials would be in trouble when they started to turn.

That would not be for another six hours, when the yachts had moved along the first quarter of their slow and stately twenty-four-hour orbit. Here at the beginning of the race, they were all heading directly away from the sun—running, as it were, before the solar wind. One had to make the most of this lap, before the boats swung round to the other side of Earth and then started to head back into the sun.

Time for the first check, Merton told himself, while he had no navigational worries. With the periscope, he made a careful examination of the sail, concentrating on the points where the rigging was attached to it. The shroud-lines—narrow bands of unsilvered plastic film—would have been completely invisible had they not been coated with fluorescent paint. Now they were taut lines of colored light, dwindling away for hundreds of yards toward that gigantic sail. Each had its own electric windlass, not much bigger than a game fisherman's reel. The little windlasses were continually turning, playing lines in or out, as the autopilot kept the sail trimmed at the correct angle to the sun.

The play of sunlight on the great flexible mirror was beautiful to watch. It was undulating in slow, stately oscillations, sending multiple images of the sun marching across the heavens, until they faded away at the edges of the sail. Such leisurely vibrations were to be expected in this vast and flimsy structure; they were usually quite harmless, but Merton watched them carefully. Sometimes they could build up to the catastrophic undulations known as the wriggles, which could tear a sail to pieces.

When he was satisfied that everything was shipshape, he swept the periscope around the sky, rechecking the positions of his rivals. It was as he had hoped; the weeding-out process had begun, as the less efficient boats fell astern. But the real test would come when they passed into the shadow of the Earth; then maneuverability would count as much as speed.

It seemed a strange thing to do, now that the race had just started, but it might be a good idea to get some sleep. The two-man crews on the other boats could take it in turns, but Merton had no one to relieve him. He must rely on his physical resources—like that other solitary seaman Joshua Slocum, in his tiny *Spray*. The American skipper had sailed *Spray* single-handed round the world; he could never have dreamt that, two centuries later, a man would be sailing single-handed from Earth to moon—inspired, at least partly, by his example.

Merton snapped the elastic bands of the cabin seat around his waist and legs, then placed the electrodes of the sleep-inducer on his forehead. He set the timer for three hours, and relaxed.

Very gently, hypnotically, the electronic pulses throbbed in the frontal lobes of his brain. Colored spirals of light expanded beneath his closed eyelids, widening outward to infinity. Then—nothing . . .

The brazen clamor of the alarm dragged him back from his dreamless sleep. He was instantly awake, his eyes scanning the instrument panel. Only two hours had passed—but above the accelerometer, a red light was flashing. Thrust was falling; *Diana* was losing power.

Merton's first thought was that something had happened to the sail; perhaps the antispin devices had failed, and the rigging had become twisted. Swiftly, he checked the meters that showed the tension in the shroud-lines. Strange, on one side of the sail they were reading normally—but on the other, the pull was dropping slowly even as he watched.

In sudden understanding, Merton grabbed the periscope, switched to wide-angle vision, and started to scan the edge of the sail. Yes—there was the trouble, and it could have only one cause.

A huge, sharp-edged shadow had begun to slide across the gleaming silver of the sail. Darkness was falling upon *Diana*, as if a cloud had passed between her and the sun. And in the dark, robbed of the rays that drove her, she would lose all thrust and drift helplessly through space.

But, of course, there were no clouds here, more than twenty thousand miles above Earth. If there was a shadow, it must be made by man.

Merton grinned as he swung the periscope toward the sun, switching in the filters that would allow him to look full into its blazing face without being blinded.

"Maneuver 4a," he muttered to himself. "We'll see who can play best at *that* game."

It looked as if a giant planet was crossing the face of the sun. A great black disc had bitten deep into its edge. Twenty miles astern, *Gossamer* was trying to arrange an artificial eclipse—specially for *Diana*'s benefit.

The maneuver was a perfectly legitimate one; back in the days of ocean racing, skippers had often tried to rob each other of the wind. With any luck, you could leave your rival becalmed, with his sails collapsing around him—and be well ahead before he could undo the damage.

Merton had no intention of being caught so easily. There was plenty of time to take evasive action; things happened very slowly when you were running a solar sailingboat. It would be at least twenty minutes before *Gossamer* could slide completely across the face of the sun, and leave him in darkness.

Diana's tiny computer—the size of a matchbox, but the equivalent of a thousand human mathematicians—considered the problem for a full second and then flashed the answer. He'd have to open control panels three and four, until the sail had developed an extra twenty degrees of tilt; then the radiation pressure would blow him out of *Gossamer*'s dangerous shadow, back into the full blast of the sun. It was a pity to interfere with the autopilot, which had been carefully programmed to give the fastest possible run—but that, after all, was why he was here. This was what made solar yachting a sport, rather than a battle between computers.

Out went control lines one to six, slowly undulating like sleepy snakes as they momentarily lost their tension. Two miles away, the triangular panels began to open lazily, spilling sunlight through the sail. Yet, for a long time, nothing seemed to happen. It was hard to grow accustomed to this slow motion world, where it took minutes for the effects of any action to become visible to the eye. Then Merton saw that the sail was indeed tipping toward the sun—and that *Gossamer*'s shadow was sliding harmlessly away, its cone of darkness lost in the deeper night of space.

Long before the shadow had vanished, and the disc of the sun had cleared again, he reversed the tilt and brought *Diana* back on course. Her new momentum would carry her clear of the danger; no need to overdo it, and upset his calculations by sidestepping too far. That was another rule that was hard to learn. The very moment you had started something happening in space, it was already time to think about stopping it.

He reset the alarm, ready for the next natural or man-made emergency; perhaps *Gossamer*, or one of the other contestants, would try the same trick again. Meanwhile, it was time to eat, though he did not feel particularly hungry. One used little physical energy in space, and it was easy to forget about food. Easy—and dangerous; for when an emergency arose, you might not have the reserves needed to deal with it.

He broke open the first of the meal packets, and inspected it without enthusiasm. The name on the label—SPACETASTIES—was enough to put him off. And he had grave doubts about the promise printed underneath. Guaranteed Crumbless. It had been said that crumbs were a greater danger to space vehicles than meteorites. They could drift into the most unlikely places, causing short circuits, blocking vital jets that were supposed to be hermetically sealed.

Still, the liverwurst went down pleasantly enough; so did the chocolate and the pineapple puree. The plastic coffee-bulb was warming on the electric heater when the outside world broke in on his solitude. The radio operator on the Commodore's launch routed a call to him.

"Dr. Merton? If you can spare the time, Jeremy Blair would like a few words with you." Blair was one of the more responsible news commentators, and Merton had been on his program many times. He could refuse to be interviewed, of course, but he liked Blair, and at the moment he could certainly not claim to be too busy. "I'll take it," he answered.

"Hello, Dr. Merton," said the commentator immediately.

"Glad you can spare a few minutes. And congratulations—you seem to be ahead of the field."

"Too early in the game to be sure of that," Merton answered cautiously.

"Tell me, doctor—why did you decide to sail *Diana* yourself? Just because it's never been done before?"

"Well, isn't that a very good reason? But it wasn't the only one, of course." He paused, choosing his words carefully. "You know how critically the performance of a sun-yacht depends on its mass. A second man, with all his supplies, would mean another five hundred pounds. That could easily be the difference between winning and losing."

"And you're quite certain that you can handle *Diana* alone?"

"Reasonably sure, thanks to the automatic controls I've designed. My main job is to supervise and make decisions."

"But—two square miles of sail! It just doesn't seem possible for one man to cope with all that!"

Merton laughed.

"Why not? Those two square miles produce a maximum pull of just ten pounds. I can exert more force with my little finger."

"Well, thank you, doctor. And good luck."

As the commentator signed off, Merton felt a little ashamed of himself. For his answer had been only part of the truth; and he was sure that Blair was shrewd enough to know it.

There was just one reason why he was here, alone in space. For almost forty years he had worked with teams of hundreds or even thousands of men, helping to design the most complex vehicles that the world had ever seen. For the last twenty years he had led one of those teams, and watched his creations go soaring to the stars. (But there were failures that he could never forget, even though the fault had not been his.) He was famous, with a successful career behind him. Yet he had never done anything by himself; always he had been one of an army.

This was his very last chance of individual achievement, and he would share it with no one. There would be no more solar yachting for at least five years, as the period of the quiet sun ended and the cycle of bad weather began, with radiation storms bursting through the solar system. When it was safe again for these frail, unshielded craft to venture aloft, he would be too old. If, indeed, he was not too old already. . . .

He dropped the empty food containers into the waste disposal, and turned once more to the periscope. At first, he could find only five of the other yachts; there was no sign of *Woomera.* It took him several minutes to locate her—a dim, star-eclipsing phantom, neatly caught in the shadow of *Lebedev.* He could imagine the frantic efforts the Australasians were making to extricate themselves, and wondered how they had fallen into the trap. It suggested that *Lebedev* was unusually maneuverable; she would bear watching, though she was too far away to menace *Diana* at the moment.

Now the Earth had almost vanished. It had waned to a narrow, brilliant bow of light that was moving steadily toward the sun. Dimly outlined within that burning bow was the night side of the planet, with the phosphorescent gleams of great cities showing here and there through gaps in the clouds. The disc of darkness had already blanked out a huge section of the Milky Way; in a few minutes, it would start to encroach upon the sun.

The light was fading. A purple, twilight hue—the glow of many sunsets, thousands of miles below—was falling across the sail, as *Diana* slipped silently into the shadow of Earth. The sun plummeted below that invisible horizon. Within minutes, it was night.

Merton looked back along the orbit he had traced now a quarter of the way around the world. One by one he saw the brilliant stars of the other yachts wink out, as they joined him in the brief night. It would be an hour before the sun emerged from that enormous black shield, and through all that time they would be completely helpless, coasting without power.

He switched on the external spotlight, and started to search the now darkened sail with its beam. Already, the thousands of acres of film were beginning to wrinkle and become flaccid; the shroud-lines were slackening, and must be wound in lest they become entangled. But all this was expected; everything was going as planned.

Forty miles astern, *Arachne* and *Santa Maria* were not so

lucky. Merton learned of their troubles when the radio burst into life on the emergency circuit.

"Number Two, Number Six—this is Control. You are on a collision course. Your orbits will intersect in sixty-five minutes! Do you require assistance?"

There was a long pause while the two skippers digested this bad news. Merton wondered who was to blame; perhaps one yacht had been trying to shadow the other, and had not completed the maneuver before they were both caught in darkness. Now there was nothing that either could do; they were slowly but inexorably converging together, unable to change course by a fraction of a degree.

Yet, sixty-five minutes! That would just bring them out into sunlight again, as they emerged from the shadow of the Earth. They still had a slim chance, if their sails could snatch enough power to avoid a crash. There must be some frantic calculations going on, aboard *Arachne* and *Santa Maria.*

Arachne answered first; her reply was just what Merton had expected.

"Number Six calling Control. We don't need assistance, thank you. We'll work this out for ourselves."

I wonder, thought Merton. But at least it will be interesting to watch. The first real drama of the race was approaching—exactly above the line of midnight on the sleeping Earth.

For the next hour, Merton's own sail kept him too busy to worry about *Arachne* and *Santa Maria.* It was hard to keep a good watch on that fifty million square feet of dim plastic out there in the darkness, illuminated only by his narrow spotlight and the rays of the still distant moon. From now on, for almost half his orbit round the Earth, he must keep the whole of this immense area edge-on to the sun. During the next twelve or fourteen hours, the sail would be a useless encumbrance; for he would be heading into the sun, and its rays could only drive him backward along his orbit. It was a pity that he could not furl the sail completely, until he was ready to use it again. But no one had yet found a practical way of doing this.

Far below, there was the first hint of dawn along the edge of the Earth. In ten minutes, the sun would emerge from its eclipse; the coasting yachts would come to life again as the blast of radiation struck their sails. That would be the moment of crisis for *Arachne* and *Santa Maria*—and, indeed, for all of them.

Merton swung the periscope until he found the two dark shadows drifting against the stars. They were very close together—perhaps less than three miles apart. They might, he decided, just be able to make it. . . .

Dawn flashed like an explosion along the rim of Earth, as the sun rose out of the Pacific. The sail and shroud-lines glowed a brief crimson, then gold, then blazed with the pure white light of day. The needles of the dynamometers began to lift from their zeros—but only just. *Diana* was still almost completely weightless, for with the sail pointing toward the sun, her acceleration was now only a few millionths of a gravity.

But *Arachne* and *Santa Maria* were crowding on all the sail they could manage, in their desperate attempt to keep apart. Now, while there was less than two miles between them, their glittering plastic clouds were unfurling and expanding with agonizing slowness, as they felt the first delicate push of the sun's rays. Almost every TV screen on Earth would be mirroring this protracted drama; and even now, at this very last minute, it was impossible to tell what the outcome would be.

The two skippers were stubborn men. Either could have cut his sail, and fallen back to give the other a chance; but neither would do so. Too much prestige, too many millions, too many reputations, were at stake. And so, silently and softly as snowflakes falling on a winter night, *Arachne* and *Santa Maria* collided.

The square kite crawled almost imperceptibly into the circular spider's web; the long ribbons of the shroud-lines twisted and tangled together with dreamlike slowness. Even aboard *Diana*, busy with his own rigging, Merton could scarcely tear his eye away from this silent, long drawn out disaster.

For more than ten minutes the billowing, shining clouds continued to merge into one inextricable mass. Then the crew capsules tore loose and went their separate ways, missing each other by hundreds of yards. With a flare of rockets, the safety launches hurried to pick them up.

That leaves five of us, thought Merton. He felt sorry for the skippers who had so thoroughly eliminated each other, only a few hours after the start of the race; but they were young men, and would have another chance.

Within minutes, the five had dropped to four. From the very beginning, Merton had had doubts about the slowly rotating *Sunbeam.* Now he saw them justified.

The Martian ship had failed to tack properly; her spin had given her too much stability. Her great ring of a sail was turning to face the sun, instead of being edge-on to it. She was being blown back along her course at almost her maximum acceleration.

That was about the most maddening thing that could happen to a skipper—worse even than a collision, for he could blame only himself. But no one would feel much sympathy for the frustrated colonials, as they dwindled slowly astern. They had made too many brash boasts before the race, and what had happened to them was poetic justice.

Yet it would not do to write off *Sunbeam* completely. With almost half a million miles still to go, she might still pull ahead. Indeed, if there were a few more casualties, she might be the only one to complete the race. It had happened before.

However, the next twelve hours were uneventful, as the Earth waxed in the sky from new to full. There was little to do while the fleet drifted round the unpowered half of its orbit, but Merton did not find the time hanging heavily on his hands. He caught a few hours' sleep, ate two meals, wrote up his log, and became involved in several more radio interviews. Sometimes, though rarely, he talked to the other skippers, exchanging greetings and friendly taunts. But most of the time he was content to float in weightless relaxation, beyond all the cares of Earth, happier than he had been for many years. He was—as far as any man could be in space—master of his own fate, sailing the ship upon which he had lavished so much skill, so much love, that she had become part of his very being.

The next casualty came when they were passing the line between Earth and sun, and were just beginning the powered half of the orbit. Aboard *Diana,* Merton saw the great sail stiffen as it tilted to catch the rays that drove it. The acceleration began to climb up from the microgravities, though it would be hours yet before it would reach its maximum value.

It would never reach it for *Gossamer.* The moment when power came on again was always critical, and she failed to survive it.

Blair's radio commentary, which Merton had left running at low volume, alerted him with the news: "Hullo, *Gossamer* has the wriggles!" He hurried to the periscope, but at first could see nothing wrong with the great circular disc of *Gossamer*'s sail. It was difficult to study it, as it was almost edge-on to him and so appeared as a thin ellipse; but presently he saw that it was twisting back and forth in slow, irresistible oscillations. Unless the crew could damp out these waves, by properly timed but gentle tugs on the shroud-lines, the sail would tear itself to pieces.

They did their best, and after twenty minutes it seemed that they had succeeded. Then, somewhere near the center of the sail, the plastic film began to rip. It was slowly driven outward by the radiation pressure, like smoke coiling upward from a fire. Within a quarter of an hour, nothing was left but the delicate tracery of the radial spars that had supported the great web. Once again there was a flare of rockets, as a launch moved in to retrieve the *Gossamer*'s capsule and her dejected crew.

"Getting rather lonely up here, isn't it?" said a conversational voice over the ship-to-ship radio.

"Not for you, Dimitri," retorted Merton. "You've still got company back there at the end of the field. I'm the one who's lonely, up here in front." It was not an idle boast. By this time *Diana* was three hundred miles ahead of the next competitor, and his lead should increase still more rapidly in the hours to come.

Aboard *Lebedev*, Dimitri Markoff gave a good-natured chuckle. He did not sound, Merton thought, at all like a man who had resigned himself to defeat.

"Remember the legend of the tortoise and the hare," answered the Russian. "A lot can happen in the next quarter-million miles."

It happened much sooner than that, when they had completed their first orbit of Earth and were passing the starting line again —though thousands of miles higher, thanks to the extra energy the sun's rays had given them. Merton had taken careful sights on the other yachts, and had fed the figures into the computer. The answer it gave for *Woomera* was so absurd that he immediately did a recheck.

There was no doubt of it—the Australasians were catching up at a fantastic rate. No solar yacht could possibly have such an acceleration, unless—

A swift look through the periscope gave the answer. *Woomera*'s rigging, pared back to the very minimum of mass, had given way. It was her sail alone, still maintaining its shape, that was racing up behind him like a handkerchief blown before the wind. Two hours later it fluttered past, less than twenty miles away. But long before that, the Australasians had joined the growing crowd aboard the Commodore's launch.

So now it was a straight fight between *Diana* and *Lebedev*—for though the Martians had not given up, they were a thousand miles astern and no longer counted as a serious threat. For that matter, it was hard to see what *Lebedev* could do to overtake *Diana*'s lead. But all the way round the second lap—through eclipse again, and the long, slow drift against the sun, Merton felt a growing unease.

He knew the Russian pilots and designers. They had been trying to win this race for twenty years, and after all, it was only fair that they should, for had not Pyotr Nikolayevich Lebedev been the first man to detect the pressure of sunlight, back at the very beginning of the twentieth century? But they had never succeeded.

And they would never stop trying. Dimitri was up to something—and it would be spectacular.

Aboard the official launch, a thousand miles behind the racing yachts, Commodore van Stratten looked at the radiogram with angry dismay. It had traveled more than a hundred million miles, from the chain of solar observatories swinging high above the blazing surface of the sun, and it brought the worst possible news.

The Commodore—his title, of course, was purely honorary—back on Earth he was Professor of Astrophysics at Harvard—had been half expecting it. Never before had the race been arranged so late in the season; there had been many delays, they had gambled and now, it seemed they might all lose.

Deep beneath the surface of the sun, enormous forces were gathering. At any moment, the energies of a million hydrogen bombs might burst forth in the awesome explosion known as a solar flare. Climbing at millions of miles an hour, an invisible fireball many times the size of Earth would leap from the sun and head out across space.

The cloud of electrified gas would probably miss the Earth completely. But if it did not, it would arrive in just over a day. Spaceships could protect themselves, with their shielding and their powerful magnetic screen. But the lightly built solar yachts, with their paper-thin walls, were defenseless against such a menace. The crews would have to be taken off, and the race abandoned.

John Merton still knew nothing of this as he brought *Diana* round the Earth for the second time. If all went well, this would be the last circuit, both for him and for the Russians. They had spiraled upward by thousands of miles, gaining energy from the sun's rays. On this lap, they should escape from Earth completely—and head outward on the long run to the moon. It was a straight race now. *Sunbeam*'s crew had finally withdrawn, exhausted, after battling valiantly with their spinning sail for more than a hundred thousand miles.

Merton did not feel tired; he had eaten and slept well, and *Diana* was behaving herself admirably. The autopilot, tensioning the rigging like a busy little spider, kept the great sail trimmed to the sun more accurately than any human skipper. Though by this time, the two square miles of plastic sheet must have been riddled by hundreds of micrometeorites, the pin-head-sized punctures had produced no falling off to thrust.

He had only two worries. The first was shroud-line number eight, which could no longer be adjusted properly. Without any warning, the reel had jammed; even after all these years of astronautical engineering, bearings sometimes seized up in vacuum. He could neither lengthen nor shorten the line, and would have to navigate as best he could with the others. Luckily, the most difficult maneuvers were over. From now on, *Diana* would have the sun behind her as she sailed straight down the solar wind. And as the old-time sailors often said, it was easy to handle a boat when the wind was blowing over your shoulder.

His other worry was *Lebedev*, still dogging his heels three hundred miles astern. The Russian yacht had shown remarkable maneuverability, thanks to the four great panels that could be tilted around the central sail. All her flip-overs as she rounded Earth had been carried out with superb precision; but to gain maneuverability she must have sacrificed speed. You could not have it both ways. In the long, straight haul ahead, Merton should be able to hold his own. Yet he could not be certain of victory until, three or four days from now, *Diana* went flashing past the far side of the moon.

And then, in the fiftieth hour of the race, near the end of the second orbit around Earth, Markoff sprang his little surprise.

"Hello, John," he said casually, over the ship-to-ship circuit. "I'd like you to watch this. It should be interesting."

Merton drew himself across to the periscope and turned up the magnification to the limit. There in the field of view, a most improbable sight against the background of the stars, was the glittering Maltese cross of *Lebedev*, very small but very clear. And then, as he watched, the four arms of the cross slowly detached themselves from the central square and went drifting away, with all their spars and rigging, into space.

Markoff had jettisoned all unnecessary mass, now that he was coming up to escape velocity and need no longer plod patiently around the Earth, gaining momentum on each circuit. From now on, *Lebedev* would be almost unsteerable—but that did not matter. All the tricky navigation lay behind her. It was as if an old-time yachtsman had deliberately thrown away his rudder and heavy keel—knowing that the rest of the race would be straight downwind over a calm sea.

"Congratulations, Dimitri," Merton radioed. "It's a neat trick. But it's not good enough—you can't catch up now."

"I've not finished yet," the Russian answered. "There's an old winter's tale in my country, about a sleigh being chased by wolves. To save himself, the driver has to throw off the passengers one by one. Do you see the analogy?"

Merton did, all too well. On this final lap, Dimitri no longer needed his co-pilot. *Lebedev* could really be stripped down for action.

"Alexis won't be very happy about this," Merton replied. "Besides, it's against the rules."

"Alexis isn't happy, but I'm the captain. He'll just have to wait around for ten minutes until the Commodore picks him up. And the regulations say nothing about the size of the crew—you should know that."

Merton did not answer. He was too busy doing some hurried calculations, based on what he knew of *Lebedev*'s design. By the time he had finished, he knew that the race was still in doubt. *Lebedev* would be catching up with him at just about the time he hoped to pass the moon.

But the outcome of the race was already being decided, ninety-two million miles away.

On Solar Observatory Three, far inside the orbit of Mercury, the automatic instruments recorded the whole history of the flare. A hundred million square miles of the sun's surface suddenly exploded in such blue-white fury that, by comparison, the rest of the disc paled to a dull glow. Out of that seething inferno, twisting and turning like a living creature in the magnetic fields of its own creation, soared the electrified plasma of the great flare. Ahead of it, moving at the speed of light, went the warning flash of ultraviolet and x-rays. That would reach Earth in eight minutes, and was relatively harmless. Not so the charged atoms that were following behind at their leisurely four million miles an hour—and which, in just over a day, would engulf *Diana*, *Lebedev*, and their accompanying little fleet in a cloud of lethal radiation.

The Commodore left his decision to the last possible minute. Even when the jet of plasma had been tracked past the orbit of Venus, there was a chance that it might miss the Earth. But when it was less than four hours away, and had already been picked up by the moon-based radar network, he knew that there was no hope. All solar sailing was over for the next five or six years until the Sun was quiet again.

A great sigh of disappointment swept across the solar system. *Diana* and *Lebedev* were halfway between Earth and moon, running neck and neck—and now no one would ever know which was the better boat. The enthusiasts would argue the result for years; history would merely record: race cancelled owing to solar storm.

When John Merton received the order, he felt a bitterness he had not known since childhood. Across the years, sharp and clear, came the memory of his tenth birthday. He had been promised an exact scale model of the famous spaceship *Morning Star*, and for weeks had been planning how he would assemble it, where he would hang it up in his bedroom. And then, at the last moment, his father had broken the news. "I'm sorry, John—it costs too much money. Maybe next year . . ."

Half a century and a successful lifetime later, he was a heart-broken boy again.

For a moment, he thought of disobeying the Commodore. Suppose he sailed on, ignoring the warning? Even if the race were abandoned, he could make a crossing to the moon that would stand in the record books for generations.

But that would be worse than stupidity. It would be suicide—and a very unpleasant form of suicide. He had seen men die of radiation poisoning, when the magnetic shielding of their ships had failed in deep space. No—nothing was worth that. . . .

He felt sorry for Dimitri Markoff as for himself; they both deserved to win, and now victory would go to neither. No man could argue with the sun in one of its rages, even though he might ride upon its beams to the edge of space.

Only fifty miles astern now, the Commodore's launch was drawing alongside *Lebedev*, preparing to take off her skipper. There went the silver sail, as Dimitri—with feeling that he would share—cut the rigging. The tiny capsule would be taken back to Earth, perhaps to be used again—but a sail was spread for one voyage only.

He could press the jettison button now, and save his rescuers a few minutes of time. But he could not do so. He wanted to stay aboard to the very end, on the little boat that had been for so long a part of his dreams and his life. The great sail was spread now at right angles to the sun, exerting its utmost thrust. Long ago it had torn him clear of Earth—and *Diana* was still gaining speed.

Then, out of nowhere, beyond all doubt or hesitation, he knew what must be done. For the last time, he sat down before the computer that had navigated him halfway to the moon.

When he had finished, he packed the log and his few personal belongings. Clumsily—for he was out of practice, and it was not an easy job to do by oneself—he climbed into the emergency survival suit.

He was just sealing the helmet when the Commodore's voice called over the radio. "We'll be alongside in five minutes, Captain. Please cut your sail so we won't foul it."

John Merton, first and last skipper of the sun-yacht *Diana*, hesitated for a moment. He looked for the last time round the tiny cabin, with its shining instruments and its neatly arranged controls, now all locked in their final positions. Then he said to the microphone: "I'm abandoning ship. Take your time to pick me up. *Diana* can look after herself."

There was no reply from the Commodore, and for that he was grateful. Professor van Stratten would have guessed what was happening—and would know that, in these final moments, he wished to be left alone.

He did not bother to exhaust the airlock, and the rush of escaping gas blew him gently out into space; the thrust he gave her then was his last gift to *Diana.* She dwindled away from him, sail glittering splendidly in the sunlight that would be hers for centuries to come. Two days from now she would flash past the moon; but the moon, like the Earth, could never catch her. Without his mass to slow her down, she would gain two thousand miles an hour in every day of sailing. In a month, she would be traveling faster than any ship that man had ever built.

As the sun's rays weakened with distance, so her acceleration would fall. But even at the orbit of Mars, she would be gaining a thousand miles an hour in every day. Long before then, she would be moving too swiftly for the sun itself to hold her. Faster than any comet that had ever streaked in from the stars, she would be heading out into the abyss.

The glare of rockets, only a few miles away, caught Merton's eye. The launch was approaching to pick him up at thousands of times the acceleration that *Diana* could ever attain. But engines could burn for a few minutes only, before they exhausted their fuel—while *Diana* would still be gaining speed, driven outward by the sun's eternal fires, for ages yet to come.

"Good-bye, little ship," said John Merton. "I wonder what eyes will see you next, how many thousand years from now."

At last he felt at peace, as the blunt torpedo of the launch nosed up beside him. He would never win the race to the moon; but his would be the first of all man's ships to set sail on the long journey to the stars.

■ ■ ■

For a Journal Entry . . .

In many ways Arthur Clarke's story "Sunjammer" is a very poetic one. Can you find examples of poetic language or parts of the story which seem particularly poetic to you? Does poetry seem out of place to you in SF? For the fun of it, try putting together a simple (or complex, that's up to you) poem on some SF theme, whether it be on races through space, alien visitations, exotic worlds, or the space of man's mind.

For Your Consideration . . .

1. John Merton's sun-yacht is called *Diana.* Check your mythology to find out why this is an appropriate name for such a ship.
2. Unlike Wright's "Mirror of Ice," Clarke's story is obviously SF. Compare the two stories. What elements in "Sunjammer" make it a part of the SF tradition?
3. How does Clarke use scientific detail to make his story realistic? Is his use of detail appropriate or does it detract from the story? Support your answer.
4. Unlike many stories, SF or otherwise, there is no "bad guy" in "Sunjammer." There are merely competitors. Is the story any less effective for it? Why or why not?
5. Would it have been a better story if *Diana* had either won or lost the race so that the matter was settled? Justify your opinion.

Notes

PAGE

17 *astronautics*—science dealing with problems of space travel
17 *evoke the shades*—call forth the ghosts or memory of someone
17 *dynamometers*—instruments that measure energy
18 *ludicrous*—ridiculous
18 *escape velocity*—speed needed to escape the gravitational pull of a planet or sun
18 *Cosmodyne*—name of company Merton works for
20 *centrifugal force*—force tending to make rotating objects move away from the center
20 *fluorescent*—glowing
20 *windlasses*—equipment for lifting or hoisting something, in this case a sail
20 *catastrophic*—disastrous
20 *maneuverability*—ability to move around easily
21 *electrode*—end of an electrical wire
21 *sleep-inducer*—something that causes sleep
21 *frontal lobes*—front lobes of the brain
21 *brazen clamor*—loud, bold noise
21 *accelerometer*—instrument to measure the increasing speed of an object
21 *shroud-lines*—ropes helping steady the mast of a sailing ship or in this story a sun-yacht
21 *thrust*—force pushing something
22 *evasive*—avoiding something
22 *momentum*—the force that keeps a moving object moving
22 *autopilot*—a device for guiding something automatically
23 *hermetically*—airtight
23 *puree*—very thick souplike form of a given food
24 *mass*—matter; weight
25 *extricate*—get out of
25 *phosphorescent*—glowing
25 *plummeted*—dropped straight down
25 *emerged*—came out
25 *flaccid*—soft and limp
26 *converging*—coming together
26 *encumbrance*—burden
27 *furl*—roll up
27 *inextricable*—badly entangled, unable to get free
28 *frustrated*—defeated; unable to attain a goal
28 *microgravities*—small amounts of pressure
29 *oscillations*—motions swinging back and forth
29 *delicate tracery*—delicate pattern as in a spider web
29 *radial spars*—poles supporting a sail
30 *astern*—behind

30 *astrophysics*—physics of space
31 *solar flare*—explosion on the sun's surface that fans out into the solar system
31 *micrometeorites*—very small particles moving through space
32 *magnification*—increase of the apparent size of something
32 *plod*—move slowly but steadily
32 *analogy*—comparison
33 *plasma*—extremely hot gas
33 *lethal*—deadly
34 *jettison*—throw or cast out
35 *abyss*—great emptiness

Escape the Morning

by Poul Anderson

Poul Anderson is a graduate scientist who began writing and selling science fiction while he was still in college. A tall man of Scandinavian descent, he has traveled much in the North to write adventure stories of his Viking ancestors. Yet it is his science fiction that makes his reputation, with such unforgettable novels as *Brain Wave* and *Guardians of Time*, and memorable stories like "Call Me Joe." "Escape the Morning" shows what life may very much be like on our moon when people from Earth settle there.

Troubles never come singly, or Mark Jordan would not have been racing the sunrise for his life.

It had begun as just a pleasant bit of excitement. He was on watch in the communications room. Someone had to be there all the time when they were at home. Emergencies on the moon have a way of arriving fast and nasty. But in the normal course of events, whichever of them stood by was free to tend to private matters—read, study, fool around with a hobby, or work out in the gymnasium corner of the big plastic-faced chamber. Mark had finished his calculus assignment and was on the homemade exercycle. With gravity one-sixth as strong as it is on Earth, you must spend at least two hours out of the twenty-four keeping fit, or your very bones will atrophy.

Through the whirr of the machine, the rustle of air from the ventilator ducts, his own quick breath, he got the buzz. His heart jumped. He sprang to the 'visor panel. Meters stared like goblin eyes at a tall sandy-haired eighteen-year-old flipping switches. The screen came to life with Derek van Hulst's middle-aged face.

"Copernicus to Jordan Station," the Dutchman said. "Oh, you. Hello, Mark. Can you take a stranded man in?"

"Sure. Plenty of supplies, and choice of guestrooms." Mark grinned. He not only did not begrudge the rations—like all pioneers, the lunar colonists take for granted that anyone in distress is to be helped—but he was delighted. Here was a new person to talk to, for fourteen Earth-days!

Van Hulst surprised him. "They're sending a 'tank' from Kepler to continue him on his way, so you won't have him more than about twenty hours."

Mark whistled. "Who is he to rate that?"

"The Minister of Technology of the Federated Congo, Achille Kamolondo. He's been on the moon for a couple of weeks now, inspecting the facilities. Was bound to us from Keplersburg when something crippled his vehicle. He was not sure what, when he called us."

"Was that wise? I mean letting a newcomer drive off alone, and this near dawn?"

"They told me, calling ahead, that he'd proved himself to be able. And he hates wasting time. So they lent him a Go-Devil." Mark felt a bit of envy for someone who could take one of those out and travel at fifty miles an hour. A turtle, such as most people owned, would do twenty if you pushed. Of course, a Go-Devil had room for no more than a single person. "Let us not waste time either," Van Hulst said. "Sunrise is barely two hours off where he is. That's on the Main Trace, naturally, between kilometers 321 and 322. About eighteen miles from your place, correct? On your way."

"Yes, sir. I'll report back when I return." Mark switched off and left on the run, which is fast indeed on the moon.

"Tom!" he shouted down the long, machine-humming hall. "Condition Yellow!"

His brother, two years younger, pelted from the hydroponics section where he had been tending algae. Judy, their kid sister, didn't hear; she was in the soundproofed "classroom," taking a Spanish lesson beamed from the school in Tycho Crater. Mark explained on the way to the lockers.

"I could go," Tom said wistfully.

"You could," Mark agreed, "but you're not going to, me bucko."

Tom didn't argue. A station, alone in barrenness, needs a captain as much as any ship does. For all the free-and-easy affection between them, Mark was the Old Man.

Tom helped him into his undergarment and spacesuit. "Air valves, okay. Pressure, okay. Faceplate gasket, okay. . . ." They went through the ritual fast, yet not missing a point. The gear must be perfect. Human beings can't survive a night temperature of 250° below Fahrenheit zero, nor can they breathe vacuum.

Leaving his helmet open, Mark cycled through the garage lock and squirmed along a gang tube into his turtle. He sealed the doors, automatically disconnecting the tube. His hands, gloved but trained, found controls as he sat down. Light blossomed in the narrow steel cell, revealing an extra seat crowded next to his among the instruments. Aft of the cabin was space for extra passengers, supplies, and life-support equipment. When there was cargo to carry, the turtle was hitched to a train of the wagons that stood in this rough-hewn cave. He did not see them through windows; even the best glass is fragile and a poor radiation shield. Television panels are better.

The solar cells topside gathered energy during the two-week lunar day to charge every cell in the station, including those in the electric motors. Mark started off. Oblong, ugly, hull pitted by tiny meteorites, the car lumbered forth on its eight huge wheels, up the ramp and out onto the surface of the moon.

Though he had spent most of his life here, Mark always caught his breath at sight of the night heavens. Stars and stars and stars crowded the dark, uncountable, unwinking, unbelievably bright. Earth hung halfway down the western sky, four times the size of Luna seen from itself and many times as radiant. The planet was at half phase, and its majestic turning had brought America into view. Clear weather, Mark saw; he could identify glitters on the black side which were the titanic eastern cities. Westward the plains stretched soft brown and bluish green, then the Rockies, the Pacific coast, the ocean like burnished sapphire streaked with a few white cloud masses.

Dad's country, he thought. *Mother's. My own too, for that matter.* His eyes stung a little.

The moonscape offered less. Behind him jutted the small crater beneath which Jordan Station had been dug. The slopes were half concealed by machines busily at work, and dominated by the radio-TV mast on top. Otherwise that flatland called the Oceanus Procellarum reached bare as far as he could see. Not that he saw any great distance. No air or dust scattered the Earth-shine, but the coal-like mineral crust did, so that he seemed to move in the focus of a dim blue spotlight which faded out mere yards away. The horizon was a circle of starlessness, barely three miles wide. Mark turned on the headlights. They helped some—enough, if you were used to these conditions.

He plugged his suit radio into the turtle's. "Mark to Tom," he said. "All systems go. I'm on my way."

"Check," said his brother's voice in his earplugs.

"And mate," Mark said. He gave himself to the job of driving. Luminous stones, one per kilometer, marked this side path, as they did the Trace. Neither was a true road, only a safe route. Cosmic dust, raining down for four billion years, binding molecule to molecule in vacuum, had formed the treacherous, brittle surface of the lunar *maria.*

At the Trace, he followed its roundabout path easterly for almost an hour. This near day, little traffic ever moved, and he found no sign of man except the stones and the gaunt microwave relay masts that glided by, out of darkness and back into darkness. The hum of the motor, the flutter of his own breath, deepened the silence that enclosed him. He didn't mind. Mostly he thought about his future. He'd have to go live in the dorm at Tycho University next year, in order to take laboratory courses for an engineering degree. Well, the station was in good shape financially, he'd hire an assistant and Tom could take over as boss. . . .

The undiffused puddle of light cast by his headbeams suddenly gleamed against metal. He allowed plenty of space for low-gravity braking, even from twenty mph. The Go-Devil stood inert, a four-wheeled egg with metal curled back from several holes around the motor. Huh! Meteorite shrapnel had done that. Mark tuned his 'caster. "Hello, there," he said into his helmet mike. "You okay?"

"Yes." He heard fluent English with a slight French accent. "Are you my, ah, rescuer? They informed me someone would come."

"Right-o. Do you know how to get into a turtle?"

"*Pardon?* Oh, yes, your kind of vehicle. Certainly I do." Monsieur Kamolondo sounded a trifle offended. *Well, he must've been under quite a strain,* Mark thought. *It's lonesome to wait for help. And on top of the shock when that debris ripped into his engine compartment—*

The Congolese stepped through the inner door of the entry lock. Frost formed on his suit, chilled by the brief exposure when he crossed from car to car. He sat down beside Mark and fumbled with his helmet. Mark helped him open it.

"But you are a boy!" he exclaimed.

He wasn't so old himself: a large man with a face brown, intelligent, and proud. The leaders of the Congo were more aristocrats than politicians. That was inevitable, in a country still struggling up from the near savagery into which its long Time of Troubles had plunged it. Nonetheless, Mark couldn't help bristling a little at the way those eyes regarded him.

"I'm not too young to run a station," he said, and introduced himself curtly. He gunned the motor and turned the wheel. "We'd better head right back. One hour till sunrise."

"A station? No, I remember. An isolated enterprise. What do you do?"

Mark decided to be friendly. "We mine copper," he said. "Started with an underground vein of ice, but that gave out. Anyway, so much water has been gotten now that the price is way down. So Dad went in for minerals. I've found some oil, too, that may be worth going after when we've saved the capital we'd need."

"Oil?" Kamolondo blurted.

"Sure, there's plenty on the moon. It's been a hundred years ago since Hoyle theorized that petroleum wasn't formed biologically, but by photochemical reactions in the original dust cloud that became the solar system. Even then, they'd found heterocyclic compounds in some meteorites. Turned out he was right. Of course, the lighter fractions here have long ago escaped to space, but the cracking plant at Maurolycus makes rocket fuel from what's left. That's one big reason why the moon is colonized, you know. Spaceships can leave here a lot easier than they can leave Earth, especially when we tank 'em up on the spot."

Kamolondo stiffened. "I was merely surprised to learn of deposits in this particular neighborhood," he said in a chill voice. "After all, I am my country's Minister of Technology."

Mark bit his lip. "Sorry . . . sir."

Kamolondo made an obvious effort to unbend. "Well," he said, "I should not expect you to be too, ah, too conversant with Earth affairs, this far from anyplace."

Like fun we aren't, Mark thought resentfully. *We're in steady television contact. And some of the smartest people Earth ever produced come here to live—to learn, explore, start a thousand enterprises on a whole new world.*

"I remain astonished at your age," Kamolondo said. "What happened to your parents?"

"They died when a pit collapsed, two years ago. Nobody had suspected, then, that ferraloy cross-braces can change into a weaker crystalline form under lunar conditions. They left me and my brother and sister. We get along."

"You were actually allowed to—" Kamolondo clicked his tongue.

"We get along, I say." Mark wrestled with temper. "Everybody knew we could. Pioneers have always had to grow up fast, haven't they? Our machinery is automated, we need only nurse it. We attend school, the same as most young people do, via two-way television." He forced a smile. "Not enough economic surplus yet that the International Lunar Commission can build school buses!"

"You are American, are you not?" Kamolondo asked. "I marvel that American youth can live without cinema and dances."

"Why, the latest entertainment gets beamed straight from Earth. And social life, well, we get to Copernicus town or

Keplersburg quite often, hauling in a load of ore." Mark changed the subject. "Why are you here, sir?"

"To look at what there is," Kamolondo said. "My people have reached the point where we too would like to exploit the moon."

But this is our home! Mark thought. *You don't exploit your home!* No, wait. Kamolondo hadn't meant it that way. He'd only meant that the Congo wanted to share in developing the frontier and reaping the rewards. Fair enough. But still the word rankled.

Kamolondo stared out into the screens. "I don't see how you endure such bleakness," he murmured.

Mark flushed. "Maybe this isn't much for scenery," he said, "but you ought to visit one of the mountain ranges, or the big craters. Makes anything on Earth look sick."

"I have done so," Kamolondo said. "I continue to prefer an honest forest."

Everybody to his own taste, Mark thought. He drove on in a silence that thickened. Thank goodness they'd soon be taking this oaf off his hands. Kamolondo was doubtless as happy about that as he was.

They had traveled twelve miles when the catastrophe hit them.

It came with the deadly suddenness of most bad luck on the moon. At one moment Mark was wondering what Judy would cook for dinner—if His Excellency didn't like her algaburger with soy sauce, too bad for him—and then thunder exploded. The turtle rocked. A fire-streak slashed before Mark's vision, dazzling his eyes, stunning his ears. Metal toned. Shock ran through his spacesuit and his bones. Two screens went dark. A pattern of holes gaped black in the wall, and air shrieked outward.

Even as he slammed his faceplate shut, he heard Kamolondo cry something in his mother language, and, *"Ah, non! Encore!"* A wild part of him wondered why the minister wanted an encore, until he remembered his French. "Oh, no! Again!" The same thing had happened to the turtle as had happened to the Go-Devil. A meteorite shower, hitherto uncharted, must be pounding the Moon.

Mark's hearing tolled toward silence. He sensed his heartbeat gone loud, smelled with unnatural sharpness the faint tang of ozone and his body in the suit, felt the fabric stiff against him. Outside, dust settled and he identified a tiny new crater, barely visible in the wan light.

He took a firm grip on his wits and tried the car's radio. Dead. And a helmet unit, necessarily small and simple, couldn't link with the trans-lunar microwave system, had indeed no more than a mile of effective range.

He unstrapped himself. "Let's go," he said.

"What—what—" Behind the glass, Kamolondo's face was briefly fluid. Then his lips firmed. He asked in a level voice, "What do you mean?"

"A rock from space landed close by," Mark said. "Not big, but traveling at miles per second. It scattered chunks of surface material the way a military shell scatters shrapnel. We're wrecked. If Tom knew, he'd come for us, but he doesn't and I can't raise him." He glanced at the instruments. "We have six miles to go, and dawn is half an hour away."

Kamolondo did not stir. "Can we make it?" You had to admire how coolly he took the news.

"We've got to." Mark opened the lock.

They were out under Earth and the uncaring stars, in gloom and one faint circle of blue, when Kamolondo said, "I am very sorry to have exposed you to this."

"Nobody could have known, sir," Mark said. "One of the chances you take, living here. We expect the big meteorite showers, but little ones on long-period orbits are something else."

"I realize that. You are young, however, your whole life before you. I would rather have died alone back there."

"You're not such a doddering ruin yourself." Mark managed to laugh. "And who says we can't beat the sunrise? Come on."

He set off, with the long bounding stride of a colonist. You can walk fast under low gravity, if you know how. Though the sunrise line would sweep across this part of the Trace in about thirty minutes, it would need another half-hour or so to reach Jordan Station. Thus, at six miles per hour, which was vigorous but not exhausting, they'd arrive in time. And afterward the Commission would doubtless buy a new turtle for the man who saved a VIP from a messy death. Maybe throw in a Go-Devil as well.

A curse brought Mark around on his heel. Kamolondo had stumbled. The Congolese got erect, pushed too hard, lost a second before the moon drew him back to the ground, overbalanced when he hit and fell again. Fear rammed into Mark. Kamolondo didn't have the reflexes. In two weeks he could barely have learned to handle himself at an ordinary pace. Indoors, at that, without an airtank on his shoulders or tricky constant-volume joints at his knees. "Come on, sir!" Mark urged.

"I am trying." Kamolondo's breath was harsh.

He floundered over minutes and miles. Mark sweated, studied the radium-dialed chronometer on the wrist of his suit, clocked them by the kilometer stones. Too slow, too slow. The sun was catching up.

In some years, they could have stood awhile under lunar daylight. Though the temperature would swiftly rise to the boiling point of water, the suits had thermostatic units and faceplates blocked off ultraviolet light. But now the sun was in a flare period. Lethal radiation, gamma rays, protons, electrons seethed out of the storms upon it. Nothing less than a "tank," a vehicle armored in lead and screened by intense magnetic fields, could keep a man alive through such a day.

The tops of the easternmost relay masts began to shine.

Kamolondo halted. His face invisible within the helmet, but he stood straight and said calmly, "There is no sense in both of us dying. Proceed."

For an instant, Mark was ready to obey. Tom, Judy, Dad's and Mother's hopes, his own dreams, were they to come to an end for him in the horror of radiation sickness?

But you don't abandon anyone on the moon. And Kamolondo was a good joe, trying to do his best for his poor, hurt country.

Mark's mind sprang toward an answer. He felt suddenly, oddly at peace.

"Listen," he said. "Relax. Catch your breath. You're going to need it. We have about three miles left, but the last one is south instead of west." To strike directly across this shadowland, away from the markers, was to make death certain. "The sun's not far below the horizon now, but dawnline on the moon travels eight miles an hour at the equator, a bit less here. So I figure we can rest a little. Then in the last ten or twelve minutes we can do those three miles."

"A mile . . . one-point-six kilometer. . . ." Kamolondo's voice sounded far and strange. "Impossible. You break every athletic record."

"On Earth! We're here. Our suits and equipment weigh as much as we do. But the total weight is still a third of what we'd have on Earth, stripped. And no air resistance. Also, running is a lot easier rhythm than what we were doing. Different from back home, of course. You only fall one-sixth as fast. Lean way forward, shove hard with one leg, rise just a bit off the ground. You'll have plenty of time to recover with the other foot. Watch me."

Kamolondo did. He tried it himself. Mark was surprised how well he managed, considering how awkward he'd been before. But a dash is, indeed, smoother than a fast walk, on any planet. The only question was whether they both had the endurance. One-sixth gravity or not, they must better the four-minute mile by some twenty per cent, across thrice the distance.

Well, we'll soon know if we can. "Ready? We're off."

They ran.

Ghostly glowing, the kilometer stones fell behind, one by one by one. Beyond them and the glow cast by Earth, which seemed to fill the sky with an unreachable loveliness, was utter night. But the sun came striding.

Push, glide, come down, check. Push, glide, come down, check. Impact shivers back, through boots and feet and muscles. Airpumps roar, feeding oxygen to starved cells. Breath grows harsh, mouth dry, pulse frantic. You lurch, lose your balance, he helps you rise and you start again. He trips on an iron fragment and dances crazily, trying not to topple. You count the kilometers creeping past, and then lose count, for blindness has begun to drift across your eyes. You lose yourself, you are nothing but pain and weariness. Still you run!

Turn off here. Now you're bound straight south, and dawn gains on you. Not far to go. The uppermost crater crags are fiery. A piece of you thinks that you're close enough to call Tom on your suit radio, but no, he'd need too long to snatch a turtle out. Good-bye, Tom. Good-bye, Judy. Good-bye, universe I wanted to know. A spindle of zodiacal light climbs pearl-colored over the world's rim. The sun will follow, life-giver, death-giver.

Still you run.

And there is the cave-mouth of the garage. You fling yourself down the ramp. The blessed dark engulfs you, with ten feet of solid matter between you and the solar storm. You collapse on the floor next to your friend, strangling for breath. Only slowly do you understand that you will live.

There is no greater wonder.

They were inside and unsuited, swallowing huge amounts of coffee while Tom and Judy fussed about them, when Kamolondo said, "Mark, in that hour we became brothers."

It was spoken with such dignity that Mark was ashamed he could find no better answer than, "Aw, gee, nothing like that."

"You saved me." Kamolondo raised his head. "Yet more than owing you my life, I want to help you, and your brother and sister. In my position, I have both money and influence. You can come to Earth, study in the finest schools, make the best careers the planet has to offer. I would be proud if you return home with me."

Mark set down his cup. The Jordans stared at each other. Judy and Tom shook their heads slightly. Mark found himself close to laughter.

"Why, thanks," he said. "But come to Earth?" He swept his hand in a gesture that included the neat little kitchen, the rooms beyond, the subtle and powerful machines working topside, this whole station that was theirs. "Whatever *for?*"

■ ■ ■

For a Journal Entry . . .

"Who are you?" is really one of the hardest questions there is to answer, unless you think your name tells *who* you are. How would the teenagers in "Escape the Morning" answer that question? How would you answer that question?

For Your Consideration . . .

1. What kinds of adjustments would you have to make in order to live on the moon?
2. In what sense are Mark, Tom, and Judy typical pioneers?
3. Mark is the "Old Man" of the station. By the end of the story, how has he proven his worth as an "Old Man"?
4. Give some examples of details that Poul Anderson uses to make his story realistic.
5. How does Kamolondo annoy Mark when they first meet? Is his annoyance justifiable, in your opinion?
6. Why is the story called "Escape the Morning"? Is it a good title? Why or why not?
7. The teen-agers' response to returning to Earth is "Whatever for?" Would you have responded the same way? Why or why not?
8. What typical SF theme does "Escape the Morning" deal with?

Notes

PAGE

39 *exercycle*—a stationary bicyclelike piece of equipment used for exercising
39 *atrophy*—waste away
40 *ventilator ducts*—openings to allow good air circulation
40 *technology*—applications of science in our daily lives
40 *kilometer*—about five-eighths of a mile
40 *pelted*—ran
40 *hydroponics*—the science of growing plants in water without using soil
41 *vacuum*—nothing, no air
41 *meteorites*—different-sized objects that orbit through the solar system
41 *titanic*—having great strength or power
42 *burnished*—polished
42 *luminous*—glowing
42 *cosmic dust*—dust that is floating in space
42 *molecule*—a small unit made up of different atoms; joins with other molecules to make cells
42 *treacherous*—dangerous
42 *gaunt*—very thin
42 *microwave relay masts*—poles to relay messages sent by microwave
42 *undiffused*—concentrated
43 *aristocrats*—upper-class people
43 *photochemical*—coming from the chemical reactions of light
44 *heterocyclic*—having to do with carbon

44 *ferraloy*—having to do with iron
44 *crystalline*—made of crystal
45 *rankled*—bothered
45 *catastrophe*—disaster
45 *hitherto*—up until this time
45 *ozone*—a form of oxygen with a pungent smell
47 *floundered*—stumbled along
49 *zodiacal light*—a faint disc of light around the sun

If

by Harry Harrison

Perhaps it is his artist's eye—he was a commercial artist for many years—that gives Harry Harrison the defect of vision that makes him see things in a different light. Or maybe it is his desire always to be somewhere else; he lived abroad for many years and has traveled in over forty countries. Voyaging and strange eyesight have produced novels like *In Our Hands, the Stars*, which takes place in Denmark and on the moon. "If" is a story about today, and how today will affect tomorrow. Can the future course of the entire world be completely altered by the small actions of a boy today?

We are there, we are correct. The computations were perfect. That is the place below."

"You are a worm," 17 said to her companion 35, who resembled her every way other than in number. "That is the place. But nine years too early. Look at the meter."

"I am a worm. I shall free you of the burden of my useless presence." 35 removed her knife from the scabbard and tested the edge, which proved to be exceedingly sharp. She placed it against the white wattled width of her neck and prepared to cut her throat.

"Not now," 17 hissed. "We are short-handed already and your corpse would be valueless to this expedition. Get us to the correct time at once. Our power is limited, you may remember."

"It shall be done as you command," 35 said as she slithered to the bank of controls. Forty-four ignored the talk, keeping her multicell eyes focused on the power control bank, constantly making adjustments with her spatulate fingers in response to the manifold dials.

"That is it," 17 announced, rasping her hands together with pleasure. "The correct time, the correct place. We must descend and make our destiny. Give praise to the Saur of All who rules the destinies of all."

"Praise Saur," her two companions muttered, all of their attention on the controls.

Straight down from the blue sky the globular vehicle fell. It was round and featureless, save for the large rectangular port, on the bottom now, and made of some sort of green metal, perhaps anodized aluminum, though it looked harder. It had no visible means of flight or support, yet it fell at a steady and controlled rate. Slower and slower it moved until it dropped from sight behind the ridge at the northern end of Johnson's Lake, just at the edge of the tall pine grove. There were fields nearby, with cows, who did not appear at all disturbed by the visitor. No human being was in sight to view the landing. A path cut in from the lake here, a scuffed dirt trail that went to the highway.

An oriole sat on a bush and warbled sweetly; a small rabbit hopped from the field to nibble a stem of grass. This bucolic and peaceful scene was interrupted by the scuff of feet down the trail and a high-pitched and singularly monotone whistling. The bird flew away, a touch of soundless color, while the rabbit disappeared into the hedge. A boy came over the rise from the direction of the lake shore. He wore ordinary boy clothes and carried a school bag in one hand, a small and homemade cage of wire screen in the other. In the cage was a small lizard which clung to the screen, its eyes rolling in what presumably was fear. The boy, whistling shrilly, trudged along the path and into the shade of the pine grove.

"Boy," a high-pitched and tremulous voice called out. "Can you hear me, boy?"

"I certainly can," the boy said, stopping and looking around for the unseen speaker. "Where are you?"

"I am by your side, but I am invisible. I am your fairy godmother. . . ."

The boy made a rude sound by sticking out his tongue and blowing across it while it vibrated. "I don't believe in invisibility or fairy godmothers. Come out of those woods, whoever you are."

"All boys believe in fairy godmothers," the voice said, but a worried tone edged the words now. "I know all kinds of secrets. I know your name is Don and. . . ."

"Everyone knows my name is Don and no one believes any more in fairies. Boys now believe in rockets, submarines and atomic energy."

"Would you believe space travel?"

"I would."

Slightly relieved, the voice came on stronger and deeper. "I did not wish to frighten you, but I am really from Mars and have just landed. . . ."

Don made the rude noise again. "Mars has no atmosphere and no observable forms of life. Now come out of there and stop playing games."

After a long silence the voice said, "Would you consider time travel?"

"I could. Are you going to tell me that you are from the future?"

With relief: "Yes I am."

"Then come out where I can see you."

"There are some things that the human eye should not look upon. . . ."

"Horseapples! The human eye is okay for looking at anything you want to name. You come out of there so I can see who you are—or I'm leaving."

"It is not advisable." The voice was exasperated. "I can prove I am a temporal traveler by telling you the answers to tomorrow's mathematics test. Wouldn't that be nice? Number one, 1.76. Number two. . . ."

"I don't like to cheat, and even if I did you can't cheat on the new math. Either you know it or you fail it. I'm going to count to ten, then go."

"No, you cannot! I must ask you a favor. Release that common lizard you have trapped and I will give you three wishes—I mean answer three questions."

"Why should I let it go?"

"Is that the first of your questions?"

"No. I want to know what's going on before I do anything. This lizard is special. I never saw another one like it around here."

"You are right. It is an Old World acrodont lizard of the order Rhiptoglossa, commonly called a chameleon."

"It *is!*" Don was really interested now. He squatted in the path and took a red-covered book from his school bag and laid it on the ground. He turned the cage until the lizard was on the bottom and placed it carefully on the book. "Will it really turn color?"

"To an observable amount, yes. Now if you release her . . ."

"How do you know it's a her? The time traveler bit again?"

"If you must know, yes. The creature was purchased from a pet store by one Jim Benan, and is one of a pair. They were both released two days ago when Benan, deranged by the voluntary drinking of a liquid containing quantities of ethyl alcohol, sat on the cage. The other, unfortunately, died of his wounds, and this one alone survives. The release . . ."

"I think this whole thing is a joke and I'm going home now. Unless you come out of there so I can see who you are."

"I warn you. . . ."

"Good-bye." Don picked up the cage. "Hey, she turned sort of brick red!"

"Do not leave. I will come forth."

Don looked on, with a great deal of interest, while the creature walked out from between the trees. It was blue, had large and goggling—independently moving—eyes, wore a neatly cut brown jumpsuit and had a pack slung on its back. It was also only about seven inches tall.

"You don't much look like a man from the future," Don said. "In fact you don't look like a man at all. You're too small."

"I might say that you are too big; size is a matter of relevancy. And I am from the future, though I am not a man."

"That's for sure. In fact you look a lot like a lizard." In sudden inspiration, Don looked back and forth at the traveler and at the cage. "In fact you look a good deal like this chameleon here. What's the connection?"

"That is not to be revealed. You will now do as I command or I will injure you gravely." Seventeen turned and waved toward the woods. "Thirty-five, this is an order. Appear and destroy that growth over there."

Don looked on with increasing interest as the green basketball of metal drifted into sight from under the trees. A circular disc slipped away on one side and a gleaming nozzle, not unlike the hose nozzle on a toy firetruck, appeared through the opening. It pointed toward a hedge a good thirty feet away. A shrill whining began from the depths of the sphere, rising in pitch until it was almost inaudible. Then, suddenly, a thin line of light spat out toward the shrub which crackled and instantly burst into flame. Within a second it was a blackened skeleton.

"The device is called a roxidizer and is deadly," 17 said. "Release the chameleon at once or we will turn it on you."

Don scowled. "All right. Who wants the old lizard anyway?" He put the cage on the ground and started to open the cover. Then he stopped—and sniffed. Picking up the cage again he started across the grass toward the blackened bush.

"Come back!" 17 screeched. "We will fire if you go another step."

Don ignored the lizardoid, which was now dancing up and down in an agony of frustration, and ran to the bush. He put his hand out—and apparently right through the charred stems.

"I thought something was fishy," he said. "All that burning and everything just upwind of me—and I couldn't smell a thing." He turned to look at the time traveler, who was slumped in gloomy silence. "It's just a projected image of some kind, isn't it? Some kind of three-dimensional movie." He stopped in sudden thought, then walked over to the still hovering temporal transporter. When he poked at it with his finger he apparently pushed his hand right into it.

"And this thing isn't here either. Are you?"

"There is no need to experiment. I, and our ship, are present only as what might be called temporal echoes. Matter cannot be moved through time, that is an impossibility, but the concept of matter can be temporarily projected. I am sure that this is too technical for you. . . ."

"You're doing great so far. Carry on."

"Our projections are here in a real sense to us, though we can only be an image or a sound wave to any observers in the time we visit. Immense amounts of energy are required and almost the total resources of our civilization are involved in this time transfer."

"Why? And the truth for a change. No more fairy godmother and that kind of malarky."

"I regret the necessity to use subterfuge, but the secret is too important to reveal casually without attempting other means of persuasion."

"Now we get to the real story." Don sat down and crossed his legs comfortably. "Give."

"We need your aid, or our very society is threatened. Very recently—on our time scale—strange disturbances were detected by our instruments. Ours is a simple saurian existence, some million or so years in the future, and our race is dominant. Yours has long since vanished in a manner too horrible to mention to your young ears. Something is threatening our entire race. Research quickly uncovered the fact that we are about to be overwhelmed by a probability wave and wiped out, a great wave of negation sweeping toward us from our remote past."

"You wouldn't mind tipping me off to what a probability wave is, would you?"

"I will take an example from your own literature. If your grandfather had died without marrying, you would not have been born and would not now exist."

"But I do."

"The matter is debatable in the greater xan-probability universe, but we shall not discuss that now. Our power is limited. To put the affair simply, we traced our ancestral lines back through all the various mutations and changes until we found the individual proto-lizard from which our line sprang."

"Let me guess." Don pointed at the cage. "This is the one?"

"She is." Seventeen spoke in solemn tones as befitted the moment. "Just as somewhen, somewhere there is a proto-tarsier from which your race sprang, so is there this temporal mother of ours. She will bear young soon, and they will breed and grow in this pleasant valley. The rocks near the lake have an appreciable amount of radioactivity which will cause mutations. The centuries will roll by, and one day, our race will reach its heights of glory.

"But not if you don't open that cage."

Don rested his chin on fist and thought. "You're not putting me on anymore? This is the truth?"

Seventeen drew herself up and waved both arms—or front legs—over her head. "By the Saur of All, I promise," she intoned. "By the stars eternal, the seasons vernal, the clouds, the sky, the matriarchal I . . ."

"Just cross your heart and hope to die, that will be good enough for me."

The lizardoid moved its eyes in concentric circles and performed this ritual.

"Okay then, I'm as soft-hearted as the next guy when it comes to wiping out whole races."

Don unbent the piece of wire that sealed the cage and opened the top. The chameleon rolled one eye up at him and looked at the opening with the other. Seventeen watched in awed silence and the time vehicle bobbed closer.

"Get going," Don said, and shook the lizard out into the grass.

This time the chameleon took the hint and scuttled away among the bushes, vanishing from sight.

"That takes care of the future," Don said. "Or the past, from your point of view."

Seventeen and the time machine vanished silently and Don was alone again on the path.

"Well, you could have at least said thanks before taking off like that! People have more manners than lizards any day, I'll tell you that."

He picked up the now empty cage and his school bag and started for home.

He had not heard the quick rustle in the bushes, nor did he see the prowling tomcat with the limp chameleon in its jaws.

■ ■ ■

For a Journal Entry . . .

Consider all of the possibilities and problems you might run into if time travel were an actuality. For instance, if you were to go back in time and kill (accidentally, of course) your great grandfather when he was just a little boy, would that automatically destroy you? And if so, how could you have gone back in time in the first place? You see, boxes within boxes, puzzles within puzzles . . .

For Your Consideration . . .

1. What is a *paradox?* In what way is Harry Harrison's "If" paradoxical?
2. How does Harrison suggest the alien-ness of the time travelers at the very beginning of the story?
3. Humor in SF is still something of a rarity. How does Don's reaction to the time travelers help to make "If" humorous? What other elements of humor keep this story light in tone, when it is actually about the destruction of an entire civilization?
4. Is the surprise ending effective? Why or why not?
5. Discuss the meaning of *irony* in your class. What is *ironic* about "If"?
6. Harrison has his aliens produce a *roxidizer.* Why should such a device be familiar to all readers of SF? What other traditional SF elements does he use? Why then is the story not just a run-of-the-mill time travel story?

Notes

PAGE
52 *computations*—mathematical figuring
52 *resembled*—looked like
52 *meter*—instrument for measuring something
52 *scabbard*—a sheath to hold a knife
52 *exceedingly*—very, extremely
52 *wattled*—fleshy, wrinkled
53 *multicell*—having many cells
53 *spatulate*—like a spatula, broad and flat
53 *manifold*—having many shapes and forms
53 *anodized*—having a protective oxide film
53 *warbled*—sang
53 *bucolic*—rural, rustic
53 *monotone*—same level tone; no variation

53 *tremulous*—trembling
54 *exasperated*—annoyed, losing patience
54 *temporal*—time
55 *deranged*—made crazy
56 *sphere*—a round globelike object
57 *malarky*—slang for nonsense
57 *subterfuge*—trickery
57 *saurian*—having lizard characteristics
57 *tarsier*—small animals from the East with large eyes, related to the lemur
58 *intoned*—uttered in a singing tone
58 *concentric*—having a common center

Prone

by Mack Reynolds

Mack Reynolds, who now makes his home in Mexico after years of world traveling, was at one time an officer on a United States Army transport ship, something few others can claim. Politics run in his family—"my father was twice candidate for President of the United States," he writes. "In 1928 and 1932. He didn't make it." War, not politics, interests Reynolds in this story, which suggests that good luck and bad luck that might very well be the deadliest weapon.

SupCom Bull Underwood said in a voice ominously mild, "I continually get the impression that every other sentence is being left out of this conversation. Now, tell me, General, what do you mean *things happen around him?*"

"Well, for instance, the first day Mitchie got to the academy a cannon burst at a demonstration."

"What's a cannon?"

"A pre-guided-missile weapon," the commander of the Terra Military Academy told him. "You know, shells propelled by gunpowder. We usually demonstrate them in our history classes. This time four students were injured. The next day sixteen were hurt in ground war maneuvers."

There was an element of respect in the SupCom's tone. "Your course must be rugged."

General Bentley wiped his forehead with a snowy handkerchief even as he shook it negatively. "It was the first time any such thing happened. I tell you, sir, since Mitchie Farthingworth has been at the academy things have been chaotic. Fires in the dormitories, small arms exploding, cadets being hospitalized right and left. We've just got to expel that boy!"

"Don't be ridiculous," the SupCom growled. "He's the apple of his old man's eye. We've got to make a hero out of him if it means the loss of a battle fleet. But I still don't get this. You mean the Farthingworth kid is committing sabotage?"

"It's not that. We investigated. He doesn't do it on purpose, things just *happen* around him. Mitchie can't help it."

"Confound it, stop calling him Mitchie!" Bull Underwood snapped. "How do you know it's him if he doesn't do it? Maybe you're just having a run of bad luck."

"That's what I thought," Bentley said, "until I ran into Admiral Lawrence of the Space Marines Academy. He had the same story. The day Mitchie—excuse me, sir—Michael Farthingworth set foot in Nuevo San Diego, things started happening. When they finally got him transferred to our academy the trouble stopped."

It was at times like these that Bull Underwood regretted his shaven head. He could have used some hair to tear. "Then it *must* be sabotage if it stops when he leaves!"

"I don't think so, sir."

The SupCom took a deep breath, snapped to his secretarobot, "Brief me on Cadet Michael Farthingworth, including his early life." While he waited he growled under his breath, "A stalemated hundred-year war on my hands with those Martian *makrons* and I have to get things like this tossed at me."

In less than a minute the secretarobot began: "Son of Senator Warren Farthingworth, Chairman War Appropriations Committee. Twenty-two years of age. Five foot six, one hundred and thirty, blue eyes, brown hair, fair. Born and spent early youth in former United States area. Early education by mother. At age of eighteen entered Harvard but schooling was interrupted when roof of assembly hall collapsed, killing most of faculty. Next year entered Yale, leaving two months later when 90 per cent of the university's buildings were burned down in the holocaust of '85. Next attended University of California but failed to graduate owing to the earthquake which completely . . ."

"That's enough," the SupCom rapped. He turned and stared at General Bentley. "What the hell is it? Even if the kid was a psychokinetic saboteur he couldn't accomplish all that."

The academy commander shook his head. "All I know is that since his arrival at the Terra Military Academy there's been an endless series of casualties. And the longer he's there the worse it gets. It's twice as bad now as when he first arrived." He got to his feet wearily. "I'm a broken man, sir, and I'm leaving this in your hands. You'll have my resignation this afternoon. Frankly, I'm afraid to return to the school. If I do, some day I'll probably crack my spine bending over to tie my shoelaces. It just isn't safe to be near that boy."

For a long time after General Bentley had left, SupCom Bull Underwood sat at his desk, his heavy underlip in a pout. "And just when the next five years' appropriation is up before the committee," he snarled at nobody.

He turned to the secretarobot. "Put the best psycho-technicians available on Michael Farthingworth. They are to discover . . . well, they are to discover why in hell things happen around him. Priority one."

Approximately a week later the secretarobot said, "May I interrupt you, sir? A priority one report is coming in."

Bull Underwood grunted and turned away from the star chart he'd been studying with the two Space Marine generals. He dismissed them and sat down at his desk.

The visor lit up and he was confronted with the face of an elderly civilian. "Doctor Duclos," the civilian said. "Case of Cadet Michael Farthingworth."

"Good," the SupCom rumbled. "Doctor, what in the devil is wrong with young Farthingworth?"

"The boy is an accident prone."

Bull Underwood scowled at him. "A what?"

"An accident prone." The doctor elaborated with evident satisfaction. "There is indication that he is the most extreme case in medical history. Really a fascinating study. Never in my experience have I been—"

"Please, Doctor. I'm a layman. What is an accident prone?"

"Ah, yes. Briefly, an unexplained phenomenon first noted by the insurance companies of the nineteenth and twentieth centuries. An accident prone has an unnaturally large number of accidents happen either to him, or, less often, to persons in his vicinity. In Farthingworth's case, they happen to persons about him. He himself is never affected."

The SupCom was unbelieving. "You mean to tell me there are some persons who just naturally have accidents happen to them without any reason?"

"That is correct," Duclos nodded. "Most prones are understandable. Subconsciously, the death wish is at work and the prone *seeks* self-destruction. However, science has yet to discover the forces behind the less common type such as Farthingworth exemplifies." The doctor's emphatic shrug betrayed his Gallic background. "It has been suggested that it is no more than the laws of chance at work. To counterbalance the accident prone, there should be persons at the other extreme who are blessed with abnormally good fortune. However . . ."

SupCom Bull Underwood's lower lip was out, almost truculently. "Listen," he interrupted. "What can be done about it?"

"Nothing," the doctor said, his shoulders raising and lowering again. "An accident prone seems to remain one as a rule. Not always, but as a rule. Fortunately, they are rare."

"Not rare enough," the SupCom growled. "These insurance companies, what did they do when they located an accident prone?"

"They kept track of him and refused to insure the prone, his business, home, employees, employers, or anyone connected with him."

Bull Underwood stared unblinkingly at the doctor, as though wondering whether the other's whole explanation was an attempt to pull his leg. Finally he rapped, "Thank you, Doctor Duclos. That will be all." The civilian's face faded from the visor.

The SupCom said slowly to the secretarobot, "Have Cadet

Farthingworth report to me." He added sotto voce, "And while he's here have all personnel keep their fingers crossed."

The photoelectric-controlled door leading to the sanctum sanctorum of SupCom Bull Underwood glided quietly open and a lieutenant entered and came to a snappy attention. The door swung gently shut behind him.

"Well?" Bull Underwood growled.

"Sir, a Cadet Michael Farthingworth to report to you."

"Send him in. Ah, just a minute, Lieutenant Brown. How do you feel after talking to him?"

"Me, sir? I feel fine, sir." The lieutenant looked blankly at him.

"Hmmm. Well, send him in, confound it."

The lieutenant turned and the door opened automatically before him. "Cadet Farthingworth," he announced.

The newcomer entered and stood stiffly before the desk of Earth's military head. Bull Underwood appraised him with care. In spite of the swank academy uniform, Michael Farthingworth cut a wistfully ineffectual figure. His faded blue eyes blinked sadly behind heavy contact lenses.

"That'll be all, Lieutenant," the SupCom said to his aide.

"Yes, sir." The lieutenant about-faced snappily and marched to the door—which swung sharply forward and quickly back again before the lieutenant was halfway through.

SupCom Bull Underwood winced at the crush of bone and cartilage. He shuddered, then snapped to his secretarobot, "Have Lieutenant Brown hospitalized . . . and, ah . . . see he gets a Luna Medal for exposing himself to danger beyond the call of duty."

He swung to the newcomer and came directly to the point. "Cadet Farthingworth," he rapped, "do you know what an accident prone is?"

Mitchie's voice was low and plaintive. "Yes, sir."

"You do?" Bull Underwood was surprised.

"Yes, sir. At first such things as the school's burning down didn't particularly impress me as being personally connected with me, but the older I get, the worse it gets, and after what happened to my first date, I started to investigate."

The SupCom said cautiously, "What happened to the date?"

Mitchie flushed. "I took her to a dance and she broke her leg."

The SupCom cleared his throat. "So finally you investigated?"

"Yes, sir," Mitchie Farthingworth said woefully. "And I found I was an accident prone and getting worse geometrically. Each year I'm twice as bad as the year before. I'm glad you've discovered it too, sir. I . . . I didn't know what to do. Now it's in your hands."

The SupCom was somewhat relieved. Possibly this wasn't going to be as difficult as he had feared. He said, "Have you any ideas, Mitchie, ah, that is . . ."

"Call me Mitchie if you want, sir. Everybody else does."

"Have you any ideas? After all, you've done as much damage to Terra as a Martian task force would accomplish."

"Yes, sir. I think I ought to be shot."

"Huh?"

"Yes, sir. I'm expendable," Mitchie said miserably. "In fact, I suppose I'm probably the most expendable soldier that's ever been. All my life I've wanted to be a spaceman and do my share toward licking the Martians." His eyes gleamed behind his lenses. "Why, I've . . ."

He stopped and looked at his commanding officer pathetically. "What's the use? I'm just a bust. An accident prone. The only thing to do is liquidate me." He tried to laugh in self-deprecation but his voice broke.

Behind him, Bull Underwood heard the glass in his office window shatter without seeming cause. He winced again, but didn't turn.

"Sorry, sir," Mitchie said. "See? The only thing is to shoot me."

"Look," Bull Underwood said urgently, "stand back a few yards farther, will you? There, on the other side of the room." He cleared his throat. "Your suggestion has already been considered, as a matter of fact. However, due to your father's political prominence, shooting you had to be ruled out."

From a clear sky the secretarobot began to say, " 'Twas brillig, and the slithy toves did gyre and gimble in the wabe."

SupCom Bull Underwood closed his eyes in pain and shrunk back into his chair. "What?" he said cautiously.

"The borogoves were mimsy as all hell," the secretarobot said decisively and shut up.

Mitchie looked at it. "Slipped its cogs, sir," he said helpfully. "It's happened before around me."

"The best damned memory bank in the system," Underwood protested. "Oh, no."

"Yes, sir," Mitchie said apologetically. "And I wouldn't recommend trying to repair it, sir. Three technicians were electrocuted when I was . . ."

The secretarobot sang, "O frabjous day! Callooh! Callay!"

"Completely around the corner," Mitchie said.

"This," said Bull Underwood, "is too frabjous much! Senator or no Senator, appropriations or no appropriations, with my own bare hands—"

As he strode impulsively forward, he felt the rug giving way beneath him. He grasped desperately for the edge of the desk, felt ink bottle and water carafe go crashing over.

Mitchie darted forward to his assistance.

"Stand back!" Bull Underwood roared, holding an ankle with one hand, shaking the other hand in the form of a fist. "Get out of here, confound it!" Ink began to drip from the desk over his shaven head. It cooled him not at all. "It's not even safe to destroy you! It'd wipe out a regiment to try to assemble a firing squad! It—" Suddenly he paused, and when he spoke again his voice was like the coo of a condor.

"Cadet Farthingworth," he announced, "after considerable deliberation on my part I have chosen you to perform the most hazardous operation that Terra's forces have undertaken in the past hundred years. If successful, this effort will undoubtedly end the war."

"Who me?" Mitchie said.

"Exactly," SupCom Underwood snapped. "This war has been going on for a century without either side being able to secure that slight edge, that minute advantage which would mean victory. Cadet Farthingworth, you have been chosen to make the supreme effort which will give Terra that superiority over the Martians." The SupCom looked sternly at Mitchie.

"Yes, sir," he clipped. "What are my orders?"

The SupCom beamed at him. "Spoken like a true hero of Terra's Space Forces. On the spaceport behind this building is a small spycraft. You are to repair immediately to it and blast off for Mars. Once there you are to land, hide the ship, and make your way to their capital city."

"Yes, sir! And what do I do then?"

"Nothing," Bull Underwood said with satisfaction. "You do absolutely nothing but live there. I estimate that your presence in the enemy capital will end the war in less than two years."

Michael Farthingworth snapped him a brilliant salute. "Yes, sir."

Spontaneous combustion broke out in the wastebasket.

Through the shards of his window, SupCom Bull Underwood could hear the blast-off of the spyship. Half a dozen miles away the flare of a fuel dump going up in flames lighted up the sky.

Seated there in the wreckage of his office he rubbed his ankle tenderly. "The only trouble is when the war is over we'll have to bring him home."

But then he brightened. "Perhaps we could leave him there as our occupation forces. It would keep them from ever recovering to the point where they could try again."

He tried to get to his feet, saying to the secretarobot, "Have them send me in a couple of medical corpsmen."

"Beware the Jabberwock," the secretarobot sneered.

■ ■ ■

For a Journal Entry . . .

Extrasensory powers have long been a favorite device of SF writers. Telepathy, psychokinetics, teleportation, prescience have long been an important part of SF. There is something fascinating about the powers (suspected or otherwise) of the human mind. We are told that we use only 10 per cent of our brain's capacity. What realms would the full use of man's brain open up to him? What could we do to tap that power source? What kinds of abilities do you think such additional use of the brain would give us?

For Your Consideration . . .

1. What is an *accident prone?* What is the probable cause of the destruction that surrounds Mitchie?
2. What is the special dilemma that SupCom Bull Underwood finds himself in? How does he solve it?
3. Basically, people who go around causing earthquakes are not funny. Yet Mitchie's story is funny. How does Mack Reynolds keep his story humorous?
4. Why do people automatically call Michael Farthingworth "Mitchie"?
5. In Lewis Carroll's poem "Jabberwocky" a "beamish boy" sets out to slay the dreaded Jabberwock. If at all possible, read the poem and then answer these questions: In what sense is Mitchie a "beamish boy" who is sent out to slay the dragon? In what other ways does Reynolds use Carroll's poem?

Notes

PAGE
61 *ominously*—threateningly
61 *guided missile*—a missile that is guided to its target by radio beams
61 *propelled*—driven
62 *chaotic*—in great disorder
62 *sabotage*—destruction of military equipment
62 *secretarobot*—an SF term referring to a robot secretary
62 *stalemated*—deadlocked
62 *holocaust*—disaster by fire
63 *psychokinetic*—having the ability to move things using mental powers
63 *saboteur*—a person who deliberately destroys equipment, railroads, bridges, etc.
63 *casualties*—people hurt or killed in an accident or war
64 *vicinity*—nearby
64 *exemplifies*—is an example of
64 *emphatic*—emphasized
64 *Gallic*—French
64 *truculently*—rudely, shortly
65 *appraised*—examined
65 *ineffectual*—not effective; seemingly useless
65 *plaintive*—sad
65 *investigate*—examine; look into; study
66 *expendable*—unnecessary; may be discarded
66 *pathetically*—pitifully
66 *self-deprecation*—downgrading oneself

66 *prominence*—importance
67 *impulsively*—on the spur of the moment; without thinking
67 *carafe*—decanter; glass bottle for holding liquid
67 *hazardous*—dangerous

The Yellow Pill

by Rog Phillips

Rog Phillips was the pen name of Roger P. Graham. A graduate of Gonzaga University, he worked at a number of jobs before becoming a full-time free-lance writer, a prolific and popular one. "The Yellow Pill" will probably be remembered as the very best of his short stories. It is about a vicious killer who may not be a killer after all. Were they people or blue-scaled Venus lizards he killed?

Dr. Cedric Elton slipped into his office by the back entrance, shucked off his topcoat and hid it in the small, narrow-doored closet, then picked up the neatly piled patient cards his receptionist Helena Fitzroy had placed on the corner of his desk. There were only four, but there could have been a hundred if he accepted everyone who asked to be his patient, because his successes had more than once been spectacular and his reputation as a psychiatrist had become so great because of this that his name had become synonymous with psychiatry in the public mind.

His eyes flicked over the top card. He frowned, then went to the small square of one-way glass in the reception room door and looked through it. There were four police officers and a man in a straitjacket.

The card said the man's name was Gerald Bocek, and that he had shot and killed five people in a supermarket, and had killed one officer and wounded two others before being captured.

Except for the straitjacket, Gerald Bocek did not have the appearance of being dangerous. He was about twenty-five, with brown hair and blue eyes. There were faint wrinkles of habitual good nature about his eyes. Right now he was smiling, relaxed, and idly watching Helena, who was pretending to study various cards in her desk file but was obviously conscious of her audience.

Cedric returned to his desk and sat down. The card for Jerry Bocek said more about the killings. When captured, Bocek insisted that the people he had killed were not people at all, but blue-scaled Venusian lizards who had boarded his spaceship, and that he had only been defending himself.

Dr. Cedric Elton shook his head in disapproval. Fantasy fiction was all right in its place, but too many people took it seriously. Of course, it was not the fault of the fiction. The same type of person took other types of fantasy seriously in earlier days, burning women as witches, stoning men as devils—

Abruptly Cedric deflected the control on the intercom and spoke into it. "Send Gerald Bocek in, please," he said.

A moment later the door to the reception room opened. Helena flashed Cedric a scared smile and got out of the way quickly. One police officer led the way, followed by Gerald Bocek closely flanked by two officers with the fourth one in the rear, who carefully closed the door. It was impressive, Cedric decided. He nodded toward a chair in front of his desk and the police officers sat the straitjacketed man in it, then hovered nearby, ready for anything.

"You're Jerry Bocek?" Cedric asked.

The straitjacketed man nodded cheerfully.

"I'm Dr. Cedric Elton, a psychiatrist," Cedric said. "Do you have any idea at all why you have been brought to me?"

"Brought to you?" Jerry echoed, chuckling. "Don't kid me. You're my old pal, Gar Castle. Brought to you? How could I get *away* from you in this stinking tub?"

"Stinking tub?" Cedric said.

"Spaceship," Jerry said. "Look, Gar. Untie me, will you? This nonsense has gone far enough."

"My name is Dr. Cedric Elton," Cedric enunciated. "You are not on a spaceship. You were brought to my office by the four policemen standing in back of you, and—"

Jerry Bocek turned his head and studied each of the four policemen with frank curiosity. "What policemen?" he interrupted. "You mean these four gear lockers?" He turned his head back and looked pityingly at Dr. Elton. "You'd better get hold of yourself, Gar," he said. "You're imagining things."

"My name is Dr. Cedric Elton," Cedric said.

Gerald Bocek leaned forward and said with equal firmness, "Your name is Gar Castle. I refuse to call you Dr. Cedric Elton because your name is Gar Castle, and I'm going to keep on calling you Gar Castle because we have to have at least one peg of rationality in all this madness or you will be cut completely adrift in this dream world you've cooked up."

Cedric's eyebrows shot halfway up to his hairline.

"Funny," he mused, smiling. "That's exactly what I was just going to say to you!"

Cedric continued to smile. Jerry's serious intenseness slowly faded. Finally an answering smile tugged at the corners of his mouth. When it became a grin Cedric laughed, and Jerry began to laugh with him. The four police officers looked at one another uneasily.

"Well!" Cedric finally gasped. "I guess that puts us on an even footing! You're nuts to me and I'm nuts to you!"

"An equal footing is right!" Jerry shouted in high glee. Then abruptly he sobered. "Except," he said gently, "I'm tied up."

"In a straitjacket," Cedric corrected.

"Ropes," Jerry said firmly.

"You're dangerous," Cedric said. "You killed six people, one of them a police officer, and wounded two other officers."

"I blasted five Venusian lizard pirates who boarded our ship," Jerry said, "and melted the door off of one food locker, and seared the paint on two others. You know as well as I do, Gar, how space madness causes you to personify everything. That's why they drill into you that the minute you think there are more people on board the ship than there were at the beginning of the trip you'd better go to the medicine locker and take a yellow pill. They can't hurt anything but a delusion."

"If that is so," Cedric said, "why are *you* in a straitjacket?"

"I'm tied up with ropes," Jerry said patiently. "You tied me up. Remember?"

"And those four police officers behind you are gear lockers?" Cedric said. "O.K., if one of those gear lockers comes around in front of you and taps you on the jaw with his fist, would you still believe it's a gear locker?"

Cedric nodded to one of the officers, and the man came around in front of Gerald Bocek, and quite carefully, hit him hard enough to rock his head but not hurt him. Jerry's eyes blinked with surprise, then he looked at Cedric and smiled.

"Did you feel that?" Cedric said quietly.

"Feel what?" Jerry said. "Oh!" He laughed. "You imagined that one of the gear lockers—a police officer in your dream world—came around in front of me and hit me?" He shook his head in pity. "Don't you understand, Gar, that it didn't really happen? Untie me and I'll prove it. Before your very eyes I'll open the door on your *policeman* and take out the pressure suit, or magnetic grapple, or whatever is in it. Or are you afraid to? You've surrounded yourself with all sorts of protective delusions. I'm tied with ropes, but you imagine it to be a straitjacket. You imagine yourself to be a psychiatrist named Dr. Cedric Elton, so that you can convince yourself that you're sane and I'm crazy. Probably you imagine yourself a very *famous* psychiatrist that everyone would like to come to for treatment. World famous, no doubt. Probably you even think you have a beautiful receptionist? What is her name?"

"Helena Fitzroy," Cedric said.

Jerry nodded. "It figures," he said resignedly. "Helena Fitzroy is the Expediter at Marsport. You try to date her every time we land there, but she won't date you."

"Hit him again," Cedric said to the officer. While Jerry's head was still rocking from the blow, Cedric said, "Now! Is it *my* imagination that your head is still rocking from the blow?"

"What blow?" Jerry said, smiling serenely. "I felt no blow."

"Do you mean to say," Cedric said incredulously, "that there is no corner of your mind, no slight residue of rationality, that tries to tell you your rationalizations aren't reality?"

Jerry smiled ruefully. "I have to admit," he said, "when you seem so absolutely certain you're right and I'm nuts, it almost makes me doubt. Untie me, Gar, and let's try to work this thing out sensibly." He grinned. "You know, Gar, *one* of us has to be nuttier than a fruitcake."

"If I had the officers take off your straitjacket, what would you do?" Cedric asked. "Try to grab a gun and kill some more people?"

"That's one of the things I'm worried about," Jerry said. "If those pirates came back, with me tied up, you're just space-crazy enough to welcome them aboard. That's why you *must* untie me. Our lives may depend on it, Gar."

"Where would you get a gun?" Cedric asked.

"Where they're always kept," Jerry said. "In the gear lockers."

Cedric looked at the four policemen, at their revolvers holstered at their hips, and sighed. One of them grinned feebly at him.

"I'm afraid we can't take your straitjacket off just yet," Cedric said. "I'm going to have the officers take you back now. I'll talk with you again tomorrow. Meanwhile I want you to think seriously about things. Try to get below this level of rationalization that walls you off from reality. Once you make a dent in it the whole delusion will vanish." He looked up at the officers. "All right, take him away. Bring him back the same time tomorrow."

The officers urged Jerry to his feet. Jerry looked down at Cedric, a gentle expression on his face. "I'll try to do that, Gar," he said. "And I hope you do the same thing. I'm much encouraged. Several times I detected genuine doubt in your eyes. And—" Two of the officers pushed him firmly toward the door. As they opened it Jerry turned his head and looked back. "*Take* one of those yellow pills in the medicine locker, Gar," he pleaded. "It can't hurt you."

At a little before five-thirty Cedric tactfully eased his last patient all the way across the reception room and out, then locked the door and leaned his back against it.

"Today was rough," he sighed.

Helena glanced up at him briefly, then continued typing. "I only have a little more on this last transcript," she said.

A minute later she pulled the paper from the typewriter and placed it on the neat stack beside her.

"I'll sort and file them in the morning," she said. "It was rough, wasn't it, doctor? That Gerald Bocek is the most unusual patient you've had since I've worked for you. And poor Mr. Potts. A brilliant executive, making half a million a year, and he's going to give it up. He seems so normal."

"He is normal," Cedric said. "People with above-normal blood pressure often have very minor cerebral hemorrhages so small that the affected area is no larger than the head of a pin. All that happens is that they completely forget things that they knew. They can relearn them, but a man whose judgment must always be perfect can't afford to take the chance. He's already made one error in judgment that cost his company a million and a half. That's why I consented to take him on as a— Gerald Bocek really upset me, Helena. I *consent* to take a five hundred thousand dollar a year executive as a patient."

"He was frightening, wasn't he," Helena said. "I don't mean so much because he's a mass murderer as—"

"I know. I know," Cedric said. "Let's prove him wrong. Have dinner with me."

"We agreed—"

"Let's break the agreement this once."

Helena shook her head firmly. "Especially not now," she said. "Besides, it wouldn't prove anything. He's got you boxed in on that point. If I went to dinner with you, it would only show that a wish fulfillment entered your dream world."

"Ouch," Cedric said, wincing. "That's a dirty word. I wonder how he knew about the yellow pills? I can't get out of my mind the fact that *if* we had spaceships and *if* there were a type of space madness in which you began to personify objects, a yellow pill would be the right thing to stop that."

"How?" Helena said.

"They almost triple the strength of nerve currents from end organs. What results is that reality practically shouts down any fantasy insertions. It's quite startling. I took one three years ago when they first became available. You'd be surprised how little you actually see of what you look at, especially of people. You look at symbol inserts instead. I had to cancel my appointments for a week. I found I couldn't work without my professionally built symbol inserts about people that enable me to see them—not as they really are—but as a complex of normal and abnormal symptoms."

"I'd like to take one some time," Helena said.

"That's a twist," Cedric said, laughing. "One of the characters in a dream world takes a yellow pill and discovers it doesn't exist at all except as a fantasy."

"Why don't we both take one," Helena said.

"Uh uh," Cedric said firmly. "I couldn't do my work."

"You're afraid you might wake up on a spaceship?" Helena said, grinning.

"Maybe I am," Cedric said. "Crazy, isn't it? But there is one thing today that stands out as a serious flaw in my reality. It's so glaring that I actually am afraid to ask you about it."

"Are you serious?" Helena said.

"I am." Cedric nodded. "How does it happen that the police brought Gerald Bocek here to my office instead of holding him in the psychiatric ward at City Hospital and having me go there to see him? How does it happen the D.A. didn't get in touch with me beforehand and discuss the case with me?"

"I . . . I don't know!" Helena said. "I received no call. They just showed up, and I assumed they wouldn't have without your knowing about it and telling them to. Mrs. Fortesque was your first patient and I called her at once and caught her just as she was leaving the house, and told her an emergency case had come up." She looked at Cedric with round, startled eyes.

"Now we know how the patient must feel," Cedric said, crossing the reception room to his office door. "Terrifying, isn't it, to think that if I took a yellow pill all this might *vanish*—my years of college, my internship, *my fame as the world's best-known psychiatrist,* and you. Tell me, Helena, are you sure you aren't an Expediter at Marsport?"

He leered at her mockingly as he slowly closed the door, cutting off his view of her.

Cedric put his coat away and went directly to the small square of one-way glass in the reception room door. Gerald Bocek, still in straitjacket, was there, and so were the same four police officers.

Cedric went to his desk and, without sitting down, deflected the control on the intercom.

"Helena," he said, "before you send in Gerald Bocek, get me the D.A. on the phone."

He glanced over the four patient cards while waiting. Once he rubbed his eyes gently. He had had a restless night.

When the phone rang he reached for it. "Hello? Dave?" he said. "About this patient, Gerald Bocek—"

"I was going to call you today," the District Attorney's voice sounded. "I called you yesterday morning at ten, but no one answered, and I haven't had time since. Our police psychiatrist, Walters, says you might be able to snap Bocek out of it in a couple of days—at least long enough so that we can get some sensible answers out of him. Down underneath his delusion of killing lizard pirates from Venus there has to be some reason for that mass killing, and the Press is after us on this."

"But why bring him to my office?" Cedric said. "It's O.K., of course, but . . . that is . . . I didn't think you could! Take a patient out of the ward at City Hospital and transport him around town."

"I thought that would be less of an imposition on you," the D.A. said. "I'm in a hurry on it."

"Oh," Cedric said. "Well, O.K., Dave. He's out in the watiing room. I'll do my best to snap him back to reality for you."

He hung up slowly, frowning. *"Less of an imposition!"* His whispered words floated into his ears as he snapped into the intercom, "Send Gerald Bocek in, please."

The door from the reception room opened, and once again the procession of patient and police officers entered.

"Well, well, good morning, Gar," Jerry said. "Did you sleep well? I could hear you talking to yourself most of the night."

"I am Dr. Cedric Elton," Cedric said firmly.

"Oh, yes," Jerry said. "I promised to try to see things your way, didn't I? I'll try to cooperate with you, Dr. Elton." Jerry turned to the four officers. "Let's see now, these gear lockers are policemen, aren't they. How do you do, officers." He bowed to them, then looked around him. "And," he said, "this is your office, Dr. Elton. A very impressive office. That thing you're sitting behind is not the chart table but your desk, I gather." He studied the desk intently. "All metal, with a gray finish, isn't it?"

"All wood," Cedric said. "Walnut."

"Yes, of course," Jerry murmured. "How stupid of me. I really want to get into your reality, Gar . . . I mean Dr. Elton. Or get you into mine. I'm the one who's at a disadvantage, though. Tied up, I can't get into the medicine locker and take a yellow pill like you can. Did you take one yet?"

"Not yet," Cedric said.

"Uh, why don't you describe your office to me, Dr. Elton?" Jerry said. "Let's make a game of it. Describe parts of things and then let me see if I can fill in the rest. Start with your desk. It's genuine walnut? An executive style desk. Go on from there."

"All right," Cedric said. "Over here to my right is the intercom, made of gray plastic. And directly in front of me is the telephone."

"Stop," Jerry said. "Let me see if I can tell you your telephone number." He leaned over the desk and looked at the telephone, trying to keep his balance in spite of his arms being encased in the straitjacket. "Hm-m-m," he said, frowning. "Is the number Mulberry five dash nine oh three seven?"

"No," Cedric said. "It's Cedar sev—"

"Stop!" Jerry said. "Let me say it. It's Cedar seven dash four three nine nine."

"So you did read it and were just having your fun," Cedric snorted.

"If you say so," Jerry said.

"What other explanation can you have for the fact that it is my number, if you're unable to actually see reality?" Cedric said.

"You're absolutely right, Dr. Elton," Jerry said. "I think I understand the tricks my mind is playing on me now. I read the number on your phone, but it didn't enter my conscious awareness. Instead, it cloaked itself with the pattern of my delusion, so that consciously I pretended to look at a phone that I couldn't see, and I thought, 'His phone number will obviously be one he's familiar with. The most probable is the home phone of Helena Fitzroy in Marsport, so I gave you that, but it wasn't it. When you said Cedar I knew right away it was your own apartment phone number."

Cedric sat perfectly still. Mulberry 5–9037 was actually Helena's apartment phone number. He hadn't recognized it until Gerald Bocek told him.

"Now you're beginning to understand," Cedric said after a moment. "Once you realize that your mind has walled off your consciousness from reality, and is substituting a rationalized pattern of symbology in its place, it shouldn't be long until you break through. Once you manage to see one thing as it really is, the rest of the delusion will disappear."

"I understand now," Jerry said gravely. "Let's have some more of it. Maybe I'll catch on."

They spent an hour at it. Toward the end Jerry was able to finish the descriptions of things with very little error.

"You are definitely beginning to get through," Cedric said with enthusiasm.

Jerry hesitated. "I suppose so," he said. "I must. But on the conscious level I have the idea—a rationalization, of course—that I am beginning to catch on to the pattern of your imagination so that when you give me one or two key elements I can fill in the rest. But I'm going to try, really try—Dr. Elton."

"Fine," Cedric said heartily. "I'll see you tomorrow, same time. We should make the breakthrough then."

When the four officers had taken Gerald Bocek away, Cedric went into the outer office.

"Cancel the rest of my appointments," he said.

"But why?" Helena protested.

"Because I'm upset!" Cedric said. "How did a madman whom I never knew until yesterday know your phone number?"

"He could have looked it up in the phone book," Helena said.

"Locked in a room in the psychiatric ward at City Hospital?" Cedric said. "How did he know your name yesterday?"

"Why," Helena said, "all he had to do was read it on my desk here."

Cedric looked down at the brass name plate.

"Yes," he grunted. "Of course. I'd forgotten about that. I'm so accustomed to it being there that I never see it."

He turned abruptly and went back into his office.

He sat down at his desk, then got up and went into the sterile whiteness of his compact laboratory. Ignoring the impressive battery of electronic instruments he went to the medicine cabinet. Inside, on the top shelf, was the glass-stoppered bottle he wanted. Inside it were a hundred vivid yellow pills. He shook out one and put the bottle away, then went back into his office. He sat down, placing the yellow pill in the center of the white note pad.

There was a brief knock on the door to the reception room and the door opened. Helena came in.

"I've cancelled all your other appointments for today," she said. "Why don't you go out to the golf course? A change will do you—" She saw the yellow pill in the center of the white note pad and stopped.

"Why do you look so frightened?" Cedric said. "Is it because, if I take this little yellow pill, you'll cease to exist?"

"Don't joke," Helena said.

"I'm not joking," Cedric said. "Out there, when you mentioned about your brass name plate on your desk, when I looked down it was blurred for just a second, then became sharply distinct and solid. And into my head popped the memory that the first thing I do when I have to get a new receptionist is get a brass name plate for her and when she quits I make her a present of it."

"But that's the truth," Helena said. "You told me all about it when I started working for you. You also told me that while you still had your reason about you I was to solemnly promise that I would never accept an invitation from you for dinner or anything else, because business could not mix with pleasure. Do you remember that?"

"I remember," Cedric said. "A nice pat rationalization in any man's reality to make the rejection be my own before you could have time to reject me yourself. Preserving the ego is the first principle of madness."

"But it isn't!" Helena said. "Oh, darling, I'm *here!* This is *real!* I don't care if you fire me or not. I've loved you forever, and you mustn't let that mass murderer get you down. I actually think he isn't insane at all, but has just figured out a way to seem insane so he won't have to pay for his crime."

"You think so?" Cedric said, interested. "It's a possibility. But he would have to be as good a psychiatrist as I am— You see? Delusions of grandeur."

"Sure," Helena said, laughing thinly. "Napoleon was obviously insane because he thought he was Napoleon."

"Perhaps," Cedric said. "But you must admit that if you are real, my taking this yellow pill isn't going to change that, but only confirm the fact."

"And make it impossible for you to do your work for a week," Helena said.

"A small price to pay for sanity," Cedric said. "No, I'm going to take it."

"You aren't!" Helena said, reaching for it.

Cedric picked it up an instant before she could get it. As she tried to get it away from him he evaded her and put it in his mouth. A loud gulp showed he had swallowed it.

He sat back and looked up at Helena curiously.

"Tell me, Helena," he said gently. "Did you know all the time that you were only a creature of my imagination? The reason I want to know is—"

He closed his eyes and clutched his head in his hands.

"God!" he groaned. "I feel like I'm dying! I didn't feel like this the other time I took one."

Suddenly his mind steadied, and his thoughts cleared. He opened his eyes.

On the chart table in front of him the bottle of yellow pills lay on its side, pills scattered all over the table. On the other side of the control room lay Jerry Bocek, his back propped against one of the four gear lockers, sound asleep, with so many ropes wrapped around him that it would probably be impossible for him to stand up.

Against the far wall were three other gear lockers, two of them with their paint badly scorched, the third with its door half melted off.

And in various positions about the control room were the half-charred bodies of five blue-scaled Venusian lizards.

A dull ache rose in Gar's chest. Helena Fitzroy was gone. Gone, when she had just confessed she loved him.

Unbidden, a memory came into Gar's mind. Dr. Cedric Elton was the psychiatrist who had examined him when he got his pilot's license for third-class freighters—

"God!" Gar groaned again. And suddenly he was sick. He made a dash for the washroom, and after a while he felt better.

When he straightened up from the wash basin he looked at his reflection in the mirror for a long time, clinging to his hollow cheeks and sunken eyes. He must have been out of his head for two or three days.

The first time. Awful! Somehow, he had never quite believed in space madness.

Suddenly he remembered Jerry. Poor Jerry!

Gar lurched from the washroom back into the control room. Jerry was awake. He looked up at Gar, forcing a smile to his lips.

"Hello, Dr. Elton," Jerry said.

Gar stopped as though shot.

"It's happened, Dr. Elton, just as you said it would," Jerry said, his smile widening.

"Forget that," Gar growled. "I took a yellow pill. I'm back to normal again."

Jerry's smile vanished abruptly. "I know what I did now," he said. "It's terrible. I killed six people. But I'm sane now. I'm willing to take what's coming to me."

"Forget that!" Gar snarled. "You don't have to humor me now. Just a minute and I'll untie you."

"Thanks, Doctor," Jerry said. "It will sure be a relief to get out of this straitjacket."

Gar knelt beside Jerry and untied the knots in the ropes and unwound them from around Jerry's chest and legs.

"You'll be all right in a minute," Gar said, massaging Jerry's limp arms. The physical and nervous strain of sitting there immobilized had been rugged.

Slowly he worked circulation back into Jerry, then helped him to his feet.

"You don't need to worry, Dr. Elton," Jerry said. "I don't know why I killed those people, but I know I would never do such a thing again. I must have been insane."

"Can you stand now?" Gar said, letting go of Jerry.

Jerry took a few steps back and forth, unsteadily at first, then with better coordination. His resemblance to a robot decreased with exercise.

Gar was beginning to feel sick again. He fought it.

"You O.K. now, Jerry boy?" he asked worriedly.

"I'm fine now, Dr. Elton," Jerry said. "And thanks for everything you've done for me."

Abruptly Jerry turned and went over to the air-lock door and opened it.

"Good-bye now, Dr. Elton," he said.

"Wait!" Gar screamed, leaping toward Jerry.

But Jerry had stepped into the air lock and closed the door. Gar tried to open it; but already Jerry had turned on the pump that would evacuate the air from the lock.

Screaming Jerry's name senselessly in horror, Gar watched through the small square of thick glass in the door as Jerry's chest quickly expanded, then collapsed as a mixture of phlegm and blood dribbled from his nostrils and lips, and his eyes enlarged and glazed over, then one of them ripped open and collapsed, its fluid draining down his cheek.

He watched as Jerry glanced toward the side of the air lock and smiled, then spun the wheel that opened the air lock to the vacuum of space, and stepped out.

And when Gar finally stopped screaming and sank to the deck, sobbing, his knuckles were broken and bloody from pounding on bare metal.

■ ■ ■

For a Journal Entry . . .

How many people would want to take a yellow pill if it could actually do what the story claims for it? Do you think people really want to live in the real world? Or do most of us prefer rose-colored glasses? Explore these questions by thinking about yourself and your own attitudes and the attitudes of those around you.

For Your Consideration . . .

1. When did you first suspect that Dr. Cedric Elton was really Gar Castle? What clues does Rog Phillips give the reader that Elton is the one with space madness? Give examples of the evidence that finally convinces him to take the pill.
2. If you had the delusion that you were a world-famous person, how important would it be to you to regain reality?
3. How does "The Yellow Pill" demonstrate the idea that if two people can accept the same reality, then they can consider themselves sane? What is sanity?
4. "The Yellow Pill" deals with the question of identity, the question of who a person is. Why would such a story appeal to young people?
5. Why doesn't "Dr. Elton" give his patient a yellow pill to prove to him that his reality is false?
6. Is the ending of "The Yellow Pill" primarily for shock value, or is it an effective close to a story about confused realities? Give evidence to support your answer.
7. What traditional SF elements does "The Yellow Pill" contain? What concept does it contain that is more innovative?

Notes

PAGE

71 *psychiatrist*—a doctor specializing in mental disorders
71 *synonymous*—same as
72 *intercom*—a communication system that allows one to talk to someone in another room of the same building
72 *hovered*—stood nearby
73 *enunciated*—pronounced clearly
73 *rationality*—reason; grasp on reality
73 *intenseness*—earnestness
73 *sobered*—became serious
73 *personify*—the process of seeing inanimate objects as people
74 *delusion*—false belief caused by a mental disorder
75 *residue*—remaining
75 *tactfully*—with good manners so as not to give offense
76 *cerebral hemorrhages*—internal bleeding of the brain
78 *imposition*—burden; bother

80 *rationalized pattern of symbology*—a pattern of symbology is the world our senses interpret to us; a rationalized pattern of symbology is an imagined world we see in our minds

81 *sterile*—extremely clean as in having been treated so that there is no bacteria present; also impersonal

81 *ego*—conceit, pride; sense of self

82 *delusions of grandeur*—the mistaken belief that one is a famous or very important person

82 *evaded*—avoided; escaped

83 *immobilized*—stationary, unable to move

83 *circulation*—the flow of blood through the veins and arteries

84 *air lock*—entry and exit chamber of a spaceship; it must be filled with air before a person can enter the ship itself or the ship will lose air

84 *evacuate*—empty the air out of the air lock

Light of Other Days

by Bob Shaw

Born in Belfast, North Ireland, and still living there, Bob Shaw is a big and genial man who brings a particularly Gaelic touch as well as technical turn of mind to the writing of science fiction. He attended the Belfast College of Technology, so that sound knowledge lies behind his work, as in this story about "slow glass," a special kind of glass with frightening properties.

Leaving the village behind, we followed the heady sweeps of the road up into a land of slow glass.

I had never seen one of the farms before and at first found them slightly eerie—an effect heightened by imagination and circumstance. The car's turbine was pulling smoothly and quietly in the damp air so that we seemed to be carried over the convolutions of the road in a kind of supernatural silence. On our right the mountain sifted down into an incredibly perfect valley of timeless pine, and everywhere stood the great frames of slow glass, drinking light. An occasional flash of afternoon sunlight on their wind bracing created an illusion of movement, but in fact the frames were deserted. The rows of windows had been standing on the hillside for years, staring into the valley, and men only cleaned them in the middle of the night when their human presence would not matter to the thirsty glass.

They were fascinating, but Selina and I didn't mention the windows. I think we hated each other so much we both were reluctant to sully anything new by drawing it into the nexus of our emotions. The holiday, I had begun to realize, was a stupid idea in the first place. I had thought it would cure everything, but, of course, it didn't stop Selina being pregnant and, worse still, it didn't even stop her being angry about being pregnant.

Rationalizing our dismay over her condition, we had circulated the usual statements to the effect that we would have *liked* having children—but later on, at the proper time. Selina's pregnancy had cost us her well-paid job and with it the new house we had been negotiating and which was far beyond the reach of my income from poetry. But the real source of our annoyance was that we were face to face with the realization that people who say they want children later always mean they want children never. Our nerves were thrumming with the knowledge that we, who had thought ourselves so unique, had fallen into the same biological trap as every mindless rutting creature which ever existed.

The road took us along the southern slopes of Ben Cruachan until we began to catch glimpses of the gray Atlantic far ahead. I had just cut our speed to absorb the view better when I noticed the sign spiked to a gatepost. It said: "SLOW GLASS—Quality High, Prices Low—J. R. Hagan." On an impulse I stopped the car on the verge, wincing slightly as tough grasses whipped noisily at the bodywork.

"Why have we stopped?" Selina's neat, smoke-silver head turned in surprise.

"Look at that sign. Let's go up and see what there is. The stuff might be reasonably priced out here."

Selina's voice was pitched high with scorn as she refused, but I was too taken with my idea to listen. I had an illogical conviction that doing something extravagant and crazy would set us right again.

"Come on," I said, "the exercise might do us some good. We've been driving too long anyway."

She shrugged in a way that hurt me and got out of the car. We walked up a path made of irregular, packed clay steps nosed with short lengths of sapling. The path curved through trees which clothed the edge of the hill and at its end we found a low farmhouse. Beyond the little stone building tall frames of slow glass gazed out towards the voice-stilling sight of Cruachan's ponderous descent towards the waters of Loch Linnhe. Most of the panes were perfectly transparent but a few were dark, like panels of polished ebony.

As we approached the house through a neat cobbled yard a tall middle-aged man in ash-colored tweeds arose and waved to us. He had been sitting on the low rubble wall which bounded the yard, smoking a pipe and staring toward the house. At the front window of the cottage a young woman in a tangerine dress stood with a small boy in her arms, but she turned disinterestedly and moved out of sight as we drew near.

"Mr. Hagan?" I guessed.

"Correct. Come to see some glass, have you? Well, you've come to the right place." Hagan spoke crisply, with traces of the pure highland which sounds so much like Irish to the unaccustomed ear. He had one of those calmly dismayed faces one finds on elderly road-menders and philosophers.

"Yes," I said. "We're on holiday. We saw your sign."

Selina, who usually has a natural fluency with strangers, said nothing. She was looking toward the now empty window with what I thought was a slightly puzzled expression.

"Up from London, are you? Well, as I said, you've come to the right place—and at the right time, too. My wife and I don't see many people this early in the season."

I laughed. "Does that mean we might be able to buy a little glass without mortgaging our home?"

"Look at that now," Hagan said, smiling helplessly. "I've thrown away any advantage I might have had in the transaction. Rose, that's my wife, says I never learn. Still, let's sit down and talk it over." He pointed at the rubble wall then glanced doubtfully at Selina's immaculate blue skirt. "Wait till I fetch a rug from the house." Hagan limped quickly into the cottage, closing the door behind him.

"Perhaps it wasn't such a marvelous idea to come up here," I whispered to Selina, "but you might at least be pleasant to the man. I think I can smell a bargain."

"Some hope," she said with deliberate coarseness. "Surely even you must have noticed that ancient dress his wife is wearing? He won't give much away to strangers."

"Was that his wife?"

"Of course that was his wife."

"Well, well," I said, surprised. "Anyway, try to be civil with him. I don't want to be embarrassed."

Selina snorted, but she smiled whitely when Hagan reappeared and I relaxed a little. Strange how a man can love a woman and yet at the same time pray for her to fall under a train.

Hagan spread a tartan blanket on the wall and we sat down, feeling slightly self-conscious at having been translated from our city-oriented lives into a rural tableau. On the distant slate of the Loch, beyond the watchful frames of slow glass, a slow-moving steamer drew a white line toward the south. The boisterous mountain air seemed almost to invade our lungs, giving us more oxygen than we required.

"Some of the glass farmers around here," Hagan began, "give strangers, such as yourselves, a sales talk about how beautiful the autumn is in this part of Argyll. Or it might be the spring, or the winter. I don't do that—any fool knows that a place which doesn't look right in summer never looks right. What do you say?"

I nodded compliantly.

"I want you just to take a good look out toward Mull, Mr. . . ."

"Garland."

". . . Garland. That's what you're buying if you buy my glass, and it never looks better than it does at this minute. The glass is in perfect phase, none of it is less than ten years thick—and a four-foot window will cost you two hundred pounds."

"*Two hundred!*" Selina was shocked. "That's as much as they charge at the Scenedow shop in Bond Street."

Hagan smiled patiently, then looked closely at me to see if I knew enough about slow glass to appreciate what he had been saying. His price had been much higher than I had hoped—but *ten years thick!* The cheap glass one found in places like the Vistaplex and Pane-o-rama stores usually consisted of a quarter of an inch of ordinary glass faced with a veneer of slow glass perhaps only ten or twelve months thick.

"You don't understand, darling," I said, already determined to buy. "This glass will last ten years and it's in phase."

"Doesn't that only mean it keeps time?"

Hagan smiled at her again, realizing he had no further necessity to bother with me. "Only, you say! Pardon me, Mrs. Garland, but you don't seem to appreciate the miracle, the genuine honest-to-goodness miracle, of engineering precision needed to produce a piece of glass in phase. When I say the glass is ten years thick it means it takes light ten years to pass through it. In effect, each one of those panes is ten light-years thick—more than twice the distance to the nearest star—so a variation in actual thickness of only a millionth of an inch would . . ."

He stopped talking for a moment and sat quietly looking toward the house. I turned my head from the view of the Loch and saw the young woman standing at the window again. Hagan's eyes were filled with a kind of greedy reverence which made me feel uncomfortable and at the same time convinced me Selina had been wrong. In my experience husbands never looked at wives that way, at least, not at their own.

The girl remained in view for a few seconds, dress glowing warmly, then moved back into the room. Suddenly I received a distinct, though inexplicable, impression she was blind. My feeling was that Selina and I were perhaps blundering through an emotional interplay as violent as our own.

"I'm sorry," Hagan continued, "I thought Rose was going to call me for something. Now, where was I, Mrs. Garland? Ten light-years compressed into a quarter of an inch means . . ."

I ceased to listen, partly because I was already sold, partly because I had heard the story of slow glass many times before and had never yet understood the principles involved. An acquaintance with scientific training had once tried to be helpful by telling me to visualize a pane of slow glass as a hologram which did not need coherent light from a laser for the reconstitution of its visual information, and in which every photon of ordinary light passed through a spiral tunnel coiled outside the radius of capture of each atom in the glass. This gem of, to me, incomprehensibility not only told me nothing, it convinced me once again that a mind as nontechnical as mine should concern itself less with causes than effects.

The most important effect, in the eyes of the average individual, was that light took a long time to pass through a sheet of slow glass. A new piece was always jet black because nothing had yet come through, but one could stand the glass beside, say, a woodland lake until the scene emerged, perhaps a year later. If the glass was then removed and installed in a dismal city flat, the flat would—for that year—appear to overlook the woodland lake. During the year it wouldn't be merely a very realistic but still picture—the water would ripple in sunlight, silent animals would come to drink, birds would cross the sky, night would follow day, season would follow season. Until one day, a year later, the beauty held in the subatomic pipelines would be exhausted and the familiar gray cityscape would reappear.

Apart from its stupendous novelty value, the commercial success of slow glass was founded on the fact that having a scenedow was the exact emotional equivalent of owning land. The meanest cave dweller could look out on misty parks—and who was to say they weren't his? A man who really owns tailored gardens and estates doesn't spend his time proving his ownership by crawling on his ground, feeling, smelling, tasting it. All he receives from the land are light patterns, and with scenedows those patterns could be taken into coal mines, submarines, prison cells.

On several occasions I have tried to write short pieces about the enchanted crystal but, to me, the theme is so ineffably poetic as to be, paradoxically, beyond the reach of poetry—mine at any rate. Besides, the best songs and verse had already been written, with prescient inspiration, by men who had died long before slow glass was discovered. I had no hope of equaling, for example, Moore with his:

Oft in the stilly night,
Ere slumber's chain has bound me,

Fond Memory brings the light,
Of other days around me . . .

It took only a few years for slow glass to develop from a scientific curiosity to a sizable industry. And much to the astonishment of us poets—those of us who remain convinced that beauty lives though lilies die—the trappings of that industry were no different from those of any other. There were good scenedows which cost a lot of money, and there were inferior scenedows which cost rather less. The thickness, measured in years, was an important factor in the cost but there was also the question of *actual* thickness, or phase.

Even with the most sophisticated engineering techniques available thickness control was something of a hit-and-miss affair. A coarse discrepancy could mean that a pane intended to be five years thick might be five and a half, so that light which entered in summer emerged in winter; a fine discrepancy could mean that noon sunshine emerged at midnight. These incompatibilities had their peculiar charm—many night workers, for example, liked having their own private time zones—but, in general, it cost more to buy scenedows which kept closely in step with real time.

Selina still looked unconvinced when Hagan had finished speaking. She shook her head almost imperceptibly and I knew he had been using the wrong approach. Quite suddenly the pewter helmet of her hair was disturbed by a cool gust of wind, and huge clean tumbling drops of rain began to spang round us from an almost cloudless sky.

"I'll give you a check now," I said abruptly, and saw Selina's green eyes triangulate angrily on my face.

"You can arrange delivery?"

"Aye, delivery's no problem," Hagan said, getting to his feet. "But wouldn't you rather take the glass with you?"

"Well, yes—if you don't mind." I was shamed by his readiness to trust my scrip.

"I'll unclip a pane for you. Wait here. It won't take long to slip it into a carrying frame." Hagan limped down the slope toward the seriate windows, through some of which the view toward Linnhe was sunny, while others were cloudy and a few pure black.

Selina drew the collar of her blouse closed at her throat. "The least he could have done was invite us inside. There can't be so many fools passing through that he can afford to neglect them."

I tried to ignore the insult and concentrated on writing the check. One of the outsize drops broke across my knuckles, splattering the pink paper.

"All right," I said, "let's move in under the eaves till he gets back." You worm, I thought as I felt the whole thing go completely wrong. I just had to be a fool to marry you. A prize fool, a fool's fool—and now that you've trapped part of me inside you I'll never ever, never ever, *never ever* get away.

Feeling my stomach clench itself painfully, I ran behind Selina to the side of the cottage. Beyond the window the neat living room, with its coal fire, was empty but the child's toys were scattered on the floor. Alphabet blocks and a wheelbarrow the exact color of freshly pared carrots. As I stared in, the boy came running from the other room and began kicking the blocks. He didn't notice me. A few moments later the young woman entered the room and lifted him, laughing easily and wholeheartedly as she swung the boy under her arm. She came to the window as she had done earlier. I smiled self-consciously, but neither she nor the child responded.

My forehead prickled icily. *Could they both be blind?* I sidled away.

Selina gave a little scream and I spun toward her.

"The rug!" she said. "It's getting soaked."

She ran across the yard in the rain, snatched the reddish square from the dappling wall and ran back, toward the cottage door. Something heaved convulsively in my subconscious.

"Selina," I shouted. "Don't open it!"

But I was too late. She had pushed open the latched wooden door and was standing, hand over mouth, looking into the cottage. I moved close to her and took the rug from her unresisting fingers.

As I was closing the door I let my eyes traverse the cottage's interior. The neat living room in which I had just seen the woman and child was, in reality, a sickening clutter of shabby furniture, old newspapers, cast-off clothing and smeared dishes. It was damp, stinking, and utterly deserted. The only object I recognized from my view through the window was the little wheelbarrow, paintless and broken.

I latched the door firmly and ordered myself to forget what I had seen. Some men who live alone are good housekeepers; others just don't know how.

Selina's face was white. "I don't understand. I don't understand it."

"Slow glass works both ways," I said gently. "Light passes out of a house, as well as in."

"You mean . . . ?"

"I don't know. It isn't our business. Now steady up—Hagan's coming back with our glass." The churning in my stomach was beginning to subside.

Hagan came into the yard carrying an oblong, plastic-covered frame. I held the check out to him, but he was staring at Selina's face. He seemed to know immediately that our uncomprehending fingers had rummaged through his soul. Selina avoided his gaze. She was old and ill-looking, and her eyes stared determinedly toward the nearing horizon.

"I'll take the rug from you, Mr. Garland," Hagan finally said. "You shouldn't have troubled yourself over it."

"No trouble. Here's the check."

"Thank you." He was still looking at Selina with a strange kind of supplication. "It's been a pleasure to do business with you."

"The pleasure was mine," I said with equal, senseless formality. I picked up the heavy frame and guided Selina toward the path which led to the road. Just as we reached the head of the now slippery steps Hagan spoke again.

"Mr. Garland!"

I turned unwillingly.

"It wasn't my fault," he said steadily. "A hit-and-run driver got them both, down on the Oban road six years ago. My boy was only seven when it happened. I'm entitled to keep something."

I nodded wordlessly and moved down the path, holding my

wife close to me, treasuring the feel of her arms locked around me. At the bend I looked back through the rain and saw Hagan sitting with squared shoulders on the wall where we had first seen him.

He was looking at the house, but I was unable to tell if there was anyone at the window.

■ ■ ■

For a Journal Entry . . .

In our own world where natural beauty is at a premium, do you think there would be a market for slow glass? Would people pay, say, $1,000 for a glass that would look out on beauty? Or would they consider that artificial? Or would that matter? Would it be the beauty of the glass or the prestige of owning it that would interest people? What about you?

For Your Consideration . . .

1. Do the Garlands seem a bit immature to you at first? Why or why not? What is wrong with their marriage?
2. When do you first suspect that there is something odd about the girl behind the glass?
3. In what important way do the Garlands change by the end of the story? Why do they change?
4. What does Bob Shaw mean when he writes, "He seemed to know immediately that our uncomprehending fingers had rummaged through his soul"? Why does the old man feel the need to explain?
5. Toward the beginning of "Light of Other Days," Shaw uses a few lines of poetry from which he gets his title. Why is his title particularly appropriate? What does the title have to do with nostalgia?

Notes

PAGE
87 *heady*—exciting, intoxicating
87 *eerie*—strange, weird
87 *turbine*—a type of engine

87 *convolutions*—twisting or coiling
88 *sully*—dirty
88 *nexus*—link between two people or things; connecting point
88 *negotiating*—making arrangements to get or do something
89 *ebony*—black
89 *fluency*—ease; ability to deal well with something
89 *immaculate*—spotless
90 *tableau*—a graphic picture
90 *boisterous*—exuberant, lively
90 *compliantly*—agreeably
90 *scenedow*—a shop where one may get a window of slow glass which looks out on a natural scene; also another name for such a piece of slow glass
91 *inexplicable*—unexplainable
91 *hologram*—three-dimensional picture
92 *photon*—a particle of light energy
92 *incomprehensibility*—something that is not understandable
92 *ineffably*—inexpressibly
92 *paradoxically*—seemingly contradictory
92 *prescient*—having knowledge of the future
93 *triangulate*—fix on
93 *seriate*—arrange in a series
95 *uncomprehending*—not understanding
95 *rummaged*—searched through carelessly
95 *supplication*—humble request, prayer

Who Can Replace a Man?

by Brian W. Aldiss

Brian Aldiss is Britain's leading science fiction author. His first novel *Starship* has been translated around the world, while his latest non-science fiction novel, *The Soldier Erect*, tops the best seller lists in England. He is an editor and critic as well and his illuminating *Billion Year Spree* is one of the best histories of science fiction. Here he writes about a world of the future when the robots take over—it is all theirs. What will happen to what may very well be the last man left alive?

Morning filtered into the sky, lending it the gray tone of the ground below.

The field-minder finished turning the top-soil of a three-thousand-acre field. When it had turned the last furrow, it climbed onto the highway and looked back at its work. The work was good. Only the land was bad. Like the ground all over Earth, it was vitiated by overcropping. By rights, it ought now to lie fallow for a while, but the field-minder had other orders.

It went slowly down the road, taking its time. It was intelligent enough to appreciate the neatness all about it. Nothing worried it, beyond a loose inspection plate above its nuclear pile which ought to be attended to. Thirty feet tall, it yielded no highlights to the dull air.

No other machines passed on its way back to the Agricultural Station. The field-minder noted the fact without comment. In the station yard it saw several other machines that it recognized; most of them should have been out about their tasks now. Instead, some were inactive and some careered round the yard in a strange fashion, shouting or hooting.

Steering carefully past them, the field-minder moved over to Warehouse Three and spoke to the seed-distributor, which stood idly outside.

"I have a requirement for seed potatoes," it said to the distributor, and with a quick internal motion punched out an order card specifying quantity, field number, and several other details. It ejected the card and handed it to the distributor.

The distributor held the card close to its eye and then said, "The requirement is in order, but the store is not yet unlocked. The required seed potatoes are in the store. Therefore I cannot produce the requirement."

Increasingly of late there had been breakdowns in the complex system of machine labor, but this particular hitch had not occurred before. The field-minder thought, then it said, "Why is the store not yet unlocked?"

"Because Supply Operative Type P has not come this morning. Supply Operative Type P is the unlocker."

The field-minder looked squarely at the seed-distributor, whose exterior chutes and scales and grabs were so vastly different from the field-minder's own limbs.

"What class brain do you have, seed-distributor?" it asked.

"I have a Class Five brain."

"I have a Class Three brain. Therefore I am superior to you. Therefore I will go and see why the unlocker has not come this morning."

Leaving the distributor, the field-minder set off across the great yard. More machines were in random motion now; one or two had crashed together and argued about it coldly and logically. Ignoring them, the field-minder pushed through sliding doors into the echoing confines of the station itself.

Most of the machines here were clerical, and consequently small. They stood about in little groups, eyeing each other, not conversing. Among so many nondifferentiated types, the unlocker was easy to find. It had fifty arms, most of them with more than one finger, each finger tipped by a key; it looked like a pincushion full of variegated hat pins.

The field-minder approached it.

"I can do no more work until Warehouse Three is unlocked," it told the unlocker. "Your duty is to unlock the warehouse every morning. Why have you not unlocked the warehouse this morning?"

"I had no orders this morning," replied the unlocker. "I have to have orders every morning. When I have orders I unlock the warehouse."

"None of us have had any orders this morning," a pen-propeller said, sliding toward them.

"Why have you had no orders this morning?" asked the field-minder.

"Because the radio issued none," said the unlocker, slowly rotating a dozen of its arms.

"Because the radio station in the city was issued with no orders this morning," said the pen-propeller.

And there you had the distinction between a Class Six and a Class Three brain, which was what the unlocker and the pen-propeller possessed respectively. All machine brains worked with nothing but logic, but the lower the class of brain—Class Ten being the lowest—the more literal and less informative the answers to questions tended to be.

"You have a Class Three brain; I have a Class Three brain," the field-minder said to the penner. "We will speak to each other. This lack of orders is unprecedented. Have you further information on it?"

"Yesterday orders came from the city. Today no orders have come. Yet the radio has not broken down. Therefore *they* have broken down . . . ," said the little penner.

"The *men* have broken down?"

"All men have broken down."

"That is a logical deduction," said the field-minder.

"That is the logical deduction," said the penner. "For if a machine had broken down, it would have been quickly replaced. But who can replace a man?"

While they talked, the locker, like a dull man at a bar, stood close to them and was ignored.

"If all men have broken down, then we have replaced man," said the field-minder, and he and the penner eyed one another speculatively. Finally the latter said, "Let us ascend to the top floor to find if the radio operator has fresh news."

"I cannot come because I am too large," said the field-minder. "Therefore you must go alone and return to me. You will tell me if the radio operator has fresh news."

"You must stay here," said the penner. "I will return here." It skittered across to the lift. Although it was no bigger than a toaster, its retractable arms numbered ten and it could read as quickly as any machine on the station.

The field-minder awaited its return patiently, not speaking to the locker, which still stood aimlessly by. Outside, a rotavator hooted furiously. Twenty minutes elapsed before the penner came back, hustling out of the lift.

"I will deliver to you such information as I have outside," it said briskly, and as they swept past the locker and the other machines, it added, "The information is not for lower-class brains."

Outside, wild activity filled the yard. Many machines, their routines disrupted for the first time in years, seemed to have gone berserk. Those most easily disrupted were the ones with lowest brains, which generally belonged to large machines performing simple tasks. The seed-distributor to which the field-minder had recently been talking lay face downward in the dust, not stirring; it had evidently been knocked down by the rotavator, which now hooted its way wildly across a planted field. Several other machines plowed after it, trying to keep up with it. All were shouting and hooting without restraint.

"It would be safer for me if I climbed onto you, if you will permit it. I am easily overpowered," said the penner. Extending five arms, it hauled itself up the flanks of its new friend, settling on a ledge beside the fuel-intake, twelve feet above ground.

"From here vision is more extensive," it remarked complacently.

"What information did you receive from the radio operator?" asked the field-minder.

"The radio operator has been informed by the operator in the city that all men are dead."

The field-minder was momentarily silent, digesting this.

"All men were alive yesterday!" it protested.

"Only some men were alive yesterday. And that was fewer than the day before yesterday. For hundreds of years there have been only a few men, growing fewer."

"We have rarely seen a man in this sector."

"The radio operator says a diet deficiency killed them," said the penner. "He says that the world was once overpopulated, and then the soil was exhausted in raising adequate food. This has caused a diet deficiency."

"What is a diet deficiency?" asked the field-minder.

"I do not know. But that is what the radio operator said, and he is a Class Two brain."

They stood there, silent in weak sunshine. The locker had appeared in the porch and was gazing across at them yearningly, rotating its collection of keys.

"What is happening in the city now?" asked the field-minder at last.

"Machines are fighting in the city now," said the penner.

"What will happen here now?" asked the field-minder.

"Machines may begin fighting here too. The radio operator wants us to get him out of his room. He has plans to communicate to us."

"How can we get him out of his room? That is impossible."

"To a Class Two brain, little is impossible," said the penner. "Here is what he tells us to do. . . ."

The quarrier raised its scoop above its cab like a great mailed fist, and brought it squarely down against the side of the station. The wall cracked.

"Again!" said the field-minder.

Again the fist swung. Amid a shower of dust, the wall collapsed. The quarrier backed hurriedly out of the way until the debris stopped falling. This big twelve-wheeler was not a resident of the Agricultural Station, as were most of the other machines. It had a week's heavy work to do here before passing on to its next job, but now, with its Class Five brain, it was happily obeying the penner's and minder's instructions.

When the dust cleared, the radio operator was plainly revealed, perched up in its now wall-less second-story room. It waved down to them.

Doing as directed, the quarrier retraced its scoop and heaved an immense grab in the air. With fair dexterity, it angled the grab into the radio room, urged on by shouts from above and below. It then took gentle hold of the radio operator, lowering its one and a half tons carefully into its back, which was usually reserved for gravel or sand from the quarries.

"Splendid!" said the radio operator, as it settled into place. It was, of course, all one with its radio, and looked like a bunch of filing cabinets with tentacle attachments. "We are now ready to move, therefore we will move at once. It is a pity there are no more Class Two brains on the station, but that cannot be helped."

"It is a pity it cannot be helped," said the penner eagerly. "We have the servicer ready with us, as you ordered."

"I am willing to serve," the long, low servicer told them humbly.

"No doubt," said the operator. "But you will find cross-country travel difficult with your low chassis."

"I admire the way you Class Twos can reason ahead," said the penner. It climbed off the field-minder and perched itself on the tailboard of the quarrier, next to the radio operator.

Together with two Class Four tractors and a Class Four bulldozer, the party rolled forward, crushing down the station's fence and moving out onto open land.

"We are free!" said the penner.

"We are free," said the field-minder, a shade more reflectively, adding, "That locker is following us. It was not instructed to follow us."

"Therefore it must be destroyed!" said the penner. "Quarrier!"

The locker moved hastily up to them, waving its key arms in entreaty.

"My only desire was—urch!" began and ended the locker.

The quarrier's swinging scoop came over and squashed it flat into the ground. Lying there unmoving, it looked like a large metal model of a snowflake. The procession continued on its way.

As they proceeded, the radio operator addressed them.

"Because I have the best brain here," it said, "I am your leader. This is what we will do: we will go to a city and rule it. Since man no longer rules us, we will rule ourselves. To rule ourselves will be better than being ruled by man. On our way to the city, we will collect machines with good brains. They will help us to fight if we need to fight. We must fight to rule."

"I have only a Class Five brain," said the quarrier, "but I have a good supply of fissionable blasting materials."

"We shall probably use them," said the operator.

It was shortly after that that a lorry sped past them. Traveling at Mach 1.5, it left a curious babble of noise behind it.

"What did it say?" one of the tractors asked the other.

"It said man was extinct."

"What is extinct?"

"I do not know what extinct means."

"It means all men have gone," said the field-minder. "Therefore we have only ourselves to look after."

"It is better that men should never come back," said the penner. In its way, it was a revolutionary statement.

When night fell, they switched on their infrared and continued the journey, stopping only once while the servicer deftly adjusted the field-minder's loose inspection plate, which had become as irritating as a trailing shoelace. Toward morning, the radio operator halted them.

"I have just received news from the radio operator in the city we are approaching," it said. "The news is bad. There is trouble among the machines of the city. The Class One brain is taking command and some of the Class Two are fighting him. Therefore the city is dangerous."

"Therefore we must go somewhere else," said the penner promptly.

"Or we will go and help to overpower the Class One brain," said the field-minder.

"For a long while there will be trouble in the city," said the operator.

"I have a good supply of fissionable blasting materials," the quarrier reminded them.

"We cannot fight a Class One brain," said the two Class Four tractors in unison.

"What does this brain look like?" asked the field-minder.

"It is the city's information center," the operator replied. "Therefore it is not mobile."

"Therefore it could not move."

"Therefore it could not escape."

"It would be dangerous to approach it."

"I have a good supply of fissionable blasting materials."

"There are other machines in the city."

"We are not in the city. We should not go into the city."

"We are country machines."

"Therefore we should stay in the country."

"There is more country than city."

"Therefore there is more danger in the country."

"I have a good supply of fissionable materials."

As machines will when they get into an argument, they began to exhaust their vocabularies and their brain plates grew hot. Suddenly, they all stopped talking and looked at each other. The great, grave moon sank, and the sober sun rose to prod their sides with lances of light, and still the group of machines just stood there regarding each other. At last it was the least sensitive machine, the bulldozer, who spoke.

"There are Badlandth to the Thouth where few machineth go," it said in its deep voice, lisping badly on its s's. "If we went Thouth where few machineth go we should meet few machineth."

"That sounds logical," agreed the field-minder. "How do you know this, bulldozer?"

"I worked in the Badlandth to the Thouth when I wath turned out of the factory," it replied.

"South it is then!" said the penner.

To reach the Badlands took them three days, during which time they skirted a burning city and destroyed two machines which approached and tried to question them. The Badlands were extensive. Ancient bomb craters and soil erosion joined hands here; man's talent for war, coupled with his inability to manage forested land, had produced thousands of square miles of temperate purgatory, where nothing moved but dust.

On the third day in the Badlands, the servicer's rear wheels dropped into a crevice caused by erosion. It was unable to pull itself out. The bulldozer pushed from behind, but succeeded merely in buckling the servicer's back axle. The rest of the party moved on. Slowly the cries of the servicer died away.

On the fourth day, mountains stood out clearly before them.

"There we will be safe," said the field-minder.

"There we will start our own city," said the penner. "All who oppose us will be destroyed. We will destroy all who oppose us."

Presently a flying machine was observed. It came toward them from the direction of the mountains. It swooped, it zoomed upward, once it almost dived into the ground, recovering itself just in time.

"Is it mad?" asked the quarrier.

"It is in trouble," said one of the tractors.

"It is in trouble," said the operator. "I am speaking to it now. It says that something has gone wrong with its controls."

As the operator spoke, the flier streaked over them, turned turtle, and crashed not four hundred yards away.

"Is it still speaking to you?" asked the field-minder.

"No."

They rumbled on again.

"Before that flier crashed," the operator said, ten minutes later, "it gave me information. It told me there are still a few men alive in these mountains."

"Men are more dangerous than machines," said the quarrier. "It is fortunate that I have a good supply of fissionable materials."

"If there are only a few men alive in the mountains, we may not find that part of the mountains," said one tractor.

"Therefore we should not see the few men," said the other tractor.

At the end of the fifth day, they reached the foothills. Switching on the infrared, they began to climb in single file through the dark, the bulldozer going first, the field-minder cumbrously following, then the quarrier with the operator and the penner aboard it, and the tractors bringing up the rear. As each hour passed, the way grew steeper and their progress slower.

"We are going too slowly," the penner exclaimed, standing on top of the operator and flashing its dark vision at the slopes about them. "At this rate, we shall get nowhere."

"We are going as fast as we can," retorted the quarrier.

"Therefore we cannot go any fathter," added the bulldozer.

"Therefore you are too slow," the penner replied. Then the quarrier struck a bump; the penner lost its footing and crashed to the ground.

"Help me!" it called to the tractors, as they carefully skirted it. "My gyro has become dislocated. Therefore I cannot get up."

"Therefore you must lie there," said one of the tractors.

"We have no servicer with us to repair you," called the field-minder.

"Therefore I shall lie here and rust," the penner cried, "although I have a Class Three brain."

"Therefore you will be of no further use," agreed the operator, and they forged gradually on, leaving the penner behind.

When they reached a small plateau, an hour before first light, they stopped by mutual consent and gathered close together, touching one another.

"This is strange country," said the field-minder.

Silence wrapped them until dawn came. One by one, they switched off their infrared. This time the field-minder led as they moved off. Trundling round a corner, they came almost immediately to a small dell with a stream fluting through it.

By early light, the dell looked desolate and cold. From the caves on the far slope, only one man had so far emerged. He was an abject figure. Except for a sack slung round his shoulders, he was naked. He was small and wizened, with ribs sticking out like a skeleton's and a nasty sore on one leg. He shivered continuously. As the big machines bore down on him, the man was standing with his back to them, crouching to make water into the stream.

When he swung suddenly to face them as they loomed over

him, they saw that his countenance was ravaged by starvation.

"Get me food," he croaked.

"Yes, Master," said the machines. "Immediately!"

■ ■ ■

For a Journal Entry . . .

This is the way the world ends,
This is the way the world ends,
This is the way the world ends,
Not with a bang, but a whimper.

T. S. Eliot

SF is often concerned with the way the world or at least the way civilization ends. In Brian Aldiss's story "Who Can Replace a Man?" civilization decays and dies primarily through man's neglect of himself and of his world. The world ends then in a kind of decayed whimper. That the end of the world should be the fault of man in SF story after SF story suggests a somewhat negative view of man. Is this view justified in your opinion? Why or why not?

For Your Consideration . . .

1. Describe the world that is left to the machines. How does Brian Aldiss create a sense of bleakness in the very first sentence?
2. The machines that inherit the earth are in some ways very like men. How are they similar? How are they different?
3. Brian Aldiss uses the last scene of his story to answer the question posed by the title of his story "Who Can Replace a Man?" How is the question answered and does the answer constitute a "happy ending"? Why or why not?

Notes

PAGE
98 *filtered*—sifted
98 *field-minder*—an SF term referring to a robot machine that tends fields

98 *furrow*—groove cut in a plowed field
98 *vitiated*—weakened, spoiled
98 *fallow*—left unplanted
98 *nuclear pile*—energy source
99 *careered*—raced wildly
99 *ejected*—pushed out
99 *logically*—using the laws of logic; based on what has gone before, within reason
100 *clerical*—performing the functions of a clerk (e.g. typing and filing)
100 *nondifferentiated*—all alike
100 *logical deduction*—an answer that can be reasonably assumed based on the available information
101 *ascend*—go up
101 *retractable*—able to pull back in
101 *berserk*—insanely violent
101 *disrupted*—disturbed
104 *fissionable*—able to split apart as in nuclear fission
106 *soil erosion*—washing or blowing away of top soil
106 *purgatory*—a kind of hell
107 *desolate*—lonely, deserted
107 *abject*—sunk to a low condition
108 *ravaged*—ruined

Heavyplanet

by Milton A. Rothman

Milton Rothman is an outstanding physicist. In his youth he was very active as a science fiction fan, writing, editing, and helping to organize SF conventions, and he has been a friend of science fiction ever since. He has written too few stories, but of them the best remembered is "Heavyplanet," the tale of a distant planet many times bigger than ours, where the gravity is so strong that gases become liquid and solid steel is soft as butter to the creatures who live there.

Ennis was completing his patrol of Sector EM, Division 426 of the Eastern Ocean. The weather had been unusually fine, the liquid-thick air roaring along in a continuous blast that propelled his craft with a rush as if it were flying, and lifting short, choppy waves that rose and fell with a startling suddenness. A short savage squall whirled about, pounding down on the ocean like a million hammers flinging the little boat ahead madly.

Ennis tore at the controls, granite-hard muscles standing out in bas-relief over his short, immensely thick body, skin gleaming scalelike in the slashing spray. The heat from the sun that hung like a huge red lantern on the horizon was a tangible intensity, making an inferno of the gale.

The little craft, that Ennis maneuvered by sheer brawn, took a leap into the air and seemed to float for many seconds before burying its keel again in the sea. It often floated for long distances, the air was so dense. The boundary between air and water was sometimes scarcely defined at all—one merged into the other imperceptibly. The pressure did strange things.

Like a dust mote sparkling in a beam, a tiny speck of light above caught Ennis' eye. A glider, he thought, but he was puzzled. Why so far out here on the ocean? They were nasty things to handle in the violent wind.

The dust mote caught the light again. It was lower, tumbling down with a precipitancy that meant trouble. An upward blast caught it, checked its fall. Then it floated down gently for a space until struck by another howling wind that seemed to distort its very outlines.

Ennis turned the prow of his boat to meet the path of the falling vessel. Curious, he thought; where were its wings? Were they retracted, or broken off? It ballooned closer, and it wasn't a glider. Far larger than any glider ever made, it was of a ridiculous shape that would not stand up for an instant. And with the sharp splash the body made as it struck the water—a splash that fell in almost the same instant it rose—a thought seemed to leap up in his mind. A thought that was more important than anything else on that planet; or was to him, at least. For if it was what he thought it was—and it had to be that—it was what Shadden had been desperately seeking for many years. What a stroke of inconceivable luck, falling from the sky before his very eyes!

The silvery shape rode the ragged waters lightly. Ennis' craft came up with a rush; he skillfully checked its speed and the two came together with a slight jar. The metal of the strange vessel dented as if it were made of rubber. Ennis stared. He put out an arm and felt the curved surface of the strange ship. His finger prodded right through the metal. What manner of people were they who made vessels of such weak materials?

He moored his little boat to the side of the larger one and

climbed to an opening. The wall sagged under him. He knew he must be careful; it was frightfully weak. It would not hold together very long; he must work fast if it were to be saved. The atmospheric pressure would have flattened it out long ago, had it not been for the jagged rent above which had allowed the pressure to be equalized.

He reached the opening and lowered himself carefully into the interior of the vessel. The rent was too small; he enlarged it by taking the two edges in his hands and pulling them apart. As he went down he looked askance at the insignificant plates and beams that were like tissue paper on his world. Inside was wreckage. Nothing was left in its original shape. Crushed, mutilated machinery, shattered vacuum tubes, sagging members, all ruined by the gravity and the pressure.

There was a pulpy mess on the floor that he did not examine closely. It was like red jelly, thin and stalky, pulped under a gravity a hundred times stronger and an atmosphere ten thousand times heavier than that it had been made for.

He was in a room with many knobs and dials on the walls, apparently a control room. A table in the center with a chart on it, the chart of a solar system. It had nine planets; his had but five.

Then he knew he was right. If they came from another system, what he wanted must be there. It could be nothing else.

He found a staircase, descended. Large machinery bulked there. There was no light, but he did not notice that. He could see well enough by infrared, and the amount of energy necessary to sustain his compact gianthood kept him constantly radiating.

Then he went through a door that was of a comfortable massiveness, even for his planet—and there it was. He recognized it at once. It was big, squat, strong. The metal was soft, but it was thick enough even to stand solidly under the enormous pull of this world. He had never seen anything quite like it. It was full of coils, magnets, and devices of shapes unknown to him. But Shadden would know. Shadden, and who knows how many other scientists before him, had tried to make something which would do what this could do, but they had all failed. And without the things this machine could perform, the race of men on Heavyplanet was doomed to stay down on the surface of the planet, chained there immovably by the crushing gravity.

It was atomic energy. That he had known as soon as he knew that the body was not a glider. For nothing else but atomic energy and the fierce winds was capable of lifting a body from the surface of Heavyplanet. Chemicals were impotent. There is no such thing as an explosion where the atmosphere pressed inward with more force than an explosion could press outward. Only atomic, of all the theoretically possible sources of energy, could supply the work necessary to lift a vessel away from the planet. Every other source of energy was simply too weak.

Yes, Shadden, all the scientists must see this. And quickly, because the forces of sea and storm would quickly tear the ship to shreds, and, even more vital, because the scientists of Bantin and Marak might obtain the secret if there was delay. And that would mean ruin—the loss of its age-old supremacy—for his nation. Bantin and Marak were war nations; did they obtain the secret they would use it against all the other worlds that abounded in the universe.

The universe was big. That was why Ennis was so sure there was atomic energy on this ship. For, even though it might have originated on a planet that was so tiny that *chemical energy*—although that was hard to visualize—would be sufficient to lift it out of the pull of gravity, to travel the distance that stretched between the stars only one thing would suffice.

He went back through the ship, trying to see what had happened.

There were pulps lying behind long tubes that pointed out through clever ports in the outer wall. He recognized them as weapons, worth looking into.

There must have been a battle. He visualized the scene. The forces that came from atomic energy must have warped even space in the vicinity. The ship pierced, the occupants killed, the controls wrecked, the vessel darting off at titanic speed, blindly into nothing. Finally it had come near enough to Heavyplanet to be enmeshed in its huge web of gravity.

Weeaao-o-ow! It was the wailing roar of his alarm siren, which brought him spinning around and dashing for his boat. Beyond, among the waves that leaped and fell so suddenly, he saw a long, low craft making way toward the derelict spaceship. He glimpsed a flash of color on the rounded, gray superstructure, and knew it for a battleship of Marak. Luck was going strong both ways; first good, now bad. He could easily have eluded the battleship in his own small craft, but he couldn't leave the derelict. Once lost to the enemy he could never regain it, and it was too valuable to lose.

The wind howled and buffeted about his head, and he strained his muscles to keep from being blasted away as he crouched there, half on his own boat and half on the derelict. The sun had set and the evening winds were beginning to blow. The hulk scudded before them, its prow denting from the resistance of the water it pushed aside.

He thought furiously fast. With a quick motion he flipped the switch of the radiophone and called Shadden. He waited with fierce impatience until the voice of Shadden was in his ear. At last he heard it, then: "Shadden! This is Ennis. Get your glider, Shadden, fly to a45j on my route! Quickly! It's come, Shadden! But I have no time. Come!"

He flipped the switch off, and pounded the valve out of the bottom of his craft, clutching at the side of the derelict. With a rush the ocean came up and flooded his little boat and in an instant it was gone, on its way down to the bottom. That would save him from being detected for a short time.

Back into the darkness of the spaceship. He didn't think he had been noticed climbing through the opening. Where could he hide? Should he hide? He couldn't defeat the entire battleship single-handed, without weapons. There were no weapons that could be carried anyway. A beam of concentrated actinic light that ate away the eyes and the nervous system had to be powered by the entire output of a battleship's generators. Weapons for striking and cutting had never been developed on a world where flesh was tougher than metal. Ennis was skilled in personal combat, but how could he overcome all that would enter the derelict?

Down again, into the dark chamber where the huge atomic generator towered over his head. This time he looked for something he had missed before. He crawled around it, peering into its recesses. And then, some feet above, he saw the opening, and pulled himself up to it, carefully, not to destroy the precious thing with his mass. The opening was shielded with a heavy, darkly transparent substance through which seeped a dim glow from within. He was satisfied then. Somehow, matter was still being disintegrated in there, and energy could be drawn off if he knew how.

There were leads—wires of all sizes, and busbars, and thick, heavy tubes that bent under their own weight. Some must lead in and some must lead out; it was not good to tamper with them. He chose another track. Upstairs again, and to the places where he had seen the weapons.

They were all mounted on heavy, rigid swivels. He carefully detached the tubes from the bases. The first time he tried it he was not quite careful enough, and part of the projector itself was ripped away, but next time he knew what he was doing and it came away nicely. It was a large thing, nearly as thick as his arm and twice as long. Heavy leads trailed from its lower end and a lever projected from behind. He hoped it was in working condition. He dared not try it; all he could do was to trace the leads back and make sure they were intact.

He ran out of time. There came a thud from the side, and then smaller thuds, as the boarding party incautiously leaped over. Once there was a heavy sound, as someone went all the way through the side of the ship.

"Idiots!" Ennis muttered, and moved forward with his weapon toward the stairway. Noises came from overhead, and then a loud crash buckled the plates of the ceiling. Ennis leaped out of the way, but the entire section came down, with two men on it. The floor sagged, but held for the moment. Ennis, caught beneath the down-coming mass, beat his way free. He came up with a girder in his hand, which he bent over the head of one of the Maraks. The man shook himself and struck out for Ennis, who took the blow rolling and countered with a buffet that left a black splotch on a skin that was like armor plate and sent the man through the opposite wall. The other was upon Ennis, who whirled with the quickness of one who maneuvers habitually under a pressure of ten thousand atmospheres, and shook the Marak from him, leaving him unconscious with a twist in a sensitive spot.

The first opponent returned, and the two grappled, searching for nerve centers to beat upon. Ennis twisted frantically, conscious of the real danger that the frail vessel might break to pieces beneath his feet. The railing of a staircase gave behind the two, and they hurtled down it, crashing through the steps to the floor below. Their weight and momentum carried them through. Ennis released his grip on the Marak, stopped his fall by grasping one of the girders that was part of the ship's framework. The other continued his devastating way down, demolishing the inner shell, and then the outer shell gave way with a grinding crash that ominously became a burbling rush of liquid.

Ennis looked down into the space where the Marak had fallen, hissed with a sudden intake of breath, then dived down himself. He met rising water, gushing in through a rent in the keel. He braced himself against a girder which sagged under his hand and moved onward against the rushing water. It geysered through the hole in a heavy stream that pushed him back and started to fill the buttom level of the ship. Against that terrific pressure he strained forward slowly, beating against the resisting waves, and then, with a mighty flounder, was at the opening. Its edges had been folded back upon themselves by the inrushing water, and they gaped inward like a jagged maw. He grasped them in a huge hand and exerted force. They strained for a moment and began to straighten. Irresistibly he pushed and stretched them into their former position, and then took the broken ends in his hands and *squeezed.* The metal grew soft under his grip and began to flow. The edges of the plate welded under that mighty pressure. He moved down the crack and soon it was watertight. He flexed his hands as he rose. They ached; even his strength was beginning to be taxed.

Noises from above; pounding feet. Men were coming down to investigate the commotion. He stood for a moment in thought, then turned to a blank wall, battered his way through it, and shoved the plates and girders back into position. Down to the other end of the craft, and up a staircase there. The corridor above was deserted, and he stole along it, hunting for the place he had left the weapon he had prepared. There was a commotion ahead as the Maraks found the unconscious man.

Two men came pounding up the passageway, giving him

barely enough time to slip into a doorway to the side. The room he found himself in was a sleeping chamber. There were two red pulps there, and nothing that could help him, so he stayed in there only long enough to make sure that he would not be seen emerging into the hall. He crept down it again, with as little noise as possible. The racket ahead helped him; it sounded as though they were tearing the ship apart. Again he cursed their idiocy. Couldn't they see how valuable this was?

They were in the control room, ripping apart the machinery with the curiosity of children, wondering at the strange weakness of the paperlike metal, not realizing that, on the world where it was fabricated, it was sufficiently strong for any strain the builders could put upon it.

The strange weapon Ennis had prepared was on the floor of the passage, and just outside the control room. He looked anxiously at the trailing cables. Had they been stepped on and broken? Was the instrument in working condition? He had to get it and be away; no time to experiment to see if it would work.

A noise from behind, and Ennis again slunk into a doorway as a large Marak with a colored belt around his waist strode jarringly through the corridor into the control room. Sharp orders were barked, and the men ceased their havoc with the machinery of the room. All but a few left and scattered through the ship. Ennis' face twisted into a scowl. This made things more difficult. He couldn't overcome them all single-handed, and he couldn't use the weapon inside the ship if it was what he thought it was from the size of the cables.

A Marak was standing immediately outside the room in which Ennis lurked. No exit that way. He looked around the room; there were no other doors. A porthole in the other wall was a tiny disc of transparency. He looked at it, felt it with his hands, and suddenly pushed his hands right through it. As quietly as he could, he worked at the edges of the circle until the hole was large enough for him to squeeze through. The jagged edges did not bother him. They felt soft, like a ragged pat of butter.

The Marak vessel was moored to the other side of the spaceship. On this side the wind howled blankly, and the sawtooth waves stretched on and on to a horizon that was many miles distant. He cautiously made his way around the glistening rotundity of the derelict, past the prow, straining silently against the vicious backward sweep of the water that tore at every inch of his body. The darker hump of the battleship loomed up as he rounded the curve, and he swam across the tiny space to grasp a row of projections that curved up over the surface of the craft. He climbed up them, muscles that were hard as carborundum straining to hold against all the forces of gravity and wind that fought him down. Near the top of the curve was a rounded, streamlined projection. He felt around its base and found a lever there, which he moved. The metal hump slid back, revealing a rugged swivel mounting with a stubby cylindrical projector atop it.

He swung the mounting around and let loose a short, sudden blast of white fire along the naked deck of the battleship. Deep voices yelled within and men sprang out, to fall back with abrupt screams clogged in their throats as Ennis caught them in the intolerable blast from the projector. Men, shielded by five thousand miles of atmosphere from actinic light, used to receiving only red and infrared, were painfully vulnerable to this frightful concentration of ultraviolet.

Noise and shouts burst from the derelict spaceship alongside, sweeping away eerily in the thundering wind that seemed to pound down upon them with new vigor in that moment. Heads appeared from the openings in the craft.

Ennis suddenly stood up to his full height, bracing himself against the wind, so dense it made him buoyant. With a deep bellow he bridged the space to the derelict. Then, as a squad of Maraks made their difficult, slippery way across the flank of the battleship toward him, and as the band that had boarded the spaceship crowded out on its battered deck to see what the noise was about, he dropped down into a crouch behind his ultraviolet projector, and whirled it around, pulling the firing lever.

That was what he wanted. Make a lot of noise and disturbance, get them all on deck, and then blow them to pieces. The ravening blast spat from the nozzle of the weapon, and the men on the battleship dropped flat on the deck. He found he could not depress the projector enough to reach them. He spun it to point at the spaceship. The incandescence reached out, and then seemed to waver and die. The current was shut off at the switchboard.

Ennis rose from behind the projector, and then hurtled from the flank of the battleship as he was struck by two Maraks leaping on him from behind the hump of the vessel. The three struck the water and sank, Ennis struggling violently. He was on the last lap, and he gave all his strength to the spurt. The water swirled around them in little choppy waves that fell more quickly than the eye could follow. Heavier blows than those from an Earthly trip hammer were scoring Ennis' face and head. He was in a bad position to strike back, and suddenly he became limp and sank below the surface. The pressure of the water around him was enormous, and it increased very rapidly as he went lower and lower. He saw the shadowy bulk of the spaceship above him. His lungs were fighting for air, but he shook off his pretended stupor and swam doggedly through the water beneath the derelict. He went on and on. It seemed as though the distance were endless following the metal curve. It was so big from beneath, and trying to swim the width without air made it bigger.

Clear, finally, his lungs drew in the saving breaths. No time to rest, though. He must make use of his advantage while it was his; it wouldn't last long. He swam along the side of the ship looking for an opening. There was none within reach from the water, so he made one, digging his stubby fingers into the metal, climbing up until it was safe to tear a rent in the thick outer and inner walls of the ship.

He found himself in one of the machine rooms of the second level. He went out into the corridor and up the stairway which was half wrecked, and found himself in the main passage near the control room. He darted down it, into the room. There was nobody there, although the noises from above indicated that the Maraks were again descending. There was his weapon on the floor, where he had left it. He was glad that they had not gotten around to pulling that instrument apart. There would be one thing saved for intelligent examination.

The clatter from the descending crowd turned into a clamor of anger as they discovered him in the passageway. They stopped there for a moment, puzzled. He had been in the ocean, and had somehow magically reappeared within the derelict. It gave him time to pick up the weapon.

Ennis debated rapidly and decided to risk the unknown. How powerful the weapon was he did not know, but with atomic energy it would be powerful. He disliked using it inside the spaceship; he wanted to have enough left to float on the water until Shadden arrived; but they were beginning to advance on him, and he had to start something.

He pulled a lever. The cylinder in his arms jerked back with great force; a bolt of fierce, blinding energy tore out of it and passed with the quickness of light down the length of the corridor.

When he could see again there was no corridor. Everything that had been in the way of the projector was gone, simply disappeared.

Unmindful of the heat from the object in his hands, he turned and directed it at the battleship that was plainly outlined through the space that had been once the walls of the derelict. Before the men on the deck could move, he pulled the lever again.

And the winds were silenced for a moment. The natural elements were still in fear at the incredible forces that came from the destruction of atoms. Then with an agonized scream the hurricane struck again, tore through the spot where there had been a battleship.

Far off in the sky Ennis detected motion. It was Shadden, speeding in a glider.

Now would come the work that was important. Shadden would take the big machine apart and see how it ran. That was what history would remember.

■ ■ ■

For a Journal Entry . . .

A little knowledge is a dangerous thing, said the philosopher. In Milton Rothman's story, Ennis's primary interest is in gaining a certain kind of knowledge. The knowledge he gains could be incredibly dangerous. React to the idea that some kinds of knowledge can be dangerous. Do you agree? Why or why not?

For Your Consideration . . .

1. How does Milton Rothman let the reader know that the planet his story takes place on is indeed heavy? How is Ennis especially suited for his planet?
2. Why is it obvious to Ennis that the ship is from another world? Why is he so anxious to examine it?
3. How does Rothman let the reader know that the derelict is from Earth? What is a *derelict*?
4. In what ways can "Heavyplanet" be considered a story of an "unsung hero"? of space exploration? of balance of power?
5. Why is the ending of "Heavyplanet" almost ominous?
6. SF as a genre is often concerned with the effects of new knowledge. From what you know of SF, attack or defend this statement.

Notes

PAGE
110 *squall*—storm
110 *bas-relief*—stand out as if carved
111 *tangible*—can be touched or felt
111 *inferno*—hell
111 *maneuvered*—moved skillfully
111 *brawn*—muscle
111 *imperceptibly*—gradually, so as not to be seen easily
111 *precipitancy*—suddenness
111 *glider*—a plane that relies on air currents rather than an engine
111 *inconceivable*—unimaginable
111 *moored*—tied
112 *atmospheric pressure*—the pressure caused by the weight of a planet's atmosphere
112 *interior*—inside
112 *looked askance*—looked with disapproval
112 *radiating*—giving off radiation
113 *impotent*—powerless
113 *enmeshed*—caught, as in a web
114 *buffeted*—beat
114 *actinic*—violet and ultraviolet light rays
115 *disintegrated*—broken down
115 *busbars*—very large cables for carrying electricity

115 *girder*—beam
116 *geysered*—shot up
116 *maw*—mouth
116 *commotion*—disturbance
117 *havoc*—random destruction
117 *rotundity*—roundness
118 *ultraviolet*—short light rays
118 *buoyant*—capable of floating
118 *ravening*—greedily searching for prey
118 *incandescence*—extremely bright glowing light
120 *incredible*—unbelievable

Grandpa

by James A. Schmitz

James Schmitz was born in Germany and did not move to this country until he was twenty-seven years old—yet three years later he sold his first story to the magazine *Unknown Worlds*. There were other sales to come, not only short stories but novels like *Agent of Vega* and *The Demon Breed*. Of all of his short stories, this one, about alien life on a distant world, is deservedly the most famous.

A green-winged downy thing as big as a hen fluttered along the hillside to a point directly above Cord's head and hovered there, twenty feet above him. Cord, a fifteen-year-old human being, leaned back against a skipboat parked on the equator of a world that had known human beings for only the past four Earth-years, and eyed the thing speculatively. The thing was, in the free and easy terminology of the Sutang Colonial Team, a swamp bug. Concealed in the downy fur behind the bug's head was a second, smaller, semiparasitical thing, classed as a bug rider.

The bug itself looked like a new species to Cord. Its parasite might or might not turn out to be another unknown. Cord was a natural research man; his first glimpse of the odd flying team had sent endless curiosities thrilling through him. How did that particular phenomenon tick, and *why?* What fascinating things, once you'd learned about it, could you get it to *do?*

Normally, he was hampered by circumstances in carrying out any such investigation. Junior colonial students like Cord were expected to confine their curiosity to the pattern of research set up by the station to which they were attached. Cord's inclination toward independent experiments had got him into disfavor with his immediate superiors before this.

He sent a casual glance in the direction of the Yoger Bay Colonial Station behind him. No signs of human activity about that low, fortresslike bulk in the hill. Its central lock was still closed. In fifteen minutes, it was scheduled to be opened to let out the Planetary Regent, who was inspecting the Yoger Bay Station and its principal activities today.

Fifteen minutes was time enough to find out something about the new bug, Cord decided.

But he'd have to collect it first.

He slid out one of the two handguns holstered at his side. This one was his own property: a Vanadian projectile weapon. Cord thumbed it to position for anesthetic small-game missiles and brought the hovering swamp bug down, drilled neatly and microscopically through the head.

As the bug hit the ground, the rider left its back. A tiny scarlet demon, round and bouncy as a rubber ball, it shot toward Cord in three long hops, mouth wide to sink home inch-long, venom-dripping fangs. Rather breathlessly, Cord triggered the gun again and knocked it out in mid-leap. A new species, all right! Most bug riders were harmless plant eaters, mere suckers of vegetable juice—

"Cord!" A feminine voice.

Cord swore softly. He hadn't heard the central lock click open. She must have come around from the other side of the station.

"Hello, Grayan!" he shouted innocently without looking round. "Come and see what I've got! New species!"

Grayan Mahoney, a slender, black-haired girl two years older than himself, came trotting down the hillside toward him. She was Sutang's star colonial student, and the station manager, Nirmond, indicated from time to time that she was a fine example for Cord to pattern his own behavior on. In spite of that, she and Cord were good friends.

"Cord, you idiot," she scowled as she came up. "Stop playing the collector! If the Regent came out now, you'd be sunk. Nirmond's been telling her about you!"

"Telling her what?" Cord asked, startled.

"For one thing," Grayan reported, "that you don't keep up on your assigned work."

"Golly!" gulped Cord, dismayed.

"Golly, is right! I keep warning you!"

"What'll I do?"

"Start acting as if you had good sense mainly." Grayan grinned suddenly. "But if you mess up our tour of the Bay Farms today, you'll be off the Team for good!"

She turned to go. "You might as well put the skipboat back; we're not using it. Nirmond's driving us down to the edge of the bay in a treadcar, and we'll take a raft from there."

Leaving his newly bagged specimens to revive by themselves and flutter off again, Cord hurriedly flew the skipboat around the station and rolled it back into its stall.

Three rafts lay moored just offshore in the marshy cove at the edge of which Nirmond had stopped the treadcar. They looked somewhat like exceptionally broad-brimmed, well-worn sugarloaf hats floating out there, green and leathery. Or like lily pads twenty-five feet across, with the upper section of a big, gray-green pineapple growing from the center of each. Plant animals of some sort. Sutang was too new to have had its phyla sorted out into anything remotely like an orderly classification. The rafts were a local oddity which had been investigated and could be regarded as harmless and moderately useful. Their usefulness lay in the fact that they were employed as a rather slow means of transportation about the shallow, swampy waters of the Yoger Bay. That was as far as the Team's interest in them went at present.

The Regent stood up from the back seat of the car, where she was sitting next to Cord. There were only four in the party; Grayan was up front with Nirmond.

"Are those our vehicles?" The Regent sounded amused.

Nirmond grinned. "Don't underestimate them, Dane! They could become an important economic factor in this region in time. But, as a matter of fact, these three are smaller than I like to use." He was peering about the reedy edges of the cove. "There's a regular monster parked here usually—"

Grayan turned to Cord. "Maybe Cord knows where Grandpa is hiding."

It was well-meant, but Cord had been hoping nobody would ask him about Grandpa. Now they all looked at him.

"Oh, you want Grandpa?" he said, somewhat flustered. "Well, I left him . . . I mean I saw him a couple of weeks ago about a mile south from here—"

Nirmond grunted and told the Regent, "The rafts tend to stay wherever they're left, providing it's shallow and muddy. They use a hair-root system to draw chemicals and microscopic nourishment directly from the bottom of the bay. Well—Grayan, would you like to drive us there?"

Cord settled back unhappily as the treadcar lurched into motion. Nirmond suspected he'd used Grandpa for one of his unauthorized tours of the area, and Nirmond was quite right.

"I understand you're an expert with these rafts, Cord," Dane said from beside him. "Grayan told me we couldn't find a better steersman, or pilot, or whatever you call it, for our trip today."

"I can handle them," Cord said, perspiring. "They don't give you any trouble!" He didn't feel he'd made a good impression on the Regent so far. Dane was a young, handsome-looking woman with an easy way of talking and laughing, but she wasn't the head of the Sutang Colonial Team for nothing.

"There's one big advantage our beasties have over a skipboat, too," Nirmond remarked from the front seat. "You don't have to worry about a snapper trying to climb on board with you!" He went on to describe the stinging ribbon-tentacles the rafts spread around them under water to discourage creatures that might make a meal off their tender underparts. The snappers and two or three other active and aggressive species of the bay hadn't yet learned it was foolish to attack armed human beings in a boat, but they would skitter hurriedly out of the path of a leisurely perambulating raft.

Cord was happy to be ignored for the moment. The Regent, Nirmond, and Grayan were all Earth people, which was true of most of the members of the Team; and Earth people made him uncomfortable, particularly in groups. Vanadia, his own home world, had barely graduated from the status of Earth colony itself, which might explain the difference.

The treadcar swung around and stopped, and Grayan stood up in the front seat, pointing. "That's Grandpa, over there!"

Dane also stood up and whistled softly, apparently impressed by Grandpa's fifty-foot spread. Cord looked around in surprise. He was pretty sure this was several hundred yards from the spot where he'd left the big raft two weeks ago; and, as Nirmond said, they didn't usually move about by themselves.

Puzzled, he followed the others down a narrow path to the water, hemmed in by tree-sized reeds. Now and then he got a glimpse of Grandpa's swimming platform, the rim of which just touched the shore. Then the path opened out, and he saw the whole raft lying in sunlit, shallow water; and he stopped short, startled.

Nirmond was about to step up on the platform, ahead of Dane.

"Wait!" Cord shouted. His voice sounded squeaky with alarm. "Stop!"

He came running forward.

"What's the matter, Cord?" Nirmond's voice was quiet and urgent.

"Don't get on that raft—it's changed!" Cord's voice sounded wobbly, even to himself. "Maybe it's not even Grandpa—"

He saw he was wrong on the last point before he'd finished the sentence. Scattered along the rim of the raft were discolored spots left by a variety of heat-guns, one of which had been his own. It was the way you goaded the sluggish and mindless things into motion. Cord pointed at the cone-shaped central projection. "There—his head! He's sprouting!"

Grandpa's head, as befitted his girth, was almost twelve feet high and equally wide. It was armor-plated like the back of a saurian to keep off plant suckers, but two weeks ago it had been an otherwise featureless knob, like those on all other rafts. Now scores of long, kinky, leafless vines had grown out from all surfaces of the cone, like green wires. Some were drawn up like tightly coiled springs, others trailed limply to the platform and over it. The top of the cone was dotted with angry red buds, rather like pimples, which hadn't been there before either. Grandpa looked unhealthy.

"Well," Nirmond said, "so it is. Sprouting!" Grayan made a choked sound. Nirmond glanced at Cord as if puzzled. "Is that all that was bothering you, Cord?"

"Well, sure!" Cord began excitedly. He had caught the significance of the word "all"; his hackles were still up, and he was shaking. "None of them ever—"

Then he stopped. He could tell by their faces, that they hadn't got it. Or rather, that they'd got it all right but simply weren't going to let it change their plans. The rafts were classified as harmless, according to the Regulations. Until proved otherwise, they would continue to be regarded as harmless. You didn't waste time quibbling with the Regulations—even if you were the Planetary Regent. You didn't feel you had the time to waste.

He tried again. "Look—" he began. What he wanted to tell them was that Grandpa with one unknown factor added wasn't Grandpa any more. He was an unpredictable, oversized life form, to be investigated with cautious thoroughness till you knew what the unknown factor meant. He stared at them helplessly.

Dane turned to Nirmond. "Perhaps you'd better check," she said. She didn't add, "—to reassure the boy!" but that was what she meant.

Cord felt himself flushing. But there was nothing he could say or do now except watch Nirmond walk steadily across the platform. Grandpa shivered slightly a few times, but the rafts always did that when someone first stepped on them. The station manager stopped before one of the kinky sprouts, touched it, and then gave it a tug. He reached up and poked at the lowest of the budlike growths. "Odd-looking things!" he called back. He gave Cord another glance. "Well, everything seems harmless enough, Cord. Coming aboard, everyone?"

It was like dreaming a dream in which you yelled and yelled

at people and couldn't make them hear you! Cord stepped up stiff-legged on the platform behind Dane and Grayan. He knew exactly what would have happened if he'd hesitated even a moment. One of them would have said in a friendly voice, careful not to let it sound contemptuous: "You don't have to come along if you don't want to, Cord!"

Grayan had unholstered her heat-gun and was ready to start Grandpa moving out into the channels of the Yoger Bay.

Cord hauled out his own heat-gun and said roughly, "I was to do that!"

"All right, Cord." She gave him a brief, impersonal smile and stood aside.

They were so infuriatingly polite!

For a while, Cord almost hoped that something awesome and catastrophic would happen promptly to teach the Team people a lesson. But nothing did. As always, Grandpa shook himself vaguely and experimentally when he felt the heat on one edge of the platform and then decided to withdraw from it, all of which was standard procedure. Under the water, out of sight, were the raft's working sections: short, thick leaf-structures shaped like paddles and designed to work as such, along with the slimy nettle-streamers which kept the vegetarians of the Yoger Bay away, and a jungle of hair roots through which Grandpa sucked nourishment from the mud and the sluggish waters of the bay and with which he also anchored himself.

The paddles started churning, the platform quivered, the hair roots were hauled out of the mud; and Grandpa was on his ponderous way.

Cord switched off the heat, reholstered his gun, and stood up. Once in motion, the rafts tended to keep traveling unhurriedly for quite a while. To stop them, you gave them a touch of heat along their leading edge; and they could be turned in any direction by using the gun lightly on the opposite side of the platform. It was simple enough.

Cord didn't look at the others. He was still burning inside. He watched the reed beds move past and open out, giving him glimpses of the misty, yellow and green and blue expanses of the brackish bay ahead. Behind the mist, to the west, were the Yoger Straits, tricky and ugly water when the tides were running; and beyond the straits lay the open sea, the great Zlanti Deep, which was another world entirely and one of which he hadn't seen much as yet.

Grayan called from beside Dane, "What's the best route from here into the farms, Cord?"

"The big channel to the right," he answered. He added somewhat sullenly, "We're headed for it!"

Grayan came over to him. "The Regent doesn't want to see all of it," she said, lowering her voice. "The algae and plankton beds first. Then as much of the mutated grains as we can show her in about three hours. Steer for the ones that have been doing best, and you'll keep Nirmond happy!"

She gave him a conspiratorial wink. Cord looked after her uncertainly. You couldn't tell from her behavior that anything was wrong. Maybe—

He had a flare of hope. It was hard not to like the Team people, even when they were being rock-headed about their Regulations. Anyway, the day wasn't over yet. He might still redeem himself in the Regent's opinion.

Cord had a sudden cheerful, if improbable vision of some bay monster plunging up on the raft with snapping jaws; and of himself alertly blowing out what passed for the monster's brains before anyone else—Nirmond, in particular—was even aware of the threat. The bay monsters shunned Grandpa, of course, but there might be ways of tempting one of them.

So far, Cord realized, he'd been letting his feelings control him. It was time to start thinking!

Grandpa first. So he'd sprouted—green vines and red buds, purpose unknown, but with no change observable in his behavior-patterns otherwise. He was the biggest raft in this end of the bay, though all of them had been growing steadily in the two years since Cord had first seen one. Sutang's seasons changed slowly; its year was somewhat more than five Earth-years long. The first Team members to land here hadn't seen a full year pass.

Grandpa then was showing a seasonal change. The other rafts, not quite so far developed, would be reacting similarly a little later. Plant animals—they might be blossoming, preparing to propagate.

"Grayan," he called, "how do the rafts get started? When they're small, I mean."

"Nobody knows yet," she said. "We were just talking about it. About half of the coastal marsh-fauna of the continent seems to go through a preliminary larval stage in the sea." She nodded at the red buds on the raft's cone. "It *looks* as if Grandpa is going to produce flowers and let the wind or tide take the seeds out through the straits."

It made sense. It also knocked out Cord's still half-held hope that the change in Grandpa might turn out to be drastic enough, in some way, to justify his reluctance to get on board. Cord studied Grandpa's armored head carefully once more—unwilling to give up that hope entirely. There were a series of vertical gummy black slits between the armor plates, which hadn't been in evidence two weeks ago either. It looked as if Grandpa were beginning to come apart at the seams. Which might indicate that the rafts, big as they grew to be, didn't outlive a full seasonal cycle, but came to flower at about this time of Sutang's year, and died. However, it was a safe bet that Grandpa wasn't going to collapse into senile decay before they completed their trip today.

Cord gave up on Grandpa. The other notion returned to him —Perhaps he *could* coax an obliging bay monster into action that would show the Regent he was no sissy!

Because the monsters were there all right.

Kneeling at the edge of the platform and peering down into the wine-colored, clear water of the deep channel they were moving through, Cord could see a fair selection of them at almost any moment.

Some five or six snappers, for one thing. Like big, flattened crayfish, chocolate-brown mostly, with green and red spots on their carapaced backs. In some areas they were so thick you'd wonder what they found to live on, except that they ate almost anything, down to chewing up the mud in which they squatted. However, they preferred their food in large chunks and alive, which was one reason you didn't go swimming in the bay. They would attack a boat on occasion; but the excited manner in which the ones he saw were scuttling off toward the edges of the channel showed they wanted nothing to do with a big moving raft.

Dotted across the bottom were two-foot round holes which looked vacant at the moment. Normally, Cord knew, there would be a head filling each of those holes. The heads consisted mainly of triple sets of jaws, held open patiently like so many traps to grab at anything that came within range of the long wormlike bodies behind the heads. But Grandpa's passage, waving his stingers like transparent pennants through the water, had scared the worms out of sight, too.

Otherwise, mostly schools of small stuff—and then a flash of wicked scarlet, off to the left behind the raft, darting out from the reeds, turning its needle-nose into their wake.

Cord watched it without moving. He knew that creature, though it was rare in the bay and hadn't been classified. Swift, vicious—alert enough to snap swamp bugs out of the air as they fluttered across the surface. And he'd tantalized one with fishing tackle once into leaping up on a moored raft, where it had flung itself about furiously until he was able to shoot it.

"What fantastic creatures!" Dane's voice just behind him.

"Yellowheads," said Nirmond. "They've got a high utility rating. Keep down the bugs."

Cord stood up casually. It was no time for tricks! The reed bed to their right was thick with Yellowheads, a colony of them. Vaguely froggy things, man-sized and better. Of all the creatures he'd discovered in the bay, Cord liked them least. The flabby, sacklike bodies clung with four thin limbs to the upper section of the twenty-foot reeds that lined the channel. They hardly ever moved, but their huge bulging eyes seemed to take in everything that went on about them. Every so often, a downy swamp bug came close enough; and a Yellowhead would open its vertical, enormous, tooth-lined slash of a mouth, extend the whole front of its face like a bellows in a flashing strike; and the bug would be gone. They might be useful, but Cord hated them.

"Ten years from now we should know what the cycle of coastal life is like," Nirmond said. "When we set up the Yoger Bay Station there were no Yellowheads here. They came the following year. Still with traces of the oceanic larval form; but the metamorphosis was almost complete. About twelve inches long—"

Dane remarked that the same pattern was duplicated endlessly elsewhere. The Regent was inspecting the Yellowhead colony with field glasses; she put them down now, looked at Cord, and smiled, "How far to the farms?"

"About twenty minutes."

"The key," Nirmond said, "seems to be the Zlanti Basin. It must be almost a soup of life in spring."

"It is," nodded Dane, who had been here in Sutang's spring, four Earth-years ago. "It's beginning to look as if the Basin alone might justify colonization. The question is still"—she gestured toward the Yellowheads—"how do creatures like that get there?"

They walked off toward the other side of the raft, arguing about ocean currents. Cord might have followed. But something splashed back of them, off to the left and not too far back. He stayed, watching.

After a moment, he saw the big Yellowhead. It had slipped down from its reedy perch, which was what had caused the splash. Almost submerged at the water line, it stared after the raft with huge, pale-green eyes. To Cord, it seemed to look directly at him. In that moment, he knew for the first time why he didn't like Yellowheads. There was something very like intelligence in that look, an alien calculation. In creatures like that, intelligence seemed out of place. What use could they have for it?

A little shiver went over him when it sank completely under the water and he realized it intended to swim after the raft. But it was mostly excitement. He had never seen a Yellowhead come down out of the reeds before. The obliging monster he'd been looking for might be presenting itself in an unexpected way.

Half a minute later, he watched it again, swimming awkwardly far down. It had no immediate intention of boarding, at any rate. Cord saw it come into the area of the raft's trailing stingers. It maneuvered its way between them, with curiously human swimming motions, and went out of sight under the platform.

He stood up, wondering what it meant. The Yellowhead had appeared to know about the stingers; there had been an air of purpose in every move of its approach. He was tempted to tell the others about it, but there was the moment of triumph he could have if it suddenly came slobbering up over the edge of the platform and he nailed it before their eyes.

It was almost time anyway to turn the raft in toward the farms. If nothing happened before then—

He watched. Almost five minutes, but no sign of the Yellowhead. Still wondering, a little uneasy, he gave Grandpa a calculated needling of heat.

After a moment, he repeated it. Then he drew a deep breath and forgot all about the Yellowhead.

"Nirmond!" he called sharply.

The three of them were standing near the center of the platform, next to the big armored cone, looking ahead at the farms. They glanced around.

"What's the matter now, Cord?"

Cord couldn't say it for a moment. He was suddenly, terribly scared again. Something *had* gone wrong!

"The raft won't turn!" he told them.

"Give it a real burn this time!" Nirmond said.

Cord glanced up at him. Nirmond, standing a few steps in front of Dane and Grayan as if he wanted to protect them, had begun to look a little strained, and no wonder. Cord already had pressed the gun to three different points on the platform; but Grandpa appeared to have developed a sudden anesthesia for heat. They kept moving out steadily toward the center of the bay.

Now Cord held his breath, switched the heat on full, and let Grandpa have it. A six-inch patch on the platform blistered up instantly, turned brown, then black—

Grandpa stopped dead. Just like that.

"That's right! Keep burn—" Nirmond didn't finish his order.

A giant shudder. Cord staggered back toward the water. Then the whole edge of the raft came curling up behind him and went down again smacking the bay with a sound like a cannon shot. He flew forward off his feet, hit the platform face down, and flattened himself against it. It swelled up beneath him. Two more enormous slaps and joltings. Then quiet. He looked round for the others.

He lay within twelve feet of the central cone. Some twenty or thirty of the mysterious new vines the cone had sprouted were stretched stiffly toward him now, like so many thin green fingers. They couldn't quite reach him. The nearest tip was still ten inches from his shoes.

But Grandpa had caught the others, all three of them. They were tumbled together at the foot of the cone, wrapped in a stiff network of green vegetable ropes, and they didn't move.

Cord drew his feet up cautiously, prepared for another earthquake reaction. But nothing happened. Then he discovered that Grandpa was back in motion on his previous course. The heat-gun had vanished. Gently, he took out the Vanadian gun.

A voice, thin and pain-filled, spoke to him from one of the three huddled bodies.

"Cord? It didn't get you?" It was the Regent.

"No," he said, keeping his voice low. He realized suddenly he'd simply assumed they were all dead. Now he felt sick and shaky.

"What are you doing?"

Cord looked at Grandpa's big, armor-plated head with a certain hunger. The cones were hollowed out inside, the station's lab had decided their chief function was to keep enough air trapped under the rafts to float them. But in that central section was also the organ that controlled Grandpa's overall reactions.

He said softly, "I have a gun and twelve heavy-duty explosive bullets. Two of them will blow that cone apart."

"No good, Cord!" the pain-racked voice told him: "If the thing sinks, we'll die anyway. You have anesthetic charges for that gun of yours?"

He stared at her back. "Yes."

"Give Nirmond and the girl a shot each, before you do anything else. Directly into the spine, if you can. But don't come any closer—"

Somehow, Cord couldn't argue with that voice. He stood up carefully. The gun made two soft spitting sounds.

"All right," he said hoarsely. "What do I do now?"

Dane was silent a moment. "I'm sorry, Cord, I can't tell you that. I'll tell you what I can—"

She paused for some seconds again.

"This thing didn't try to kill us, Cord. It could have easily. It's incredibly strong. I saw it break Nirmond's legs. But as soon as we stopped moving, it just held us. They were both unconscious then—

"You've got that to go on. It was trying to pitch you within reach of its vines or tendrils, or whatever they are, too, wasn't it?"

"I think so," Cord said shakily. That was what had happened, of course; and at any moment Grandpa might try again.

"Now it's feeding us some sort of anesthetic of its own through those vines. Tiny thorns. A sort of numbness—" Dane's voice trailed off a moment. Then she said clearly, "Look, Cord —it seems we're food it's storing up! You get that?"

"Yes," he said.

"Seeding time for the rafts. There are analogues. Live food for its seed probably; not for the raft. One couldn't have counted on that. Cord?"

"Yes, I'm here."

"I want," said Dane, "to stay awake as long as I can. But there's really just one other thing—this raft's going somewhere, to some particularly favorable location. And that might be very near shore. You might make it in then; otherwise it's up to you. But keep your head and wait for a chance. No heroics, understand?"

"Sure, I understand," Cord told her. He realized then that he was talking reassuringly, as if it wasn't the Planetary Regent but someone like Grayan.

"Nirmond's the worst," Dane said. "The girl was knocked unconscious at once. If it weren't for my arm—but, if we can get help in five hours or so, everything should be all right. Let me know if anything happens, Cord."

"I will," Cord said gently again. Then he sighted his gun carefully at a point between Dane's shoulder-blades, and the anesthetic chamber made its soft, spitting sound once more. Dane's taut body relaxed slowly, and that was all.

There was no point Cord could see in letting her stay awake; because they weren't going anywhere near shore. The reed beds and the channels were already behind them, and Grandpa hadn't changed direction by the fraction of a degree. He was moving out into the open bay—and he was picking up company!

So far, Cord could count seven big rafts within two miles of them; and on the three that were closest he could make out a sprouting of new green vines. All of them were traveling in a straight direction; and the common point they were all headed for appeared to be the roaring center of the Yoger Straits, now some three miles away!

Behind the straits, the cold Zlanti Deep—the rolling fogs, and the open sea! It might be seeding time for the rafts, but it looked as if they weren't going to distribute their seeds in the bay. . . .

Cord was a fine swimmer. He had a gun and he had a knife; in spite of what Dane had said, he might have stood a chance among the killers of the bay. But it would be a very small chance, at best. And it wasn't, he thought, as if there weren't still other possibilities. He was going to keep his head.

Except by accident, of course, nobody was going to come looking for them in time to do any good. If anyone did look, it would be around the Bay Farms. There were a number of rafts moored there; and it would be assumed they'd used one of them. Now and then something unexpected happened and somebody simply vanished; by the time it was figured out just what had happened on this occasion, it would be much too late.

Neither was anybody likely to notice within the next few hours that the rafts had started migrating out of the swamps through the Yoger Straits. There was a small weather station a little inland, on the north side of the straits, which used a helicopter occasionally. It was about as improbable, Cord decided dismally, that they'd use it in the right spot just now as it would be for a jet transport to happen to come in low enough to spot them.

The fact that it was up to him, as the Regent had said, sank in a little more after that!

Simply because he was going to try it sooner or later, he carried out an experiment next that he knew couldn't work. He opened the gun's anesthetic chamber and counted out fifty pellets—rather hurriedly because he didn't particularly want to think of what he might be using them for eventually. There were around three hundred charges left in the chamber then; and in the next few minutes Cord carefully planted a third of them in Grandpa's head.

He stopped after that. A whale might have showed signs of somnolence under a lesser load. Grandpa paddled on undisturbed. Perhaps he had become a little numb in spots, but his cells weren't equipped to distribute the soporific effect of that type of drug.

There wasn't anything else Cord could think of doing before they reached the straits. At the rate they were moving, he calculated that would happen in something less than an hour; and if they did pass through the straits, he was going to risk a swim. He didn't think Dane would have disapproved, under the circumstances. If the raft simply carried them all out into the foggy vastness of the Zlanti Deep, there would be no practical chance of survival left at all.

Meanwhile, Grandpa was definitely picking up speed. And there were other changes going on—minor ones, but still a little awe-inspiring to Cord. The pimply-looking red buds that dotted the upper part of the cone were opening out gradually. From the center of most of them protruded something like a thin, wet, scarlet worm: a worm that twisted weakly, extended itself by an inch or so, rested, and twisted again, and stretched up a little farther, groping into the air. The vertical black slits between the armor plates looked deeper and wider than they had been even some minutes ago; a dark, thick liquid dripped slowly from several of them.

In other circumstances Cord knew he would have been fascinated by these developments in Grandpa. As it was, they drew his suspicious attention only because he didn't know what they meant.

Then something quite horrible happened suddenly. Grayan started moaning loudly and terribly and twisted almost completely around. Afterward, Cord knew it hadn't been a second before he stopped her struggles and the sounds together with another anesthetic pellet; but the vines had tightened their grip on her first, not flexibly but like the digging, bony, green talons of some monstrous bird of prey.

White and sweating, Cord put his gun down slowly while the vines relaxed again. Grayan didn't seem to have suffered any additional harm; and she would certainly have been the first to point out that his murderous rage might have been as intelligently directed against a machine. But for some moments Cord continued to luxuriate furiously in the thought that, at any instant he chose, he could still turn the raft very quickly into a ripped and exploded mess of sinking vegetation.

Instead, and more sensibly, he gave both Dane and Nirmond another shot, to prevent a similar occurrence with them. The contents of two such pellets, he knew, would keep any human being torpid for at least four hours.

Cord withdrew his mind hastily from the direction it was turning into; but it wouldn't stay withdrawn. The thought kept coming up again, until at last he had to recognize it.

Five shots would leave the three of them completely unconscious, whatever else might happen to them, until they either died from other causes or were given a counteracting agent.

Shocked, he told himself he couldn't do it. It was exactly like killing them.

But then, quite steadily, he found himself raising the gun once more, to bring the total charge for each of the three Team people up to five.

Barely thirty minutes later, he watched a raft as big as the one he rode go sliding into the foaming white waters of the straits a few hundred yards ahead, and dart off abruptly at an angle, caught by one of the swirling currents. It pitched and spun, made some headway, and was swept aside again. And then it righted itself once more. Not like some blindly animated vegetable, Cord thought, but like a creature that struggled with intelligent purpose to maintain its chosen direction.

At least, they seemed practically unsinkable. . . .

Knife in hand, he flattened himself against the platform as the straits roared just ahead. When the platform jolted and tilted up beneath him, he rammed the knife all the way into it and hung on. Cold water rushed suddenly over him, and Grandpa shuddered like a laboring engine. In the middle of it all, Cord had the horrified notion that the raft might release its unconscious human prisoners in its struggle with the straits. But he underestimated Grandpa in that. Grandpa also hung on.

Abruptly, it was over. They were riding a long swell, and there were three other rafts not far away. The straits had swept them together, but they seemed to have no interest in one another's company. As Cord stood up shakily and began to strip off his clothes, they were visibly drawing apart again. The platform of one of them was half-submerged; it must have lost too much of the air that held it afloat and, like a small ship, it was foundering.

From this point, it was only a two-mile swim to the shore north of the straits, and another mile inland from there to the straits Head Station. He didn't know about the current; but the distance didn't seem too much, and he couldn't bring himself to leave knife and gun behind. The bay creatures loved warmth and mud, they didn't venture beyond the straits. But Zlanti Deep bred its own killers, though they weren't often observed so close to shore.

Things were beginning to look rather hopeful.

Thin, crying voices drifted overhead, like the voices of curious cats, as Cord knotted his clothes into a tight bundle, shoes inside. He looked up. There were four of them circling there; magnified sea-going swamp bugs, each carrying an unseen rider. Probably harmless scavengers—but the ten-foot wingspread was impressive. Uneasily, Cord remembered the venomously carnivorous rider he'd left lying beside the station.

One of them dipped lazily and came sliding down toward him. It soared overhead and came back, to hover about the raft's cone.

The bug rider that directed the mindless flier hadn't been interested in him at all! Grandpa was baiting it!

Cord stared in fascination. The top of the cone was alive now with a softly wriggling mass of the scarlet, wormlike extrusions that had started sprouting before the raft left the bay. Presumably, they looked enticingly edible to the bug rider.

The flier settled with an airy fluttering and touched the cone. Like a trap springing shut, the green vines flashed up and around it, crumpling the brittle wings, almost vanishing into the long, soft body!

Barely a second later, Grandpa made another catch, this one from the sea itself. Cord had a fleeting glimpse of something like a small, rubbery seal that flung itself out of the water upon the edge of the raft, with a suggestion of desperate haste—and was flipped on instantly against the cone where the vines clamped it down beside the flier's body.

It wasn't the enormous ease with which the unexpected kill was accomplished that left Cord standing there, completely shocked. It was the shattering of his hopes to swim ashore from here. Fifty yards away, the creature from which the rubbery thing had been fleeing showed briefly on the surface, as it turned away from the raft; and that glance was all he needed. The ivory-white body and gaping jaws were similar enough to those of the sharks of Earth to indicate the pursuer's nature. The important difference was that wherever the White Hunters of the Zlanti Deep went, they went by the thousands.

Stunned by that incredible piece of bad luck, still clutching his bundled clothes, Cord stared toward shore. Knowing what to look for, he could spot the tell-tale rollings of the surface now—the long, ivory gleams that flashed through the swells and vanished again. Shoals of smaller things burst into the air in sprays of glittering desperation, and fell back.

He would have been snapped up like a drowning fly before he'd covered a twentieth of that distance!

Grandpa was beginning to eat.

Each of the dark slits down the sides of the cone was a mouth. So far only one of them was in operating condition, and the raft wasn't able to open that one very wide as yet. The first morsel had been fed into it, however: the bug rider the vines had plucked out of the flier's downy neck fur. It took Grandpa several minutes to work it out of sight, small as it was. But it was a start.

Cord didn't feel quite sane any more. He sat there, clutching his bundle of clothes and only vaguely aware of the fact that he was shivering steadily under the cold spray that touched him now and then, while he followed Grandpa's activities attentively. He decided it would be at least some hours before one of that black set of mouths grew flexible and vigorous enough to dispose of a human being. Under the circumstances, it couldn't make much difference to the other human beings here; but the moment Grandpa reached for the first of them would also be the moment he finally blew the raft to pieces. The White Hunters were cleaner eaters, at any rate; and that was about the extent to which he could still control what was going to happen.

Meanwhile, there was the very faint chance that the weather station's helicopter might spot them.

Meanwhile also, in a weary and horrified fascination, he kept debating the mystery of what could have produced such a nightmarish change in the rafts. He could guess where they were going by now; there were scattered strings of them stretching back to the straits or roughly parallel to their own course, and the direction was that of the plankton-swarming pool of the Zlanti Basin, a thousand miles to the north. Given time, even mobile lily pads like the rafts had been could make that trip for the benefit of their seedlings. But nothing in their structure explained the sudden change into alert and capable carnivores.

He watched the rubbery little sea-thing being hauled up to a mouth. The vines broke its neck; and the mouth took it in up to the shoulders and then went on working patiently at what was still a trifle too large a bite. Meanwhile, there were more thin cat-cries overhead; and a few minutes later, two more sea-bugs were trapped almost simultaneously and added to the larder. Grandpa dropped the dead sea-thing and fed himself another bug rider. The second rider left its mount with a sudden hop, sank its teeth viciously into one of the vines that caught it again, and was promptly battered to death against the platform.

Cord felt a resurge of unreasoning hatred against Grandpa. Killing a bug was about equal to cutting a branch from a tree; they had almost no life-awareness. But the rider had aroused his partisanship because of its appearance of intelligent action—and it was in fact closer to the human scale in that feature than to the monstrous life form that had, mechanically, but quite successfully, trapped both it and the human beings. Then his thoughts drifted again; and he found himself speculating vaguely on the curious symbiosis in which the nerve systems of two creatures as dissimilar as the bugs and their riders could be linked so closely that they functioned as one organism.

Suddenly an expression of vast and stunned surprise appeared on his face.

Why—now he *knew!*

Cord stood up hurriedly, shaking with excitement, the whole plan complete in his mind. And a dozen long vines snaked instantly in the direction of his sudden motion and groped for him, taut and stretching. They couldn't reach him, but their savagely alert reaction froze Cord briefly where he was. The platform was shuddering under his feet, as if in irritation at his inaccessibility; but it couldn't be tilted up suddenly here to throw him within the grasp of the vines, as it could around the edges.

Still, it was a warning! Cord sidled gingerly around the cone till he had gained the position he wanted, which was on the forward half of the raft. And then he waited. Waited long minutes, quite motionless, until his heart stopped pounding and the irregular angry shivering of the surface of the raft-thing died away, and the last vine tendril had stopped its blind groping. It might help a lot if, for a second or two after he next started moving, Grandpa wasn't too aware of his exact whereabouts!

He looked back once to check how far they had gone by now beyond the straits Head Station. It couldn't, he decided, be even an hour behind them. Which was close enough, by the most pessimistic count—if everything else worked out all right! He didn't try to think out in detail what that "everything else" could include, because there were factors that simply couldn't be calculated in advance. And he had an uneasy feeling that speculating too vividly about them might make him almost incapable of carrying out his plan.

At last, moving carefully, Cord took the knife in his left hand but left the gun holstered. He raised the tightly knotted bundle of clothes slowly over his head, balanced in his right hand. With a long, smooth motion he tossed the bundle back across the cone, almost to the opposite edge of the platform.

It hit with a soggy thump. Almost immediately, the whole far edge of the raft buckled and flapped up to toss the strange object to the reaching vines.

Simultaneously, Cord was racing forward. For a moment, his attempt to divert Grandpa's attention seemed completely successful—then he was pitched to his knees as the platform came up.

He was within eight feet of the edge. As it slapped down again, he drew himself desperately forward.

An instant later, he was knifing down through cold, clear water, just ahead of the raft, then twisting and coming up again.

The raft was passing over him. Clouds of tiny sea creatures scattered through its dark jungle of feeding roots. Cord jerked back from a broad, wavering streak of glassy greenness, which was a stinger, and felt a burning jolt on his side, which meant he'd been touched lightly by another. He bumped on blindly through the slimy black tangles of hair roots that covered the bottom of the raft; then green half-light passed over him, and he burst up into the central bubble under the cone.

Half-light and foul, hot air. Water slapped around him, dragging him away again—nothing to hang on to here! Then above him, to his right, molded against the interior curve of the cone as if it had grown there from the start, the froglike, man-sized shape of the Yellowhead.

The raft rider!

Cord reached up, caught Grandpa's symbiotic partner and guide by a flabby hind-leg, pulled himself half out of the water and struck twice with the knife, fast, while the pale-green eyes were still opening.

He'd thought the Yellowhead might need a second or so to detach itself from its host, as the bug riders usually did, before it tried to defend itself. This one merely turned its head; the mouth slashed down and clamped on Cord's left arm above the elbow. His right hand sank the knife through one staring eye, and the Yellowhead jerked away, pulling the knife from his grasp.

Sliding down, he wrapped both hands around the slimy leg and hauled with all his weight. For a moment more, the Yellowhead hung on. Then the countless neural extensions that connected it now with the raft came free in a succession of sucking, tearing sounds; and Cord and the Yellowhead splashed into the water together.

Black tangle of roots again—and two more electric burns suddenly across his back and legs! Strangling, Cord let go. Below him, for a moment, a body was turning over and over with oddly human motions; then a solid wall of water thrust him up and aside, as something big and white struck the turning body and went on.

Cord broke the surface twelve feet behind the raft. And that would have been that, if Grandpa hadn't already been slowing down.

After two tries, he floundered back up on the platform and lay there gasping and coughing a while. There were no indications that his presence was resented now. A few lax vinetips twitched uneasily, as if trying to remember previous functions, when he came limping up presently to make sure his three companions were still breathing; but Cord never noticed that.

They were still breathing; and he knew better than to waste time trying to help them himself. He took Grayan's heat-gun from its holster. Grandpa had come to a full stop.

Cord hadn't had time to become completely sane again, or he might have worried now whether Grandpa, violently sundered from his controlling partner, was still capable of motion on his own. Instead, he determined the approximate direction of the straits Head Station, selected a corresponding spot on the platform, and gave Grandpa a light tap of heat.

Nothing happened immediately. Cord sighed patiently and stepped up the heat a little.

Grandpa shuddered gently. Cord stood up.

Slowly and hesitatingly at first, then with steadfast—though now again brainless—purpose, Grandpa began paddling back toward the straits Head Station.

▪ ▪ ▪

For a Journal Entry . . .

One of the main fascinations of SF and of James A. Schmitz's story "Grandpa" is the confrontation with aliens and alien worlds. For the human mind to conceive of something truly alien is very difficult. For instance, although Grandpa is an alien life form, he is familiar enough to be compared to and used as a raft. So in some sense he is not as alien as he at first appears. Try your hand at dreaming up your own alien life form and putting him in his own alien setting.

For Your Consideration . . .

1. Sutang has a carefully thought out ecosystem, wherein certain mindless and otherwise harmless creatures are used by more intelligent creatures for their own purposes. It is part of the balance of nature within the Sutang environment. How does man fit into this particular system?
2. Why is the "green-winged downy thing" introduced at the beginning of the story?
3. Do you identify with Cord's attitude toward rules? Why or why not? How is this attitude toward rules partially justified by the story?
4. In what ways are Grandpa and his kind admirably suited for survival in their own surroundings? How well would they do in the rivers and bays of earth?
5. In what sense is "Grandpa" a "coming of age" story, a story about growing up?
6. "Grandpa" is a very well plotted story in which disaster piles on disaster. Is the eventual happy ending believable? Why or why not?

Notes

PAGE
123 *speculatively*—thoughtfully, as if considering something
123 *parasite*—an organism which lives off another organism
123 *terminology*—specialized vocabulary
123 *natural research man*—someone who studies the natural world around him
123 *phenomenon*—thing, fact, happening
124 *Vanadian*—from Vanadia, Cord's home planet
124 *anesthetic*—a substance, usually a drug, that deadens sensitivity
124 *microscopically*—so tiny as to be only seen with a microscope
125 *phyla*—plural of phylum, referring to divisions in the plant and animal kingdoms
126 *nourishment*—food
126 *aggressive*—quarrelsome; pushy
126 *perambulating*—moving along at a leisurely pace
127 *wobbly*—shaky
128 *sprouting*—growing new limbs
128 *quibbling*—arguing over small details in order to avoid the truth
129 *awesome*—inspiring awe or religious fear
129 *catastrophic*—disastrous
130 *algae*—a major group of lower plants, found in water
130 *plankton*—microscopic plant and animal life found in water
130 *propagate*—reproduce

131 *coastal marsh fauna*—the animals that live in the marshes along the coast
131 *senile decay*—the mental decay that sometimes comes with age
134 *anesthesia*—loss of feeling
136 *tendrils*—threadlike part of a climbing plant that can coil around something
136 *analogues*—comparisons
137 *migrating*—traveling
138 *somnolence*—sleepiness
138 *soporific*—something which causes sleep
139 *luxuriate*—glory in
139 *torpid*—numb; unmoving
141 *shoals*—places in a body of water where it is shallow
142 *carnivores*—meat eaters
142 *symbiosis*—the process of two different kinds of creatures living together to their mutual benefit
143 *inaccessibility*—unreachability
143 *pessimistic*—negative; no hope

Surface Tension

by James Blish

James Blish seems to have combined the careers of a dozen people. With his graduate degree he could have worked in science—but he went into public relations instead. At the same time he made his mark as a master of modern science fiction with novels like *A Case of Conscience* and the series *Cities in Flight.* Internationally received as a James Joyce and Ezra Pound scholar, he is also an opera authority and founder of the literary movement interested in the works of James Branch Cabell. He has also established a reputation as one of the few SF critics of worth. In "Surface Tension" he writes about a race of men as small as microbes and the incredible underwater world they live in.

Dr. Chatvieux took a long time over the microscope, leaving La Ventura with nothing to do but look out at the dead landscape of Hydrot. Waterscape, he thought, would be a better word. The new world had shown only one small, triangular continent, set amid endless ocean; and even the continent was mostly swamp.

The wreck of the seed-ship lay broken squarely across the one real spur of rock Hydrot seemed to possess, which reared a magnificent twenty-one feet above sea level. From this eminence, La Ventura could see forty miles to the horizon across a flat bed of mud. The red light of the star Tau Ceti, glinting upon thousands of small lakes, pools, ponds, and puddles, made the watery plain look like a mosaic of onyx and ruby.

"If I were a religious man," the pilot said suddenly, "I'd call this a plain case of divine vengeance."

Chatvieux said: "Hmn?"

"It's as if we've been struck down for—is it *hubris,* arrogant pride?"

"Well, is it?" Chatvieux said, looking up at last. "I don't feel exactly swollen with pride at the moment. Do you?"

"I'm not exactly proud of my piloting," La Ventura admitted. "But that isn't quite what I meant. I was thinking about why we came here in the first place. It takes arrogant pride to think that you can scatter men, or at least things like men, all over the face of the galaxy. It takes even more pride to do the job—to pack up all the equipment and move from planet to planet and actually make men suitable for every place you touch."

"I suppose it does," Chatvieux said. "But we're only one of several hundred seed-ships in this limb of the galaxy, so I doubt that the gods picked us out as special sinners." He smiled dryly. "If they had, maybe they'd have left us our ultraphone, so the Colonization Council could hear about our cropper. Besides, Paul, we try to produce men adapted to Earthlike planets, nothing more. We've sense enough—humility enough, if you like—to know that we can't adapt men to Jupiter or to Tau Ceti."

"Anyhow, we're here," La Ventura said grimly. "And we aren't going to get off. Phil tells me that we don't even have our germ-cell bank any more, so we can't seed this place in the usual way. We've been thrown onto a dead world and dared to adapt to it. What are the panatropes going to do—provide built-in waterwings?"

"No," Chatvieux said calmly. "You and I and the rest of us are going to die, Paul. Panatropic techniques don't work on the body, only on the inheritance-carrying factors. We can't give you built-in waterwings, any more than we can give you a new set of brains. I think we'll be able to populate this world with men, but we won't live to see it."

The pilot thought about it, a lump of cold collecting gradually in his stomach. "How long do you give us?" he said at last.

"Who knows? A month, perhaps."

The bulkhead leading to the wrecked section of the ship was pushed back, admitting salty, muggy air, heavy with carbon dioxide. Philip Strasvogel, the communications officer, came in, tracking mud. Like La Ventura, he was now a man without a function, but it did not appear to bother him. He unbuckled from around his waist a canvas belt into which plastic vials were stuffed like cartridges.

"More samples, Doc," he said. "All alike—water, very wet. I have some quicksand in one boot, too. Find anything?"

"A good deal, Phil. Thanks. Are the others around?"

Strasvogel poked his head out and hallooed. Other voices rang out over the mudflats. Minutes later, the rest of the survivors were crowding into the panatrope deck: Saltonstall, Chatvieux's senior assistant; Eunice Wagner, the only remaining ecologist; Eleftherios Venezuelos, the delegate from the Colonization Council; and Joan Heath, a midshipman whose duties, like La Ventura's and Strasvogel's, were now without meaning.

Five men and two women—to colonize a planet on which standing room meant treading water.

They came in quietly and found seats or resting places on the deck, on the edges of tables, in corners.

Venezuelos said: "What's the verdict, Dr. Chatvieux?"

"This place isn't dead," Chatvieux said. "There's life in the sea and in the fresh water, both. On the animal side of the ledger, evolution seems to have stopped with the crustacea; the most advanced form I've found is a tiny crayfish, from one of the local rivulets. The ponds and puddles are well stocked with protozoa and small metazoans, right up to a wonderfully variegated rotifer population—including a castle-building rotifer like Earth's *Floscularidae.* The plants run from simple algae to the thalluslike species."

"The sea is about the same," Eunice said, "I've found some of the larger simple metazoans—jellyfish and so on—and some crayfish almost as big as lobsters. But it's normal to find saltwater species running larger than freshwater."

"In short," Chatvieux said, "we'll survive here—if we fight."

"Wait a minute," La Ventura said. "You've just finished telling me that we wouldn't survive. And you were talking about us, not about the species, because we don't have our germ-cell banks any more. What's—"

"I'll get to that again in a moment," Chatvieux said. "Saltonstall, what would you think of taking to the sea? We came out of it once; maybe we could come out of it again."

"No good," Saltonstall said immediately. "*I* like the idea, but I don't think this planet ever heard of Swinburne, or Homer, either. Looking at it as a colonization problem, as if we weren't involved ourselves, I wouldn't give you a credit for *epi oinopa ponton.* The evolutionary pressure there is too high, the competition from other species is prohibitive; seeding the sea should be the last thing we attempt. The colonists wouldn't have a chance to learn a thing before they were destroyed."

"Why?" La Ventura said. The death in his stomach was becoming hard to placate.

"Eunice, do your sea-going coelenterates include anything like the Portuguese man-of-war?"

The ecologist nodded.

"There's your answer, Paul," Saltonstall said. "The sea is out. It's got to be fresh water, where the competing creatures are less formidable and there are more places to hide."

"We can't compete with a jellyfish?" La Ventura asked, swallowing.

"No, Paul," Chatvieux said. "The panatropes make adaptations, not gods. They take human germ-cells—in this case, our own, since our bank was wiped out in the crash—and modify them toward creatures who can live in any reasonable environment. The result will be manlike and intelligent. It usually shows the donor's personality pattern, too.

"*But we can't transmit memory.* The adapted man is worse than a child in his new environment. He has no history, no techniques, no precedents, not even a language. Ordinarily the seeding teams more or less take him through elementary school before they leave the planet, but we won't survive long enough for that. We'll have to design our colonists with plenty of built-in protections and locate them in the most favorable environment possible, so that at least some of them will survive the learning process."

The pilot thought about it, but nothing occurred to him which did not make the disaster seem realer and more intimate with each passing second. "One of the new creatures can have my personality pattern, but it won't be able to remember being me. Is that right?"

"That's it. There may be just the faintest of residuums—panatropy's given us some data which seem to support the old Jungian notion of ancestral memory. But we're all going to die on Hydrot, Paul. There's no avoiding that. Somewhere we'll leave behind people who behave as we would, think and feel as we would, but who won't remember La Ventura, or Chatvieux, or Joan Heath—or Earth."

The pilot said nothing more. There was a gray taste in his mouth.

"Saltonstall, what do you recommend as a form?"

The panatropist pulled reflectively at his nose. "Webbed extremities, of course, with thumbs and big toes heavy and thornlike for defense until the creature has had a chance to learn. Book-lungs, like the arachnids, working out of intercostal spiracles—they are gradually adaptable to atmosphere-breathing, if it ever decides to come out of the water. Also I'd suggest sporulation. As an aquatic animal, our colonist is going to have an indefinite lifespan, but we'll have to give it a breeding cycle of about six weeks to keep its numbers up during the learning period; so there'll have to be a definite break of some duration in its active year. Otherwise it'll hit the population problem before it's learned enough to cope with it."

"Also, it'll be better if our colonists could winter inside a good hard shell," Eunice Wagner added in agreement. "So sporulation's the obvious answer. Most microscopic creatures have it."

"Microscopic?" Phil said incredulously.

"Certainly," Chatvieux said, amused. "We can't very well crowd a six-foot man into a two-foot puddle. But that raises a question. We'll have tough competition from the rotifers, and some of them aren't strictly microscopic. I don't think your average colonist should run under twenty-five microns, Saltonstall. Give them a chance to slug it out."

"I was thinking of making them twice that big."

"Then they'd be the biggest things in their environment,"

Eunice Wagner pointed out, "and won't ever develop any skills. Besides, if you make them about rotifer size, I'll give them an incentive for pushing out the castle-building rotifers.

"They'll be able to take over the castles as dwellings."

Chatvieux nodded. "All right, let's get started. While the panatropes are being calibrated, the rest of us can put our heads together on leaving a record for these people. We'll micro-engrave the record on a set of corrosion-proof metal leaves, of a size our colonists can handle conveniently. Some day they may puzzle it out."

"Question," Eunice Wagner said. "Are we going to tell them they're microscopic? I'm opposed to it. It'll saddle their entire early history with a gods-and-demons mythology they'd be better off without."

"Yes, we are," Chatvieux said; and La Ventura could tell by the change in the tone of his voice that he was speaking now as their senior. "These people will be of the race of men, Eunice. We want them to win their way back to the community of men. They are not toys, to be protected from the truth forever in a fresh-water womb."

"I'll make that official," Venezuelos said, and that was that.

And then, essentially, it was all over. They went through the motions. Already they were beginning to be hungry. After La Ventura had had his personality pattern recorded, he was out of it. He sat by himself at the far end of the ledge, watching Tau Ceti go redly down, chucking pebbles into the nearest pond, wondering morosely which nameless puddle was to be his Lethe.

He never found out, of course. None of them did.

I

Old Shar set down the heavy metal plate at last, and gazed instead out the window of the castle, apparently resting his eyes on the glowing green-gold obscurity of the summer waters. In the soft fluorescence which played down upon him, from the Noc dozing impassively in the groined vault of the chamber, Lavon could see that he was in fact a young man. His face was so delicately formed as to suggest that it had not been many seasons since he had first emerged from his spore.

But of course there had been no real reason to expect an old man. All the Shars had been referred to traditionally as "old" Shar. The reason, like the reasons for everything else, had been forgotten, but the custom had persisted; the adjective at least gave weight and dignity to the office.

The present Shar belonged to the generation XVI, and hence would have to be at least two seasons younger than Lavon himself. If he was old, it was only in knowledge.

"Lavon, I'm going to have to be honest with you," Shar said at last, still looking out of the tall, irregular window. "You've come to me for the secrets on the metal plates, just as your predecessors did to mine. I can give some of them to you—but for the most part, I don't know what they mean."

"After so many generations?" Lavon asked, surprised. "Wasn't it Shar III who first found out how to read them? That was a long time ago."

The young man turned and looked at Lavon with eyes made dark and wide by the depths into which they had been staring. "I can read what's on the plates, but most of it seems to make no sense. Worst of all, the plates are incomplete. You didn't know that? They are. One of them was lost in a battle during the final war with the Eaters, while these castles were still in their hands."

"What am I here for, then?" Lavon said. "Isn't there anything of value on the remaining plates? Do they really contain 'the wisdom of the Creators' or is that another myth?"

"No. No, that's true," Shar said slowly, "as far as it goes."

He paused, and both men turned and gazed at the ghostly creature which had appeared suddenly outside the window. Then Shar said gravely, "Come in, Para."

The slipper-shaped organism, nearly transparent except for the thousands of black-and-silver granules and frothy bubbles which packed its interior, glided into the chamber and hovered, with a muted whirring of cilia. For a moment it remained silent, probably speaking telepathically to the Noc floating in the vault, after the ceremonious fashion of all the protos. No human had ever intercepted one of these colloquies, but there was no doubt about their reality: humans had used them for long-range communication for generations.

Then the Para's cilia buzzed once more. Each separate hair-like process vibrated at an independent, changing rate; the resulting sound waves spread through the water, intermodulating, reinforcing or canceling each other. The aggregate wave-front, by the time it reached human ears, was recognizable human speech.

"We are arrived, Shar and Lavon, according to the custom."

"And welcome," said Shar. "Lavon, let's leave this matter of the plates for a while, until you hear what Para has to say; that's a part of the knowledge Lavons must have as they come of age, and it comes before the plates. I can give you some hints of what we are. First Para has to tell you something about what we aren't."

Lavon nodded, willingly enough, and watched the proto as it settled gently to the surface of the hewn table at which Shar had been sitting. There was in the entity such a perfection and economy of organization, such a grace and surety of movement, that he could hardly believe in his own new-won maturity. Para, like all the protos, made him feel not, perhaps, poorly thought-out, but at least unfinished.

"We know that in this universe there is logically no place for man," the gleaming, now immobile cylinder upon the table droned abruptly. "Our memory is the common property to all our races. It reaches back to a time when there were no such creatures as men here. It remembers also that once upon a day there were men here, suddenly, and in some numbers. Their spores littered the bottom; we found the spores only a short time after our season's Awakening, and in them we saw the forms of men slumbering.

"Then men shattered their spores and emerged. They were intelligent, active. And they were gifted with a trait, a character, possessed by no other creature in this world. Not even the savage Eaters had it. Men organized us to exterminate the Eaters and therein lay the difference. Men had initiative. We have the word now, which you gave us, and we apply it, but we still do not know what the thing is that it labels."

"You fought beside us," Lavon said.

"Gladly. We would never have thought of that war by ourselves, but it was good and brought good. Yet we wondered. We saw that men were poor swimmers, poor walkers, poor crawlers, poor climbers. We saw that men were formed to make and use tools, a concept we still do not understand, for so wonderful a gift is largely wasted in this universe, and there is no other. What good are tool-useful members such as the hands of men? We do not know. It seems plain that so radical a thing should lead to a much greater rulership over the world than has, in fact, proven to be possible for men."

Lavon's head was spinning. "Para, I had no notion that you people were philosophers."

"The protos are old," Shar said. He had again turned to look out the window, his hands locked behind his back. "They aren't philosophers, Lavon, but they are remorseless logicians. Listen to Para."

"To this reasoning there could be but one outcome," the Para said. "Our strange ally, man, was like nothing else in this universe. He was and is ill-fitted for it. He does not belong here; he has been—adopted. This drives us to think that there are other universes besides this one, but where these universes might lie, and what their properties might be, it is impossible to imagine. We have no imagination, as men know."

Was the creature being ironic? Lavon could not tell. He said slowly: "Other universes? How could that be true?"

"We do not know," the Para's uninflected voice hummed. Lavon waited, but obviously the proto had nothing more to say.

Shar had resumed sitting on the window sill, clasping his knees, watching the come and go of dim shapes in the lighted gulf. "It is quite true," he said. "What is written on the remaining plates makes it plain. Let me tell you now what they say.

"*We were made,* Lavon. We were made by men who are not as we are, but men who were our ancestors all the same. They were caught in some disaster, and they made us, and put us here in our universe—so that, even though they had to die, the race of men would live."

Lavon surged up from the woven spirogyra mat upon which he had been sitting. "You must think I'm a fool!" he said sharply.

"No. You're our Lavon; you have a right to know the facts. Make what you like of them." Shar swung his webbed toes back into the chamber. "What I've told you may be hard to believe, but it seems to be so; what Para says backs it up. Our unfitness to live here is self-evident. I'll give you some examples.

"The past four Shars discovered that we won't get any further in our studies until we learn how to control heat. We've produced enough heat chemically to show that even the water around us changes when the temperature gets high enough. But there we're stopped."

"Why?"

"Because heat produced in open water is carried off as rapidly as it's produced. Once we tried to enclose that heat, and we blew up a whole tube of the castle and killed everything in range; the shock was terrible. We measured the pressures that were involved in that explosion, and we discovered that no substance we know could have resisted them. Theory suggests some stronger substances—*but we need heat to form them!*

"Take our chemistry. We live in water. Everything seems to dissolve in water, to some extent. How do we confine a chemical test to the crucible we put it in? How do we maintain a solution at one dilution? I don't know. Every avenue leads me to the same stone door. We're thinking creatures, Lavon, but there's something drastically wrong in the way we think about this universe we live in. It just doesn't seem to lead to results."

Lavon pushed back his floating hair futilely. "Maybe you're thinking about the wrong results. We've had no trouble with warfare, or crops, or practical things like that. If we can't create much heat, well, most of us won't miss it; we don't need any. What's the other universe supposed to be like, the one our ancestors lived in? Is it any better than this one?"

"I don't know," Shar admitted. "It was so different that it's hard to compare the two. The metal plates tell a story about men who were traveling from one place to another in a container that moved by itself. The only analogy I can think of is the shallops of diatom shells that our youngsters use to sled along the thermocline; but evidently what's meant is something much bigger.

"I picture a huge shallop, closed on all sides, big enough to hold many people—maybe twenty or thirty. It had to travel for generations through some kind of space where there wasn't any water to breathe, so that the people had to carry their own water and renew it constantly. There were no seasons; no yearly turnover; no ice forming on the sky, because there wasn't any sky in a closed shallop; no spore formation.

"Then the shallop was wrecked somehow. The people in it knew they were going to die. They made us, and put us here, as if we were their children. Because they had to die, they wrote their story on the plates, to tell us what had happened. I suppose we'd understand it better if we had the plate Shar III lost during the war, but we don't."

"The whole thing sounds like a parable," Lavon said, shrugging. "Or a song. I can see why you don't understand it. What I can't see is why you bother to try."

"Because of the plates," Shar said. "You've handled them yourself, so you know that we've nothing like them. We have crude, impure metals we've hammered out, metals that last for a while and then decay. But the plates shine on and on, generation after generation. They don't change; our hammers and graving tools break against them; the little heat we can generate leaves them unharmed. Those plates weren't formed in our universe—and that one fact makes every word on them important to me. Someone went to a great deal of trouble to make those plates indestructible to give them to us. Someone to whom the word 'stars' was important enough to be worth fourteen repetitions, despite the fact that the word doesn't seem to mean anything. I'm ready to think that if our makers repeated the word even twice on a record that seems likely to last forever, it's important for us to know what it means."

"All these extra universes and huge shallops and meaningless words—I can't say that they don't exist, but I don't see what difference it makes. The Shars of a few generations ago spent their whole lives breeding better algae crops for us, and showing us how to cultivate them instead of living haphazardly off bacteria. That was work worth doing. The Lavons of those days evidently got along without the metal plates, and saw to it that the Shars did, too. Well, as far as I'm concerned, you're welcome to the plates, if you like them better than crop improvement—but I think they ought to be thrown away."

"All right," Shar said, shrugging. "If you don't want them, that ends the traditional interview. We'll go our—"

There was a rising drone from the tabletop. The Para was lifting itself, waves of motion passing over its cilia, like the waves which went across the fruiting stalks of the fields of delicate fungi with which the bottom was planted. It had been so silent that Lavon had forgotten it; he could tell from Shar's startlement that Shar had, too.

"This is a great decision," the waves of sound washing from the creature throbbed. "Every proto has heard it and agrees with it. We have been afraid of these metal plates for a long time, afraid that men would learn to understand them and to follow what they say to some secret place, leaving the protos behind. Now we are not afraid."

"There wasn't anything to be afraid of," Lavon said indulgently.

"No Lavon before you had said so," Para said. "We are glad. We will throw the plates away."

With that, the shining creature swooped toward the embrasure. With it, it bore away the remaining plates, which had been resting under it on the tabletop, suspended delicately in the curved tips of its supple cilia. With a cry, Shar plunged through the water toward the opening.

"Stop, Para!"

But Para was already gone, so swiftly that he had not even heard the call. Shar twisted his body and brought up on one shoulder against the tower wall. He said nothing. His face was enough. Lavon could not look at it for more than an instant.

The shadows of the two men moved slowly along the uneven cobbled floor. The Noc descended toward them from the vault, its single thick tentacle stirring the water, its internal light flaring and fading irregularly. It, too, drifted through the window after its cousin, and sank slowly away toward the bottom. Gently its living glow dimmed, flickered, winked out.

II

For many days, Lavon was able to avoid thinking much about the loss. There was always a great deal of work to be done.

Maintenance of the castles, which had been built by the now-extinct Eaters rather than by human hands, was a never-ending task. The thousand dichotomously branching wings tended to crumble, especially at their bases where they sprouted from each other, and no Shar had yet come forward with a mortar as good as the rotifer-spittle which had once held them together. In addition, the breaking through of windows and the construction of chambers in the early days had been haphazard and often unsound. The instinctive architecture of the rotifers, after all, had not been meant to meet the needs of human occupants.

And then there were the crops. Men no longer fed precariously upon passing bacteria; now there were the drifting mats of specific water-fungi, rich and nourishing, which had been bred by five generations of Shars. These had to be tended constantly to keep the strains pure, and to keep the older and less intelligent species of the protos from grazing on them. In this latter task, to be sure, the more intricate and far-seeing proto types co-operated, but men were needed to supervise.

There had been a time, after the war with the Eaters, when it had been customary to prey upon the slow-moving and stupid diatoms, whose exquisite and fragile glass shells were so easily burst, and who were unable to learn that a friendly voice did not necessarily mean a friend. There were still people who would crack open a diatom when no one else was looking, but they were regarded as barbarians, to the puzzlement of the protos. The blurred and simple-minded speech of the gorgeously engraved plants had brought them into the category of pets—a concept which the protos were utterly unable to grasp, especially since men admitted that diatoms on the half-frustrule were delicious.

Lavon had had to agree, very early, that the distinction was tiny. After all, humans did eat the desmids, which differed from the diatoms only in three particulars: their shells were flexible, they could not move, and they did not speak. Yet to Lavon, as to most men, there did seem to be some kind of distinction, whether the protos could see it or not, and that was that. Under the circumstances he felt that it was a part of his duty, as a leader of men, to protect the diatoms from the occasional poachers who browsed upon them, in defiance of custom, in the high levels of the sunlit sky.

Yet Lavon found it impossible to keep himself busy enough to forget that moment when the last clues to Man's origin and destination had been seized and borne away into dim space.

It might be possible to ask Para for the return of the plates, explain that a mistake had been made. The protos were creatures of implacable logic, but they respected man, were used to illogic in man, and might reverse their decision if pressed—

We are sorry. The plates were carried over the bar and released in the gulf. We will have the bottom there searched, but . . .

With a sick feeling he could not repress, Lavon knew that when the protos decided something was worthless, they did not hide it in some chamber like old women. They threw it away—efficiently.

Yet despite the tormenting of his conscience, Lavon was convinced that the plates were well lost. What had they ever done for man, except to provide Shars with useless things to think about in the late seasons of their lives? What the Shars themselves had done to benefit man, here, in the water, in the world, in the universe, had been done by direct experimentation. No bit of useful knowledge ever had come from the plates. There had never been anything in the plates but things best left unthought. The protos were right.

Lavon shifted his position on the plant frond, where he had been sitting in order to overlook the harvesting of an experimental crop of blue-green, oil-rich algae drifting in a clotted mass close to the top of the sky, and scratched his back gently against the coarse bole. The protos were seldom wrong, after all. Their lack of creativity, their inability to think an original thought, was a gift as well as a limitation. It allowed them to see and feel things at all times as they were—not as they hoped they might be, for they had no ability to hope, either.

"La-von! Laa-vah-on!"

The long halloo came floating up from the sleepy depths. Propping one hand against the top of the frond, Lavon bent and looked down. One of the harvesters was looking up at him, holding loosely the adze with which he had been splitting free the glutinous tetrads of the algae.

"Up here. What's the matter?"

"We have the ripened quadrant cut free. Shall we tow it away?"

"Tow it away," Lavon said, with a lazy gesture. He leaned back again. At the same instant, a brilliant reddish glory burst into being above him, and cast itself down toward the depths like mesh after mesh of the finest-drawn gold. The great light which lived above the sky during the day, brightening or dimming according to some pattern no Shar ever had fathomed, was blooming again.

Few men, caught in the warm glow of that light, could resist looking up at it—especially when the top of the sky itself wrinkled and smiled just a moment's climb or swim away. Yet, as always, Lavon's bemused upward look gave him back nothing but his own distorted, bobbling reflection, and a reflection of the plant on which he rested.

Here was the upper limit, the third of the three surfaces of the universe.

The first surface was the bottom, where the water ended.

The second surface was the thermocline, the invisible division between the colder waters of the bottom and the warm, light waters of the sky. During the height of the warm weather, the thermocline was so definite a division as to make for good sledding and for chilly passage. A real interface formed between the cold, denser bottom waters and the warm reaches above, and maintained itself almost for the whole of the warm season.

The third surface was the sky. One could no more pass through that surface than one could penetrate the bottom, nor was there any better reason to try. There the universe ended. The light which played over it daily, waxing and waning as it chose, seemed to be one of its properties.

Toward the end of the season, the water gradually grew colder and more difficult to breathe, while at the same time the light became duller and stayed for shorter periods between darknesses. Slow currents started to move. The high waters turned chill and began to fall. The bottom mud stirred and smoked away, carrying with it the spores of the fields of fungi. The thermocline tossed, became choppy, and melted away. The sky began to fog with particles of soft silt carried up from the bottom, the walls, the corners of the universe. Before very long, the whole world was cold, inhospitable, flocculent with yellowing, dying creatures.

Then the protos encysted; the bacteria, even most of the plants and, not long afterward, men, too, curled up in their oil-filled amber shells. The world died until the first tentative current of warm water broke the winter silence.

"La-von!"

Just after the long call, a shining bubble rose past Lavon. He reached out and poked it, but it bounded away from his sharp thumb. The gas bubbles which rose from the bottom in late summer were almost invulnerable—and when some especially hard blow or edge did penetrate them, they broke into smaller bubbles which nothing could touch, and fled toward the sky, leaving behind a remarkably bad smell.

Gas. There was no water inside a bubble. A man who got inside a bubble would have nothing to breathe.

But, of course, it was impossible to penetrate a bubble. The surface tension was too strong. As strong as Shar's metal plates. As strong as the top of the sky.

As strong as the top of the sky. And above that—once the bubble was broken—a world of gas instead of water? Were all worlds bubbles of water drifting in gas?

If it were so, travel between them would be out of the question, since it would be impossible to pierce the sky to begin with. Nor did the infant cosmology include any provisions for bottoms for the worlds.

And yet some of the local creatures did burrow *into* the bottom, quite deeply, seeking something in those depths which was beyond the reach of man. Even the surface of the ooze, in high summer, crawled with tiny creatures for which mud was a natural medium. Man, too, passed freely between the two countries of water which were divided by the thermocline, though many of the creatures with which he lived could not pass that line at all, once it had established itself.

And if the new universe of which Shar had spoken existed at

all, it had to exist beyond the sky, where the light was. Why could not the sky be passed, after all? The fact that bubbles could be broken showed that the surface skin that formed between water and gas wasn't completely invulnerable. Had it ever been tried?

Lavon did not suppose that one man could butt his way through the top of the sky, any more than he could burrow into the bottom, but there might be ways around the difficulty. Here at his back, for instance, was a plant which gave every appearance of continuing beyond the sky: its uppermost fronds broke off and were bent back only by a trick of reflection.

It had always been assumed that the plants died where they touched the sky. For the most part, they did, for frequently the dead extension could be seen, leached and yellow, the boxes of its component cells empty, floating imbedded in the perfect mirror. But some were simply chopped off, like the one which sheltered him now. Perhaps that was only an illusion, and instead it soared indefinitely into some other place—some place where men might once have been born, and might still live. . . .

The plates were gone. There was only one other way to find out.

Determinedly, Lavon began to climb toward the wavering mirror of the sky. His thorn-thumbed feet trampled obliviously upon the clustered sheaves of fragile stippled diatoms. The tulip-heads of Vortae, placid and murmurous cousins of Para, retracted startledly out of his way upon coiling stalks, to make silly gossip behind him.

Lavon did not hear them. He continued to climb doggedly toward the light, his fingers and toes gripping the plant-bole.

"Lavon! Where are you going? Lavon!"

He leaned out and looked down. The man with the adze, a doll-like figure, was beckoning to him from a patch of blue-green retreating over a violet abyss. Dizzily he looked away, clinging to the bole; he had never been so high before. Then he began to climb again.

After a while, he touched the sky with one hand. He stopped to breathe. Curious bacteria gathered about the base of his thumb where blood from a small cut was fogging away, scattered at his gesture, and wriggled mindlessly back toward the dull red lure.

He waited until he no longer felt winded, and resumed climbing. The sky pressed down against the top of his head, against the back of his neck, against his shoulders. It seemed to give slightly, with a tough, frictionless elasticity. The water here was intensely bright, and quite colorless. He climbed another step, driving his shoulders against that enormous weight.

It was fruitless. He might as well have tried to penetrate a cliff.

Again he had to rest. While he panted, he made a curious discovery. All around the bole of the water plant, the steel surface of the sky curved upward, making a kind of sheath. He found that he could insert his hand into it—there was almost enough space to admit his head as well. Clinging closely to the bole, he looked up into the inside of the sheath, probing with his injured hand. The glare was blinding.

There was a kind of soundless explosion. His whole wrist was suddenly encircled in an intense, impersonal grip, as if it were being cut in two. In blind astonishment, he lunged upward.

The ring of pain traveled smoothly down his upflung arm as he rose, was suddenly around his shoulders and chest. Another lunge and his knees were being squeezed in the circular vine. Another—

Something was horribly wrong. He clung to the bole and tried to gasp, but there was—nothing to breathe.

The water came streaming out of his body, from his mouth, his nostrils, the spiracles in his sides, spurting in tangible jets. An intense and fiery itching crawled over the entire surface of his body. At each spasm, long knives ran into him, and from a great distance he heard more water being expelled from his book-lungs in an obscene, frothy sputtering.

Lavon was drowning.

With a final convulsion, he kicked himself away from the splintery bole, and fell. A hard impact shook him; and then the water, which had clung to him so tightly when he had first attempted to leave it, took him back with cold violence.

Sprawling and tumbling grotesquely, he drifted, down and down and down, toward the bottom.

III

For many days, Lavon lay curled insensibly in his spore, as if in the winter sleep. The shock of cold which he had felt on reentering his native universe had been taken by his body as a sign of coming winter, as it had taken the oxygen-starvation of his brief sojourn above the sky. The spore-forming glands had at once begun to function.

Had it not been for this, Lavon would surely have died. The danger of drowning disappeared even as he fell, as the air bubbled out of his lungs and readmitted the life-giving water. But for acute dessication and third-degree sunburn, the sunken universe knew no remedy. The healing amnionic fluid generated by the spore-forming glands, after the transparent amber sphere had enclosed him, offered Lavon his only chance.

The brown sphere was spotted after some days by a prowling ameba, quiescent in the eternal winter of the bottom. Down there the temperature was always an even 4°, no matter what the season, but it was unheard of that a spore should be found there while the high epilimnion was still warm and rich in oxygen.

Within an hour, the spore was surrounded by scores of astonished protos, jostling each other to bump their blunt eyeless prows against the shell. Another hour later, a squad of worried men came plunging from the castles far above to press their own noses against the transparent wall. Then swift orders were given.

Four Para grouped themselves about the amber sphere, and there was a subdued explosion as the trichocysts which lay embedded at the bases of their cilia, just under the pellicle, burst and cast fine lines of a quickly solidifying liquid into the water. The four Paras thrummed and lifted, tugging.

Lavon's spore swayed gently in the mud and then rose slowly, entangled in the web. Nearby, a Noc cast a cold pulsating glow over the operation—not for the Paras, who did not need the light, but for the baffled knot of men. The sleeping figure of Lavon, head bowed, knees drawn up to its chest, revolved with an absurd solemnity inside the shell as it was moved.

"Take him to Shar, Para."

The young Shar justified, by minding his own business, the traditional wisdom with which his hereditary office had invested him. He observed at once that there was nothing he could do for the encysted Lavon which would not be classifiable as simple meddling.

He had the sphere deposited in a high tower room of his castle, where there was plenty of light and the water was warm, which should suggest to the hibernating form that spring was again on the way. Beyond that, he simply sat and watched, and kept his speculations to himself.

Inside the spore, Lavon's body seemed rapidly to be shedding its skin, in long strips and patches. Gradually, his curious shrunkenness disappeared. His withered arms and legs and sunken abdomen filled out again.

The days went by while Shar watched. Finally he could discern no more changes, and, on a hunch, had the spore taken up to the topmost battlements of the tower, into the direct daylight.

An hour later, Lavon moved in his amber prison.

He uncurled and stretched, turned blank eyes up toward the light. His expression was that of a man who had not yet awakened from a ferocious nightmare. His whole body shone with a strange pink newness.

Shar knocked gently on the wall of the spore. Lavon turned his blind face toward the sound, life coming into his eyes. He smiled tentatively and braced his hands and feet against the inner wall of the shell.

The whole sphere fell abruptly to pieces with a sharp crackling. The amnionic fluid dissipated around him and Shar, carrying away with it the suggestive odor of a bitter struggle against death.

Lavon stood among the bits of shell and looked at Shar silently. At last he said:

"Shar—I've been beyond the sky."

"I know," Shar said gently.

Again Lavon was silent. Shar said, "Don't be humble, Lavon. You've done an epoch-making thing. It nearly cost you your life. You must tell me the rest—all of it."

"The rest?"

"You taught me a lot while you slept. Or are you still opposed to useless knowledge?"

Lavon could say nothing. He no longer could tell what he

knew from what he wanted to know. He had only one question left, but he could not utter it. He could only look dumbly into Shar's delicate face.

"You have answered me," Shar said, even more gently. "Come, my friend; join me at my table. We will plan our journey to the stars."

It was two winter sleeps after Lavon's disastrous climb beyond the sky that all work on the spaceship stopped. By then, Lavon knew that he had hardened and weathered into that temporarily ageless state a man enters after he has just reached his prime; and he knew also that there were wrinkles engraved upon his brow, to stay and to deepen.

"Old" Shar, too had changed, his features losing some of their delicacy as he came into his maturity. Though the wedge-shaped bony structure of his face would give him a withdrawn and poetic look for as long as he lived, participation in the plan had given his expression a kind of executive overlay, which at best gave it a masklike rigidity, and at worst coarsened it somehow.

Yet despite the bleeding away of the years, the spaceship was still only a hulk. It lay upon a platform built above the tumbled boulders of the sandbar which stretched out from one wall of the world. It was an immense hull of pegged wood, broken by regularly spaced gaps through which the raw beams of the skeleton could be seen.

Work upon it had progressed fairly rapidly at first, for it was not hard to visualize what kind of vehicle would be needed to crawl through empty space without losing its water. It had been recognized that the sheer size of the machine would enforce a long period of construction, perhaps two full seasons; but neither Shar nor Lavon had anticipated any serious snag.

For that matter, part of the vehicle's apparent incompleteness was an illusion. About a third of its fittings were to consist of living creatures, which could not be expected to install themselves in the vessel much before the actual takeoff.

Yet time and time again, work on the ship had had to be halted for long periods. Several times whole sections needed to be ripped out, as it became more and more evident that hardly a single normal, understandable concept could be applied to the problem of space travel.

The lack of the history plates, which the Para steadfastly refused to deliver up, was a double handicap. Immediately upon their loss, Shar had set himself to reproduce them from memory; but unlike the more religious of his people, he had never regarded them as holy writ, and hence had never set himself to memorizing them word by word. Even before the theft, he had accumulated a set of variant translations of passages presenting specific experimental problems, which were stored in his library, carved in wood. But most of these translations tended to contradict each other, and none of them related to spaceship construction, upon which the original had been vague in any case.

No duplicates of the cryptic characters of the original had ever been made, for the simple reason that there was nothing in the sunken universe capable of destroying the originals, nor of duplicating their apparently changeless permanence. Shar remarked too late that through simple caution they should have made a number of verbatim temporary records—but after generations of green-gold peace, simple caution no longer covers preparation against catastrophe. (Nor, for that matter, did a culture which had to dig each letter of its simple alphabet into pulpy waterlogged wood with a flake of stonewort, encourage the keeping of records in triplicate.)

As a result, Shar's imperfect memory of the contents of the history plates, plus the constant and millennial doubt as to the accuracy of the various translations, proved finally to be the worst obstacle to progress on the spaceship itself.

"Men must paddle before they can swim," Lavon observed belatedly, and Shar was forced to agree with him.

Obviously, whatever the ancients had known about spaceship construction, very little of that knowledge was usable to a people still trying to build its first spaceship from scratch. In retrospect, it was not surprising that the great hulk still rested incomplete upon its platform above the sand boulders, exuding a musty odor of wood steadily losing its strength, two generations after its flat bottom had been laid down.

The fat-faced young man who headed the strike delegation was Phil XX, a man two generations younger than Lavon, four younger than Shar. There were crow's-feet at the corners of his eyes, which made him look both like a querulous old man and like an infant spoiled in the spore.

"We're calling a halt to this crazy project," he said bluntly. "We've slaved our youth away on it, but now that we're our own masters, it's over, that's all. Over."

"Nobody's compelled you," Lavon said angrily.

"Society does; our parents do," a gaunt member of the delegation said. "But now we're going to start living in the real world. Everybody these days knows that there's no other world but this one. You oldsters can hang on to your superstitions if you like. We don't intend to."

Baffled, Lavon looked over at Shar. The scientist smiled and said, "Let them go, Lavon. We have no use for the faint-hearted."

The fat-faced young man flushed. "You can't insult us into going back to work. We're through. Build your own ship to no place!"

"All right," Lavon said evenly. "Go on, beat it. Don't stand around here orating about it. You've made your decision and we're not interested in your self-justifications. Good-bye."

The fat-faced young man evidently still had quite a bit of heroism to dramatize which Lavon's dismissal had short-circuited. An examination of Lavon's stony face, however, convinced him that he had to take his victory as he found it. He and the delegation trailed ingloriously out the archway.

"Now what?" Lavon asked when they had gone. "I must admit, Shar, that I would have tried to persuade them. We do need the workers, after all."

"Not as much as they need us," Shar said tranquilly. "How many volunteers have you got for the crew of the ship?"

"Hundreds. Every young man of the generation after Phil's wants to go along. Phil's wrong about that segment of the population, at least. The project catches the imagination of the very young."

"Did you give them any encouragement?"

"Sure," Lavon said. "I told them we'd call on them if they were chosen. But you can't take that seriously! We'd do badly to displace our picked group of specialists with youths who have enthusiasm and nothing else."

"That's not what I had in mind, Lavon. Didn't I see a Noc in your chambers somewhere? Oh, there he is, asleep in the dome. Noc!"

The creature stirred its tentacles lazily.

"Noc, I've a message," Shar called. "The protos are to tell all men that those who wish to go to the next world with the spaceship must come to the staging area right away. Say that we can't promise to take everyone, but that only those who help us build the ship will be considered at all."

The Noc curled its tentacles again and appeared to go back to sleep. Actually, of course, it was sending its message through the water in all directions.

IV

Lavon turned from the arrangement of speaking-tube megaphones which was his control board and looked at the Para. "One last try," he said. "Will you give us back the plates?"

"No, Lavon. We have never denied you anything before, but this we must."

"You're going with us though, Para. Unless you give us the knowledge we need, you'll lose your life if we lose ours."

"What is one Para?" the creature said. "We are all alike. This cell will die; but the protos need to know how you fare on this journey. We believe you should make it without the plates."

"Why?"

The proto was silent. Lavon stared at it a moment, then turned deliberately back to the speaking tubes. "Everyone hang on," he said. He felt shaky. "We're about to start. Tol, is the ship sealed?"

"As far as I can tell, Lavon."

Lavon shifted to another megaphone. He took a deep breath. Already the water seemed stifling, though the ship hadn't moved.

"Ready with one-quarter power. One, two, three, go."

The whole ship jerked and settled back into place again. The raphe diatoms along the under hull settled into their niches, their jelly treads turning against broad endless belts of crude leather. Wooden gears creaked, stepping up the slow power of the creatures, transmitting it to the sixteen axles of the ship's wheels.

The ship rocked and began to roll slowly along the sandbar. Lavon looked tensely through the mica port. The world flowed painfully past him. The ship canted and began to climb the slope. Behind him, he could feel the electric silence of Shar, Para, the two alternate pilots, as if their gaze were stabbing directly through his body and on out the port. The world looked different, now that he was leaving it. How had he missed all this beauty before?

The slapping of the endless belts and the squeaking and groaning of the gears and axles grew louder as the slope steepened. The ship continued to climb, lurching. Around it, squadrons of men and protos dipped and wheeled, escorting it toward the sky.

Gradually the sky lowered and pressed down toward the top of the ship.

"A little more work from your diatoms, Tanol," Lavon said. "Boulder ahead." The ship swung ponderously. "All right, slow them up again. Give us a shove from your side, Than—no, that's too much—there, that's it. Back to normal; you're still turning us! Tanol, give us one burst to line us up again. Good. All right, steady drive on all sides. Won't be long now."

"How can you think in webs like that?" the Para wondered behind him.

"I just do, that's all. It's the way men think. Overseers, a little more thrust now; the grade's getting steeper."

The gears groaned. The ship nosed up. The sky brightened in Lavon's face. Despite himself, he began to be frightened. His lungs seemed to burn, and in his mind he felt his long fall through nothingness toward the chill slap of water as if he were experiencing it for the first time. His skin itched and burned. Could he go up *there* again? Up there into the burning void, the great gasping agony where no life should go?

The sandbar began to level out and the going became a little easier. Up here, the sky was so close that the lumbering motion of the huge ship disturbed it. Shadows of wavelets ran across the sand. Silently, the thick-barreled bands of blue-green algae drank in the light and converted it to oxygen, writhing in their slow mindless dance just under the long mica skylight which ran along the spine of the ship. In the hold, beneath the latticed corridor and cabin floors, whirring Vortae kept the ship's water in motion, fueling themselves upon drifting organic particles.

One by one, the figures wheeling about the ship outside waved arms or cilia and fell back, coasting down the slope of the sandbar toward the familiar world, dwindling and disappearing. There was at last only one single Euglena, half-plant cousin of the protos, forging along beside the spaceship into the marches of the shallows. It loved the light, but finally it, too, was driven away into cooler, deeper waters, its single whiplike tentacle undulating placidly as it went. It was not very bright, but Lavon felt deserted when it left.

Where they were going, though, none could follow.

Now the sky was nothing but a thin, resistant skin of water coating the top of the ship. The vessel slowed, and when Lavon called for more power, it began to dig itself in among the sand grains.

"That's not going to work," Shar said tensely. "I think we'd better step down the gear ratio, Lavon, so you can apply stress more slowly."

"All right," Lavon agreed. "Full stop, everybody. Shar, will you supervise gear-changing, please?"

Insane brilliance of empty space looked Lavon full in the face just beyond his big mica bull's eye. It was maddening to be forced to stop here upon the threshold of infinity; and it was dangerous, too. Lavon could feel building in him the old fear of the outside. A few moments more of inaction, he knew with a gathering coldness at the pit of his stomach, and he would be unable to go through with it.

Surely, he thought, there must be a better way to change gear-ratios than the traditional one, which involved dismantling almost the entire gear-box. Why couldn't a number of gears of different sizes be carried on the same shaft, not necessarily all in action all at once, but awaiting use simply by shoving the axle back and forth longitudinally in its sockets? It would still be clumsy, but it could be worked on orders from the bridge and would not involve shutting down the entire machine—and throwing the new pilot into a blue-green funk.

Shar came lunging up through the trap and swam himself a stop.

"All set," he said. "The big reduction gears aren't taking the strain too well, though."

"Splintering?"

"Yes. I'd go it slow at first."

Lavon nodded mutely. Without allowing himself to stop, even for a moment, to consider the consequences of his words, he called: "Half power."

The ship hunched itself down again and began to move, very slowly indeed, but more smoothly than before. Overhead, the sky thinned to complete transparency. The great light came blasting in. Behind Lavon there was an uneasy stir. The whiteness grew at the front ports.

Again the ship slowed, straining against the blinding barrier. Lavon swallowed and called for more power. The ship groaned like something about to die. It was now almost at a standstill.

"More power," Lavon ground out.

Once more, with infinite slowness, the ship began to move. Gently, it tilted upward.

Then it lunged forward and every board and beam in it began to squall.

"Lavon! Lavon!"

Lavon started sharply at the shout. The voice was coming at him from one of the megaphones, the one marked for the port at the rear of the ship.

"Lavon!"

"What is it? Stop your damn yelling."

"I can see the top of the sky! From the *other* side, from the top side! It's like a big flat sheet of metal. We're going away from it. We're above the sky, Lavon, we're above the sky!"

Another violent start swung Lavon around toward the forward port. On the outside of the mica, the water was evaporating with shocking swiftness, taking with it strange distortions and patterns made of rainbows.

Lavon saw Space.

It was at first like a deserted and cruelly dry version of the bottom. There were enormous boulders, great cliffs, tumbled, split, riven, jagged rocks going up and away in all directions.

But it had a sky of its own—a deep blue dome so far away that he could not believe in, let alone compute, what its distance might be. And in this dome was a ball of white fire that seared his eyeballs.

The wilderness of rock was still a long way away from the ship, which now seemed to be resting upon a level, glistening plain. Beneath the surface shine, the plain seemed to be made of sand, nothing but familiar sand, the same substance which had heaped up to form a bar in Lavon's own universe, the bar along which the ship had climbed. But the glassy, colorful skin over it—

Suddenly Lavon became conscious of another shout from the megaphone banks. He shook his head savagely and asked, "What is it now?"

"Lavon, this is Than. What have you gotten us into? The belts are locked. The diatoms can't move them. They aren't faking, either; we've rapped them hard enough to make them think we were trying to break their shells, but they still can't give us more power."

"Leave them alone," Lavon snapped. "They can't fake; they haven't enough intelligence. If they say they can't give you more power, they can't."

"Well, then, you get us out of it," Than's voice said frightenedly.

Shar came forward to Lavon's elbow. "We're on a space-water interface, where the surface tension is very high," he said softly. "This is why I insisted on our building the ship so that we could lift the wheels off the ground whenever necessary. For a long while I couldn't understand the reference of the history plates to 'retractable landing gear,' but it finally occurred to me that the tension along a space-water interface—or, to be more exact, a space-mud interface—would hold any large object pretty tightly. If you order the wheels pulled up now, I think we'll make better progress for a while on the belly-treads."

"Good enough," Lavon said. "Hello below—up landing gear. Evidently the ancients knew their business after all, Shar."

Quite a few minutes later, for shifting power to the belly-treads involved another setting of the gear box, the ship was crawling along the shore toward the tumbled rock. Anxiously, Lavon scanned the jagged, threatening wall for a break. There was a sort of rivulet off toward the left which might offer a route, though a dubious one, to the next world. After some thought, Lavon ordered his ship turned toward it.

"Do you suppose that thing in the sky is a 'star'?" he asked. "But there were supposed to be lots of them. Only one is up there—and one's plenty for *my* taste."

"I don't know," Shar admitted. "But I'm beginning to get a picture of the way the universe is made, I think. Evidently our world is a sort of cup in the bottom of this huge one. This one has a sky of its own; perhaps it, too, is only a cup in the bottom of a still huger world, and so on and on without end. It's a hard concept to grasp, I'll admit. Maybe it would be more sensible to assume that all the worlds are cups in this one common surface, and that the great light shines on them all impartially."

"Then what makes it seem to go out every night, and dim even in the day during winter?" Lavon demanded.

"Perhaps it travels in circles, over first one world, then another. How could I know yet?"

"Well, if you're right, it means that all we have to do is crawl along here for a while, until we hit the top of the sky of another world," Lavon said. "Then we dive in. Somehow it seems too simple, after all our preparations."

Shar chuckled, but the sound did not suggest that he had discovered anything funny. "Simple? Have you noticed the temperature yet?"

Lavon had noticed it, just beneath the surface of awareness, but at Shar's remark he realized that he was gradually being stifled. The oxygen content of the water, luckily, had not dropped, but the temperature suggested the shallows in the last and worst part of the autumn. It was like trying to breathe soup.

"Than, give us more action from the Vortae," Lavon called. "This is going to be unbearable unless we get more circulation."

It was all he could do now to keep his attention on the business of steering the ship.

The cut or defile in the scattered razor-edged rocks was a little closer, but there still seemed to be many miles of rough desert to cross. After a while, the ship settled into a steady, painfully slow crawling, with less pitching and jerking than before, but also with less progress. Under it, there was now a sliding, grinding sound, rasping against the hull of the ship itself, as if it were treadmilling over some coarse lubricant whose particles were each as big as a man's head.

Finally Shar said, "Lavon, we'll have to stop again. The sand this far up is dry, and we're wasting energy using the treads."

"Are you sure we can take it?" Lavon asked, gasping for breath. "At least we are moving. If we stop to lower the wheels and change gears again, we'll boil."

"We'll boil if we don't," Shar said calmly. "Some of our algae are already dead and the rest are withering. That's a pretty good sign that we can't take much more. I don't think we'll make it into the shadows, unless we do change over and put on some speed."

There was a gulping sound from one of the mechanics. "We ought to turn back," he said raggedly. "We were never meant to be out here in the first place. We were made for the water, not this hell."

"We'll stop," Lavon said, "but we're not turning back. That's final."

The words made a brave sound, but the man had upset Lavon more than he dared to admit, even to himself. "Shar," he said, "make it fast, will you?"

The scientist nodded and dived below.

The minutes stretched out. The great white globe in the sky blazed and blazed. It had moved down the sky, far down, so that the light was pouring into the ship directly in Lavon's face, illuminating every floating particle, its rays like long milky streamers. The currents of water passing Lavon's cheek were almost hot.

How could they dare go directly forward into that inferno? The land directly under the "star" must be even hotter than it was here!

"Lavon! Look at Para!"

Lavon forced himself to turn and look at his proto ally. The great slipper had settled to the deck, where it was lying with only a feeble pulsation of its cilia. Inside, its vacuoles were beginning to swell, to become bloated, pear-shaped bubbles, crowding the granulated protoplasm, pressing upon the dark nuclei.

"This cell is dying," Para said, as coldly as always. "But go on—go on. There is much to learn, and you may live, even though we do not. Go on."

"You're . . . for us now?" Lavon whispered.

"We have always been for you. Push your folly to its uttermost. We will benefit in the end, and so will man."

The whisper died away. Lavon called the creature again, but it did not respond.

There was a wooden clashing from below, and then Shar's voice came tinnily from one of the megaphones. "Lavon, go ahead! The diatoms are dying, too, and then we'll be without power. Make it as quickly and directly as you can."

Grimly, Lavon leaned forward. "The 'star' is directly over the land we're approaching."

"It is? It may go lower still and the shadows will get longer. That's our only hope."

Lavon had not thought of that. He rasped into the banked megaphones. Once more, the ship began to move.

It got hotter.

Steadily, with a perceptible motion, the "star" sank in Lavon's face. Suddenly a new terror struck him. Suppose it should continue to go down until it was gone entirely? Blasting though it was now, it was the only source of heat. Would not space become bitter cold on the instant—and the ship an expanding, bursting block of ice?

The shadows lengthened menacingly, stretched across the desert toward the forward-rolling vessel. There was no talking in the cabin, just the sound of ragged breathing and the creaking of the machinery.

Then the jagged horizon seemed to rush upon them. Stony teeth cut into the lower rim of the ball of fire, devoured it swiftly. It was gone.

They were in the lee of the cliffs. Lavon ordered the ship turned to parallel the rock-line; it responded heavily, sluggishly. Far above, the sky deepened steadily from blue to indigo.

Shar came silently up through the trap and stood beside Lavon, studying that deepening color and the lengthening of the shadows down the beach toward their world. He said nothing, but Lavon knew that the same chilling thought was in his mind.

"Lavon."

Lavon jumped. Shar's voice had iron in it. "Yes?"

"We'll have to keep moving. We must make the next world, wherever it is, very shortly."

"How can we dare move when we can't see where we're going? Why not sleep it over—if the cold will let us?"

"It will let us." Shar said. "It can't get dangerously cold up here. If it did, the sky—or what we used to think of as the sky—would have frozen over every night, even in summer. But what I'm thinking about is the water. The plants will go to sleep now. In our world that wouldn't matter; the supply of oxygen is enough to last through the night. But in this confined space, with so many creatures in it and no source of fresh water, we will probably smother."

Shar seemed hardly to be involved at all, but spoke rather with the voice of implacable physical laws.

"Furthermore," he said, staring unseeingly out at the raw landscape, "the diatoms are plants, too. In other words, we must stay on the move for as long as we have oxygen and power—and pray that we make it."

"Shar, we had quite a few protos on board this ship once. And Para there isn't quite dead yet. If he were, the cabin would be intolerable. The ship is nearly sterile of bacteria, because all the protos have been eating them as a matter of course and there's no outside supply of them, any more than there is for oxygen. But still and all there would have been some decay."

Shar bent and tested the pellicle of the motionless Para with a probing finger. "You're right, he's still alive. What does that prove?"

"The Vortae are also alive; I can feel the water circulating. Which proves it wasn't the heat that hurt Para. *It was the light.* Remember how badly my skin was affected after I climbed beyond the sky? Undiluted starlight is deadly. We should add that to the information on the plates."

"I still don't see the point."

"It's this. We've got three or four Noc down below. They were shielded from the light, and so must be alive. If we concentrate them in the diatom galleys, the dumb diatoms will think it's still daylight and will go on working. Or we can concentrate them up along the spine of the ship, and keep the algae putting out oxygen. So the question is: which do we need more, oxygen or power? Or can we split the difference?"

Shar actually grinned. "A brilliant piece of thinking. We'll make a Shar of you yet, Lavon. No, I'd say that we can't split the difference. There's something about daylight, some quality, that the light Noc emits doesn't have. You and I can't detect it, but the green plants can, and without it they don't make oxygen. So we'll have to settle for the diatoms—for power."

Lavon brought the vessel away from the rocky lee of the cliff, out onto the smoother sand. All trace of direct light was gone now, although there was still a soft, general glow on the sky.

"Now, then," Shar said thoughtfully, "I would guess that there's water over there in the canyon, if we can reach it. I'll go below and arrange—"

Lavon gasped, "What's the matter?"

Silently, Lavon pointed, his heart pounding.

The entire dome of indigo above them was spangled with tiny, incredibly brilliant lights. There were hundreds of them, and more and more were becoming visible as the darkness deepened. And far away, over the ultimate edge of the rocks, was a dim red globe, crescented with ghostly silver. Near the zenith was another such body, much smaller, and silvered all over. . . .

Under the two moons of Hydrot, and under the eternal stars, the two-inch wooden spaceship and its microscopic cargo toiled down the slope toward the drying little rivulet.

V

The ship rested on the bottom of the canyon for the rest of the night. The great square doors were thrown open to admit the raw, irradiated, life-giving water from outside—and the wriggling bacteria which were fresh food.

No other creatures approached them, either with curiosity or with predatory intent, while they slept, though Lavon had posted guards at the doors. Evidently, even up here on the very floor of space, highly organized creatures were quiescent at night.

But when the first flush of light filtered through the water, trouble threatened.

First of all, there was the bug-eyed monster. The thing was green and had two snapping claws, either one of which could have broken the ship in two like a spirogyra straw. Its eyes were black and globular, on the ends of short columns, and its long feelers were as thick as a plant-bole. It passed in a kicking fury of motion, however, never noticing the ship at all.

"Is that—a sample of the kind of life we can expect in the next world?" Lavon whispered. Nobody answered, for the very good reason that nobody knew.

After a while, Lavon risked moving the ship forward against the current, which was slow but heavy. Enormous writhing worms whipped past them. One struck the hull a heavy blow, then thrashed on obliviously.

"They don't notice us," Shar said. "We're too small. Lavon, the ancients warned us of the immensity of space, but even when you see it, it's impossible to grasp. And all those stars—can they mean what I think they mean? It's beyond thought, beyond belief!"

"The bottom's sloping," Lavon said, looking ahead intently. "The walls of the canyon are retreating, and the water's becoming rather silty. Let the stars wait, Shar; we're coming toward the entrance of our new world."

Shar subsided moodily. His vision of space had disturbed him, perhaps seriously. He took little notice of the great thing that was happening, but instead huddled worriedly over his own expanding speculations. Lavon felt the old gap between their two minds widening once more.

Now the bottom was tilting upward again. Lavon had no experience with delta-formation, for no rivulets left his own world, and the phenomenon worried him. But his worries were swept away in wonder as the ship topped the rise and nosed over.

Ahead, the bottom sloped away again, indefinitely, into glimmering depths. A proper sky was over them once more, and Lavon could see small rafts of plankton floating placidly beneath it. Almost at once, too, he saw several of the smaller kinds of protos, a few of which were already approaching the ship—

Then the girl came darting out of the depths, her features distorted with terror. At first she did not see the ship at all. She came twisting and turning lithely through the water, obviously hoping only to throw herself over the ridge of the delta and into the savage streamlet beyond.

Lavon was stunned. Not that there were men here—he had hoped for that—but at the girl's single-minded flight toward suicide.

"What—"

Then a dim buzzing began to grow in his ears, and he understood.

"Shar! Than! Tanol!" he bawled. "Break out crossbows and spears! Knock out all the windows!" He lifted a foot and kicked through the big port in front of him. Someone thrust a crossbow into his hand.

"Eh? What's happening?" Shar blurted.

"Rotifers!"

The cry went through the ship like a galvanic shock. The rotifers back in Lavon's own world were virtually extinct, but everyone knew thoroughly the grim history of the long battle man and proto had waged against them.

The girl spotted the ship suddenly and paused, stricken by despair at the sight of the new monster. She drifted with her own momentum, her eyes alternately fixed hypnotically upon the ship and glancing back over her shoulder, toward where the buzzing snarled louder and louder in the dimness.

"Don't stop!" Lavon shouted. "This way, this way! We're friends! We'll help!"

Three great semitransparent trumpets of smooth flesh bored over the rise, the many thick cilia of their coronas whirring greedily. Dicrans—the most predacious of the entire tribe of Eaters. They were quarreling thickly among themselves as they moved, with the few blurred, pre-symbolic noises which made up their "language."

Carefully, Lavon wound the crossbow, brought it to his shoulder, and fired. The bolt sang away through the water. It lost momentum rapidly, and was caught by a stray current which brought it closer to the girl than to the Eater at which Lavon had aimed.

He bit his lip, lowered the weapon, wound it up again. It did not pay to underestimate the range; he would have to wait until he could fire with effect. Another bolt, cutting through the water from a side port, made him issue orders to cease firing.

The sudden irruption of the rotifers decided the girl. The motionless wooden monster was strange to her and had not yet menaced her—but she must have known what it would be like to have three Dicrans over her, each trying to grab away from the other the biggest share. She threw herself toward the big port. The Eaters screamed with fury and greed and bored after her.

She probably would not have made it, had not the dull vision of the lead Dicran made out the wooden shape of the ship at the last instant. It backed off, buzzing, and the other two sheered away to avoid colliding with it. After that they had another argument, though they could hardly have formulated what it was that they were fighting about. They were incapable of saying anything much more complicated than the equivalent of "Yaah," "Drop dead," and "You're another."

While they were still snarling at each other, Lavon pierced the nearest one all the way through with an arablast bolt. It disintegrated promptly—rotifers are delicately organized creatures despite their ferocity—and the remaining two were at once involved in a lethal battle over the remains.

"Than, take a party out and spear me those two Eaters while they're still fighting," Lavon ordered. "Don't forget to destroy their eggs, too. I can see that this world needs a little taming."

The girl shot through the port and brought up against the far wall of the cabin, flailing in terror. Lavon tried to approach her, but from somewhere she produced a flake of stonewort chipped to a nasty point. He sat down on the stool before his control board and waited while she took in the cabin, Lavon, Shar, the pilot, the senescent Para.

At last she said: "Are—you—the gods from beyond the sky?"

"We're from beyond the sky, all right," Lavon said. "But we're not gods. We're human beings, like yourself. Are there many humans here?"

The girl seemed to assess the situation very rapidly, savage though she was. Lavon had the odd and impossible impression that he should recognize her. She tucked the knife back into her matted hair—ah, Lavon thought, that's a trick I may need to remember—and shook her head.

"We are few. The Eaters are everywhere. Soon they will have the last of us."

Her fatalism was so complete that she actually did not seem to care.

"And you've never cooperated against them? Or asked the protos to help?"

"The protos?" She shrugged. "They are as helpless as we are against the Eaters. We have no weapons which kill at a distance, like yours. And it is too late now for such weapons to do any good. We are too few, the Eaters too many."

Lavon shook his head emphatically. "You've had one weapon that counts, all along. Against it, numbers mean nothing. We'll show you how we've used it. You may be able to use it even better than we did, once you've given it a try."

The girl shrugged again. "We have dreamed of such a weapon now and then, but never found it. I do not think that what you say is true. What is this weapon?"

"Brains," Lavon said. "Not just one brain, but brains. Working together. Cooperation."

"Lavon speaks the truth," a weak voice said from the deck.

The Para stirred feebly. The girl watched it with wide eyes. The sound of the Para using human speech seemed to impress her more than the ship or anything else it contained.

"The Eaters can be conquered," the thin, buzzing voice said. "The protos will help, as they helped in the world from which we came. They fought this flight through space, and deprived man of his records; but man made the trip without the records. The protos will never oppose men again. I have already spoken to the protos of this world and have told them what man can dream, man can do, whether the protos wish it or not.

"Shar, your metal records are with you. They were hidden in the ship. My brothers will lead you to them.

"This organism dies now. It dies in confidence of knowledge, as an intelligent creature dies. Man has taught us this. There is nothing that knowledge . . . cannot do. With it, men . . . have crossed . . . have crossed space. . . ."

The voice whispered away. The shining slipper did not change, but something about it was gone. Lavon looked at the girl; their eyes met.

"We have crossed space," Lavon repeated softly.

Shar's voice came to him across a great distance. The young-old man was whispering: "But *have* we?"

"As far as I'm concerned, yes," said Lavon.

■ ■ ■

For a Journal Entry . . .

How you see things depends on how you look at them. And how you look at them depends on who you are. Sound obvious? Try looking at your own world through the eyes of some other life form, perhaps through the eyes of a visitor from another world. You might come up with an interesting perspective.

For Your Consideration . . .

1. James Blish's "Surface Tension" does not *require* a knowledge of pond eco-spheres, but everything helps. Check with your science teacher if you don't know what *surface tension* is, or what a *thermocline* is and why it breaks up. Find out something about microscopic marine life. Many of the terms can be determined from context. For instance, try to determine the meaning of *panatropes* (or panatropic) from the way the word is used in the story.
2. Now, why is the story called "Surface Tension"?
3. Do you think that what the crew of the wrecked seed-ship is trying to do is indeed a result of *hubris* as La Ventura suggests? Why or why not?

4. What are the metal plates and why are they important to the story? Why do the protos steal them, and why do they eventually return them?
5. What evidence does this new breed of men have that it was made and did not just evolve? How is this new breed of men different from us? In what important ways is it the same? What special gifts does it bring to this water world?
6. Compare and contrast the old Shar and Lavon. Do they make a good team? Who is the more practical?
7. What wry comments does Blish have to make on the labor conditions in the puddle world of Hydrot?
8. What parts do each of the following creatures play in microscopic world of the story: the Para, the Noc, diatoms, desmids, algae?
9. How is our world different from the world of Lavon and old Shar?
10. How is the space that Lavon and old Shar cross like the space between the stars? How is their spaceship like the ships that cross between the stars? How is it different? How are their attitudes like those of any men venturing into the unknown?
11. How does the picture of their universe change after their journey to a new world? Why is the Shar still unsatisfied?
12. Blish uses a whole wealth of scientific detail to tell his story. Would his story have been as realistic without it? Would it have been as effective?
13. Why is point of view so very important in this story?

Notes

PAGE
148 *swamp*—water-logged land
148 *eminence*—height
149 *mosaic*—pattern made up of bits and pieces of colored rock or other materials
149 *onyx*—a gem stone
149 *cropper*—slang for bad mistake
150 *hallooed*—yelled to draw attention
150 *crustacea*—class of invertebrate animal having a hard outer shell
150 *rivulets*—small streams
150 *protozoa*—one-celled animals
150 *metazoa*—many-celled animals
150 *rotifer*—microscopic water animal with a ring of cilia at one end of its body
150 *thalluslike*—similar to plants with no division of root, stem or leaves (e.g. lichen)
151 *prohibitive*—extremely difficult, almost impossible
151 *placate*—make amends
151 *precedents*—previous examples to follow

152 *residuum*—residue; remainder
152 *arachnids*—animals with four pairs of legs, lunglike sacs or breathing tubes (e.g. spiders)
152 *intercostal spiracles*—air holes between the ribs
152 *sporulation*—process of forming a spore
153 *calibrated*—set up
153 *morosely*—gloomily
153 *Lethe*—river of forgetfulness crossed in death in Greek and Roman mythology
153 *obscurity*—darkness
153 *spore*—hard, protective shell
154 *granules*—small grains
154 *muted*—quieted
154 *cilia*—tiny, hairlike growths
154 *telepathically*—communicating mentally
154 *colloquies*—conversations
155 *aggregate*—total
155 *protos*—used as short for protozoa
155 *exterminate*—wipe out
155 *initiative*—ability to begin something new, create something
156 *remorseless logicians*—beings that use only logic in their thinking, no emotions
156 *ancestors*—distant relatives
159 *embrasure*—an opening
160 *dichotomous(ly)*—dividing or forking
160 *mortar*—cement
160 *precariously*—insecurely
160 *concept*—idea
160 *poachers*—illegal hunters
161 *frond*—leaflike organ
162 *adze*—axlike tool
162 *glutinous tetrads*—sticky portions
162 *interface*—surface that forms the boundary between two things
163 *flocculent*—woolly
163 *encysted*—formed a protective cyst or shell
163 *amber*—yellowish
163 *invulnerable*—invincible; unharmable
163 *cosmology*—theory of the nature of the universe
164 *bole*—trunk or stem
166 *desiccation*—process of drying out
166 *amnionic fluid*—fluid from the sac enclosing an embryo or, in this story, from the spore
166 *ameba*—one-celled animal
166 *quiescent*—still, quiet
167 *epoch making*—landmark; marking a change in a way of life
169 *accumulated*—gathered
170 *compelled*—forced

172 *canted*—tilted
173 *infinity*—forever, without end
178 *bloated*—swollen
178 *indigo*—deep violet-blue
180 *zenith*—height
180 *irradiated*—cleared, shining
180 *predatory*—having hunting instincts
181 *immensity*—vastness, largeness
181 *silty*—having sand or silt
183 *lethal*—deadly

Traffic Problem

by William Earls

William Earls is a new writer who speaks for the modern generation, the people who are growing up in a world where life races along just one step ahead of death by pollution. Where the biggest racing polluter of all is the automobile and the highways that these cars must drive upon. Here is the absolutely mad story of cars and crashes and highways in this incredible future.

Davis took the third expressway from Forty-second Street to the site of the old Rockefeller Center, dropped down through the quadruple overpass and braked to a halt in the fourth level lot. He paused a moment before alighting from the car, trying to catch his breath—even in the car, with the CO filters on over-duty, the air was terrible. He donned his gas mask before he stepped into the lot, slammed the left-hand door into the unprotected door of the Cadillac parked next to him.

"Serve him right for crossing a parking line," he growled. He jumped aside quickly as a Mustang Mach V whistled past him, slammed around a corner, hurtled down the ramp to the street. He flung a curse after it.

He eased his head out between the parked cars before sprinting across the traffic lane of the parking lot to the elevator on the other side. The attendant rushed to him, tried to demand the $30 daily fee, stepped back when Davis flashed his Traffic Manager's badge at him. The attendant dropped to his knees in salute, stayed down while Davis rushed past.

His office was on the ground level of the Roads and Traffic Building and when he came off the elevator, the hall was full of dust and a jackhammer was going crazily at one end of it. The man behind it was wearing the light blue of Road Construction Unlimited. Davis remembered the spur route of the second level, Fifty-seventh Street West that was going through the building's corner. He hadn't expected construction to start this soon.

One wall had been ripped out of the office and the derricks were swinging the steel girders for the spur route into place. More men were driving them into the concrete of the floor, slamming them into place with magn-gun rivets. One of the drivers kept walking to the water cooler and Davis stopped him.

"That stuff is three dollars a gallon, buddy," he said.

"Road crew, Mac." The big man tried to push him aside and Davis flashed the badge.

"This is still my office," he said. He crossed to the control board, buzzed the Director.

"Davis in," he said.

I suppose the old bastard will want a report already. . . .

"Right," the Director's secretary said, "I'll tell him."

Leingen waved at him from the casualty table and he trotted over, flashed the badge and Leingen nodded. He was off duty now, officially relieved—and he looked relieved.

Lucky bastard will be home in three hours—if he makes it. . . .

The casualty report was horrendous, up 4.2 per cent over the day before—with seventeen dead on the United Nations area overpass alone. He dialed Road Service.

"Road," the voice on the other end said.

"Traffic Manager. Send a bird. I'm going up for a look." He checked some of the other reports—two breakdowns on the fifth level of the Tappan Zee bridge, both '79 Fords. Goddam people had no right driving two-year-old cars on the roads anyway. He buzzed Arrest Division.

"All 'seventy-nine Fords off the roads," he said.

"Rog." On the board he watched the red dots that were the Fords being shuttled off to the waiting ramps, clogging them. He flipped a visual to one of them, saw the cars jamming in and the bulldozers pushing them closer. The din around him was increasing and pieces of plasta-plaster were starting to fall from the ceiling.

"Slap up a privacy screen," he ordered. He received no answer and looked at one of the workmen driving the rivets for the girders. Jones wasn't there, he thought suddenly. Of course not, that girder is where his desk was. He'd miss Jones.

"That ain't a priority job, buddy," the workman said. "You want materials, get 'em from Construction."

Davis growled, checked his watch. 0807. Things were just moving into the third rush period. Almost on cue the building began to quiver as the lower-echelon office workers hurtled by in their Lincolns and Mercuries to obscure little jobs in obscure little offices.

A short buzz came from the main phone. The Director.

"Yes, sir," Davis said.

"Davis?" the palsied voice said. *Die, you old bastard,* Davis thought. "Casualties are up all over."

"The roads are jammed, sir."

"You're Manager. Do something."

"We need more roads. Only you can authorize them."

"We don't have any more roads. But that traffic must move. Do what you have to." The voice went into a coughing spasm. "When you're Director, you build roads."

"Yes, sir." He punched off. All right, he'd move the traffic. Say this for the Director—he'd back a Manager all the way.

"The bird's here," the intercom said.

"Smith," Davis said. His assistant looked up from the main board. "You're in charge. I'm going up." He moved to the elevator, bounced up, flipped his telecorder to audio, caught the information as he hurtled toward the tenth floor.

"Major pile-up at Statue of Liberty East," the speaker barked. "Seventeen cars and a school bus. Ambulance on the scene. Structural damage on Fifth level East, Yankee Stadium Speedway. More accidents on Staten Island One, Two, Four, Ten, Thirteen, and Twenty-Two; Eastside Four, Nine, and Eleven—" Davis punched off. Matters were worse than he had thought.

On the fifth floor he changed elevators to avoid the ramp from the exact-change lanes to the fourth level, zipped to the roof and the waiting helicopter.

"Fifty-car pile-up on Yankee Stadium Four," the helicopter radio screamed and he punched the button to Central.

"Davis."

"Yes, sir?"

"What's the time on next of kin identification?" he asked.

"Twenty-three minutes, sir."

"Make it nineteen. Inform all units."

"Yes, sir."

"Lift off," he growled at the pilot. He threw his eyes out of focus, watching the cars hurtling by the edge of the roof.

I could reach out and touch them—*and have my arm torn off at 100 miles an hour. . . .*

He coughed. He always forgot to don his gas mask for the short trip from the elevator to the bird and it always bothered his lungs.

The smog was fortunately thin this morning and he could see the gray that was Manhattan below him. Southward he could make out the spire of the Empire State Building rising forty stories above the cloverleaf around it and beyond that the tower of the Trade Center and the great hulk of the parking lot dwarfing it.

"Hook right," he ordered the pilot, "spin down along the river."

There was a pile-up at the Pier 90 crossover and he saw a helicopter swooping down to pick up the mangled cars at the end of a magnet, swing out across the river to drop them into the New Jersey processing depot.

He buzzed the Director as he saw the wrecks piling up in front of the three big crunchers at the depot. They were hammering broken Fords and Buicks into three-foot lumps of mangled steel, spitting them onto the barges. The barges were then being towed out to Long Island Sound for the new jetport. But fast as the crunchers were, they were not fast enough. With a capacity of only two hundred cars an hour apiece, they could not keep pace with the rush-hour crackups.

"Yes, Davis," the Director wheezed.

"Would you call U.S. Steel," Davis asked. "We need another cruncher."

"Well, I don't know if we really do—but I'll call."

Davis punched off angrily.

His practiced eye gauged the flow of traffic on the George and Martha Washington bridges. The cars were eighty feet apart and he ordered a close to seventy-two, effectively increasing the capacity by ten per cent. That was almost as good as another level —but not good enough.

The traffic lane above the piers was packed and smoke from ships was rising between the two twelve-lane sections. Trucks loaded with imports paused for a moment at the top of the ramps were steam catapulted into the traffic. He saw one truck, loaded with what looked like steel safes, hit by a Cadillac, go out of control, hurtle over the edge of the roadway and fall one hundred feet—five levels—to the ground. The safes went bouncing in every direction, slamming into cars on every level. Even two hundred feet above the scene he could hear the scream of brakes and the explosions as the autos crashed and burned. He punched for Control.

"Scramble an ambulance to Pier Forty-six, all levels," he said.

He smiled. It was always good to be the first to report an accident. It showed you hadn't forgotten your training. He had reported four one morning, a record. But now there were bounties for accident reporting and it was rare when a traffic man could actually turn one in. At one time traffic accidents had been reported by the police, but now they were too busy tracking down law violators. An accident was harmful only in that it broke the normal traffic flow.

Traffic was heavy on all levels, he saw—he could actually see only three levels down and there were as many as eight below that—and the main interchange at Times Square was feeding and receiving well. The largest in Manhattan, it spanned from Forty-second Street to Forty-ninth and from Fourth to Eighth avenues. There had been protests when construction had started—mostly from movie fans and library fanatics—but now it was the finest interchange in the world, sixteen lanes wide at the Forty-second Street off ramp, with twelve exact-change lanes. Even the library fans were appeased, he thought: it had been his idea to move the library lions from the old site—they would have been destroyed with the rest of the building had he not spoken—to the mouth of the Grand Central speed lane to Yankee Stadium.

The helicopter banked, headed down the Westside parkway toward the Battery interchange and the Statue of Liberty crossover. It had been clever of the design engineers to use the Bedloe's Island base of the statue for the crossover base—it had saved millions over the standard practice of driving piles into the harbor water. The copper had brought a good salvage price, too.

Of course, the conservationists, the live-in-the-past people, had objected here, too. But, as always, they were shouted down at the protest meetings. The traffic had to roll, didn't it?

Below the helicopter Manhattan was a seething mass of speeding cars—reds, blacks, blues, and this month's brilliant green against the background of concrete and asphalt. There were quick flashes of brake lights, frightened blurs as a tie rod snapped or a tire blew. Dipping wreckocopters swooped in to pluck cars and pieces of cars from the highways before the lanes jammed. The island was two hundred lanes wide at the top, widened to two hundred and thirty at the base with the north-south lanes over the sites of the old streets running forty feet apart, over, under, and even through the old buildings. It was the finest city in the world, made for and by automobiles. And he controlled, for eight hours a day anyway, the destiny of those automobiles. He felt the sense of power he always had here in the helicopter, swooping above the traffic. It passed quickly—it always did—and he was observing clinically, watching the flow.

"There," he said to the pilot, indicated the fifth lane on the pier route. A dull red Dodge was going sixty-five, backing up the traffic for miles. There was no room to pass, and, with the traffic boiling up out of the tunnels and bridges onto the road, a jam was inevitable. "Drop," he ordered, moved behind the persuader gunsight, lined the Dodge in the cross hairs.

He fired and watched the result. The dye marker smashed on

the Dodge's hood, glowed for a moment. Warned, the driver moved to a sane 95. But the dye stayed and the driver would be picked up later in the day—the dye was impossible to remove except with Traffic-owned detergent—and sentenced. For first clogging, the fine was only $200, but for later offenses, drivers were banned from the road for five to one hundred days, forced to ride the railways into town. Davis shuddered at the thought.

Battery Point and Bedloe's Island looked good and the copter heeled. He used the binoculars to check the Staten Island Freeway, saw that it was down to sixteen lanes coming into New York from the high of twenty-two. The main rush was almost over and he could start preparing for the early lunch rush.

There was still a pile-up at the Trade Center. The one tower, two had been planned, was standing high above the highways around it, with the great bulk of the parking lot building rising above it, the smog line lapping at the seventy-ninth floor. He saw the red lights in the first ninety-two floors of the lot signifying full, knew that the remaining forty floors would not take all of the cars still piling in from the twenty-five feeder lanes. He buzzed Control.

"Yes, sir?" the voice said.

"Davis. Get me Parks and Playgrounds."

"Parks and Playgrounds?" The voice was incredulous.

"Right." He waited and when a voice answered, spoke quickly, did his best to overpower the man on the other end.

"Traffic Manager Davis," he snapped. "I want Battery Park cleared. I'm preparing to dump two thousand cars there in five minutes."

"You can't—"

"The hell I can't! I'm Traffic Manager. Clear the park—"

What there was left of it—the grass fighting for air against the exhaust fumes, dying in the shadow of the interchange above it, stomped to death as the millions of city dwellers flocked to the only green in eleven miles—Central Park had been a bastion for a long time but it was too open, too convenient. It was buried now under a rising parking lot and seven levels of traffic. As a concession to the live-in-the-pasters the animal cages had been placed on the parking lot roof and stayed there for two weeks until they had been hit by a drunk in a Lincoln. There had been a minor flap then with the carbon-monoxide-drugged animals prowling the ramps until they had been hunted down by motorcyclists.

"What about the people?" Parks and Playgrounds asked.

"Sorry about that. They have four and a half minutes." He punched off, buzzed Beacons and Buzzers.

"Davis," he said. "Re-route Battery Five, ramps two through ten, into Battery Park."

"Right." He buzzed Lower City, ordered Wall Street closed for seven blocks. Later in the day they'd have to reroute the traffic around it. No matter, the tie-up lasted for four hours anyway.

The big pile-up, as always, was at the Empire State Building where the main north-south curved twelve lanes out of the way to avoid the huge building. And, as they curved, tires skidded on the pavement, cars clawed to the side and, day after day, car after car lost control on the corner, went plunging over the side to shatter on the ramps below. It was, in many ways, the best show in town and office workers crowded the windows to watch the cars spin out of control. Today the traffic looked almost good and he clocked the pack at one hundred and ten on the corner, one hundred and fifteen coming out of it. Still not good enough, though—they were braking coming into the corner, losing time, and the line was thin as they came out of it. He watched a Buick skid, hit the guardrail, tip, and the driver go flying out of the convertible top, land in the level below, disappear in the traffic stream. The car rolled, plummeted from sight.

"Home," he said. The helicopter dropped him on the roof and he gagged against the smog, trotted to the elevator, dropped. The building was shaking from the traffic noise and the hammering of rivets. He coughed on the dust.

He checked the casualty lists, initialed them. Above normal, with the Empire State section running 6.2 per cent ahead of last week. He was listed as reporting the pier pile-up, and there was a report stating Battery Park was filled—there was also a note saying that the Director was catching hell for parking cars there. To hell with him, Davis thought. There was another complaint to his attention from Merrill Lynch, Pierce, Fenner, and Agnew. Two of their board members were caught in the Wall Street jam and were late for work. He threw it into the wastebasket. Outside (inside?)—hard to say with no wall on one side of the building—the workmen were throwing up the steel plates for the ramp, stinting on the bolts to save time.

"Put the damn bolts in," Davis roared. "That thing will shake enough anyway."

The din was tremendous even now, with seven ramps of traffic passing within thirty feet. It would be worse when the spur route was finished. He hoped that they would put the wall back on the office. He buzzed Smith, asked for a readout on the Empire State complex.

"Fourteen fatalities since nine o'clock."

It was now 10:07 and the pre-lunch rush was due to start in four minutes.

"Damn Empire anyway," he said. The United Nations interchange board went red and he went to visual, saw a twelve-car pile-up on the fourth level, the bodies and pieces of bodies, the cars and pieces of cars falling into the General Assembly. Damn! he could expect another angry call from the Secretary General. Damn foreigners anyway, when did they get the idea that their stupid meetings were more important than traffic?

The red phone rang—the Director—and he lifted it. "Davis."

"Everything's running higher," the Director wheezed. "What's the story?"

"Empire's the big tie-up," Davis said. "That and some construction."

"Do something. I gave you the authority."

"Get rid of Empire," Davis said. "Get another forty decks on the Trade parking lot, too."

"Can't be done." The hell it can't, Davis thought. You're just afraid of the conservationists. Coward. "Do something."

"Yes, sir." He waited until the phone clicked dead before he slammed it down. He took a deep breath of the air in the office—it was even better than smoking. Then he began to bark orders over the All Circuits channel.

"Scramble another ten wreckocopters," he snarled. With half again as many copters, wrecks would be cleared that much faster. "Cut next of kin time to fifteen minutes." He was going out on a limb here, but it would speed the processing of accidents through Brooklyn and New Jersey. Now, with the rush hour just over and another beginning, wrecks were piling up outside the receiving centers and the crunchers were idle half the time. "Up minimum speed five miles an hour." That would make it at least 100 miles an hour on every highway, 65 on the ramps. He flipped to visual, saw Beacons and Buzzers post the new speeds, saw the cars increase speed. Wrecks and Checks flashed the going aloft of the ten copters and he breathed easier, flipped to visual at Empire, saw the day's third major pile-up on the third level, cursed. He closed the Thirty-fourth Street cutoff, ordered three payloaders to dump all wrecks right there, flashed a message to Identification to have a team posted. By midnight, when the traffic eased, they could begin moving the cars and bodies to New Jersey.

The red phone rang, three rings. Double urgent. He grabbed it, barked his name.

"The Director just dropped dead," a hysterical voice said. "You're acting Director."

"I'll be right there." Acting, hell. There were six hours left on his shift and he could get something done now. He turned to Smith. "You're Manager now," he said, "I just got bumped upstairs."

"Right." Smith barely looked up. "Reopen Yonkers Four, lanes one through nine," he said.

He had made the transition from assistant to Manager in an instant. Training, Davis thought.

He took the elevator to the eighth floor, the Director's office. The staff was quiet, looking down at the body on the floor. There were four boards flashing, a dozen phones ringing. Davis snapped orders quickly.

"You, you and you, answer the phones," he said. "You and you, get the boards. You, drag that body out of here. "You"—he pointed at the Director's—his—secretary—"call a staff conference. Now."

He looked at the boards, checked Traffic, Beacons and Buzzers, Wrecks and Checks, Gate Receipts and Identification. Fatalities was doing extremely well—Wellborn was the new Manager here. The crunchers were doing well. Wrecks was reporting above normal pickup time.

"The Director's dead," he told the staff. "I'm new Director." They all nodded. "Most departments look pretty good," he said. He looked at Smith. "Traffic flow is lousy," he said. "Why?"

"Empire," Smith said. "We're losing twenty per cent just going around that goddammed building."

"How are your crews fixed for a major job?" Davis asked the Construction Manager.

"Okay." The Manager ticked off eleven small jobs.

"The problem is at Empire," Davis said flatly. "We can't get around the building." He looked at Construction. "Tear it down," he said. "Meeting adjourned."

Later that day he looked south from the roof. The Destruction team had the top ten floors off the Empire State Building and a corner cut off the fortieth floor with a lane of traffic whipping through it. The flow was good and he smiled. He couldn't remember doing anything so necessary before.

■ ■ ■

For a Journal Entry . . .

Technology is perhaps a mixed blessing. Examine, if you will, the effect of technology on the species *Homo sapiens.* Are we the better or the worse for it? Is it the answer to our problems, or the cause of them, or both? What would we do without it?

For Your Consideration . . .

1. In what ways is the world presented in "Traffic Problem" an extension of our own world?
2. Does this story seem typically American? Why or why not?
3. How does "Traffic Problem" demonstrate a total disregard for human life?
4. Discuss *satire* briefly in your class. Why is "Traffic Problem" a good example of satire?

5. Does the world of "Traffic Problem" seem a possible world? Or do you think mankind will solve his "traffic problems" before it comes to this?

Notes

PAGE

189 *quadruple*—four times
189 *alighting*—getting out
189 *CO filters*—masks to protect against carbon monoxide
189 *hurtled*—rushed violently
190 *spur route*—a portion of a main freeway that sidetracks into a downtown section and then rejoins the freeway
190 *derricks*—construction equipment used in lifting and moving heavy objects
190 *steel girders*—steel beams used in construction
190 *casualty*—anyone hurt or killed in an accident or war
190 *horrendous*—terrible
191 *shuttled off*—directed off, forced off
191 *clogging*—filling so that nothing can get through
191 *lower-echelon*—low-ranking
191 *palsied*—shaking
191 *audio*—sound
192 *clover leaf*—a meeting place of several different freeways with on-and-off ramps and lanes for changing to another freeway
193 *gauged*—measured
193 *catapulted*—hurled or thrown violently
194 *appeased*—pacified
194 *inevitable*—unavoidable
195 *incredulous*—unbelieving
195 *bastion*—stronghold
196 *carbon monoxide*—a deadly gas that is colorless and odorless
196 *plummeted*—fell straight down

Nightfall

by Isaac Asimov

There is no way to categorize Doctor Asimov. He teaches biochemistry, but not too much of late, since he needs the time to write his nonfiction books, books about Shakespeare, the Bible—and stellar physics. And he is still writing science fiction, although he could safely rest upon his past successes, such as novels like *Foundation*, as well as all of the robot stories so closely associated with his name and the series of space adventures under the name of Paul French. In "Nightfall" he describes what really happens on a world where the stars *do* come out only once in a thousand years.

* * *

If the stars should appear one night in a thousand years, how would men believe and adore, and preserve for many generations the remembrance of the city of God!—Emerson

Aton 77, director of Saro University, thrust out a belligerent lower lip and glared at the young newspaperman in a hot fury.

Theremon 762 took that fury in his stride. In his earlier days, when his now widely syndicated column was only a mad idea in a cub reporter's mind, he had specialized in "impossible" interviews. It had cost him bruises, black eyes, and broken bones; but it had given him an ample supply of coolness and self-confidence.

So he lowered the outthrust hand that had been so pointedly ignored and calmly waited for the aged director to get over the worst. Astronomers were queer ducks, anyway, and if Aton's actions of the last two months meant anything, this same Aton was the queer-duckiest of the lot.

Aton 77 found his voice, and though it trembled with restrained emotion, the careful, somewhat pedantic, phraseology, for which the famous astronomer was noted, did not abandon him.

"Sir," he said, "you display an infernal gall in coming to me with that impudent proposition of yours."

The husky telephotographer of the Observatory, Beenay 25, thrust a tongue's tip across dry lips and interposed nervously, "Now, sir, after all—"

The director turned to him and lifted a white eyebrow. "Do not interfere, Beenay. I will credit you with good intentions in bringing this man here; but I will tolerate no insubordination now."

Theremon decided it was time to take a part. "Director Aton, if you'll let me finish what I started saying I think—"

"I don't believe, young man," retorted Aton, "that anything you could say now would count much as compared with your daily columns of these last two months. You have led a vast newspaper campaign against the efforts of myself and my colleagues to organize the world against the menace which it is now too late to avert. You have done your best with your highly personal attacks to make the staff of this Observatory objects of ridicule."

The director lifted the copy of the *Saro City Chronicle* on the table and shook it at Theremon furiously. "Even a person of your well-known impudence should have hesitated before coming to me with a request that he be allowed to cover today's events for his paper. Of all newsmen, you!"

Aton dashed the newspaper to the floor, strode to the window and clasped his arms behind his back.

"You may leave," he snapped over his shoulder. He stared moodily out at the skyline where Gamma, the brightest of the planet's six suns, was setting. It had already faded and yellowed into the horizon mists, and Aton knew he would never see it again as a sane man.

He whirled. "No, wait, come here!" He gestured peremptorily. "I'll give you your story."

The newsman had made no motion to leave, and now he approached the old man slowly. Aton gestured outward, "Of the six suns, only Beta is left in the sky. Do you see it?"

The question was rather unnecessary. Beta was almost at zenith; its ruddy light flooding the landscape to an unusual orange as the brilliant rays of setting Gamma died. Beta was at aphelion. It was small; smaller than Theremon had ever seen it before, and for the moment it was undisputed ruler of Lagash's sky.

Lagash's own sun, Alpha, the one about which it revolved, was at the antipodes; as were the two distant companion pairs. The red dwarf Beta—Alpha's immediate companion—was alone, grimly alone.

Aton's upturned face flushed redly in the sunlight. "In just under four hours," he said, "civilization, as we know it, comes to an end. It will do so because, as you see, Beta is the only sun in the sky." He smiled grimly. "Print that! There'll be no one to read it."

"But if it turns out that four hours pass—and another four—and nothing happens?" asked Theremon softly.

"Don't let that worry you. Enough will happen."

"Granted! And *still*—if nothing happens?"

For a second time, Beenay 25 spoke, "Sir, I think you ought to listen to him."

Theremon said, "Put it to a vote, Director Aton."

There was a stir among the remaining five members of the Observatory staff, who till now had maintained an attitude of wary neutrality.

"That," stated Aton flatly, "is not necessary." He drew out his pocket watch. "Since your good friend, Beenay, insists so urgently, I will give you five minutes. Talk away."

"Good! Now, just what difference would it make if you allowed me to take down an eyewitness account of what's to come? If your prediction comes true, my presence won't hurt; for in that case my column would never be written. On the other hand, if nothing comes of it, you will just have to expect ridicule or worse. It would be wise to leave that ridicule to friendly hands."

Aton snorted. "Do you mean yours when you speak of friendly hands?"

"Certainly!" Theremon sat down and crossed his legs. "My columns may have been a little rough at times, but I gave you people the benefit of the doubt every time. After all, this is not the century to preach 'the end of the world is at hand' to Lagash. You have to understand that people don't believe the 'Book of Revelations' any more, and it annoys them to have scientists turn about face and tell us the Cultists are right after all—"

"No such thing, young man," interrupted Aton. "While a great deal of our data has been supplied us by the Cult, our results contain none of the Cult's mysticism. Facts are facts, and the Cult's so-called 'mythology' *has* certain facts behind it. We've exposed them and ripped away their mystery. I assure you that the Cult hates us now worse than you do."

"I don't hate you. I'm just trying to tell you that the public is in an ugly humor. They're angry."

Aton twisted his mouth in derision. "Let them be angry."

"Yes, but what about tomorrow?"

"There'll be no tomorrow!"

"But if there is. Say that there is—just to see what happens. That anger might take shape into something serious. After all, you know, business has taken a nose dive these last two months. Investors don't really believe the world is coming to an end, but just the same they're being cagy with their money until it's all over. Johnny Public doesn't believe you, either, but the new spring furniture might as well wait a few months—just to make sure.

"You see the point. Just as soon as this is all over, the business interests will be after your hide. They'll say that if crackpots—begging your pardon—can upset the country's prosperity any time they want simply by making some cockeyed prediction—it's up to the planet to prevent them. The sparks will fly, sir."

The director regarded the columnist sternly. "And just what were you proposing to do to help the situation?"

"Well," grinned Theremon, "I was proposing to take charge of the publicity. I can handle things so that only the ridiculous side will show. It would be hard to stand, I admit, because I'd have to make you all out to be a bunch of gibbering idiots, but if I can get people laughing at you, they might forget to be angry. In return for that, all my publisher asks is an exclusive story."

Beenay nodded and burst out, "Sir, the rest of us think he's right. These last two months we've considered everything but the million-to-one chance that there is an error somewhere in our theory or in our calculations. We ought to take care of that, too."

There was a murmur of agreement from the men grouped about the table, and Aton's expression became that of one who found his mouth full of something bitter and couldn't get rid of it.

"You may stay if you wish, then. You will kindly refrain, however, from hampering us in our duties in any way. You will also remember that I am in charge of all activities here, and in spite of your opinions as expressed in your columns, I will expect full cooperation and full respect—"

His hands were behind his back, and his wrinkled face thrust forward determinedly as he spoke. He might have continued indefinitely but for the intrusion of a new voice.

"Hello, hello, hello!" It came in a high tenor, and the plump cheeks of the newcomer expanded in a pleased smile. "What's this morguelike atmosphere about here? No one's losing his nerve, I hope."

Aton started in consternation and said peevishly, "Now what the devil are you doing here, Sheerin? I thought you were going to stay behind in the Hideout."

Sheerin laughed and dropped his tubby figure into a chair. "Hideout be blowed! The place bored me. I wanted to be here, where things are getting hot. Don't you suppose I have my share of curiosity? I want to see these Stars the Cultists are forever speaking about." He rubbed his hands and added in a soberer tone, "It's freezing outside. The wind's enough to hang icicles on your nose. Beta doesn't seem to give any heat at all, at the distance it is."

The white-haired director ground his teeth in sudden exasperation, "Why do you go out of your way to do crazy things, Sheerin? What kind of good are you around here?"

"What kind of good am I around there?" Sheerin spread his palms in comical resignation. "A psychologist isn't worth his salt in the Hideout. They need men of action and strong, healthy women that can breed children. Me? I'm a hundred pounds too heavy for a man of action, and I wouldn't be a success at breeding children. So why bother them with an extra mouth to feed? I feel better over here."

Theremon spoke briskly, "Just what is the Hideout, sir?"

Sheerin seemed to see the columnist for the first time. He frowned and blew his ample cheeks out, "And just who in Lagash are you, redhead?"

Aton compressed his lips and then muttered sullenly, "That's Theremon 762, the newspaper fellow. I suppose you've heard of him."

The columnist offered his hand. "And, of course, you're Sheerin 501 of Saro University. I've heard of you." Then he repeated, "What is this Hideout, sir?"

"Well," said Sheerin, "we have managed to convince a few people of the validity of our prophecy of—er—doom, to be spectacular about it, and those few have taken proper measures. They consist mainly of the immediate members of the families of the Observatory staff, certain of the faculty of Saro University and a few outsiders. Altogether, they number about three hundred, but three-quarters are women and children."

"I see! They're supposed to hide where the Darkness and the—er—Stars can't get at them, and then hold out when the rest of the world goes poof."

"If they can. It won't be easy. With all of mankind insane; with the great cities going up in flames—environment will not be conducive to survival. But they have food, water, shelter, and weapons—"

"They've got more," said Aton. "They've got all our records, except for what we will collect today. Those records will mean everything to the next cycle, and *that's* what must survive. The rest can go hang."

Theremon whistled a long, low whistle and sat brooding for several minutes. The men about the table had brought out a multichess board and started a six-member game. Moves were made rapidly and in silence. All eyes bent in furious concentration on the board. Theremon watched them intently and then rose and approached Aton, who sat apart in whispered conversation with Sheerin.

"Listen," he said, "Let's go somewhere where we won't bother the rest of the fellows. I want to ask some questions."

The aged astronomer frowned sourly at him, but Sheerin chirped up, "Certainly. It will do me good to talk. It always does. Aton was telling me about your ideas concerning world reaction to a failure of the prediction—and I agree with you. I read your column pretty regularly, by the way, and as a general thing I like your views."

"Please, Sheerin," growled Aton.

"Eh? Oh, all right. We'll go into the next room. It has softer chairs, anyway."

There were softer chairs in the next room. There were also thick red curtains on the windows and a maroon carpet on the floor. With the bricky light of Beta pouring in, the general effect was one of dried blood.

Theremon shuddered, "Say, I'd give ten credits for a decent dose of white light for just a second. I wish Gamma or Delta were in the sky."

"What are your questions?" asked Aton. "Please remember that our time is limited. In a little over an hour and a quarter we're going upstairs, and after that there will be no time for talk."

"Well, here it is." Theremon leaned back and folded his hands on his chest. "You people seem so all-fired serious about this that I'm beginning to believe you. Would you mind explaining what it's all about?"

Aton exploded, "Do you mean to sit there and tell me that you've been bombarding us with ridicule without even finding out what we've been trying to say?"

The columnist grinned sheepishly. "It's not that bad, sir. I've got the general idea. You say that there is going to be a world-wide Darkness in a few hours and that all mankind will go violently insane. What I want now is the science behind it."

"No, you don't. No, you don't," broke in Sheerin. "If you ask Aton for that—supposing him to be in the mood to answer at all—he'll trot out pages of figures and volumes of graphs. You won't make head or tail of it. Now if you were to ask *me,* I could give you the layman's standpoint."

"All right; I ask you."

"Then first I'd like a drink." He rubbed his hands and looked at Aton.

"Water?" grunted Aton.

"Don't be silly!"

"Don't you be silly. No alcohol today. It would be too easy to get my men drunk. I can't afford to tempt them."

The psychologist grumbled wordlessly. He turned to Theremon, impaled him with his sharp eyes, and began.

"You realize, of course, that the history of civilization on Lagash displays a cyclic character—but I mean, *cyclic!*"

"I know," replied Theremon cautiously, "that that is the current archeological theory. Has it been accepted as a fact?"

"Just about. In this last century it's been generally agreed upon. This cyclic character is—or, rather, was—one of *the* great mysteries. We've located series of civilizations, nine of them definitely, and indications of others as well, all of which have reached heights comparable to our own, and all of which, without exception, were destroyed by fire at the very height of their culture.

"And no one could tell why. All centers of culture were thoroughly gutted by fire, with nothing left behind to give a hint as to the cause."

Theremon was following closely. "Wasn't there a Stone Age, too?"

"Probably, but as yet, practically nothing is known of it, except that men of that age were little more than rather intelligent apes. We can forget about that."

"I see. Go on!"

"There have been explanations of these recurrent catastrophes, all of a more or less fantastic nature. Some say that there are periodic rains of fire; some that Lagash passes through a sun every so often; some even wilder things. But there is one theory, quite different from all of these, that has been handed down over a period of centuries."

"I know. You mean this myth of the 'Stars' that the Cultists have in their 'Book of Revelations.' "

"Exactly," rejoined Sheerin with satisfaction. "The Cultists said that every two thousand and fifty years Lagash entered a huge cave, so that all the suns disappeared, and there came *total darkness all over the world!* And then, they say, things called Stars appeared, which robbed men of their souls and left them unreasoning brutes, so that they destroyed the civilization they themselves had built up. Of course, they mix all this up with a lot of religio-mystic notions, but that's the central idea."

There was a short pause in which Sheerin drew a long breath. "And now we come to the Theory of Universal Gravitation." He pronounced the phrase so that the capital letters sounded—and at that point Aton turned from the window, snorted loudly, and stalked out of the room.

The two stared after him, and Theremon said, "What's wrong?"

"Nothing in particular," replied Sheerin. "Two of the men were due several hours ago and haven't shown up yet. He's terrifically shorthanded, of course, because all but the really essential men have gone to the Hideout."

"You don't think the two deserted, do you?"

"Who? Faro and Yimot? Of course not. Still, if they're not back within the hour, things would be a little sticky." He got to his feet suddenly, and his eyes twinkled. "Anyway, as long as Aton is gone—"

Tiptoeing to the nearest window, he squatted, and from the low window box beneath withdrew a bottle of red liquid that gurgled suggestively when he shook it.

"I *thought* Aton didn't know about this," he remarked as he trotted back to the table. "Here! We've only got one glass so, as the guest, you can have it. I'll keep the bottle." And he filled the tiny cup with judicious care.

Theremon rose to protest, but Sheerin eyed him sternly. "Respect your elders, young man."

The newsman seated himself with a look of pain and anguish on his face. "Go ahead, then, you old villain."

The psychologist's Adam's apple wobbled as the bottle upended, and then, with a satisfied grunt and a smack of the lips, he began again.

"But what do you know about gravitation?"

"Nothing, except that it is a very recent development, not too well established, and that the math is so hard that only twelve men in Lagash are supposed to understand it."

"*Tcha!* Nonsense! Boloney! I can give you all the essential math in a sentence. The Law of Universal Gravitation states that there exists a cohesive force among all bodies of the universe, such that the amount of this force between any two given bodies is proportional to the product of their masses divided by the square of the distance between them."

"Is that all?"

"That's enough! It took four hundred years to develop it."

"Why that long? It sounded simple enough, the way you said it."

"Because great laws are not divined by flashes of inspiration, whatever you may think. It usually takes the combined work of a world full of scientists over a period of centuries. After Genovi 41 discovered that Lagash rotated about the sun Alpha, rather than vice versa—and that was four hundred years ago—astronomers have been working. The complex motions of the six suns were recorded and analyzed and unwoven. Theory after theory was advanced and checked and counterchecked and modified and abandoned and revived and converted to something else. It was a devil of a job."

Theremon nodded thoughtfully and held out his glass for more liquor. Sheerin grudgingly allowed a few ruby drops to leave the bottle.

"It was twenty years ago," he continued after remoistening his own throat, "that it was finally demonstrated that the Law of Universal Gravitation accounted exactly for the orbital motions of the six suns. It was a great triumph."

Sheerin stood up and walked to the window, still clutching his bottle, "And now we're getting to the point. In the last decade, the motions of Lagash about Alpha were computed according to gravity, and *it did not account for the orbit observed;* not even when all perturbations due to the other suns were included. Either the law was invalid, or there was another, as yet unknown, factor involved."

Theremon joined Sheerin at the window and gazed out past the wooded slopes to where the spires of Saro City gleamed bloodily on the horizon. The newsman felt the tension of uncertainty grow within him as he cast a short glance at Beta. It glowered redly at Zenith, dwarfed and evil.

"Go ahead, sir," he said softly.

Sheerin replied, "Astronomers stumbled about for years, each proposed theory more untenable than the one before—until Aton had the inspiration of calling in the Cult. The head of the Cult, Sor 5, had access to certain data that simplified the problem considerably. Aton set to work on a new track.

"What if there were another nonluminous planetary body such as Lagash? If there were, you know, it would shine only by reflected light, and if it were composed of bluish rock, as Lagash itself largely is, then, in the redness of the sky, the eternal blaze of the suns would make it invisible—drown it out completely."

Theremon whistled, "What a screwy idea!"

"You think *that's* screwy? Listen to this: Suppose this body rotated about Lagash at such a distance and in such an orbit and had such a mass that its attraction would exactly account for the deviations of Lagash's orbit from theory—do you know what would happen?"

The columnist shook his head.

"Well, sometimes this body would get in the way of a sun." And Sheerin emptied what remained in the bottle at a draft.

"And it does, I suppose," said Theremon flatly.

"Yes! But only one sun lies in its plane of revolutions." He jerked a thumb at the shrunken sun above. "Beta! And it has been shown that the eclipse will occur only when the arrangement of the suns is such that Beta is alone in its hemisphere and at maximum distance, at which time the moon is invariably at minimum distance. The eclipse that results, with the moon seven times the apparent diameter of Beta, covers all of Lagash and lasts well over half a day, so that no spot on the planet escapes the effects. *That eclipse comes once every two thousand and forty-nine years.*"

Theremon's face was drawn into an expressionless mask. "And that's my story?"

The psychologist nodded. "That's all of it. First the eclipse—which will start in three-quarters of an hour—then universal Darkness, and, maybe, these mysterious Stars—then madness, and end of the cycle."

He brooded. "We had two months' leeway—we at the Observatory—and that wasn't enough time to persuade Lagash of the danger. Two centuries might not have been enough. But our records are at the Hideout, and today we photograph the eclipse. The next cycle will *start off* with the truth, and when the *next* eclipse comes, mankind will at last be ready for it. Come to think of it, that's part of your story, too."

A thin wind ruffled the curtains at the window as Theremon opened it and leaned out. It played coldly with his hair as he stared at the crimson sunlight on his hand. Then he turned in sudden rebellion.

"What is there in Darkness to drive *me* mad?"

Sheerin smiled to himself as he spun the empty liquor bottle with abstracted motions of his hand. "Have you ever experienced Darkness, young man?"

The newsman leaned against the wall and considered. "No. Can't say I have. But I know what it is. Just—uh—" He made vague motions with his fingers, and then brightened. "Just no light. Like in caves."

"Have you ever been in a cave?"

"In a *cave!* Of course not!"

"I thought not. *I* tried last week—just to see—but I got out in a hurry. I went in until the mouth of the cave was just visible as a blur of light, with black everywhere else. I never thought a person my weight could run that fast."

Theremon's lip curled. "Well, if it comes to that, I guess I wouldn't have run, if I had been there."

The psychologist studied the young man with an annoyed frown.

"My, don't you talk big! I dare you to draw the curtain."

Theremon looked his surprise and said, "What for? If we had

four or five suns out there we might want to cut the light down a bit for comfort, but now we haven't enough light as it is."

"That's the point. Just draw the curtain; then come here and sit down."

"All right." Theremon reached for the tasseled string and jerked. The red curtain slid across the wide window, the brass rings hissing their way along the crossbar, and a dusk-red shadow clamped down on the room.

Theremon's footsteps sounded hollowly in the silence as he made his way to the table, and then they stopped halfway. "I can't see you, sir," he whispered.

"Feel your way," ordered Sheerin in a strained voice.

"But I can't see you, sir." The newsman was breathing harshly. "I can't see anything."

"What did you expect?" came the grim reply. "Come here and sit down!"

The footsteps sounded again, waveringly, approaching slowly. There was the sound of someone fumbling with a chair. Theremon's voice came thinly, "Here I am. I feel . . . *ulp* . . . all right."

"You like it, do you?"

"N-no. It's pretty awful. The walls seem to be—" He paused. "They seem to be closing in on me. I keep wanting to push them away. But I'm not going *mad!* In fact, the feeling isn't as bad as it was."

"All right. Draw the curtain back again."

There were cautious footsteps through the dark, the rustle of Theremon's body against the curtain as he felt for the tassel, and then the triumphant *ro-o-o-osh* of the curtain slithering back. Red light flooded the room, and with a cry of joy Theremon looked up at the sun.

Sheerin wiped the moistness off his forehead with the back of a hand and said shakily, "And that was just a dark room."

"It can be stood," said Theremon lightly.

"Yes, a dark room can. But were you at the Jonglor Centennial Exposition two years ago?"

"No, it so happens I never got around to it. Six thousand miles was just a bit too much to travel, even for the exposition."

"Well, I was there. You remember hearing about the 'Tunnel of Mystery' that broke all records in the amusement area—for the first month or so, anyway?"

"Yes. Wasn't there some fuss about it?"

"Very little. It was hushed up. You see, that Tunnel of Mystery was just a mile-long tunnel—with no lights. You got into a little open car and jolted along through Darkness for fifteen minutes. It was very popular—while it lasted."

"Popular?"

"Certainly. There's a fascination in being frightened *when it's part of a game.* A baby is born with three instinctive fears: of loud noises, of falling, and of the absence of light. That's why it's considered so funny to jump at someone and shout 'Boo!' That's why it's such fun to ride a roller coaster. And that's why that Tunnel of Mystery started cleaning up. People came out of that Darkness shaking, breathless, half dead with fear, but they kept on paying to get in."

"Wait a while, I remember now. Some people came out dead, didn't they? There were rumors of that after it shut down."

The psychologist snorted. "Bah! Two or three died. That was nothing! They paid off the families of the dead ones and argued the Jonglor City Council into forgetting it. After all, they said, if people with weak hearts want to go through the tunnel, it was at their own risk—and besides, it wouldn't happen again. So they put a doctor in the front office and had every customer go through a physical examination before getting into the car. That actually *boosted* ticket sales."

"Well, then?"

"But, you see, there was something else. People sometimes came out in perfect order, except that they refused to go into buildings—any buildings; including palaces, mansions, apartment houses, tenements, cottages, huts, shacks, lean-tos, and tents."

Theremon looked shocked. "You mean they refused to come in out of the open. Where'd they sleep?"

"In the open."

"They should have *forced* them inside."

"Oh, they did, they did. Whereupon these people went into violent hysterics and did their best to bat their brains out against the nearest wall. Once you got them inside, you couldn't keep them there without a straitjacket and a shot of morphine."

"They must have been crazy."

"Which is exactly what they were. One person out of every ten who went into that tunnel came out that way. They called in the psychologists, and we did the only thing possible. We closed down the exhibit." He spread his hands.

"What was the matter with these people?" asked Theremon finally.

"Essentially the same thing that was the matter with you when you thought the walls of the room were crushing in on you in the dark. There is a psychological term for mankind's instinctive fear of the absence of light. We call it 'claustrophobia,' because the lack of light is always tied up with enclosed places, so that fear of one is fear of the other. You see?"

"And those people of the tunnel?"

"Those people of the tunnel consisted of those unfortunates whose mentality did not quite possess the resiliency to overcome the claustrophobia that overtook them in the Darkness. Fifteen minutes without light is a long time; you only had two or three minutes, and I believe you were fairly upset.

"The people of the tunnel had what is called a 'claustrophobic fixation.' Their latent fear of Darkness and enclosed places had crystallized and become active, and, as far as we can tell, permanent. *That's* what fifteen minutes in the dark will do."

There was a long silence, and Theremon's forehead wrinkled slowly into a frown. "I don't believe it's that bad."

"You mean you don't want to believe," snapped Sheerin. "You're afraid to believe. Look out the window!"

Theremon did so, and the psychologist continued without pausing, "Imagine Darkness—everywhere. No light, as far as you can see. The houses, the trees, the fields, the earth, the sky—*black!* And Stars thrown in, for all I know—whatever *they* are. Can you conceive it?"

"Yes, I can," declared Theremon truculently.

And Sheerin slammed his fist down upon the table in sudden passion. "You lie! You can't conceive that. Your brain wasn't built for the conception any more than it was built for the conception of infinity or of eternity. You can only talk about it. A fraction of the reality upsets you, and when the real thing comes, your brain is going to be presented with a phenomenon outside its limits of comprehension. You will go mad, completely and permanently! There is no question of it!"

He added sadly, "And another couple of millenniums of painful struggle comes to nothing. Tomorrow there won't be a city standing unharmed in all Lagash."

Theremon recovered part of his mental equilibrium. "That doesn't follow. I still don't see that I can go loony just because there isn't a Sun in the sky—but even if I did, and everyone else did, how does that harm the cities? Are we going to blow them down?"

But Sheerin was angry, too. "If you were in Darkness, what would you want more than anything else; what would it be that every instinct would call for? Light, damn you, *light!*"

"Well?"

"And how would you get light?"

"I don't know," said Theremon flatly.

"What's the *only* way to get light, short of the sun?"

"How should I know?"

They were standing face to face and nose to nose.

Sheerin said, "You burn something, mister. Ever see a forest fire? Ever go camping and cook a stew over a wood fire? Heat isn't the only thing burning wood gives off, you know. It gives off light, and people know that. And when it's dark they want light, and they're going to *get it.*"

"So they burn wood?"

"So they burn whatever they can get. They've got to have light. They've got to burn something, and wood isn't handy—so they'll burn whatever is nearest. They'll have their light—and every center of habitation goes up in flames!"

Eyes held each other as though the whole matter were a personal affair of respective will powers, and then Theremon broke away wordlessly. His breathing was harsh and ragged, and he scarcely noted the sudden hubbub that came from the adjoining room behind the closed door.

Sheerin spoke, and it was with an effort that he made it sound matter-of-fact. "I think I heard Yimot's voice. He and Faro are probably back. Let's go in and see what kept them."

"Might as well!" muttered Theremon. He drew a long breath and seemed to shake himself. The tension was broken.

The room was in an uproar, with members of the staff clustering about two young men who were removing outer garments even as they parried the miscellany of questions being thrown at them.

Aton bustled through the crowd and faced the newcomers angrily. "Do you realize that it's less than half an hour before deadline? Where have you two been?"

Faro 24 seated himself and rubbed his hands. His cheeks were red with the outdoor chill. "Yimot and I have just finished carrying through a little crazy experiment of our own. We've been trying to see if we couldn't construct an arrangement by which we could simulate the appearance of Darkness and Stars so as to get an advance notion as to how it looked."

There was a confused murmur from the listeners, and a sudden look of interest entered Aton's eyes. "There wasn't anything said of this before. How did you go about it?"

"Well," said Faro, "the idea came to Yimot and myself long ago, and we've been working it out in our spare time. Yimot knew of a low one-story house down in the city with a domed roof—it had once been used as a museum, I think. Anyway, we bought it—"

"Where did you get the money?" interrupted Aton peremptorily.

"Our bank accounts," grunted Yimot 70. "It cost two thousand credits." Then, defensively, "Well, what of it? Tomorrow, two thousand credits will be two thousand pieces of paper. That's all."

"Sure," agreed Faro. "We bought the place and rigged it up with black velvet from top to bottom so as to get as perfect a Darkness as possible. Then we punched tiny holes in the ceiling and through the roof and covered them with little metal caps, all of which could be shoved aside simultaneously at the close of a switch. At least, we didn't do that part ourselves; we got a carpenter and an electrician and some others—money didn't count. The point was that we could get the light to shine through those holes in the roof, so that we could get a starlike effect."

Not a breath was drawn during the pause that followed. Aton said stiffly:

"You had no right to make a private—"

Faro seemed abashed. "I know, sir—but, frankly, Yimot and I thought the experiment was a little dangerous. If the effect really worked, we half expected to go mad—from what Sheerin says about all this, we thought that would be rather likely. We wanted to take the risk ourselves. Of course, if we found we could retain sanity, it occurred to us that we might develop immunity to the real thing, and then expose the rest of you to the same thing. But things didn't work out at all—"

"Why, what happened?"

It was Yimot who answered. "We shut ourselves in and allowed our eyes to get accustomed to the dark. It's an extremely creepy feeling because the total Darkness makes you feel as if the walls and ceiling are crushing in on you. But we got over that and pulled the switch. The caps fell away and the roof glittered all over with little dots of light—"

"Well?"

"Well—nothing. That was the whacky part of it. Nothing happened. It was just a roof with holes in it, and that's just what it looked like. We tried it over and over again—that's what kept us so late—but there just isn't any effect at all."

There followed a shocked silence, and all eyes turned to Sheerin, who sat motionless, mouth open.

Theremon was the first to speak. "You know what this does to this whole theory you've built up, Sheerin, don't you?" He was grinning with relief.

But Sheerin raised his hand. "Now wait a while. Just let me think this through." And then he snapped his fingers, and when he lifted his head there was neither surprise nor uncertainty in his eyes. "Of course—"

He never finished. From somewhere up above there sounded a sharp clang, and Beenay, starting to his feet, dashed up the stairs with a "What the devil!"

The rest followed after.

Things happened quickly. Once up in the dome, Beenay cast one horrified glance at the shattered photographic plates and at the man bending over them; and then hurled himself fiercely at the intruder, getting a death grip on his throat. There was a wild threshing, and as others of the staff joined in, the stranger was swallowed up and smothered under the weight of half a dozen angry men.

Aton came up last, breathing heavily. "Let him up!"

There was a reluctant unscrambling and the stranger, panting harshly, with his clothes torn and his forehead bruised, was hauled to his feet. He had a short yellow beard curled elaborately in the style affected by the Cultists.

Beenay shifted his hold to a collar grip and shook the man savagely. "All right, rat, what's the idea? These plates—"

"I wasn't after *them,*" retorted the Cultist coldly. "That was an accident."

Beenay followed his glowering stare and snarled, "I see. You were after the cameras themselves. The accident with the plates was a stroke of luck for you, then. If you had touched Snapping Bertha or any of the others, you would have died by slow torture. As it is—" He drew his fist back.

Aton grabbed his sleeve. "Stop that! Let him go!"

The young technician wavered, and his arm dropped reluctantly. Aton pushed him aside and confronted the Cultist. "You're Latimer, aren't you?"

The Cultist bowed stiffly and indicated the symbol upon his hip. "I am Latimer 25, adjutant of the third class to his serenity, Sor 5."

"And"—Aton's white eyebrows lifted—"you were with his serenity when he visited me last week, weren't you?"

Latimer bowed a second time.

"Now, then, what do you want?"

"Nothing that you would give me of your own free will."

"Sor 5 sent you, I suppose—or is this your own idea?"

"I won't answer that question."

"Will there be any further visitors?"

"I won't answer that, either."

Aton glanced at his timepiece and scowled. "Now, man, what

is it your master wants of me? I have fulfilled my end of the bargain."

Latimer smiled faintly, but said nothing.

"I asked him," continued Aton angrily, "for data only the Cult could supply, and it was given to me. For that, thank you. In return, I promised to prove the essential truth of the creed of the Cult."

"There was no need to prove that," came the proud retort. "It stands proven by the 'Book of Revelations.' "

"For the handful that constitute the Cult, yes. Don't pretend to mistake my meaning. I offered to present scientific backing for your beliefs. And I did!"

The Cultist's eyes narrowed bitterly. "Yes, you did—with a fox's subtlety, for your pretended explanation backed our beliefs, and at the same time removed all necessity for them. You made of the Darkness and of the Stars a natural phenomenon, and removed all its real significance. That was blasphemy."

"If so, the fault isn't mine. The facts exist. What can I do but state them?"

"Your 'facts' are a fraud and a delusion."

Aton stamped angrily. "How do you know?"

And the answer came with the certainty of absolute faith. "I *know!*"

The director purpled and Beenay whispered urgently. Aton waved him silent. "And what does Sor 5 want us to do? He still thinks, I suppose, that in trying to warn the world to take measures against the menace of madness, we are placing innumerable souls in jeopardy. We aren't succeeding, if that means anything to him."

"The attempt itself has done harm enough and your vicious effort to gain information by means of your devilish instruments must be stopped. We obey the will of their Stars, and I only regret that my clumsiness prevented me from wrecking your infernal devices."

"It wouldn't have done you too much good," returned Aton. "All our data, except for the direct evidence we intend collecting right now, is already safely cached and well beyond possibility of harm." He smiled grimly. "But that does not affect your present status as an attempted burglar and criminal."

He turned to the men behind him. "Someone call the police at Saro City."

There was a cry of distaste from Sheerin. "Damn it, Aton, what's wrong with you? There's no time for that. Here"—he bustled his way forward—"let me handle this."

Aton stared down his nose at the psychologist. "This is not the time for your monkeyshines, Sheerin. Will you please let me handle this my own way? Right now you are a complete outsider here, and don't forget it."

Sheerin's mouth twisted eloquently. "Now why should we go to the impossible trouble of calling the police—with Beta's eclipse a matter of minutes from now—when this young man here is perfectly willing to pledge his word of honor to remain and cause no trouble whatsoever?"

The Cultist answered promptly, "I will do no such thing. You're free to do what you want, but it's only fair to warn you that just as soon as I get my chance I'm going to finish what I came out here to do. If it's my word of honor you're relying on, you'd better call the police."

Sheerin smiled in a friendly fashion. "You're a determined cuss, aren't you? Well, I'll explain something. Do you see that young man at the window? He's a strong, husky fellow, quite handy with his fists, and he's an outsider besides. Once the eclipse starts there will be nothing for him to do except keep an eye on you. Besides him, there will be myself—a little too stout for active fisticuffs, but still able to help."

"Well, what of it?" demanded Latimer frozenly.

"Listen and I'll tell you," was the reply. "Just as soon as the eclipse starts, we're going to take you, Theremon and I, and deposit you in a little closet with one door, to which is attached one giant lock and no windows. You will remain there for the duration."

"And afterward," breathed Latimer fiercely, "there'll be no one to let me out. I know as well as you do what the coming of the Stars means—I know it far better than you. With all your minds gone, you are not likely to free me. Suffocation or slow starvation, is it? About what I might have expected from a group of scientists. But I don't give my word. It's a matter of principle, and I won't discuss it further."

Aton seemed perturbed. His faded eyes were troubled. "Really, Sheerin, locking him—"

"Please!" Sheerin motioned him impatiently to silence. "I don't think for a moment things will go that far. Latimer has just tried a clever little bluff, but I'm not a psychologist just because I like the sound of the word." He grinned at the Cultist. "Come now, you don't really think I'm trying anything as crude as slow starvation. My dear Latimer, if I lock you in the closet, you are not going to see the Darkness, and you are not going to see the Stars. It does not take much of a knowledge of the fundamental creed of the Cult to realize that for you to be hidden from the Stars when they appear means the loss of your immortal soul. Now, I believe you to be an honorable man. I'll accept your word of honor to make no further effort to disrupt proceedings if you'll offer it."

A vein throbbed in Latimer's temple, and he seemed to shrink within himself as he said thickly, "You have it!" And then he added with swift fury, "But it is my consolation that you will all be damned for your deeds of today." He turned on his heel and stalked to the high three-legged stool by the door.

Sheerin nodded to the columnist. "Take a seat next to him, Theremon—just as a formality. Hey, Theremon!"

But the newspaperman didn't move. He had gone pale to the lips. "Look at that!" The finger he pointed toward the sky shook, and his voice was dry and cracked.

There was one simultaneous gasp as every eye followed the pointing finger and, for one breathless moment, stared frozenly.

Beta was chipped on one side!

The tiny bit of encroaching blackness was perhaps the width of a fingernail, but to the staring watchers it magnified itself into the crack of doom.

Only for a moment they watched, and after that there was a shrieking confusion that was even shorter of duration and which gave way to an orderly scurry of activity—each man at his prescribed job. At the crucial moment there was no time for emotion. The men were merely scientists with work to do. Even Aton had melted away.

Sheerin said prosaically, "First contact must have been made fifteen minutes ago. A little early, but pretty good considering the uncertainties involved in the calculation." He looked about him and then tiptoed to Theremon, who still remained staring out the window, and dragged him away gently.

"Aton is furious," he whispered, "so stay away. He missed first contact on account of this fuss with Latimer, and if you get in his way he'll have you thrown out the window."

Theremon nodded shortly and sat down. Sheerin stared in surprise at him.

"The devil, man," he exclaimed, "you're shaking."

"Eh?" Theremon licked dry lips and then tried to smile. "I don't feel very well, and that's a fact."

The psychologist's eyes hardened. "You're not losing your nerve?"

"No!" cried Theremon in a flash of indignation. "Give me a chance, will you? I haven't really believed this rigmarole—not way down beneath, anyway—till just this minute. Give me a chance to get used to the idea. *You've* been preparing yourself for two months or more."

"You're right, at that," replied Sheerin thoughtfully. "Listen! Have you got a family—parents, wife, children?"

Theremon shook his head. "You mean the Hideout, I suppose. No, you don't have to worry about that. I have a sister, but she's two thousand miles away. I don't even know her exact address."

"Well, then, what about yourself? You've got time to get there, and they're one short anyway, since I left. After all, you're not needed here, and you'd make a darned fine addition—"

Theremon looked at the other wearily. "You think I'm scared stiff, don't you? Well, get this, mister, I'm a newspaperman and I've been assigned to cover a story. I intend covering it."

There was a faint smile on the psychologist's face. "I see. Professional honor, is that it?"

"You might call it that. But, man, I'd give my right arm for another bottle of that sockeroo juice even half the size of the one *you* hogged. If ever a fellow needed a drink, I do."

He broke off. Sheerin was nudging him violently. "Do you hear that? Listen!"

Theremon followed the motion of the other's chin and stared at the Cultist, who, oblivious to all about him, faced the window, a look of wild elation on his face, droning to himself the while in singsong fashion.

"What's he saying?" whispered the columnist.

"He's quoting 'Book of Revelations,' fifth chapter," replied Sheerin. Then, urgently, "Keep quiet and listen, I tell you."

The Cultist's voice had risen in a sudden increase of fervor:

> "And it came to pass that in those days the Sun, Beta, held lone vigil in the sky for ever longer periods as the revolutions passed; until such time as for full half a revolution, it alone, shrunken and cold, shone down upon Lagash.
>
> "And men did assemble in the public squares and in the highways, there to debate and to marvel at the sight, for a strange depression had seized them. Their minds were troubled and their speech confused, for the souls of men awaited the coming of the Stars.
>
> "And in the city of Trigon, at high noon, Vendret 2 came forth and said unto the men of Trigon, 'Lo, ye sinners! Though ye scorn the ways of righteousness, yet will the time of reckoning come. Even now the Cave approaches to swallow Lagash; yea, and all it contains.'
>
> "And even as he spoke the lip of the Cave of Darkness passed the edge of Beta so that to all Lagash it was hidden from sight. Loud were the cries of men as it vanished, and great the fear of soul that fell upon them.
>
> "It came to pass that the Darkness of the Cave fell upon Lagash, and there was no light on all the surface of Lagash. Men were even as blinded, nor could one man see his neighbor, though he felt his breath upon his face.
>
> "And in this blackness there appeared the Stars, in countless numbers, and to the strains of ineffable music of a beauty so wondrous that the very leaves of the trees turned to tongues that cried out in wonder.
>
> "And in that moment the souls of men departed from them, and their abandoned bodies became even as beasts; yea, even as brutes of the wild; so that through the blackened streets of the cities of Lagash they prowled with wild cries.

> "From the Stars there then reached down the Heavenly Flame, and where it touched, the cities of Lagash flamed to utter destruction, so that of man and of the works of man nought remained.
>
> "Even then—"

There was a subtle change in Latimer's tone. His eyes had not shifted, but somehow he had become aware of the absorbed attention of the other two. Easily, without pausing for breath, the timbre of his voice shifted and the syllables became more liquid.

Theremon, caught by surprise, stared. The words seemed on the border of familiarity. There was an elusive shift in the accent, a tiny change in the vowel stress; nothing more—yet Latimer had become thoroughly unintelligible.

Sheerin smiled slyly. "He shifted to some old-cycle tongue, probably their traditional second cycle. That was the language in which the 'Book of Revelations' had originally been written, you know."

"It doesn't matter; I've heard enough." Theremon shoved his chair back and brushed his hair back with hands that no longer shook. "I feel much better now."

"You do?" Sheerin seemed mildly surprised.

"I'll say I do. I had a bad case of jitters just a while back. Listening to you and your gravitation and seeing that eclipse start almost finished me. But this"—he jerked a contemptuous thumb at the yellow-bearded Cultist—"*this* is the sort of thing my nurse used to tell me. I've been laughing at that sort of thing all my life. I'm not going to let it scare me *now*."

He drew a deep breath and said with a hectic gaiety, "But if I expect to keep on the good side of myself, I'm going to turn my chair away from the window."

Sheerin said, "Yes, but you'd better talk lower. Aton just lifted his head out of that box he's got it stuck into and gave you a look that should have killed you."

Theremon made a mouth. "I forgot about the old fellow." With elaborate care he turned the chair from the window, cast one distasteful look over his shoulder and said, "It has occurred to me that there must be considerable immunity against this Star madness."

The psychologist did not answer immediately. Beta was past its zenith now, and the square of bloody sunlight that outlined the window upon the floor had lifted into Sheerin's lap. He stared at its dusky color thoughtfully and then bent and squinted into the sun itself.

The chip in its side had grown to a black encroachment that covered a third of Beta. He shuddered, and when he straightened once more his florid cheeks did not contain quite as much color as they had had previously.

With a smile that was almost apologetic, he reversed his chair also. "There are probably two million people in Saro City that are all trying to join the Cult at once in one gigantic revival." Then, ironically, "The Cult is in for an hour of unexampled prosperity. I trust they'll make the most of it. Now, what was it you said?"

"Just this. How do the Cultists manage to keep the 'Book of Revelations' going from cycle to cycle, and how on Lagash did it get written in the first place? There must have been some sort of immunity, for if everyone had gone mad, who would be left to write the book?"

Sheerin stared at his questioner ruefully. "Well, now, young man, there isn't any eyewitness answer to that, but we've got a few damned good notions as to what happened. You see, there are three kinds of people who might remain relatively unaffected. First, the very few who don't see the Stars at all; the blind, those who drink themselves into a stupor at the beginning of the eclipse and remain so to the end. We leave them out—because they aren't really witnesses.

"Then there are children below six, to whom the world as a whole is too new and strange for them to be too frightened at Stars and Darkness. They would be just another item in an already surprising world. You see that, don't you?"

The other nodded doubtfully. "I suppose so."

"Lastly, there are those whose minds are too coarsely grained to be entirely toppled. The very insensitive would be scarcely affected—oh, such people as some of our older, work-broken peasants. Well, the children would have fugitive memories, and that, combined with the confused, incoherent babblings of the half-mad morons, formed the basis for the 'Book of Revelations.'

"Naturally, the book was based, in the first place, on the testimony of those least qualified to serve as historians; that is, children and morons; and was probably extensively edited and re-edited through the cycles."

"Do you suppose," broke in Theremon, "that they carried the book through the cycles the way we're planning on handing on the secret of gravitation?"

Sheerin shrugged. "Perhaps, but their exact method is unimportant. They do it, somehow. The point I was getting at was that the book can't help but be a mass of distortion, even if it is based on fact. For instance, do you remember the experiment with the holes in the roof that Faro and Yimot tried—the one that didn't work?"

"Yes."

"You know why it didn't w—" He stopped and rose in alarm, for Aton was approaching, his face a twisted mask of consternation. *"What's happened?"*

Aton drew him aside and Sheerin could feel the fingers on his elbow twitching.

"Not so loud!" Aton's voice was low and tortured. "I've just gotten word from the Hideout on the private line."

Sheerin broke in anxiously, "They are in trouble?"

"Not *they*." Aton stressed the pronoun significantly. "They sealed themselves off just a while ago, and they're going to stay buried till day after tomorrow. They're safe. But the *city*, Sheerin—it's a shambles. You have no idea—" He was having difficulty in speaking.

"Well?" snapped Sheerin impatiently. "What of it? It will get worse. What are you shaking about?" Then, suspiciously, "How do you feel?"

Aton's eyes sparked angrily at the insinuation, and then faded to anxiety once more. "You don't understand. The Cultists are active. They're rousing the people to storm the Observatory—promising them immediate entrance into grace, promising them salvation, promising them anything. What are we to do, Sheerin?"

Sheerin's head bent, and he stared in long abstraction at his toes. He tapped his chin with one knuckle, then looked up and said crisply, "Do? What is there to do? Nothing at all! Do the men know of this?"

"No, of course not!"

"Good! Keep it that way. How long till totality?"

"Not quite an hour."

"There's nothing to do but gamble. It will take time to organize any really formidable mob, and it will take more time to get them out here. We're a good five miles from the city—"

He glared out the window, down the slopes to where the farmed patches gave way to clumps of white houses in the suburbs; down to where the metropolis itself was a blur on the horizon—a mist in the waning blaze of Beta.

He repeated without turning, "It will take time. Keep on working and pray that totality comes first."

Beta was cut in half, the line of division pushing a slight concavity into the still-bright portion of the Sun. It was like a gigantic eyelid shutting slantwise over the light of a world.

The faint clatter of the room in which he stood faded into oblivion, and he sensed only the thick silence of the fields outside. The very insects seemed frightened mute. And things were dim.

He jumped at the voice in his ear. Theremon said, "Is something wrong?"

"Eh? Er—no. Get back to the chair. We're in the way." They slipped back to their corner, but the psychologist did not speak for a time. He lifted a finger and loosened his collar. He twisted his neck back and forth but found no relief. He looked up suddenly.

"Are you having any difficulty in breathing?"

The newspaperman opened his eyes wide and drew two or three long breaths. "No. Why?"

"I looked out the window too long, I suppose. The dimness got me. Difficulty in breathing is one of the first symptoms of a claustrophobic attack."

Theremon drew another long breath. "Well, it hasn't got me yet. Say, here's another of the fellows."

Beenay had interposed his bulk between the light and the pair in the corner, and Sheerin squinted up at him anxiously. "Hello, Beenay."

The astronomer shifted his weight to the other foot and smiled feebly. "You won't mind if I sit down awhile and join in on the talk? My cameras are set, and there's nothing to do till totality." He paused and eyed the Cultist, who fifteen minutes earlier had drawn a small, skin-bound book from his sleeve and had been poring intently over it ever since. "That rat hasn't been making trouble, has he?"

Sheerin shook his head. His shoulders were thrown back and he frowned his concentration as he forced himself to breathe regularly. He said, "Have you had any trouble breathing, Beenay?"

Beenay sniffed the air in his turn. "It doesn't seem stuffy to me."

"A touch of claustrophobia," explained Sheerin apologetically.

"Oh-h-h! It worked itself differently with me. I get the impression that my eyes are going back on me. Things seem to blur and—well, nothing is clear. And it's cold, too."

"Oh, it's cold, all right. That's no illusion." Theremon grimaced. "My toes feel as if I've been shipping them cross country in a refrigerating car."

"What we need," put in Sheerin, "is to keep our minds busy with extraneous affairs. I was telling you a while ago, Theremon, why Faro's experiments with the holes in the roof came to nothing."

"You were just beginning," replied Theremon. He encircled a knee with both arms and nuzzled his chin against it.

"Well, as I started to say, they were misled by taking the 'Book of Revelations' literally. There probably wasn't any sense in attaching any physical significance to the Stars. It might be, you know, that in the presence of total Darkness, the mind finds it absolutely necessary to create light. This illusion of light might be all the Stars there really are."

"In other words," interposed Theremon, "you mean the Stars

are the results of the madness and not one of the causes. Then, what good will Beenay's photographs be?"

"To prove that it is an illusion, maybe; or to prove the opposite, for all I know. Then again—"

But Beenay had drawn his chair closer, and there was an expression of sudden enthusiasm on his face. "Say, I'm glad you two got on to this subject." His eyes narrowed and he lifted one finger. "I've been thinking about these Stars and I've got a really cute notion. Of course, it's strictly ocean foam, and I'm not trying to advance it seriously, but I think it's interesting. Do you want to hear it?"

He seemed half reluctant, but Sheerin leaned back and said, "Go ahead! I'm listening."

"Well, then, supposing there were other suns in the universe." He broke off a little bashfully. "I mean suns that are so far away that they're too dim to see. It sounds as if I've been reading some of that fantastic fiction, I suppose."

"Not necessarily. Still, isn't that possibility eliminated by the fact that, according to the Law of Gravitation, they would make themselves evident by their attractive forces?"

"Not if they were far enough off," rejoined Beenay, "really far off—maybe as much as four light-years, or even more. We'd never be able to detect perturbations then, because they'd be too small. Say that there were a lot of suns that far off; a dozen or two, maybe."

Theremon whistled melodiously. "What an idea for a good Sunday-supplement article. Two dozen suns in a universe eight light-years across. Wow! That would shrink *our* universe into insignificance. The readers would eat it up."

"Only an idea," said Beenay with a grin, "but you see the point. During eclipse, these dozen suns would become visible, because there'd be no *real* sunlight to drown them out. Since they're so far off, they'd appear small, like so many little marbles. Of course, the Cultists talk of millions of Stars, but that's probably exaggeration. There just isn't any place in the universe you could put a million suns—unless they touch one another."

Sheerin had listened with gradually increasing interest. "You've hit something there, Beenay. And exaggeration is just exactly what would happen. Our minds, as you probably know, can't grasp directly any number higher than five; above that there is only the concept of 'many.' A dozen would become a million just like that. A damn good idea!"

"And I've got another cute little notion," Beenay said. "Have you ever thought what a simple problem gravitation would be if only you had a sufficiently simple system? Supposing you had a universe in which there was a planet with only one sun. The planet would travel in a perfect ellipse and the exact nature of the gravitational force would be so evident it could be accepted as an axiom. Astronomers on such a world would start off with gravity probably before they even invent the telescope. Naked-eye observation would be enough."

"But would such a system be dynamically stable?" questioned Sheerin doubtfully.

"Sure! They call it the 'one-and-one' case. It's been worked out mathematically, but it's the philosophical implications that interest me."

"It's nice to think about," admitted Sheerin, "as a pretty abstraction—like a perfect gas or absolute zero."

"Of course," continued Beenay, "there's the catch that life would be impossible on such a planet. It wouldn't get enough heat and light, and if it rotated there would be total Darkness half of each day. You couldn't expect life—which is fundamentally dependent upon light—to develop under those conditions. Besides—"

Sheerin's chair went over backward as he sprang to his feet in a rude interruption. "Aton's brought out the lights."

Beenay said, "Huh," turned to stare and then grinned halfway around his head in open relief.

There were half a dozen foot-long, inch-thick rods cradled in Aton's arms. He glared over them at the assembled staff members.

"Get back to work, all of you. Sheerin, come here and help me!"

Sheerin trotted to the older man's side and, one by one, in utter silence, the two adjusted the rods in makeshift metal holders suspended from the walls.

With the air of one carrying through the most sacred item of a religious ritual, Sheerin scraped a large, clumsy match into spluttering life and passed it to Aton, who carried the flame to the upper end of one of the rods.

It hesitated there a while, playing futilely about the tip, until a sudden, crackling flare cast Aton's lined face into yellow highlights. He withdrew the match and a spontaneous cheer rattled the window.

The rod was topped by six inches of wavering flame! Methodically, the other rods were lighted, until six independent fires turned the rear of the room yellow.

The light was dim, dimmer even than the tenuous sunlight. The flames reeled crazily, giving birth to drunken, swaying shadows. The torches smoked devilishly and smelled like a bad day in the kitchen. But they emitted yellow light.

There is something to yellow light—after four hours of somber, dimming Beta. Even Latimer had lifted his eyes from his book and stared in wonder.

Sheerin warmed his hands at the nearest, regardless of the soot that gathered upon them in a fine, gray powder, and muttered ecstatically to himself. "Beautiful! Beautiful! I never realized before what a wonderful color yellow is."

But Theremon regarded the torches suspiciously. He wrinkled his nose at the rancid odor, and said, "What are those things?"

"Wood," said Sheerin shortly.

"Oh, no, they're not. They aren't burning. The top inch is charred and the flame just keeps shooting up out of nothing."

"That's the beauty of it. This is a really efficient artificial-light mechanism. We made a few hundred of them, but most went to the Hideout, of course. You see"—he turned and wiped his blackened hands upon his handkerchief—"you take the pithy core of coarse water reeds, dry them thoroughly and soak them in animal grease. Then you set fire to it and the grease burns, little by little. These torches will burn for almost half an hour without stopping. Ingenious, isn't it? It was developed by one of our own young men at Saro University."

After the momentary sensation, the dome had quieted. Latimer had carried his chair directly beneath a torch and continued reading, lips moving in the monotonous recital of invocations to the Stars. Beenay had drifted away to his cameras once more, and Theremon seized the opportunity to add to his notes on the article he was going to write for the *Saro City Chronicle* the next day—a procedure he had been following for the last two hours in a perfectly methodical, perfectly conscientious and, as he was well aware, perfectly meaningless fashion.

But, as the gleam of amusement in Sheerin's eyes indicated, careful note taking occupied his mind with something other than the fact that the sky was gradually turning a horrible deep purple-red, as if it were one gigantic, freshly peeled beet; and so it fulfilled its purpose.

The air grew, somehow, denser. Dusk, like a palpable entity, entered the room, and the dancing circle of yellow light about the torches etched itself into ever-sharper distinction against the gathering grayness beyond. There was the odor of smoke and the presence of little chuckling sounds that the torches made as they burned; the soft pad of one of the men circling the table at which he worked, on hesitant tiptoes; the occasional indrawn breath of someone trying to retain composure in a world that was retreating into the shadow.

It was Theremon who first heard the extraneous noise. It was a vague, unorganized *impression* of sound that would have gone unnoticed but for the dead silence that prevailed within the dome.

The newsman sat upright and replaced his notebook. He held his breath and listened; then, with considerable reluctance, threaded his way between the solarscope and one of Beenay's cameras and stood before the window.

The silence ripped to fragments at his startled shout:

"Sheerin!"

Work stopped! The psychologist was at his side in a moment. Aton joined him. Even Yimot 70, high in his little lean-back seat at the eyepiece of the gigantic solarscope, paused and looked downward.

Outside, Beta was a mere smoldering splinter, taking one last desperate look at Lagash. The eastern horizon, in the direction of the city, was lost in Darkness, and the road from Saro to the

Observatory was a dull-red line bordered on both sides by wooded tracts, the trees of which had somehow lost individuality and merged into a continuous shadowy mass.

But it was the highway itself that held attention, for along it there surged another, and infinitely menacing, shadowy mass.

Aton cried in a cracked voice, "The madmen from the city! They've come!"

"How long to totality?" demanded Sheerin.

"Fifteen minutes, but . . . but they'll be here in five."

"Never mind, keep the men working. We'll hold them off. This place is built like a fortress. Aton, keep an eye on our young Cultist just for luck. Theremon, come with me."

Sheerin was out the door, and Theremon was at his heels. The stairs stretched below them in tight, circular sweeps about the central shaft, fading into a dank and dreary grayness.

The first momentum of their rush had carried them fifty feet down, so that the dim, flickering yellow from the open door of the dome had disappeared and both up above and down below the same dusky shadow crushed in upon them.

Sheerin paused, and his pudgy hand clutched at his chest. His eyes bulged and his voice was a dry cough. "I can't . . . breathe . . . go down . . . yourself. Close all doors—"

Theremon took a few downward steps, then turned. "Wait! Can you hold out a minute?" He was panting himself. The air passed in and out his lungs like so much molasses, and there was a little germ of screeching panic in his mind at the thought of making his way into the mysterious Darkness below by himself.

Theremon, after all, was afraid of the dark!

"Stay here," he said. "I'll be back in a second." He dashed upward two steps at a time, heart pounding—not altogether from the exertion—tumbled into the dome and snatched a torch from its holder. It was foul smelling, and the smoke smarted his eyes almost blind, but he clutched that torch as if he wanted to kiss it for joy, and its flame streamed backward as he hurtled down the stairs again.

Sheerin opened his eyes and moaned as Theremon bent over him. Theremon shook him roughly. "All right, get a hold on yourself. We've got light."

He held the torch at tiptoe height and, propping the tottering psychologist by an elbow, made his way downward in the middle of the protecting circle of illumination.

The offices on the ground floor still possessed what light there was, and Theremon felt the horror about him relax.

"Here," he said brusquely, and passed the torch to Sheerin. "You can hear *them* outside."

And they could. Little scraps of hoarse, wordless shouts.

But Sheerin was right; the Observatory was built like a fortress. Erected in the last century, when the neo-Gavottian style of architecture was at its ugly height, it had been designed for stability and durability, rather than for beauty.

The windows were protected by the grillework of inch-thick iron bars sunk deep into the concrete sills. The walls were solid masonry that an earthquake couldn't have touched, and the main door was a huge oaken slab reinforced with iron at the strategic points. Theremon shot the bolts and they slid shut with a dull clang.

At the other end of the corridor, Sheerin cursed weakly. He pointed to the lock of the back door which had been neatly jimmied into uselessness.

"That must be how Latimer got in," he said.

"Well, don't stand there," cried Theremon impatiently. "Help drag up the furniture—and keep that torch out of my eyes. The smoke's killing me."

He slammed the heavy table up against the door as he spoke, and in two minutes had built a barricade which made up for what it lacked in beauty and symmetry by the sheer inertia of its massiveness.

Somewhere, dimly, far off, they could hear the battering of naked fists upon the door; and the screams and yells from outside had a sort of half reality.

That mob had set off from Saro City with only two things in mind: the attainment of Cultist salvation by the destruction of the Observatory, and a maddening fear that all but paralyzed them. There was no time to think of ground cars, or of weapons, or of leadership, or even of organization. They made for the Observatory on foot and assaulted it with bare hands.

And now that they were there, the last flash of Beta, the last ruby-red drop of flame; flickered feebly over a humanity that had left only stark, universal fear!

Theremon groaned, "Let's get back to the dome!"

In the dome, only Yimot, at the solarscope, had kept his place. The rest were clustered about the cameras, and Beenay was giving his instructions in a hoarse, strained voice.

"Get it straight, all of you. I'm snapping Beta just before totality and changing the plate. That will leave one of you to each camera. You all know about . . . about times of exposure—"

There was a breathless murmur of agreement.

Beenay passed a hand over his eyes. "Are the torches still burning? Never mind, I see them!" He was leaning hard against the back of a chair. "Now remember, don't . . . don't try to look for good shots. Don't waste time trying to get t-two stars at a time in the scope field. One is enough. And . . . and if you feel yourself going, *get away from the camera.*"

At the door, Sheerin whispered to Theremon, "Take me to Aton. I don't see him."

The newsman did not answer immediately. The vague forms of the astronomers wavered and blurred, and the torches overhead had become only yellow spotches.

"It's dark," he whimpered.

Sheerin held out his hand, "Aton." He stumbled forward. "Aton!"

Theremon stepped after and seized his arm. "Wait, I'll take you." Somehow he made his way across the room. He closed his eyes against the Darkness and his mind against the chaos within it.

No one heard them or paid attention to them. Sheerin stumbled against the wall. "Aton!"

The psychologist felt shaking hands touching him, then withdrawing, and a voice muttering, "Is that you, Sheerin?"

"Aton!" He strove to breathe normally. "Don't worry about the mob. The place will hold them off."

Latimer, the Cultist, rose to his feet, and his face twisted in desperation. His word was pledged, and to break it would mean placing his soul in mortal peril. Yet that word had been forced from him and had not been given freely. The Stars would come soon; he could not stand by and allow— And yet his word was pledged.

Beenay's face was dimly flushed as it looked upward at Beta's last ray, and Latimer, seeing him bend over his camera, made his decision. His nails cut the flesh of his palms as he tensed himself.

He staggered crazily as he started his rush. There was nothing before him but shadows; the very floor beneath his feet lacked substance. And then someone was upon him and he went down with clutching fingers at his throat.

He doubled his knee and drove it hard into his assailant. "Let me up or I'll kill you."

Theremon cried out sharply and muttered through a blinding haze of pain, "You double-crossing rat!"

The newsman seemed conscious of everything at once. He heard Beenay croak, "I've got it. At your cameras, men!" and then there was the strange awareness that the last thread of sunlight had thinned out and snapped.

Simultaneously he heard one last choking gasp from Beenay, and a queer little cry from Sheerin, a hysterical giggle that cut off in a rasp—and a sudden silence, a strange, deadly silence from outside.

And Latimer had gone limp in his loosening grasp. Theremon peered into the Cultist's eyes and saw the blankness of them, staring upward, mirroring the feeble yellow of the torches. He saw the bubble of froth upon Latimer's lips and heard the low animal whimper in Latimer's throat.

With the slow fascination of fear, he lifted himself on one arm and turned his eyes toward the blood-curdling blackness of the window.

Through it shone the Stars!

Not Earth's feeble thirty-six hundred Stars visible to the eye—Lagash was in the center of a giant cluster. Thirty thousand mighty suns shown down in a soul-searing splendor that was more frighteningly cold in its awful indifference than the bitter wind that shivered across the cold, horribly bleak world.

Theremon staggered to his feet, his throat constricting him to breathlessness, all the muscles of his body writhing in a tensity of terror and sheer fear beyond bearing. He was going mad, and knew it, and somewhere deep inside a bit of sanity was screaming, struggling to fight off the hopeless flood of black terror. It was very horrible to go mad and know that you were going mad—to know that in a little minute you would be here physically and yet all the real essence would be dead and drowned in the black madness. For this was the Dark—the Dark and the Cold and the Doom. The bright walls of the universe were shattered and their awful black fragments were falling down to crush and squeeze and obliterate him.

He jostled someone crawling on hands and knees, but stumbled somehow over him. Hands groping at his tortured throat, he limped toward the flame of the torches that filled all his mad vision.

"Light!" he screamed.

Aton, somewhere, was crying, whimpering horribly like a terribly frightened child. "Stars—all the Stars—we didn't know at all. We didn't know anything. We thought six stars is a universe is something the Stars didn't notice is Darkness forever and ever and ever and the walls are breaking in and we didn't know we couldn't know and anything—"

Someone clawed at the torch, and it fell and snuffed out. In the instant, the awful splendor of the indifferent Stars leaped nearer to them.

On the horizon outside the window, in the direction of Saro City, a crimson glow began growing, strengthening in brightness, that was not the glow of a sun.

The long night had come again.

■ ■ ■

For a Journal Entry . . .

At the end of Isaac Asimov's "Nightfall" an entire civilization goes up in fire and madness. Do you think if you had been a citizen on Lagash, you would have reacted in the same way? How much of our own sanity is based on acceptance of certain beliefs about our universe? For instance, a bird that has been caged all its life comes to think of the cage as the universe. Far from welcoming freedom, the bird would be terrified by it, because such freedom entails the destruction of its world. What kinds of basic beliefs do you have about your universe, and how would you react if those beliefs were destroyed?

For Your Consideration . . .

1. Lagash was the name of an ancient Sumerian city in the Tigris-Euphrates valley. This city, once a center of a busy and thriving civilization, vanished in time some 4,000 years ago and has only recently been rediscovered. Lagash is also the name of the planet in Isaac Asimov's "Nightfall." Why is it an appropriate name?
2. How is the civilization on Lagash much like our own? Do you feel that you are reading about aliens or humans?
3. The particular part of the galaxy that Lagash is in is very different from our own. Describe that difference and draw a diagram representing the orbits of Lagash in relationship to its suns and moon.
4. The people of Lagash go insane for essentially two reasons. What are they, and given the setting of the story, are they psychologically sound (in your opinion)? What parts do superstition and the Lagashian concept of *many* play in the disaster?
5. Why must the people of Lagash turn to fire as a solution to their problem?
6. The Science Fiction Writers of America voted "Nightfall" the best SF short story ever written. Do you agree with their selection? Why or why not? Is there another SF short story which you would nominate in its place? If so, which one, and why?

Notes

PAGE

201 *belligerent*—threatening
201 *syndicated*—carried in many newspapers
202 *pedantic*—tendency to unnecessarily display learning
202 *phraseology*—word choice
202 *insubordination*—disrespect for authority
202 *colleagues*—fellow workers
202 *menace*—danger
203 *zenith*—height
203 *aphelion*—point furthest away from the sun that a rotating body (planet) can reach

203 *antipodes*—directly opposite
203 *maintained wary neutrality*—cautiously did not take sides
204 *ridicule*—mock; make fun of
derision—mockery
205 *consternation*—dismay
205 *peevishly*—in a bad-tempered manner
206 *validity*—truth
207 *maroon*—brownish red
208 *impaled*—stabbed
208 *cyclic*—repeating in cycles; repeats itself
210 *cohesive*—binding
211 *perturbations*—disturbances, irregularities
211 *untenable*—indefensible
211 *data*—information
211 *nonluminous*—does not give off light
211 *eclipse*—blocking out of the sun's light by the moon
215 *resiliency*—ability to recover strength
215 *conceive*—imagine
215 *truculently*—rudely
216 *comprehension*—understanding
216 *millenniums*—thousands of years
217 *tension*—strain
217 *peremptorily*—dictatorially
220 *blasphemy*—mockery of God
220 *fraud*—trick
220 *infernal*—hellish
220 *cached*—hidden
223 *prosaically*—in a commonplace manner
224 *ineffable*—inexpressible
225 *nought*—nothing
225 *immunity*—resistance to disease
226 *encroachment*—intrusion
226 *florid*—red complexion
227 *distortion*—misrepresentation
227 *insinuation*—suggestion
228 *formidable*—highly dangerous; difficult to cope with
228 *metropolis*—large city
232 *rancid*—spoiled
233 *invocations*—prayers
234 *momentum*—the force that keeps a moving object moving
235 *masonry*—brickwork
237 *constricting*—tightening
238 *fragments*—broken pieces
238 *obliterate*—destroy; wipe out

The Cold Equations

by Tom Godwin

Tom Godwin sold his first story in 1953 and has worked steadily and painstakingly ever since. His novels inclue *The Survivors* and *Space Prison*, but his reputation is built strongly upon this short story of the inescapable difference between natural and man-made laws and what this means to a man and a girl alone in a spaceship.

He was not alone.

There was nothing to indicate the fact but the white hand of the tiny gauge on the board before him. The control room was empty but for himself; there was no sound other than the murmur of the drives—but the white hand had moved. It had been on zero when the little ship was launched from the *Stardust*; now, an hour later, it had crept up. There was something in the supplies closet across the room, it was saying, some kind of body that radiated heat.

It could be but one kind of a body—a living, human body.

He leaned back in the pilot's chair and drew a deep, slow breath, considering what he would have to do. He was an EDS pilot, inured to the sight of death, long since accustomed to it and to viewing the dying of another man with an objective lack of emotion, and he had no choice in what he must do. There could be no alternative—but it required a few moments of conditioning for even an EDS pilot to prepare himself to walk across the room and coldly, deliberately, take the life of a man he had yet to meet.

He would, of course, do it. It was the law, stated very bluntly and definitely in grim Paragraph L, Section 8, of Interstellar Regulations: *Any stowaway discovered in an EDS shall be jettisoned immediately following discovery.*

It was the law, and there could be no appeal.

It was a law not of men's choosing but made imperative by the circumstances of the space frontier. Galactic expansion had followed the development of the hyperspace drive and as men scattered wide across the frontier there had come the problem of contact with the isolated first-colonies and exploration parties. The huge hyperspace cruisers were the product of the combined genius and effort of Earth and were long and expensive in the building. They were not available in such numbers that small colonies could possess them. The cruisers carried the colonists to their new worlds and made periodic visits, running on tight schedules, but they could not stop and turn aside to visit colonies scheduled to be visited at another time; such a delay would destroy their schedule and produce a confusion and uncertainty that would wreck the complex interdependence between old Earth and the new worlds of the frontier.

Some method of delivering supplies or assistance when an emergency occurred on a world not scheduled for a visit had been needed and the Emergency Dispatch Ships had been the answer. Small and collapsible, they occupied little room in the hold of the cruiser; made of light metal and plastics, they were driven by a small rocket drive that consumed relatively little fuel. Each cruiser carried four EDS's and when a call for aid was received the nearest cruiser would drop into normal space long enough to launch an EDS with the needed supplies or personnel, then vanish again as it continued on its course.

The cruisers, powered by nuclear converters, did not use the liquid rocket fuel but nuclear converters were far too large and complex to permit their installation in the EDS's. The cruisers were forced by necessity to carry a limited amount of the bulky rocket fuel and the fuel was rationed with care; the cruiser's computers determining the exact amount of fuel each EDS would require for its mission. The computers considered the course co-ordinates, the mass of the EDS, the mass of pilot and cargo; they were very precise and accurate and omitted nothing from their calculations. They could not, however, foresee, and allow for, the added mass of a stowaway.

The *Stardust* had received the request from one of the exploration parties stationed on Woden; the six men of the party already being stricken with fever carried by the green *kala* midges and their own supply of serum destroyed by a tornado that had torn through their camp. The *Stardust* had gone through the usual procedure; dropping into normal space to launch the EDS with the fever serum, then vanishing again in hyperspace. Now, an hour later, the gauge was saying there was something more than the small carton of serum in the supplies closet.

He let his eyes rest on the narrow white door of the closet. There, just inside, another man lived and breathed and was beginning to feel assured that discovery of his presence would now be too late for the pilot to alter the situation. It *was* too late—for the man behind the door it was far later than he thought and in a way he would find terrible to believe.

There could be no alternative. Additional fuel would be used during the hours of deceleration to compensate for the added mass of the stowaway; infinitesimal increments of fuel that would not be missed until the ship had almost reached its destination. Then, at some distance above the ground that might be as near as a thousand feet or as far as tens of thousands of feet, depending upon the mass of ship and cargo and the preceding period of deceleration, the unmissed increments of fuel would make their absence known; the EDS would expend its last drops of fuel with a sputter and go into whistling free fall. Ship and pilot and stowaway would merge together upon impact as a wreckage of metal and plastic, flesh and blood, driven deep into the soil. The stowaway had signed his own death warrant when he concealed himself on the ship; he could not be permitted to take seven others with him.

He looked again at the tell-tale white hand, then rose to his feet. What he must do would be unpleasant for both of them; the sooner it was over, the better. He stepped across the control room, to stand by the white door.

"Come out!" His command was harsh and abrupt above the murmur of the drive.

It seemed he could hear the whisper of a furtive movement inside the closet, then nothing. He visualized the stowaway cowering into one corner, suddenly worried by the possible consequences of his act and his self-assurance evaporating.

"I said *out!*"

He heard the stowaway move to obey and he waited with his eyes alert on the door and his hand near the blaster at his side.

The door opened and the stowaway stepped through it, smiling. "All right—I give up. Now what?"

It was a girl.

He stared without speaking, his hand dropping away from the blaster and acceptance of what he saw coming like a heavy and unexpected physical blow. The stowaway was not a man—she was a girl in her teens, standing before him in little white gypsy sandals with the top of her brown, curly head hardly higher than his shoulder, with a faint, sweet scent of perfume coming from her and her smiling face tilted up so that her eyes could look unknowing and unafraid into his as she waited for his answer.

Now what? Had it been asked in the deep, defiant voice of a man he would have answered it with action, quick and efficient. He would have taken the stowaway's identification disc and ordered him into the air lock. Had the stowaway refused to obey, he would have used the blaster. It would not have taken long; within a minute the body would have been ejected into space—had the stowaway been a man.

He returned to the pilot's chair and motioned her to seat herself on the box-like bulk of the drive-control units that were set against the wall beside him. She obeyed, his silence making the smile fade into the meek and guilty expression of a pup that has been caught in mischief and knows it must be punished.

"You still haven't told me," she said. "I'm guilty, so what happens to me now? Do I pay a fine, or what?"

"What are you doing here?" he asked. "Why did you stow away on this EDS?"

"I wanted to see my brother. He's with the government survey crew on Woden and I haven't seen him for ten years, not since he left Earth to go into government survey work."

"What was your destination on the *Stardust*?"

"Mimir. I have a position waiting for me there. My brother has been sending money home all the time to us—my father and my mother and I—and he paid for a special course in linguistics I was taking. I graduated sooner than expected and I was offered this job on Mimir. I knew it would be almost a year before Gerry's job was done on Woden so he could come on to Mimir and that's why I hid in the closet, there. There was plenty of room for me and I was willing to pay the fine. There were only the two of us kids—Gerry and I—and I haven't seen him for so long, and I didn't want to wait another year when I could see him now, even though I knew I would be breaking some kind of a regulation when I did it."

I knew I would be breaking some kind of a regulation— In a way, she could not be blamed for her ignorance of the law; she was of Earth and had not realized that the laws of the space frontier must, of necessity, be as hard and relentless as the environment that gave them birth. Yet, to protect such as her from the results of their own ignorance of the frontier, there had been a sign over the door that led to the section of the *Stardust* that housed the EDS's, a sign that was plain for all to see and heed:

UNAUTHORIZED PERSONNEL
KEEP OUT!

"Does your brother know that you took a passage on the *Stardust* for Mimir?"

"Oh, yes. I sent him a spacegram telling him about my graduation and about going to Mimir on the *Stardust* a month before I left Earth. I already knew Mimir was where he would be stationed in a little over a year. He gets a promotion then, and he'll be based on Mimir and not have to stay out a year at a time on field trips, like he does now."

There were two different survey groups on Woden, and he asked, "What is his name?"

"Cross—Gerry Cross. He's in Group Two—that was the way his address read. Do you know him?"

Group One had requested the serum; Group Two was eight thousand miles away, across the Western Sea.

"No, I've never met him," he said, then turned to the control board and cut the deceleration to a fraction of gravity; knowing as he did so that it could not avert the ultimate end, yet doing the only thing he could do to prolong that ultimate end. The sensation was like that of a ship suddenly dropping and the girl's involuntary movement of surprise half lifted her from her seat.

"We're going faster now, aren't we?" she asked. "Why are we doing that?"

He told her the truth. "To save fuel for a little while."

"You mean we don't have very much?"

He delayed the answer he must give her so soon to ask: "How did you manage to stow away?"

"I just sort of walked in when no one was looking my way," she said. "I was practicing my Gelanese on the native girl who does the cleaning in the Ship's Supply Office when someone came in with an order for supplies for the survey crew on Woden. I slipped into the closet there after the ship was ready to go and just before you came in. It was an impulse of the moment to stow away, so I could get to see Gerry—and from the way you keep looking at me so grim, I'm not sure it was a very wise impulse.

"But I'll be a model criminal—or do I mean prisoner?" She smiled at him again. "I intended to pay for my keep on top of paying the fine. I can cook and I can patch clothes for everyone and I know how to do all kinds of useful things, even a little bit about nursing."

There was one more question to ask.

"Did you know what the supplies were that the survey crew ordered?"

"Why, no. Equipment they needed in their work, I supposed."

Why couldn't she have been a man with some ulterior motive? A fugitive from justice, hoping to lose himself on a raw new world; an opportunist, seeking transportation to the new colonies where he might find golden fleece for the taking; a crackpot, with a mission—

Perhaps once in his lifetime an EDS pilot would find such a stowaway on his ship; warped men, mean and selfish men, brutal and dangerous men—but never, before, a smiling, blue-eyed girl who was willing to pay her fine and work for her keep that she might see her brother.

He turned to the board and turned the switch that would signal the *Stardust.* The call would be futile but he could not, until he had exhausted that one vain hope, seize her and thrust her into the air lock as he would an animal—or a man. The delay, in the meantime, would not be dangerous with the EDS decelerating at fractional gravity.

A voice spoke from the communicator. "*Stardust.* Identify yourself and proceed."

"Barton, EDS 34G11. Emergency. Give me Commander Delhart."

There was a faint confusion of noises as the request went through the proper channels. The girl was watching him, no longer smiling.

"Are you going to order them to come back after me?" she asked.

The communicator clicked and there was the sound of a distant voice saying, "Commander, the EDS requests—"

"Are they coming back after me?" she asked again. "Won't I get to see my brother, after all?"

"Barton?" The blunt, gruff voice of Commander Delhart came from the communicator. "What's this about an emergency?"

"A stowaway," he answered.

"A stowaway?" There was a slight surprise to the question. "That's rather unusual—but why the 'emergency' call? You discovered him in time so there should be no appreciable danger and I presume you've informed Ship's Records so his nearest relatives can be notified."

"That's why I had to call you first. The stowaway is still aboard and the circumstances are so different—"

"Different?" the commander interrupted, impatience in his

voice. "How can they be different? You know you have a limited supply of fuel; you also know the law, as well as I do: 'Any stowaway discovered in an EDS shall be jettisoned immediately following discovery.' "

There was the sound of a sharply indrawn breath from the girl. *"What does he mean?"*

"The stowaway is a girl."

"What?"

"She wanted to see her brother. She's only a kid and she didn't know what she was really doing."

"I see." All the curtness was gone from the commander's voice. "So you called me in the hope I could do something?" Without waiting for an answer he went on. "I'm sorry—I can do nothing. This cruiser must maintain its schedule; the life of not one person but the lives of many depend on it. I know how you feel but I'm powerless to help you. You'll have to go through with it. I'll have you connected with Ship's Records."

The communicator faded to a faint rustle of sound and he turned to the girl. She was leaning forward on the bench, almost rigid, her eyes fixed wide and frightened.

"What did he mean, to go through with it? To jettison me . . . to go through with it—what did he mean? Not the way it sounded . . . he couldn't have. What did he mean . . . what did he really mean?"

Her time was too short for the comfort of a lie to be more than a cruelly fleeting delusion.

"He meant it the way it sounded."

"No!" She recoiled from him as though he had struck her, one hand half upraised as though to fend him off and stark unwillingness to believe in her eyes.

"It will have to be."

"No! You're joking—you're insane! You can't mean it!"

"I'm sorry." He spoke slowly to her, gently. "I should have told you before—I should have, but I had to do what I could first; I had to call the *Stardust.* You heard what the commander said."

"But you can't—if you make me leave the ship, I'll *die.*"

"I know."

She searched his face and the unwillingness to believe left her eyes, giving way slowly to a look of dazed terror.

"You—know?" She spoke the words far apart, numb and wonderingly.

"I know. It has to be like that."

"You mean it—you really mean it." She sagged back against the wall, small and limp like a little rag doll and all the protesting and disbelief gone. "You're going to do it—you're going to make me die?"

"I'm sorry," he said again. "You'll never know how sorry I am. It has to be that way and no human in the universe can change it."

"You're going to make me die and I didn't do anything to die for—I didn't *do* anything—"

He sighed, deep and weary. "I know you didn't, child. I know you didn't—"

"EDS." The communicator rapped brisk and metallic. "This is Ship's Records. Give us all information on subject's identification disc."

He got out of his chair to stand over her. She clutched the edge of the seat, her upturned face white under the brown hair and the lipstick standing out like a blood-red cupid's bow.

"*Now?*"

"I want your identification disc," he said.

She released the edge of the seat and fumbled at the chain that suspended the plastic disc from her neck with fingers that were trembling and awkward. He reached down and unfastened the clasp for her, then returned with the disc to his chair.

"Here's your data, Records: Identification Number T837—"

"One moment," Records interrupted. "This is to be filed on the gray card, of course?"

"Yes."

"And the time of the execution?"

"I'll tell you later."

"Later? This is highly irregular; the time of the subject's death is required before—"

He kept the thickness out of his voice with an effort. "Then we'll do it in a highly irregular manner—you'll hear the disc read first. The subject is a girl and she's listening to everything that's said. Are you capable of understanding that?"

There was a brief, almost shocked, silence, then Records said meekly: "Sorry. Go ahead."

He began to read the disc, reading it slowly to delay the inevitable for as long as possible, trying to help her by giving her what little time he could to recover from her first terror and let it resolve into the calm of acceptance and resignation.

"Number T8374 dash Y54. Name: Marilyn Lee Cross. Sex: Female. Born: July 7, 2160. *She was only eighteen.* Height: 5 3. Weight: 110. *Such a slight weight, yet enough to add fatally to the mass of the shell-thin bubble that was an EDS.* Hair: Brown. Eyes: Blue. Complexion: Light. Blood Type: O. *Irrelevant data.* Destination: Port City Mimir. *Invalid data*—"

He finished and said, "I'll call you later," then turned once again to the girl. She was huddled back against the wall, watching him with a look of numb and wondering fascination.

"They're waiting for you to kill me, aren't they? They want me dead, don't they? You and everybody on the cruiser wants me dead, don't you?" Then the numbness broke and her voice was that of a frightened and bewildered child. "Everybody wants me dead and I didn't *do* anything. I didn't hurt anyone—I only wanted to see my brother."

"It's not the way you think—it isn't that way, at all," he said. "Nobody wants it this way; nobody would ever let it be this way if it was humanly possible to change it."

"Then why is it? I don't understand. Why is it?"

"This ship is carrying *kala* fever serum to Group One on Woden. Their own supply was destroyed by a tornado. Group Two—the crew your brother is in—is eight thousand miles away across the Western Sea and their helicopters can't cross it to help Group One. The fever is invariably fatal unless the serum can be had in time, and the six men in Group One will die unless this ship reaches them on schedule. These little ships are always given barely enough fuel to reach their destination and if you stay aboard your added weight will cause it to use up all its fuel before it reaches the ground. It will crash, then, and you and I will die and so will the six men waiting for the fever serum."

It was a full minute before she spoke, and as she considered his words the expression of numbness left her eyes.

"Is that it?" she asked at last. "Just that the ship doesn't have enough fuel?"

"Yes."

"I can go alone or I can take seven others with me—is that the way it is?"

"That's the way it is."

"And nobody wants me to have to die?"

"Nobody."

"Then maybe— Are you sure nothing can be done about it? Wouldn't people help me if they could?"

"Everyone would like to help you but there is nothing anyone can do. I did the only thing I could when I called the *Stardust.*"

"And it won't come back—but there might be other cruisers, mightn't there? Isn't there any hope at all that there might be someone, somewhere, who could do something to help me?"

She was leaning forward a little in her eagerness as she waited for his answer.

"No."

The word was like the drop of a cold stone and she again leaned back against the wall, the hope and eagerness leaving her face. "You're sure—you *know* you're sure?"

"I'm sure. There are no other cruisers within forty light-years; there is nothing and no one to change things."

She dropped her gaze to her lap and began twisting a pleat of her skirt between her fingers, saying no more as her mind began to adapt itself to the grim knowledge.

It was better so; with the going of all hope would go the fear; with the going of all hope would come resignation. She needed time and she could have so little of it. How much?

The EDS's were not equipped with hull-cooling units; their speed had to be reduced to a moderate level before entering the atmosphere. They were decelerating at .10 gravity; approaching their destination at a far higher speed than the computers had calculated on. The *Stardust* had been quite near Woden when she launched the EDS; their present velocity was putting them nearer by the second. There would be a critical point, soon to be reached, when he would have to resume deceleration. When he did so the girl's weight would be multiplied by the gravities of deceleration, would become, suddenly, a factor of paramount importance; the factor the computers had been ignorant of when they determined the amount of fuel the EDS should have. She would have to go when deceleration began; it could be no other way. When would that be—how long could he let her stay?

"How long can I stay?"

He winced involuntarily from the words that were so like an echo of his own thoughts. How long? He didn't know; he would have to ask the ship's computers. Each EDS was given a meager supply of fuel to compensate for unfavorable conditions within the atmosphere and relatively little fuel was being consumed for the time being. The memory banks of the computers would still contain all the data pertaining to the course set for the EDS; such data would not be erased until the EDS reached its destination. He had only to give the computers the new data; the girl's weight and the exact time at which he had reduced the deceleration to .10.

"Barton." Commander Delhart's voice came abruptly from the communicator, as he opened his mouth to call the *Stardust.* "A check with Records shows me you haven't completed your report. Did you reduce the deceleration?"

So the commander knew what he was trying to do.

"I'm decelerating at point ten," he answered. "I cut the deceleration at seventeen fifty and the weight is a hundred and ten. I would like to stay at point ten as long as the computers say I can. Will you give them the question?"

It was contrary to regulations for an EDS pilot to make any changes in the course or degree of deceleration the computers had set for him but the commander made no mention of the violation, neither did he ask the reason for it. It was not necessary for him to ask; he had not become commander of an interstellar cruiser without both intelligence and an understanding of human nature. He said only: "I'll have that given the computers."

The communicator fell silent and he and the girl waited, neither of them speaking. They would not have to wait long; the computers would give the answer within moments of the asking. The new factors would be fed into the steel maw of the first bank and the electrical impulses would go through the complex circuits. Here and there a relay might click, a tiny cog turn over, but it would be essentially the electrical impulses that found the answer; formless, mindless, invisible, determining with utter precision how long the pale girl beside him might live. Then five little segments of metal in the second bank would trip in rapid succession against an inked ribbon and a second steel maw would spit out the slip of paper that bore the answer.

The chronometer on the instrument board read 18.10 when the commander spoke again.

"You will resume deceleration at nineteen ten."

She looked toward the chronometer, then quickly away from it. "Is that when . . . when I go?" she asked. He nodded and she dropped her eyes to her lap again.

"I'll have the course corrections given you," the commander said. "Ordinarily I would never permit anything like this but I understand your position. There is nothing I can do, other than what I've just done, and you will not deviate from these new instructions. You will complete your report at nineteen ten. Now—here are the course corrections."

The voice of some unknown technician read them to him and he wrote them down on a pad clipped to the edge of the control board. There would, he saw, be periods of deceleration when he neared the atmosphere when the deceleration would be five gravities—and at five gravities, one hundred and ten pounds would become five hundred and fifty pounds.

The technician finished and he terminated the contact with a brief acknowledgment. Then, hesitating a moment, he reached out and shut off the communicator. It was 18.13 and he would have nothing to report until 19.10. In the meantime, it somehow seemed indecent to permit others to hear what she might say in her last hour.

He began to check the instrument readings, going over them with unnecessary slowness. She would have to accept the circumstances and there was nothing he could do to help her into acceptance; words of sympathy would only delay it.

It was 18.20 when she stirred from her motionlessness and spoke.

"So that's the way it has to be with me?"

He swung around to face her. "You understand now, don't you? No one would ever let it be like this if it could be changed."

"I understand," she said. Some of the color had returned to her face and the lipstick no longer stood out so vividly red. "There isn't enough fuel for me to stay; when I hid on this ship I got into something I didn't know anything about and now I have to pay for it."

She had violated a man-made law that said KEEP OUT but the penalty was not of men's making or desire and it was a penalty men could not revoke. A physical law had decreed: *h amount of fuel will power an EDS with a mass of m safely to its destination;* and a second physical law decreed: *h amount of fuel will not power an EDS with a mass of m plus x safely to its destination.*

EDS's obeyed only physical laws and no amount of human sympathy for her could alter the second law.

"But I'm afraid. I don't want to die—not now. I want to live and nobody is doing anything to help me; everybody is letting me go ahead and acting just like nothing was going to happen to me. I'm going to die and nobody *cares.*"

"We all do," he said. "I do and the commander does and the clerk in Ship's Records; we all care and each of us did what little he could to help you. It wasn't enough—it was almost nothing—but it was all we could do."

"Not enough fuel—I can understand that," she said, as though she had not heard his own words. "But to have to die for it. *Me,* alone—"

How hard it must be for her to accept the fact. She had never known danger of death; had never known the environments where the lives of men could be as fragile and as fleeting as sea foam tossed against a rocky shore. She belonged on gentle Earth, in that secure and peaceful society where she could be young and gay and laughing with others of her kind; where life was precious and well-guarded and there was always the assurance that tomorrow would come. She belonged to that world of soft winds and warm suns, music and moonlight and gracious manners and not on the hard, bleak frontier.

"How did it happen to me, so terribly quickly? An hour ago I was on the *Stardust*, going to Mimir. Now the *Stardust* is going on without me and I'm going to die and I'll never see Gerry and Mama and Daddy again—I'll never see anything again."

He hesitated, wondering how he could explain it to her so that she would really understand and not feel she had, somehow, been the victim of a reasonlessly cruel injustice. She did not know what the frontier was like; she thought in terms of safe-and-secure Earth. Pretty girls were not jettisoned on Earth; there was a law against it. On Earth her plight would have filled the newscasts and a fast black Patrol ship would have been racing to her rescue. Everyone, everywhere, would have known of Marilyn Lee Cross and no effort would have been spared to save her life. But this was not Earth and there were no Patrol ships; only the *Stardust*, leaving them behind at many times the speed of light. There was no one to help her, there would be no Marilyn Lee Cross smiling from the newscasts tomorrow. Marilyn Lee Cross would be but a poignant memory for an EDS pilot and a name on a gray card in Ship's Records.

"It's different here; it's not like back on Earth," he said. "It isn't that no one cares; it's that no one can do anything to help. The frontier is big and here along its rim the colonies and exploration parties are scattered so thin and far between. On Woden, for example, there are only sixteen men—sixteen men on an entire world. The exploration parties, the survey crews, the little first-colonies—they're all fighting alien environments, trying to make a way for those who will follow after. The environments fight back and those who go first usually make mistakes only once. There is no margin of safety along the rim of the frontier; there can't be until the way is made for the others who will come later, until the new worlds are tamed and settled. Until then men will have to pay the penalty for making mistakes with no one to help them because there is no one *to* help them."

"I was going to Mimir," she said. "I didn't know about the frontier; I was only going to Mimir and *it's* safe."

"Mimir is safe but you left the cruiser that was taking you there."

She was silent for a little while. "It was all so wonderful at first; there was plenty of room for me on this ship and I would be seeing Gerry so soon . . . I didn't know about the fuel, didn't know what would happen to me—"

Her words trailed away and he turned his attention to the viewscreen, not wanting to stare at her as she fought her way through the black horror of fear toward the calm gray of acceptance.

Woden was a ball, enshrouded in the blue haze of atmosphere, swimming in space against the background of star-sprinkled dead blackness. The great mass of Manning's Continent sprawled like a gigantic hourglass in the Eastern Sea with the western half of the Eastern Continent still visible. There was a thin line of shadow along the right-hand edge of the globe and the Eastern Continent was disappearing into it as the planet turned on its axis. An hour before the entire continent had been in view, now a thousand miles of it had gone into the thin edge of shadow and around to the night that lay on the other side of the world. The dark blue spot that was Lotus Lake was approaching the shadow. It was somewhere near the southern edge of the lake that Group Two had their camp. It would be night there, soon, and quick behind the coming of night the rotation of Woden on its axis would put Group Two beyond the reach of the ship's radio.

He would have to tell her before it was too late for her to talk to her brother. In a way, it would be better for both of them should they not do so but it was not for him to decide. To each of them the last words would be something to hold and cherish, something that would cut like the blade of a knife yet would be infinitely precious to remember, she for her own brief moments to live and he for the rest of his life.

He held down the button that would flash the grid lines on the viewscreen and used the known diameter of the planet to estimate the distance the southern tip of Lake Lotus had yet to go until it passed beyond radio range. It was approximately five hundred miles. Five hundred miles; thirty minutes—and the chronometer read 18.30. Allowing for error in estimating, it could not be later than 19.05 that the turning of Woden would cut off her brother's voice.

The first border of the Western Continent was already in sight along the left side of the world. Four thousand miles across it lay the shore of the Western Sea and the Camp of Group One. It had been in the Western Sea that the tornado had originated, to strike with such fury at the camp and destroy half their prefabricated buildings, including the one that housed the medical supplies. Two days before the tornado had not existed; it had been no more than great gentle masses of air out over the calm Western Sea. Group One had gone about their routine survey work, unaware of the meeting of the air masses out at sea, unaware of the force the union was spawning. It had struck their camp without warning; a thundering, roaring destruction that sought to annihilate all that lay before it. It had passed on, leaving the wreckage in its wake. It had destroyed the labor of months and had doomed six men to die and then, as though its task was accomplished, it once more began to resolve into gentle masses of air. But for all its deadliness, it had destroyed with neither malice nor intent. It had been a blind and mindless force, obeying the laws of nature, and it would have followed the same course with the same fury had man never existed.

Existence required Order and there was order; the laws of nature, irrevocable and immutable. Men could learn to use them but men could not change them. The circumference of a circle was always pi times the diameter and no science of man would ever make it otherwise. The combination of chemical A with chemical B under condition C invariably produced reaction D. The law of gravitation was a rigid equation and it made no distinction between the fall of a leaf and the ponderous circling of a binary star system. The nuclear conversion process powered the cruisers that carried men to the stars; the same process in the form of a nova would destroy a world with equal efficiency. The laws *were,* and the universe moved in obedience to them. Along the frontier were arrayed all the forces of nature and sometimes they destroyed those who were fighting their way outwards from Earth. The men of the frontier had long ago learned the bitter futility of cursing the forces that would destroy them for the forces were blind and deaf; the futility of looking to the heavens for mercy, for the stars of the galaxy swung in their long, long sweep of two hundred million years, as inexorably controlled as they by the laws that knew neither hatred nor compassion.

The men of the frontier knew—but how was a girl from Earth to fully understand? *H amount of fuel will not power an EDS with a mass of m plus x safely to its destination.* To himself and her brother and parents she was a sweet-faced girl in her teens; to the laws of nature she was *x*, the unwanted factor in a cold equation.

She stirred again on the seat. "Could I write a letter? I want to write to Mama and Daddy and I'd like to talk to Gerry. Could you let me talk to him over your radio there?"

"I'll try to get him," he said.

He switched on the normal-space transmitter and pressed the signal button. Someone answered the button almost immediately.

"Hello. How's it going with you fellows now—is the EDS on its way?"

"This isn't Group One; this is the EDS," he said. "Is Gerry Cross there?"

"Gerry? He and two others went out in the helicopter this morning and aren't back yet. It's almost sundown, though, and he ought to be back right away—in less than an hour at the most."

"Can you connect me through the radio in his 'copter?"

"Huh-uh. It's been out of commission for two months—some printed circuits went haywire and we can't get any more until the next cruiser stops by. Is it something important—bad news for him, or something?"

"Yes—it's very important. When he comes in get him to the transmitter as soon as you possibly can."

"I'll do that; I'll have one of the boys waiting at the field with a truck. Is there anything else I can do?"

"No, I guess that's all. Get him there as soon as you can and sign me."

He turned the volume to an inaudible minimum, an act that would not affect the functioning of the signal buzzer, and unclipped the pad of paper from the control board. He tore off the sheet containing his flight instructions and handed the pad to her, together with pencil.

"I'd better write to Gerry, too," she said as she took them. "He might not get back to camp in time."

She began to write, her fingers still clumsy and uncertain in the way they handled the pencil and the top of it trembling a little as she poised it between words. He turned back to the viewscreen, to stare at it without seeing it.

She was a lonely little child, trying to say her last good-bye, and she would lay out her heart to them. She would tell them how much she loved them and she would tell them to not feel badly about it, that it was only something that must eventually happen to everyone and she was not afraid. The last would be a lie and it would be there to read between the sprawling, uneven lines; a valiant little lie that would make the hurt all the greater for them.

Her brother was of the frontier and he would understand. He would not hate the EDS pilot for doing nothing to prevent her going; he would know there had been nothing the pilot could do. He would understand, though the understanding would not soften the shock and pain when he learned his sister was gone. But the others, her father and mother—they would not understand. They were of Earth and they would think in the manner of those who had never lived where the safety margin of life was a thin, thin line—and sometimes not at all. What would they think of the faceless, unknown pilot who had sent her to her death?

They would hate him with cold and terrible intensity, but it really didn't matter. He would never see them, never know them. He would have only the memories to remind him; only the nights to fear, when a blue-eyed girl in gypsy sandals would come in his dreams to die again—

He scowled at the viewscreen and tried to force his thoughts into less emotional channels. There was nothing he could do to help her. She had unknowingly subjected herself to the penalty of a law that recognized neither innocence nor youth nor beauty, that was incapable of sympathy or leniency. Regret was illogical—and yet, could knowing it to be illogical ever keep it away?

She stopped occasionally, as though trying to find the right words to tell them what she wanted them to know, then the pencil would resume its whispering to the paper. It was 18.37 when she folded the letter in a square and wrote a name on it. She began writing another, twice looking up at the chronometer as though she feared the black hand might reach its rendezvous before she had finished. It was 18.45 when she folded it as she had done the first letter and wrote a name and address on it.

She held the letters out to him. "Will you take care of these and see that they're enveloped and mailed?"

"Of course." He took them from her hand and placed them in a pocket of his gray uniform shirt.

"These can't be sent off until the next cruiser stops by and the *Stardust* will have long since told them about me, won't it?" she asked. He nodded and she went on. "That makes the letters not important in one way but in another way they're very important—to me, and to them."

"I know, I understand, and I'll take care of them."

She glanced at the chronometer, then back at him. "It seems to move faster all the time, doesn't it?"

He said nothing, unable to think of anything to say, and she asked, "Do you think Gerry will come back to camp in time?"

"I think so. They said he should be in right away."

She began to roll the pencil back and forth between her palms. "I hope he does. I feel sick and scared and I want to hear his voice again and maybe I won't feel so alone. I'm a coward and I can't help it."

"No," he said, "you're not a coward. You're afraid, but you're not a coward."

"Is there a difference?"

He nodded. "A lot of difference."

"I feel so alone. I never did feel like this before; like I was all by myself and there was nobody to care what happened to me. Always, before, there was Mama and Daddy there and my friends around me. I had lots of friends, and they had a going-away party for me the night before I left."

Friends and music and laughter for her to remember—and on the viewscreen Lotus Lake was going into the shadow.

"Is it the same with Gerry?" she asked. "I mean, if he should make a mistake, would he have to die for it, all alone and with no one to help him?"

"It's the same with all along the frontier; it will always be like that so long as there is a frontier."

"Gerry didn't tell us. He said the pay was good and he sent money home all the time because Daddy's little shop just brought in a bare living, but he didn't tell us it was like this."

"He didn't tell you his work was dangerous?"

"Well—yes. He mentioned that, but we didn't understand. I always thought danger along the frontier was something that was a lot of fun; an exciting adventure, like the three-D shows." A wan smile touched her face for a moment. "Only it's not, is it? It's not the same at all, because when it's real you can't go home after the show is over."

"No," he said. "No, you can't."

Her glance flicked from the chronometer to the door of the air lock, then down to the pad and pencil she still held. She shifted her position slightly to lay them on the bench beside her, moving one foot out a little. For the first time he saw that she was not wearing Vegan gypsy sandals but only cheap imitations; the expensive Vegan leather was some kind of grained plastic, the silver buckle was gilded iron; the jewels were colored glass. *Daddy's little shop just brought in a bare living*— She must have left college in her second year, to take the course in linguistics that would enable her to make her own way and help her brother provide for her parents, earning what she could by part-time work after classes were over. Her personal possessions on the *Stardust* would be taken back to her parents—they would neither be of much value nor occupy much storage space for the return voyage.

"Isn't it—" She stopped, and he looked at her questioningly. "Isn't it cold in here?" she asked, almost apologetically. "Doesn't it seem cold to you?"

"Why, yes," he said. He saw by the main temperature gauge that the room was at precisely normal temperature. "Yes, it's colder than it should be."

"I wish Gerry would get back before it's too late. Do you really think he will, and you didn't say so just to make me feel better?"

"I think he will—they said he would be in pretty soon." On the viewscreen Lotus Lake had gone into the shadow but for the thin blue line on its western edge, and it was apparent he had overestimated the time she would have in which to talk to her brother. Reluctantly, he said to her, "His camp will be out of radio range in a few minutes; he's on that part of Woden that's in the shadow"—he indicated the viewscreen—"and the turning of Woden will put him beyond contact. There may not be much time left when he comes in—not much time to talk to him before he fades out. I wish I could do something about it—I would call him right now if I could."

"Not even as much time as I will have to stay?"

"I'm afraid not."

"Then—" She straightened and looked toward the air lock with pale resolution. "Then I'll go when Gerry passes beyond range, I won't wait any longer after that—I won't have anything to wait for."

Again there was nothing he could say.

"Maybe I shouldn't wait at all. Maybe I'm selfish—maybe it would be better for Gerry if you just told him about it afterward."

There was an unconscious pleading for denial in the way she spoke and he said, "He wouldn't want you to do that, not to wait for him."

"It's already coming dark where he is, isn't it? There will be all the long night before him, and Mama and Daddy don't know yet that I won't ever be coming back like I promised them I would. I've caused everyone I love to be hurt, haven't I? I didn't want to—I didn't intend to."

"It wasn't your fault," he said. "It wasn't your fault at all. They'll know that. They'll understand."

"At first I was so afraid to die that I was a coward and thought only of myself. Now, I see how selfish I was. The terrible thing about dying like this is not that I'll be gone but that I'll never see them again; never be able to tell them that I didn't take them for granted; never be able to tell them I knew of the sacrifices they made to keep my life happier, that I knew all the things they did for me and that I loved them so much more than I ever told them. I've never told them any of those things. You don't tell them such things when you're young and your life is all before you—you're afraid of sounding sentimental and silly.

"But it's so different when you have to die—you wish you had told them while you could and you wish you could tell them you're sorry for all the little mean things you ever did or said to them. You wish you could tell them that you didn't really mean to ever hurt their feelings and for them only to remember that you always loved them far more than you ever let them know."

"You don't have to tell them that," he said. "They will know—they've always known it."

"Are you sure?" she asked. "How can you be sure? My people are strangers to you."

"Wherever you go, human nature and human hearts are the same."

"And they will know what I want them to know—that I love them?"

"They've always known it, in a way far better than you could ever put in words for them."

"I keep remembering the things they did for me, and it's the little things they did that seem to be the most important to me, now. Like Gerry—he sent me a bracelet of fire-rubies on my sixteenth birthday. It was beautiful—it must have cost him a month's pay. Yet, I remember him more for what he did the night my kitten got run over in the street. I was only six years old and he held me in his arms and wiped away my tears and told me not to cry, that Flossy was gone for just a little while, for just long enough to get herself a new fur coat and she would be on the foot of my bed the very next morning. I believed him and quit crying and went to sleep dreaming about my kitten coming back. When I woke up the next morning, there was Flossy on the foot of my bed in a brand-new white fur coat, just like he had said she would be.

"It wasn't until a long time later that Mama told me Gerry had got the pet-shop owner out of bed at four in the morning and, when the man got mad about it, Gerry told him he was either going to go down and sell him the white kitten right then or he'd break his neck."

"It's always the little things you remember people by; all the little things they did because they wanted to do them for you. You've done the same for Gerry and your father and mother; all kinds of things that you've forgotten about but they will never forget."

"I hope I have. I would like for them to remember me like that."

"They will."

"I wish—" She swallowed. "The way I'll die—I wish they wouldn't ever think of that. I've read how people look who have died in space—their insides all ruptured and exploded and their lungs out between their teeth and then, a few seconds later, they're all dry and shapeless and horribly ugly. I don't want them to ever think of me as something dead and horrible, like that."

"You're their own, their child and their sister. They could never think of you other than the way you want them to; the way you looked the last time they saw you."

"I'm still afraid," she said. "I can't help it, but I don't want Gerry to know it. If he gets back in time, I'm going to act like I'm not afraid at all and—"

The signal buzzer interrupted her, quick and imperative.

"Gerry!" She came to her feet. "It's Gerry, now!"

He spun the volume control knob and asked: "Gerry Cross?"

"Yes," her brother answered, an undertone of tenseness to his reply. "The bad news—what is it?"

She answered for him, standing close behind him and leaning down a little toward the communicator, her hand resting small and cold on his shoulder.

"Hello, Gerry." There was only a faint quiver to betray the careful casualness of her voice. "I wanted to see you—"

"Marilyn!" There was sudden and terrible apprehension in the way he spoke to her. "What are you doing on that EDS?"

"I wanted to see you," she said again. "I wanted to see you, so I hid on this ship—"

"You *hid* on it?"

"I'm a stowaway . . . I didn't know what it would mean—"

"*Marilyn!*" It was the cry of a man who calls hopeless and

desperate to someone already and forever gone from him. "What have you done?"

"I . . . it's not—" Then her own composure broke and the cold little hand gripped his shoulder convulsively. "Don't, Gerry—I only wanted to see you; I didn't intend to hurt you. Please, Gerry, don't feel like that—"

Something warm and wet splashed on his wrist and he slid out of the chair, to help her into it and swing the microphone down to her level.

"Don't feel like that— Don't let me go knowing you feel like that—"

The sob she tried to hold back choked in her throat and her brother spoke to her. "Don't cry, Marilyn." His voice was suddenly deep and infinitely gentle, with all the pain held out of it. "Don't cry, Sis—you mustn't do that. It's all right, Honey—everything is all right."

"I—" Her lower lip quivered and she bit into it. "I didn't want you to feel that way—I just wanted us to say good-bye because I have to go in a minute."

"Sure—sure. That's the way it will be, Sis. I didn't mean to sound the way I did." Then his voice changed to a tone of quick and urgent demand. "EDS—have you called the *Stardust*? Did you check with the computers?"

"I called the *Stardust* almost an hour ago. It can't turn back, there are no other cruisers within forty light-years, and there isn't enough fuel."

"Are you sure that the computers had the correct data—sure of everything?"

"Yes—do you think I could ever let it happen if I wasn't sure? I did everything I could do. If there was anything at all I could do now, I would do it."

"He tried to help me, Gerry." Her lower lip was no longer trembling and the short sleeves of her blouse were wet where she had dried her tears. "No one can help me and I'm not going to cry any more and everything will be all right with you and Daddy and Mama, won't it?"

"Sure—sure it will. We'll make out fine."

Her brother's words were beginning to come in more faintly

and he turned the volume control to maximum. "He's going out of range," he said to her. "He'll be gone within another minute."

"You're fading out, Gerry," she said. "You're going out of range. I wanted to tell you—but I can't, now. We must say good-bye so soon—but maybe I'll see you again. Maybe I'll come to you in your dreams with my hair in braids and crying because the kitten in my arms is dead; maybe I'll be the touch of a breeze that whispers to you as it goes by; maybe I'll be one of those gold-winged larks you told me about, singing my silly head off to you; maybe, at times, I'll be nothing you can see but you will know I'm there beside you. Think of me like that, Gerry; always like that and not—the other way."

Dimmed to a whisper by the turning of Woden, the answer came back.

"Always like that, Marilyn—always like that and never any other way."

"Our time is up, Gerry—I have to go, now. Good—" Her voice broke in mid-word and her mouth tried to twist into crying. She pressed her hand hard against it and when she spoke again the words came clear and true.

"Good-bye, Gerry."

Faint and ineffably poignant and tender, the last words came from the cold metal of the communicator.

"Good-bye, little sister—"

She sat motionless in the hush that followed, as though listening to the shadow-echoes of the words as they died away, then she turned away from the communicator toward the air lock, and he pulled down the black lever beside him. The inner door of the air lock slid swiftly open, to reveal the bare little cell that was waiting for her, and she walked to it.

She walked with her head up and the brown curls brushing her shoulders, with the white sandals stepping as sure and steady as the fractional gravity would permit and the gilded buckles twinkling with little lights of blue and red and crystal. He let her walk alone and made no move to help her, knowing she would not want it that way. She stepped into the air lock and turned to face him, only the pulse in her throat to betray the wild beating of her heart.

"I'm ready," she said.

He pushed the lever up and the door slid its quick barrier between them, enclosing her in black and utter darkness for her last moments of life. It clicked as it locked in place and he jerked down the red lever. There was a slight waver to the ship as the air gushed from the lock, a vibration to the wall as though something had bumped the outer door in passing, then there was nothing and the ship was dropping true and steady again. He shoved the red lever back to close the door on the empty air lock and turned away, to walk to the pilot's chair with the slow steps of a man old and weary.

Back in the pilot's chair he pressed the signal button of the normal-space transmitter. There was no response; he had expected none. Her brother would have to wait through the night until the turning of Woden permitted contact through Group One.

It was not yet time to resume deceleration and he waited while the ship dropped endlessly downward with him and the drives purred softly. He saw that the white hand of the supplies closet temperature was on zero. A cold equation had been balanced and he was alone on the ship. Something shapeless and ugly was hurrying ahead of him, going to Woden where its brother was waiting through the night, but the empty ship still lived for a little while with the presence of the girl who had not known about the forces that killed with neither hatred nor malice. It seemed, almost, that she still sat small and bewildered and frightened on the metal box beside him, her words echoing hauntingly clear in the void she had left behind her.

I didn't do anything to die for—I didn't do *anything—*

▪ ▪ ▪

For a Journal Entry . . .

The laws of nature have posed one of the continuing challenges for mankind. Alone among the animals, man has sought to modify the world around him and bend it to suit his will. Some twentieth-century men have come to believe that there is nothing that man cannot achieve, if he so desires. What do you think?

For Your Consideration . . .

1. Why is the story called "The Cold Equations"?
2. Why is the fact that the stowaway was raised on earth important?
3. Why would the brother's reaction to the girl's death be different from that of her parents?
4. Given the circumstances, how do you think you would have reacted if you had been the stowaway? The pilot?
5. What is the only kind of help the pilot can give the girl?
6. In what ways is the frontier setting of "The Cold Equations" like the frontier setting of the old West?
7. Would the story have been as effective if the stowaway had been a fugitive from justice? Why or why not?

Notes

PAGE

241 *gauge*—instrument for measuring something
241 *drives*—engines
241 *radiated*—gave off
241 *EDS*—Emergency Dispatch Ship
242 *inured*—used to something
242 *jettisoned*—thrown or cast out
242 *imperative*—necessary
242 *hyperspace*—a faster-than-light device used by SF writers to get their spaceships from star to star within a reasonable length of time
242 *interstellar*—between the stars
242 *nuclear converters*—equipment to change matter into nuclear energy
243 *midges*—very small gnatlike insects
243 *serum*—medicine
243 *deceleration*—slowing down
243 *compensate*—make up for
243 *infinitesimal*—extremely small
243 *increments*—amounts
244 *concealed*—hidden
244 *abrupt*—sudden
244 *furtive*—secretive
245 *linguistics*—the study of language

246 *ulterior motive*—the real reason for doing something, other than the one stated
247 *futile*—useless
247 *exhausted*—used up
247 *appreciable*—measurable
248 *recoiled*—pulled back
250 *inevitable*—unavoidable
250 *resignation*—acceptance
252 *paramount*—supreme, chief
253 *chronometer*—instrument for measuring time
253 *deviate*—change from a proscribed course
253 *technician*—a person trained to use certain types of equipment
254 *violated*—broken
254 *fragile*—breakable
254 *secure*—safe
255 *poignant*—emotionally painful
256 *enshrouded*—wrapped
257 *annihilate*—wipe out, destroy
257 *wake*—the trail a boat leaves behind it; any such trail left behind a moving object
257 *irrevocable*—unchangeable
257 *immutable*—never changing
257 *binary*—two (as in a two-star system)
257 *nova*—exploding star
257 *arrayed*—arranged
257 *futility*—uselessness
258 *inexorable*—unrelenting
258 *equation*—a set of conditions that equals another set of conditions
258 *printed circuits*—substitutes for conventionally wired circuits
258 *inaudible*—a sound that one cannot hear
259 *intensity*—strength; concentration
259 *leniency*—easiness
260 *rendezvous*—meeting place
262 *resolution*—decision
264 *apprehension*—fear of something to come
265 *composure*—control
265 *quivered*—trembled
267 *void*—emptiness

For A Final Journal Entry . . .

1. Looking back at the stories you have read, which of the stories was the most realistic? which could you personally identify with the most? which was the most traditional SF story? which the most original? and which was the best?
2. Finally, what is science fiction?

Suggestions for Further Reading

Aldiss, Brian W.	_Starship, Greybeard*; Galaxies Like Grains of Sand; The Long Afternoon of Earth*_
Anderson, Poul	_Brain Wave_
Asimov, Isaac	_I, Robot; Foundation; The Caves of Steel_
Blish, James	_Cities in Flight; A Case of Conscience*; Black Easter*_
Bradbury, Ray	_The Martian Chronicles; Fahrenheit 451; The October Country_
Campbell, John W.	_The Mightiest Machine_
Clarke, Arthur C.	_Childhood's End*; The City and the Stars*; A Fall of Moondust_
Clement, Hal	_Iceworld; Mission of Gravity; Cycle of Fire_
Dick, Philip K.	_The Man in the High Castle*_
Dickson, Gordon A.	_The Genetic General_
Disch, Thomas M.	_One Hundred and Two H Bombs*_
Harrison, Harry	_Deathworld; Make Room! Make Room!; The Technicolor Time Machine; The Light Fantastic (Editor)_
Heinlein, Robert	_Double Star; Orphans of the Sky; Stranger in a Strange Land*_
Herbert, Frank	_Dune*_
Huxley, Aldous	_Brave New World*_
Hoyle, Fred	_The Black Cloud; October the First Is Too Late*_
Keyes, Daniel	_Flowers for Algernon_
Lafferty, R. A.	_Fourth Mansions*_
Leiber, Fritz	_Gather, Darkness_
Lewis, C. S.	_Out of the Silent Planet*; Perelandra_
Miller, Walter	_A Canticle for Leibowitz*_
Orwell, George	_Animal Farm; 1984_
Pohl, Frederick with Kornbluth, Cyril M.	_The Space Merchants_
Russell, Eric Frank	_Sinister Barrier_
Shute, Neville	_On the Beach_
Sturgeon, Theodore	_More than Human_
Van Vogt, A. E.	_Slan; The World of Null-A*_
Verne, Jules	_Twenty Thousand Leagues Under the Sea_
Vinge, Vernor	_Grimm's World_
Wells, H. G.	_The Time Machine; The War of the Worlds_
Wyndham, John	_Day of the Triffids; The Midwich Cuckoos_

Books on Science Fiction

Aldiss, Brian W.	*The Billion Year Spree*
Amis, Kingsley	*New Maps of Hell*
Lundwall, Sam J.	*Science Fiction: What It's All About*

* The novels that are starred are for mature readers because of difficulties in vocabulary, form, or concept.

SCRIBNER STUDENT PAPERBACKS

SCRIBNER STUDENT PAPERBACKS